Praise for Jon Hassler and *The Love Hunter*

"The author's capacity for physical description can be impressive. . . . His prose is clean and evocative, his plot twists graceful, and his narrative talent abundant."
—*The Washington Post*

"Ever since his remarkable first novel *Staggerford*, [Hassler] has moved surely forward in the perfection of his art. His prose is flawless, his characters are decent, believable people about whom you care immensely, his stories are strong. He writes about what he knows so that we may know it too and find therein the power of understanding."
—*The Cleveland Plain Dealer*

"Jon Hassler . . . once again comes to grips with a stark, disturbing theme and handles it with unpretentious dignity for a third novel that confirms the depth of his talent. . . . *The Love Hunter* is excellent fare, a sound and moving novel written with candor and skill."
—*Anniston Star*

"*The Love Hunter* is, most assuredly, a novel of suspense. But it is far more than that. In beautiful, straightforward prose, filled with startling descriptions of both nature and feeling, Jon Hassler has written a novel of love, of friendship, and of decent people caught by circumstances they cannot control."
—*The Chapel Hill Newspaper*

Please turn the page for more reviews. . . .

THE LOVE
HUNTER

BY JON HASSLER

Staggerford
Simon's Night
The Love Hunter
A Green Journey
Grand Opening
North of Hope
Dear James
Rookery Blues

For young adults
Four Miles to Pinecone
Jemmy

THE LOVE HUNTER

Jon Hassler

BALLANTINE BOOKS • NEW YORK

http://www.randomhouse.com

Library of Congress Catalog Card Number: 96-96671

ISBN: 345-41019-X

This edition published by arrangement with William Morrow and Company, Inc.

Manufactured in the United States of America

First Ballantine Books Mass Market Edition: April 1988
First Ballantine Books Trade Edition: August 1996

10 9 8 7 6 5 4 3 2 1

The author is grateful for the fellowship provided him by the Minnesota State Arts Board and funded by the Minnesota State Legislature.

That death's unnatural that kills for loving.

OTHELLO

PART ONE

— ❖ —

1

*A*T THE APPOINTED TIME—sunrise—
Chris arrived at the Quinns' house in his mint-green
Chevrolet. He stopped at the curb under the giant elm
and saw the front door open and Larry come shuffling
out into the sparkling, rain-soaked morning. Before
dawn a thunderstorm had drenched the city, stripping the
trees of half their golden leaves and opening this yard to
sunlight where yesterday there had been shadow. Larry
blinked. His movements were tentative. His face was an
oval of ivory and his pale, wispy hair, what remained of
it, lifted in the breeze. His brown eyes were dark and
damaging; even from this distance they pierced Chris's
heart.

Behind Larry came Rachel in her blue robe. She laid a
hand lightly on her husband's shoulder and the two of
them moved slowly along the short walk as Chris
stepped around the car to open Larry's door and then
stood under the dripping elm watching them—watching
her—approach. This was Rachel the actress, Rachel the
jogger, Rachel the woman of compassion and quick
moves and brimming good nature. In the sun she was
radiant. She, too, pierced Chris's heart, but not with
sorrow or pity or whatever it was that Larry inflicted;
when Chris looked at Rachel he was shot through with
joy. And longing. Against the ivy clinging thickly to the
front of the house—ivy darkening from green to rust—
Rachel's sunlit hair was the color of fire.

"A perfect morning," said Chris.

"Yes," they said together, she making a chirp of it,
Larry a groan. Smiling, she took Chris's hand for an in-

3

stant, squeezed it; then as Chris helped Larry into the
car she folded shut the walker and put it into the back
seat.

"I'll get his things," she said, returning to the house.

"This is all nonsense," said Larry. He sat on the pas-
senger side of the front seat like a small boy acting prim,
his legs tight together, his hands folded on his knees.
Except when he fell asleep in a chair, his sitting posture
was always stiff, as though he feared relaxing into pain.
He looked up from under the bill of his brown corduroy
cap. His eyes were murky, his nose bony and pointed,
his smile slightly bilious. "This is all nonsense and, mind
you, I'm going only because we're both agreed that it's
all nonsense."

Chris, standing with one foot in the leafy gutter,
stooped to roll down the window. He shut the door. "But
on the other hand," he said through the window, "it
might be the hunt of a lifetime."

Larry said, "How exciting." At the sides of Larry's
mouth the muscles designed for sarcasm—lemon-
sucking muscles—were well developed; they brought
down the corners of his smile, tightening it. "How utterly
exciting."

Chris said, "Don't go away," and as he turned to follow Rachel, he met a paperboy, who handed him the
Quinns' copy of the *Rookery Morning Call*, which was
lumpy with moisture. Going up the walk, he scanned the
front page—Thursday, October 4, 1979: three thousand
Soviet troops in Cuba; sunshine in the forecast; a sea of
spilled oil washing up on the beaches of Texas; the Pope
and his cardinals flying to Iowa to say mass on a farm;
Gene Autry and his Angels flying to Baltimore for the
playoffs.

In the living room Larry's hunting gear was heaped in
front of the cold fireplace. Rachel, avoiding Chris's eyes,
opened the bulging duffel bag and lifted out the shaving
kit containing Larry's medicine. "This is the pill he takes
for pain, and this one whenever his head aches."

"I know."

She sorted through the shaving equipment with her

large, nimble hands, her nails painted blood-red. She drew out a string of eight or ten capsules pressed between foil and clear plastic. "And this is Ayrozil—one each day. Unless he gets depressed—then two."

"I know."

"I *know* you know, Chris, but I've got to go over it with you, to ease my conscience." She gave him what he called her in-between smile—half sincere and half stagecraft. "I'm facing four days of freedom and already I'm feeling guilty."

"Four days in what—fourteen years? No wonder you feel guilty." It had been fourteen years since Larry's decline from vigor was diagnosed as multiple sclerosis, and Rachel's roles had been multiplying ever since. She had trained herself to be his nurse, his psychiatrist, his dietitian, his breadwinner, his will to live—all this besides being his wife and the mother of Bruce, whose heavy footsteps they now heard upstairs.

Chris pressed his hand on her lean hip. "Why don't you get the hell out of town for four days? Drive down to Minneapolis and take in some plays?"

She bent to the duffel bag, replacing the shaving kit, then bobbed up and gripped him tightly by both forearms and brought the point of her nose forward to the point of his chin. "I may drive down Saturday, but first I'm going to lie in bed and read for a day and a half." Her voice, an instrument of many registers, was low now, a purr. "I'm not going to dress until tomorrow noon. I'll have Bruce bring me peanut butter sandwiches."

Through a wisp of her red hair he kept an eye on the stairway as he kissed her between the eyebrows.

"Remember, Chris, don't push him." She spoke to his throat. "He's finally got to the point where he no longer tries to exert himself beyond his limits, so just let him go at his own pace. If he doesn't feel like climbing into a boat or sitting all day in a duck blind, please don't force him."

He lifted her chin and they kissed quickly, not as fervently as he had hoped. How many hours, days, had he spent weighing the fervency of Rachel's kisses? How

many nights had he lain awake, alone, trying to understand if her love for him matched his for her? He knew
she loved him. She had told him so. But that was months
ago, before declaring that only in her widowhood would
she permit anything more to be said—or done—about
their love. It was distressing—crippling, actually—for
Chris to realize that the male lead in last winter's production of *Barefoot in the Park* had tasted more of Rachel's
kisses than he himself ever had.

"Oh, I almost forgot your lunch." She darted into the
kitchen and returned with a sack. "Here are four ham-
on-ryes and a few apples—for snacking as you drive."
She picked up Larry's boots and sleeping bag and went
out the front door as Bruce, barefoot, came padding
down the stairs in his pajamas.

Scarcely awake now, his yellow hair stringy on his
forehead, his eyes puffy, Bruce said, "Hi, Chris. Remember to aim before you shoot."

"Show respect."

Bruce was seventeen and a hulk—an amiable giant
with bruises on his face from football. North High was
halfway through its eight-game schedule and if the team
finished with as many as four wins, Bruce's immovable
presence in the line would have a lot to do with it. He
loved to knock people down and crush them under his
two hundred pounds and then get to his feet and exult.
Among the characteristic sounds of a North High game,
among the clicking impact of pads and helmets and the
grunts of exertion and the thunder of stampeding cleats,
was the howling laughter of Bruce Quinn. Larry and Rachel and Chris attended all the home games—they
watched from lawn chairs near the end zone so Larry
wouldn't have to climb into the bleachers—and last Friday night they sat within ten feet of Bruce as he dumped
the Lincoln High quarterback behind the goal line, then
jumped to his feet and howled at the sky. What was the
source of that ecstatic howl? Had it come down to Bruce
from his four-legged ancestors, or was it the purely
human joy one feels in being good at what he does? Or

was it an act? Chris suspected that Bruce, like his mother, was an actor.

"Are you hunting this weekend?"

"Yeah, this afternoon after practice and tomorrow afternoon before the game. With a couple of friends. We're going to hunt the Badbattle River about ten miles downstream." He hoisted his father's heavy duffel bag to his shoulder and went out to the car.

Chris followed with Larry's shotgun and string bag of shells, certain that although he and Larry were setting off for Canada's prime duck country, neither of them was really interested in ducks. He was convinced that Larry sought oblivion—he wanted, literally, to die. How many times in the past two years had Larry told him he'd prefer nonexistence to the misery he endured? Surely he wouldn't be making the superhuman effort that hunting required of a man in his condition if he weren't hunting for death, not ducks.

And myself? thought Chris, stepping out into ribbons of sunlight. I'm hunting for love.

2

THE GEAR STOWED, THE sun climbing,
Chris got in behind the wheel. He looked across at Rachel and Bruce, their heads framed in Larry's window.
Yawning, Bruce said something that sounded like "God
love you both." It may have been just that, for Bruce (to
his father's disdain and his mother's wonderment) was
currently religious. Weekends he sang in a gospel quartet; he and three of his friends from the football team
delivered their repertoire of sacred songs in a shoulder-
wagging, knee-flexing style that was much in demand at
three Rookery churches: Assemblies of God, United
Baptist, Parkview Methodist.

"Go back to bed," Larry told him. "You look half-
asleep. Your eyes are gummy."

"You betcha," said Bruce. No school today and tomorrow—the state teacher's convention. When Chris
first proposed this trip to Canada, Larry had considered
taking Bruce along. Delta Marsh would be farther than
they had ever before traveled for ducks, and Larry imagined himself going forth with his son, shoulder to
shoulder, man to man (the son being more of a man these
days than the father)—one last hunting trip for Larry to
savor and, after he died, for Bruce to cherish. But football was keeping Bruce home. He had practice this afternoon and a game tomorrow night.

Rachel put her head in at the window. Her lips hov-
ered before her husband, brushing light kisses across his
forehead and temple. Backing away, she looked across at
Chris with her most genuine smile, the one he read as a
sign of their love, a sad and splendid smile. He started

8

the car. In his mind's eye, the faces of those he loved were always the most elusive, and as he called goodbye and pulled away from the curb, he kept his gaze on Rachel, trying to inscribe her face in his memory. He did this whenever they parted. Last time he had concentrated on her gray eyes, blue at the center. The time before that, on the matched pair of curving creases that parenthesised her lovely mouth. Now he took in her cheekbones. They were prominent cheekbones, wide and lightly freckled. They colored with feeling as she waved goodbye.

"Better watch where you're going," said Larry.

Chris wrenched the wheel to avoid running up on the curb. He switched on the windshield wipers (the car had been plastered by wet leaves from the Quinns' elm) and thought how essential were good cheekbones to a woman's beauty. Cheekbones guided you into her eyes, into her soul. He looked in the mirror and caught a glimpse of Rachel turning in a pirouette on her way to the house—her arms out, the hem of her bathrobe floating wide, her head thrown back. In this little dance signifying the joy of release, her hair was a blur of copper sunlight, her robe a swirl of blue. Her ankles flashed white against the dripping shrubbery.

Larry said, "I didn't sleep well last night." He leaned forward and pushed in the lighter, then fumbled in the pockets of his jacket for a cigarette. He found none. "I can't walk, Chris. What the hell am I going hunting for?"

Chris switched off the wipers, turned a corner and speeded up. "Don't tell me I'm in for four days of self-pity. Get happy, we're off on a holiday."

Larry turned to him, blinking. "Tell you what, I'll lay off the self-pity if you lay off the goddamn happiness." He crossed his arms and looked perturbed.

"Fair enough."

"This weekend let's try not to think of you as a counselor and me as an invalid."

"Right."

"Let's try not to think of this trip as therapy. As long

as we're going duck hunting, let's think of it as a duck-hunting trip, okay?"

"Fair enough."

"So get your mind off counseling for a while. Put it where it belongs—on the stinking muck of Delta Marsh."

Which was precisely where Chris's mind had been for the past sixty days—the Manitoba bogland, where Larry, between now and Sunday, would die.

Speeding west, they met a glut of traffic moving into the city—factory workers, nurses, gas pumpers, janitors, policemen and all others whose shift would begin at eight. Ordinarily Chris's day, too, began at eight, but he was on a two-day leave—to settle some business, he had told the dean. It was the truth.

Beside the highway were clusters of pine trees—angular, green-brown. Also clusters of garish signs announcing hamburgers and gas. The signs diminished as they drove, the pines grew thicker. It had been a summer and autumn of ample rain. The forestland was luxuriant. Last night's downpour had snarled and matted the thick weeds in the roadside ditches. The highway curved around a lake. Larry gazed at the water.

"Chris, you know what I'd like to do more than anything else in the world?" He sounded wistful.

"Yes."

"No, you don't."

"But I do. You'd like to write a history of Minnesota." For as long as Chris had known him—eighteen years—Larry had been meaning to write the definitive state history.

"No, that's out of the question. What I'd like more than anything is to stop and buy a pack of Old Golds."

"Fine."

"And another thing I'd like more than anything is to eat breakfast at a truck stop. I've had this great urge the last few years to someday eat breakfast at a truck stop. I told Rachel no breakfast this morning, we'd eat along the way."

"We'll do that. We're about ten minutes from Buster's."

"What's Buster's?"

"Buster's Truck Corral. Buster has it all—sassy waitresses, picture postcards, Old Golds."

"Park close to the door. My walker isn't designed for long distances."

In a moment Larry was asleep, his arms crossed, his head drooping forward, his cheek flexing in a spasm of nerves.

3

AT BUSTER'S TRUCK CORRAL, Chris lifted the walker out from the back seat, snapped it open and set it before Larry's door on its rubber-tipped feet. Larry swung, or rather threw, his legs out onto the ground and Chris helped him to stand.

The walker was new. Until this fall Larry had used a crutch; before that, two canes; before that, one cane. Two years ago his two legs were enough. As Larry's legs failed him, Chris had been fascinated by Rachel's reaction. About the time Larry got his first cane, Rachel began taking long slow walks with him in the late afternoon when she got home from work (her work that year was social work); and when he got his second cane and she could no longer draw him away from their yard, she set off alone, jogging. By the time he got his crutch she was jogging twice a day in a new running outfit—maroon with white piping, shorts in warm weather, sweatpants in cold. The day he got his walker she became a compulsive runner; now she ran six miles a day if it wasn't raining, two miles if it was. She ran in the narrow valley behind her house—an eye-shaped depression of land at the center of the city through which the Badbattle River flowed. From her back door she followed a path downhill through a cemetery and came out on Badbattle Drive, which led along the east side of the river to an amusement park half a mile downstream. There she crossed the river on a wooden footbridge and came back along a bike trail on the west bank, crossed another bridge and returned home through the cemetery. High above the bike trail on the west bank stood the apartment building where Chris lived. Chris was not a jogger —he didn't even walk very fast—but home from work and sipping gin in his seventh-floor window, he loved to follow Rachel along the dips and turns of her course. She vanished behind lilacs and cedars and under the framework that held up the roller coaster; then she appeared farther on, her hair bouncing, her chin up. She had slim legs and a pert rump. He noticed how drab her maroon outfit appeared against the colors of the carnival, how colorful it appeared against the drab tombstones. In fair weather Larry was often sitting at the picnic table in his backyard at this time of day. Larry was a birdwatcher and hung a pair of binoculars around his neck whenever he went outside. Occasionally he aimed them into the valley and watched his wife run. Now and then, when Chris couldn't endure another day without speaking to Rachel, without seeing her up close and hearing her voice, he would leave his apartment, descend into the valley and intercept her along the bike trail; her breathless smile was always breathtaking as it moved swiftly toward him, as she came to a stop before him, as they stood a little apart from each other and chatted for a minute, both of them aware that Larry might be at the picnic table or at the window of his den, straining his weakening eyesight as he peered down on them from above.

"Behold, Buster's," said Chris as they moved slowly across the parking lot.

"A dream come true," said Larry.

There were no bad meals at Buster's Truck Corral, but you had to ignore the bathrooms and the grit under your shoes. Chris and Larry slid into opposite sides of a booth by a window. The sun was warm through the glass. Larry fixed his eyes on Chris. For all their murkiness, they were intense eyes—owllike—and they made Chris nervous. As Larry's flesh paled and his hair receded, his eyes seemed to be growing at once smaller and more prominent. The skin of Larry's face, lately so lifeless, so expressionless, made Chris think of paper—

gray paper, newsprint without the news—and his small, round eyes, by contrast, were points of ink. Returning Larry's stare, struggling not to be intimidated by it, Chris thought he detected, behind it, a hint of apprehension. Chris nervously looked away. Surely Larry was betraying the natural anxiety of a man who had been spirited away from the doting care of his wife and the vitality of his hulking son. Surely this man who could barely walk and who often saw double and who had muscle spasms that sometimes sent him sprawling must feel uneasy about a two-day hunt in a Manitoba marsh—particularly since his doctor, when he heard of it, had advised him not to go. Surely he could not know that Chris intended to steer him into some remote estuary of the bogland and press his face into the shallow water and not let him up for air.

This shallow water—it was green with algae—had first appeared to Chris in a dream. The dream returned on four different nights before he understood it to be prophetic. In recent weeks he was seeing the green water by day as well as by night. The algae was growing thicker, the water deeper, the mudbanks spongier. The meaning was clear. The time had come to deliver Larry from his misery, Rachel from her burden, Chris himself from loneliness. Chris was a counselor. He made his living telling people what was good for them, telling them which dreams were worth pursuing. Sometimes a counselor had to counsel himself:

You love Rachel?

Yes, yes.

Then you shall have her.

Ah.

And you love Larry?

He is my closest friend. My only friend.

Then you must kill him.

They were handed menus by a waitress in a miniskirt ten years after the fashion—a fashion good for business, given the clientele. She went away and in twenty seconds she came back. "Are you guys ready to order?"

She held to her breast—her wrists crossed—an order pad and the stub of a pencil and she looked intently at Larry. Her eyes widened. "Hey, my God, you're Doctor Quinn! My favorite history prof! You've lost weight or something." She bent down to him, frowning deeply.

Larry patted her cheek. "Miss Olson, right?"

"Nelson."

"Yes, of course—Nelson. Class of about '74."

She nodded, frowning, still bent to Larry for a close look, her eyes outlined in broad strokes of black, her hay-colored hair stacked on her head in a tight bundle. She had a long pretty neck. "I heard about your... trouble, Doctor Quinn. Oh, God, I could just cry." She did, a little. She took a paper napkin from the dispenser and dabbed carefully at the corners of her eyes.

"Sausage, scrambled eggs and one pancake," said Larry. "And coffee and orange juice. Warm the syrup and cool the juice, if you please. And a pack of Old Golds."

She wrote fast.

"Just coffee," said Chris. "I've already eaten."

Larry exploded. "Jesus, you mean you ate breakfast before you picked me up? You sat there in your spooky apartment and ate breakfast all alone! Sometimes you act very strange, Chris. How come you did that—ate breakfast before you picked me up?"

Chris recoiled. It had not occurred to him that Larry would want to eat breakfast along the way. His first reaction to Larry's temper, now as always, was a flinch of surprise and a little anger. Which he suppressed. "Well, maybe some toast. With jam."

"That's all?" said Miss Nelson.

Chris nodded, closing his menu.

"How come you already ate?" said Miss Nelson.

Chris looked up, amazed. He couldn't believe her boldness.

"How come you ate breakfast before you picked up Doctor Quinn?" If this was a joke, there was nothing in her stern face to confirm it.

"We had made no plans for breakfast."

"There, Doctor Quinn, you see—he wasn't being un-friendly after all." She went to the kitchen and hung their order on a wire.

"Class of '74," said Larry. "History major."

"A brain?"

"B minus and bewildered. But loyal. A hard worker."

They watched her serving three truck drivers at the counter. She had the ruddy look of a tomboy and the frown of a troubled past—a permanent frown, insolent, careworn; it said *hard as nails* and *approach at your own risk.*

"Who's she mad at?" said Chris.

"It used to vary. In History Four-oh-eight it was Harry Truman for dropping the bomb. Today I think it's you."

"Too bad a girl with her good looks has to go through life scowling."

"There are worse things to go through life with." He drilled Chris with his eyes.

"No self-pity, you promised."

Larry nodded.

"You said no happiness and I agreed to that, and I said no self-pity and you agreed to that, and I'm doing my best to hold up my end. I'm trying to suppress my happiness." Even as he spoke, he wished he didn't adopt Larry's irony so easily. With others he was able to keep his sarcasm blunted, but in Larry's company it grew sharp. Larry enjoyed helping him hone it.

Chris turned in his booth and looked across the horse-shoe counter at the booths on the other side of the room. He saw a family of four that reminded him of his own. Father and son faced mother and daughter across a table. They were sipping water, waiting. The mother's hair was dark, almost black, like Karen's. The boy looked about nine, the girl seven—the ages of Billy and Kay ten years ago. Chris studied the father, a serious-looking man in a sportcoat and turtleneck sweater, and he saw himself in 1969. At that time Karen was over-coming, again, her enslavement to the bottle (this vic-tory, more lasting than the others, was to leave her sober for nearly ten months) and Billy and Kay were showing signs of turning into the kinds of people he wanted them to be—generous without being careless of themselves, even-tempered without being docile. They were nine and seven—ages that filled a father with hope.

He turned back to Larry. "I've never told you about my last Father's Day card."

Larry's eyes were on Miss Nelson. "That girl's legs will give out early, Chris. I'd say she's got five years at the outside; then she'll have to start wearing longer skirts."

"That may be true, but let me tell you the story of my Father's Day card."

"Still, she strikes my fancy, Chris. She's fundamentally attractive."

"Yes, now my story begins last June, the Saturday before Father's Day."

"It's about your kids, isn't it?" Larry gave him his attention. "You're trying to soften me."

"It's about my kids. . . ."

Miss Nelson brought coffee and sat down in the booth next to Larry. She turned her frown on him, close up, as though reading fine print. "Give it to me straight, Doctor Quinn. Tell me how you are."

"As they say in nursing homes, I'm doing as well as can be expected, thank you. I'm still able to get around with the help of that device of aluminum tubing over there by the wall. See it?"

"I watched you come in. God, I didn't know it was you." Her brow twisted into large and small creases.

"I get around. I understand that at the Rookery Civic Festival next year they're going to have a footrace for those of us who use walkers. It'll be a downhill race along Basswood Avenue and it will come between the potato-sack race and the wheelchair race."

"Careful, Larry."

Miss Nelson glowered at Chris for interrupting.

Larry nodded and took a different tack. He put his face close to Miss Nelson's and said, "And how is it

going with you? Is this where a B.A. in history leads
these days? To Buster's?"

"It's where *mine* has led." She leaned away slightly
from the power of his eyes.

"I guess teaching jobs are scarce."

"Oh, I had a teaching job. I taught in a little town in
North Dakota for two years. History. Sophomores, jun-
iors and seniors. Right away they nailed me to the wall.
The most despicable hellraisers you ever saw. Finally I
broke down in class and cried. God, was *that* a disaster.
Kids like that see you're vulnerable and they move in for
the kill. Luckily it was near the end of the year when I
went to pieces, and I had the summer to pull myself together. I signed up for another year. I wanted to prove
myself, you know. Plus there weren't any other jobs. So
I went back—and I had a nervous breakdown. I'll sling
hash till the cows come home rather than return to
teaching. I mean, I really went out of my mind. To this
day, you show me a grade book or a piece of chalk and
I'll scream."

Larry chuckled and she looked at him fondly. She almost smiled.

He put his arm around her and gave her a squeeze.
"Life is cruel and you're a dear and where are my
scrambled eggs?"

A bell dinged.

"Just a sec." She sprang away to fetch them.

"I think her first name is Carmelita. Isn't that a
strange combination? Carmelita Nelson?"

She returned and skidded Chris's toast across the
table, then set Larry's three plates carefully before him.
"What else can I bring you?"

Larry took stock of his food.

Chris said he'd like some jam.

"Catsup for your hash browns, Doctor Quinn?"

"If you please. And some cream."

"And jam," said Chris.

Next time past their booth she dropped off catsup and
cream. Larry ate.

"The story of my Father's Day card, Part One."

Larry nodded as he swallowed, permitting the story to proceed.

"Part One takes place on the day before Father's Day. I was waiting for the mailman and I had this feeling that both of my kids had forgotten about Father's Day. I hadn't got a birthday card from Kay in February and Billy's Christmas gift—golf balls—came a month late. Golf balls. I don't play golf. And after the golf balls no word from either of them. No letters. No calls. I write or phone them every week, but they never write or phone me."

"You should have ordered hash browns. They're very good."

"Larry, you're going to hear this story in its entirety, make up your mind to it."

"I'm listening." Larry fed himself shakily, hungrily. "Golf balls from Billy." He chewed fast. "No card from Kay."

"Billy's clerking in a record store in Fresno. Kay's a junior in high school. They've changed a lot. Ever since the divorce, when Karen took them west, I've felt they're out of my reach. When we do communicate, we aren't really on the same wavelength. There's no give-and-take. Only courteous small talk."

Miss Nelson was serving the family of four. Chris paused to watch the napkin-tucking, the salting and peppering. Like Kay's, the girl's eyes were wide apart and pretty. So Karen's had been before she acquired the squint of anxiety and the blear of booze. The father cut a sausage in two and gave it to his children. The boy handed his mother a slice of pickled apple. The mother handed the father a slice of toast. The girl handed her father a sprig of parsley.

"They're not the same Billy and Kay I used to know. But they're on my mind all the time. Especially holidays. Stupid of me, I know—as if Father's Day were anything but a contrivance for selling cuff links and shaving lotion —but there I was in the entryway as the mailman came up the walk, and I opened the door for him. 'A refreshing rain,' I told him, but my eyes were on the mail he carried. 'Damn wet,' said the mailman—angrily, I thought. I suppose the poor man had walked about seven miles in it since breakfast. He began stuffing mail into the wall of boxes. 'Which one are you?' he said. 'MacKensie,' I told him. 'Christopher MacKensie?' he asked, and I said yes and he handed me a single piece of mail, and what do you suppose it was?"

"A Father's Day card. Your stories usually have happy endings."

"It was a flyer from the Franklin Mint, advertising a new series of commemorative coins."

"Not a happy ending?"

"Not an ending at all. I've just begun."

Miss Nelson returned. She held a tiny plastic container of jam, and instead of placing it on the table, she waited for Chris to put his hand out for it; then she dropped it next to his plate. She sat down beside Larry, cramping his eating elbow. "Doctor Quinn, you were one of the two best teachers I ever had in my life."

"I'm flattered."

"What you had was commitment to your subject, Doctor Quinn. You were enthusiastic. I told myself I would be the same way when I became a teacher, but what can you do when five senior boys get you in a corner of the classroom during American history and *undress* you?"

The bell dinged. She got up and ran.

"Jesus, did you hear that?" said Larry.

"I did. And I've heard worse. I've heard of teachers knifed and shot."

"In North Dakota?"

"No, not in North Dakota."

"She's talking about being undressed in North Dakota for God's sake."

"When I was in Fresno this summer, Karen told me that in the school Kay goes to, the students curse at the teachers."

Chris's portion of jelly (apple, said the label) covered half a slice of toast. It was perfectly tasteless. They ate in silence, the Father's Day story paling in the light of what Miss Nelson had told them. A Greyhound bus pulled up outside and unloaded all its riders.

Refilling their coffee cups, Miss Nelson had time for only a few words: "And the other favorite of mine was Mr. Summers in audio-visual. Again it was commitment to subject matter that impressed me. Mr. Summers was in love with his cassettes and his projectors and his closed-circuit TV."

And later, back with their check: "But by and large teachers are a crummy bunch these days. It's become a profession of malcontents. It seemed that every teacher in that little town in North Dakota had hopes of either retiring early or going into carpet sales. Will there be anything else?"

Larry said, "Your first name is Carmelita, right?"

"Yes." She smiled, frowning. "You remembered."

"And you wrote your senior paper on Truman."

"That fink! Will there be anything else?"

"Carmelita, how about you and me getting a room somewhere?"

She blanched, bereft of her frown. "Doctor *Quinn*! What are you saying?"

"I'm saying, let's make love in a motel. Or better yet, how about coming to Canada with us? When we get there, we'll ditch our driver and make love in a duck blind. Get your coat." Gripping the back of the booth with one hand and the edge of the table with the other, Larry heaved himself to his feet.

She backed away only slightly. She spoke close to his ear, confidentially. "Listen, Doctor Quinn, I'm not above that sort of thing and God knows if you had proposed it when I was in college, I'd have been in seventh heaven, but now I'm older and I'm harder to get. Let's just be friends, okay? Let me just be your former student and your waitress, okay?"

Chris moved quickly to the walker and set it between them. Larry leaned on it, humping his back. "Damn it, Carmelita, everything in my whole *life* is former!" Larry's voice, whenever he raised it, was full of sharp cracks. It caused people to stare. "You're a former student and I'm a former teacher and the bike my son rides was formerly my bike and the sweatshirt my wife wears when she cleans house was formerly my sweatshirt because I've shrunken to the point where it's baggier on me than it is on her. And pretty soon my wife will be my former wife and my son will be my former son and this friend of mine here will be my former friend because I'm *dying*, Carmelita Nelson, I'm *dying!*"

The stream of entering bus riders stopped in their tracks. The three truckers turned on their stools. The family of four quit eating.

"Dying!"

Chris, check in hand, tried to get Larry started toward the cash register, but they were stalled by Carmelita, in whose face high color had suddenly returned, in whose eyes tears brimmed. She threw her arms around Larry's neck. All activity in Buster's stopped, all serving, talking, chewing. Everyone stared at their awkward embrace—this shaky man clinging to this leggy waitress, the walker between them, she telling him something soft in his ear.

Chris had foreseen the difficulties in moving Larry from his house in Rookery to his death in the Marsh, but they had been of another kind—physical difficulties—moving Larry around in the bog, his lameness, his failing sight. He had not thought to worry about his state of mind. His medication was supposed to keep him from going crazy.

"Come on, Larry, let's get moving." He nudged him. The bell dinged. Carmelita let Larry go. Weeping, she stepped behind the cash register and took Chris's money and gave him change.

"Take care of him," she said, her mascara holding, tearproof. "He's a dear, dear man." She went to the door and opened it for Larry and helped him out; she exchanged with him a few words Chris couldn't hear. She called out as they set off toward the car: "You were my inspiration, Doctor Quinn." She scampered back inside to answer the dinging bell.

Larry shuffled and clumped across the asphalt. "She's

a sucker for disease, Chris. Remember this: if you ever die before you're old, there's a certain type of girl you can always get by telling them you're dying."

They stood aside to let a drumming, smoking diesel-powered truck roll by, and Larry had to yell to make Chris understand: "You can tell who they are by their course of study. History majors are suckers for a line like that. Tell a history major you're dying and you unlock a great reservoir of feeling. Notice how Carmelita Nelson now wants to be my mother and my lover. She's a sucker for disease."

The truck rumbled away, following the stream of black exhaust flowing out of its chimney pipe. While they were eating, a strong wind had risen from the west.

"I never knew you to chase women," said Chris.

"Well, I'm thinking of turning over a new leaf."

4

IN THE CAR LARRY lit a cigarette. He turned on the radio and tried several stations: a computer picking the Orioles and Pirates to win the playoffs, a weatherman predicting fair and warmer, the Pope defining love as giving. And woven among these messages the sound of drums and amplified guitars—a rumbling, savage music.

"How many shells did you bring?" said Chris.

"Six boxes." Larry switched off the radio. "What about you?"

"Six."

"When did we ever shoot up twelve boxes of shells?"

"I guess never."

"So what sort of delusions are we having about this trip?"

"We're trying, just once, to get into the middle of a thousand flocks of ducks."

"Nonsense."

"And we're shaking off the dust of Rookery. You and I are getting dusty, Larry. You're in that house all day and I'm in my office all day and we need airing out. I swear I've counseled more troubled students this term than I usually do in a whole year. I'm drained." This was only partially true. What drained Chris was not his work but the anxiety brought on by his vision of the algae-green water. He had been on edge since August, when he first planned this trip, this murder.

They were driving through forestland, swampland, rocky farmland. The sky was pieced with blocks of cloud. The sun dimmed and brightened. The wind blew leaves across the highway.

"You confirmed our reservation?"

"Last night I called the fellow who runs the camp. His name is Blackie LaVoi. His exact words were: 'Get your ass up here, there's a million ducks flying.' He sounded half in the bag. . . . And now, moving ahead with my Father's Day story—"

"I've already heard it. You waited for the mailman and he gave you a letter from the Franklin Mint and it was raining. A hell of a good story, all right, but I've heard it."

"Not all of it, you haven't. There's another chapter. It's about a girl named Wanda Schultz."

"I'm all ears."

"Wanda Schultz had neither father nor mother."

Larry nodded. "An orphan."

"Last fall, a year ago, Wanda Schultz moved to Rookery from somewhere in Kansas. She was eighteen. She moved in with a shirttail relative, a woman who runs the Mama Louisa Café."

"That would be Mama Louisa."

"No, no, it's a woman named Mattie Jergens. There's a whole chain of Mama Louisa Cafés."

Larry blew a smoke ring. "Oh."

"Have you ever eaten at the Mama Louisa's in Rookery?"

"I've never heard of it."

"It's over on the east side, near the railroad yards. It's Italian-American—the best of both. You eat spaghetti off plastic plates and drink wine out of plastic tumblers. Anyhow, this Wanda Schultz enrolled at the college with the intention of earning a degree in office management, and she came to me for counseling all the time. She was always in need of help. Her schedule needed revising or Mattie Jergens was getting on her nerves or she was flunking a course."

"Not a strong student."

"Not a very interested one. Right away I could see that she wasn't aimed in the right direction. She wasn't the least bit interested in office management. An uncle or somebody had told her to go into office management and she obeyed him. That's the way she was—the obliging sort. So I gave her an aptitude test and we had a number of conferences and I finally discovered what she really wanted to do with her life. She wanted to groom dogs."

"You're right." Larry drew deeply on his cigarette. "This story is a spellbinder."

"But though she wanted to groom dogs, she stayed in the office management program, amassing credits at about half the rate of her classmates, and during winter term she became very obviously pregnant. She told me the father was someone who had passed through the city on his way to the coalfields of Wyoming. He stopped in at Mama Louisa's for lunch and told Wanda he loved her and for that he got a bed for the night. In the morning he was gone." Chris picked a pair of sunglasses off the dash and put them on.

Larry lit a second cigarette with the stub of his first.

"Wanda Schultz had a sunny disposition, but it was a mask. In spite of her troubles, she was always pleasant and sunny and only I as her counselor knew what an effort it was for her to be sunny. You see, underneath it all, Wanda Schultz was inclined to melancholy."

"Who isn't?"

"I mean, when you really got to know Wanda Schultz, you discovered this great empty place at the core of her, Larry. This tremendous lack."

"Like mine."

"And her sunny disposition was her disguise, her attempt to cover up the lack."

"That's what mine is."

Chris laughed softly for half a mile. Larry watched him out of the corner of his eye, pleased to have been amusing.

"Even pregnant she was sunny. During the last three months of her pregnancy, when she was very sunny on the outside and very melancholy on the inside and very big all around, she was enrolled in this course of mine called Academic Adjustment."

"A.A."

"Some call it A.A. and others called it Bonehead Coping, but the catalogue calls it Academic Adjustment and it consists of speed-reading drills and lectures on study habits and some individual counseling—you know the sort of thing we do nowadays for the sake of enrollment."

"Trying to make college material out of people who would be happier grooming dogs."

"Exactly. Now picture Wanda Schultz, at her sunniest and saddest, raising her hand in class and telling me that she had just lined up a job for herself in a veterinary clinic where her main work would be cutting and combing the hair of poodles. She said this without a trace of embarrassment, even though her classmates were listening and looking down their noses at her. In her eyes I saw happiness. But it was a tight sort of happiness. Behind her happiness, as always, I could see apprehension. I saw it in the tight way she crossed her legs and crossed her arms and hunched her shoulders. She was always tight like that. I told her I was glad she had found a job to her liking. I asked if she was dropping out of college. Not until the end of the term, she said—she had paid her tuition and would stay around and get her money's worth. Well and good, I told her, and I went ahead with my lecture on how to avoid getting lost in the library, and Wanda raised her hand again. She said—in front of everybody—that I had done a great deal for her during her time on campus and she could never thank me enough and there was one more favor she wanted to ask. She wondered if it would be all right if she called me Dad."

Chris glanced at Larry, who was holding his cigarette an inch from his mouth. His eyes were closed.

"Are you listening, Larry?"

"She wanted to call you Dad."

"Yes. And I laughed. I didn't mean to make light of her request. I think I laughed cheerfully, in response to the cheer in her eyes, forgetting for a moment her great need. I laughed as I told her it was fine with me if she wanted to call me Dad. I said—facetiously—that she had made a wise choice, that there was nothing in the line of fatherhood that I couldn't handle. I said I had had two teenagers of my own and they had given me some tough training. 'If you need a father,' I said, 'I'm your man.' Then she said, 'I don't expect you to actually *do* anything, Mr. MacKensie—I'd just like to be able to call you Dad once in a while. I get this strong urge to call somebody Dad and if you'll just let me say, "Hi, Dad," when we meet in the halls it would do me a lot of good.'

"'Permission granted,' I told her, hoping for her sake that she would stop there. Her classmates were grinning at each other and rolling their eyes. They were a roomful of students on the verge of flunking out of college, and Wanda with her fatherless child and her ambition to be a dog groomer and her forced cheerfulness and her poorly concealed melancholy—in other words, Wanda in all her misery—was giving them a chance to feel superior. One of them even laughed out loud—a laugh I would have squelched if I hadn't just laughed out loud myself. But there was no stopping Wanda. She pressed on. She wasn't the least bit intimidated by the others. She said, 'I spend a lot of time thinking about people like you who are living what I imagine is a very full life, Mr. MacKensie. I mean, you've got a wife and kids—I see pictures of your kids in your office—and I don't have anybody I feel close to, so what I sometimes do is pretend I'm part of a family. I don't think it's crazy or anything. It's just a thing I do. Some days when I leave the campus, I pretend that I'm going home to my family—and what I imagine is usually a mother and a father, not a husband. It's just harmless pretending, don't you agree?'

"Picture it, Larry. Along with her smile she was looking at me with this apprehensive squint, as though she were afraid I might see the depth of her need. 'Perfectly harmless,' I told her. 'And perfectly flattering,' I added. And with that, she let me go ahead with my lecture."

"It's a touching story, and I know why she chose you as her father."

"Yes, it was obvious. I'd been counseling her all year."

"I don't think so. I think she chose you because you *look* so much like a father."

"What do you mean? All men look like fathers."

"Like hell they do. Most men these days, with their mustaches, look like John Wilkes Booth. I've never told you this, Chris, but I'm telling you now: you have a very paternal look about you. You're graying and your jowls are starting to sag and you slouch when you walk. You're slump-shouldered, Chris, and the way you carry yourself seems to say that from now on hardly anything in life is going to strike you as urgent."

"My jowls sag?"

"And consider your face, Chris. You've got a weary face. It's a philosopher's face. Your face is settling into an expression of resignation. What are you, forty-six?"

"I'm forty-five."

"Well, you have the look of a man a lot older. When I look at your face, I see not only fatherhood, I see *grand*-fatherhood—but get on with your story."

Chris turned the mirror on himself. "My jowls aren't sagging."

"Get on with your story."

Chris glanced several times between the road and the mirror. He had thought he looked younger than forty-five. His hair was graying, but slowly; at its darkest it had been medium brown and now it was only half a shade lighter. His color was always on the high side, particularly the color of his nose after his third Martini. Though he was wrinkled around the eyes, his face was holding firm. He guessed he was eight or ten years away from the grand sag. Eight or ten years till his flesh gave way and slid into pouches and puffs. Before readjusting the mirror, he checked his twenty-four-hour whiskers (he never shaved on a hunting day) and here his age was apparent. His whiskers were white. Two years ago, after the divorce, he had grown a beard, but its whiteness alarmed him, and he shaved it off in its seventh week.

"Get on with your story, Chris, I feel a nap coming on."

"For the rest of spring term, whenever I met Wanda in the hallways—I'd be walking along, you know, slump-shouldered and resigned, my jowls sagging—I'd say, 'Hello, Wanda,' and she'd say, 'Hi, Dad.'"

"And you're going to tell me that she went into dog grooming and she's extremely happy and the reason everything turned out so well is that calling you Dad filled up her emptiness."

"No, all I can say for sure is that she had her baby and gave it up for adoption and went into dog grooming. I don't know how happy she is or whether she's been cured of her emptiness. But I do know that that bit of role-playing left its mark."

"How do you know?"

"Because the mark is on me."

Larry put out his cigarette. "Let me guess. It aged you. Whereas you used to look at pretty coeds and fantasize about being their lover, now you fantasize about being their father."

"Something like that."

The highway cut through the middle of a low-lying pond and a gust of wind gripped the car, swaying it. Ahead and very high a V of geese moved south. Ahead at treetop level a ragged string of a hundred crows moved north.

Larry rested his head on the back of the seat. "Wake me for lunch."

"Wait, there's more to my story."

"Mmmmmmmmmmmm."

"On Saturday, as I said, I got no card in the mail. Then on Sunday, Father's Day, I got no phone call from California. So on Monday I was standing in the entryway again as the mailman came in and handed me a piece of mail. It was the shape of a greeting card—surely, I thought, a Father's Day card; my fatherhood was somehow valid once more; I was remembered by at least one of my kids. I ripped open the envelope and there, printed across the front of the card—over a picture of a tennis racket and a fishing rod and an antique car and all the other things fathers are supposed to be interested in— were the words 'To a Swell Dad.' My sigh of pleasure must have been audible because the mailman turned and gave me a curious look. I opened the card and inside, it said, 'Love always,' and guess whose signature I saw."

"Billy and Kay's."

"Nope."

"It was somebody else's card. The mailman made a mistake."

"No, it was my card all right."

"Oh, I get it—a card from Wanda Schultz."

"A card from Wanda Schultz. I thought, damn! two kids of my own and the best I can do is a card from this girl with the big empty place at the core of her. I almost tore it up. But I didn't. And later I was glad I hadn't. Later I got to thinking how much better it was to get a card from Wanda Schultz than to get no card at all. The more I thought about it, the nicer it seemed. The card meant that as of last June, Wanda Schultz was still playing out her role as my daughter and asking nothing from me except that I allow it. Really, it was a kind of love. A kind of pure, undemanding love. You don't find that sort of love very often, Larry."

"Except in dogs."

"And thinking about that card over the summer, I realized that Wanda Schultz wasn't alone in her role-playing. I, too, was pretending."

Larry, relaxing, let his head roll toward the window on his right. He said, "We'll have to stop pretty soon, I've got to piss."

Chris drove a mile before he said, "I, too, was pretending, Larry. You see, at first the father-daughter pretense was derived from Wanda's emptiness, but during the summer I came to see that it was my *own* emptiness that made the card so affecting."

Another mile. "Larry, there's an emptiness at the core of me."

Larry was asleep, or pretending to be. Chris hoped he was sleeping, for he was a little embarrassed at having spoken so candidly. It wasn't his style to pour out his heart. Perhaps as a reaction to his job, which consisted of hashing over the emotions of others, he buried his own very deeply. Besides, he knew it wasn't safe to get confidential with Larry. It made you vulnerable. In his bitterness Larry often twisted your heartfelt statements and sent them flying back at you in a way that made you flinch.

Another mile. "Anyhow, I saved the card."

No reply from Larry. His hands lay inert in his lap.

Another mile and Larry began to snore.

5

THIS WOULD BE LARRY'S third winter of too much sleep. If he lived. Again this fall, Larry was heading into a pit of depression. Chris and Rachel and Bruce saw it coming. Larry himself saw it coming. They recognized the signals they had seen two years earlier—1977—when despondency settled over Larry in October and locked him into a housebound, humorless state through the winter and didn't ease up until spring. He raged and he sulked for seven months. He slept, if left alone, like a hibernating animal. Not the restorative sleep of fatigue or even boredom, but the restive sleep of affliction and despair.

Driving northwest now, toward clearing skies, Chris looked back at 1977, the year that Larry—forty-five and too broken-down to teach—had been forced to retire. It was also the year that Chris—forty-three and freshly divorced—had moved to Rookery and renewed his friendship with the Quinns after fifteen years of being friendly from a distance. Theirs was an eighteen-year friendship with a fifteen-year hole in the middle.

The Quinns and the MacKensies came together in the small town of Owl Brook in 1961, the year that Larry (history) and Chris (English) joined the Owl Brook High School faculty. Larry was twenty-nine and Chris was twenty-seven and this was to be the third teaching position for each of them. In those days of burgeoning enrollments, teachers could change jobs at will, and did. They moved for good reasons and bad, and for no reason at all. Few of them left the state they were trained in, for

crossing the state line would have wiped out their retirement fund and required recertification, but within the
borders of their home state—in this case Minnesota—
teachers were seldom long in one place. They moved
from north to south because the winters were milder, and
they moved from south to north because the fishing was
better. They moved from the country to the city so husbands could be close to the Twins and the Vikings and
wives could be close to the shops of their desiring, and
they moved from the city to the country to escape what
they called the rat race.

Chris's memory of those years was crowded with
moving days, his own and others'. All teachers, never
mind their competence or lack of it in the classroom,
became efficient, if slapdash, movers. Several times
each summer the faculty men would be called upon to
help a fellow teacher load his belongings into a rented
truck, and a day or two later be called upon to unload the
truck of the teacher who came to take his place. Movers
were always paid in beer or wine, consumed on the job,
and therefore, the last pieces they handled incurred more
scratches and dents and lost casters than the earlier
pieces, and the heirloom whose marred surface made the
teacher's wife moan with dismay was never found at the
front of the truck but always near the tailgate.

Larry and Rachel Quinn had moved to Owl Brook
early in the summer, and so Larry was called upon to
help when Chris and Karen and Billy MacKensie arrived
in August. Standing beside the moving van, Chris and
Larry were introduced by Superintendent Johansson,
who had hired them. The superintendent, a thick-bellied
man with thick glasses and a thin brain, showed up for a
few minutes at the beginning of every moving day, as
though to consecrate it, and then disappeared before
someone asked him to lift something. Chris and Larry
were friends from the moment they shook hands. They
were the same height and found the same things funny
and shared the premonition that whatever the issue,
large or small, they would see eye to eye. Larry had
sandy hair and a pointed nose and penetrating brown

eyes. He smiled easily, but it was a tight-lipped smile. His laugh was deliberate and dry. One of his front teeth was discolored and Chris wondered if his desire to conceal it accounted for his manner of smiling and laughing. It was Chris's belief that what people thought of their teeth had a lot to do with how they came to terms with humor.

As a mover Larry had flashes of brilliance but no staying power. He got into the MacKensies' considerable liquor supply and before the truck was half-empty, he was pickled. He placed a dining room chair in the flower bed near the front door and sat down and devoted the rest of the morning to singing songs and making supervisory remarks. Karen took Chris aside and asked him to tell Larry that she wasn't amused. Chris refused.

The next day—Sunday—Larry phoned and invited the MacKensies to the city park where he and Rachel were going to have a picnic. Karen threw together a salad and they took along a blanket and a couple of extra diapers for Billy and they spent the afternoon in the shade of the oaks along the river. They ate hot dogs and drank beer and worked with the Quinns' Hula-Hoop until the sun sank low and the mosquitoes began to bite. Karen MacKensie, though fretting about the house she hadn't yet settled into, was relaxed by the beer, and the two couples had a good time. This day fell almost exactly between the two Hula-Hoop crazes, the craze of the late fifties and the craze of the mid-sixties, and it was typical of Larry and Rachel—as Chris came to know them—that they should be Hula-Hooping during the nadir of its popularity. They liked being out of step. Later, when Hula-Hoops were back, the Quinns were learning the Charleston, and when the Charleston again became the rage, they were wild about chess.

Larry Quinn had left his previous job, in southern Minnesota, for a reason which, though extraordinary, was not unique in the profession: he had been fired for marrying one of his students. Rachel was eighteen. She did not impress Chris that day in the park as being especially attractive or vivacious or witty or wise. She was simply young. Her face was heart-shaped, the cheek-bones wide, the chin narrow, the skin totally unblemished by any mark of woe or want. Her voice was strong and musical. If Chris sensed in her the indomitable and lovely woman she would become, it was only a fleeting observation, for compared to his own wife, Karen, who was twenty-five and pregnant for the second time and opinionated and articulate (especially when she was upset), Rachel struck him as unformed and only slightly interesting. That Rachel was breathlessly in love with Larry, that she couldn't quite believe her good fortune in marrying him was apparent in the way she looked at him all day in the park and in the things she said. There was a childlike, not to say daughterly, ardor in her eyes, and late in the afternoon Chris overheard her say to Karen, across the bean crock, "And to think only a few weeks ago I was calling him Mr. Quinn."

The school year began with a reprimand: Chris and Larry were called into the superintendent's office and told that their behavior in the park on a recent Sunday afternoon had been observed and judged scandalous—they had drunk beer outdoors in broad daylight. Superintendent Johansson asked them to apologize and promise to reform. They refused to apologize on the grounds that they had not been duly informed of what constituted scandal in Owl Brook, but they did promise to reform. Larry said he would never again drink beer outdoors except in the dead of night. Chris said that hereafter he would drink beer only in his house, and then with the shades drawn. The superintendent said he was glad to have the matter cleared up. This interview evolved into a silly three-minute skit which Chris and Larry performed at faculty parties—early in the evening, before the Johanssons arrived; or late, after they went home.

Meddling administration aside, Chris and Larry liked their new jobs. The native stock of Owl Brook was Americanized Scandinavian—hardworking shopkeepers and farmers whose school-age children, though largely unimaginative, were alert and diligent and respectful of authority. They were the sort of students a teacher could leave unsupervised for twenty minutes while he sneaked across the street to the Boxcar Café, which, by decree of the superintendent, was off limits to the faculty between eight in the morning and four in the afternoon. But the superintendent's window faced another direction and so Chris and Larry, happy as truants, met there each morning at ten for a cup of coffee and a smoke. It was in the Boxcar Café one day in late September that Larry asked, "Are you ready for duck season? Got your shells and license?"

Chris said he had never hunted ducks. "I'm not sure I'd know a duck in flight from a woodpecker."

"Never?" Larry drew back in amazement. "I can't believe it."

"I used to hunt pheasants as a boy—and squirrels. But hunting really doesn't interest me."

"Listen, this is prime duck country and Saturday's opening day. I'm hunting a pond just six miles east of here. Come along."

"No, really, I'm a very poor shot."

"Hell, shooting's only a small part of it. You bring a thermos of coffee and you watch the sunrise and you listen to the waves and you tell stories. Come on, get yourself a license. I'll pick you up at a quarter after five Saturday morning. We'll be back in town by noon—and if it's good hunting, we'll try it again on Sunday."

Chris found it hard to say no to Larry, who not only was two years older, but had done more with his twenties than Chris was doing. He had been around. He had served in the army (Chris had been exempted first for scholarship, then for asthma); he had begun work on his doctorate in history at the University of Iowa (Chris had been planning, vaguely, to work on his master's); he had hunted elk in Montana and he had toured France on a bike. Moreover, he was a superb teacher. He loved to tell stories from American history—his course was a cavalcade of heroes, traitors, fools and humanitarians—and you could see at a glance through the open door of his classroom that he inspired—electrified—his students.

On each of the next three Saturdays, when Larry came for him, Chris was dressed in brown and sitting on his front step with his thermos beside him and his shotgun across his knees. Chris drove on Sundays. They traveled west on a gravel road and then followed a long driveway through an aspen wood and around the south side of a ten-acre pond and up a hill to the farmyard of Amos Peterson, who, at first light, was busy in his barn. They parked the car beside the barn and walked downhill between the house and the machine shed and through a stand of pines and a thick cluster of willows and they stepped out across a low-lying pasture and came to the north side of the ten-acre pond. Here they slipped into the blind which Larry had built of hay bales, pine boughs and cornstalks—a high-sided enclosure with openings for scanning the sky and water. They drank coffee and told stories and laughed. Quite often their talk was interrupted by the whir and rush of wings—ducks flying in from behind them, from ponds to the north and west, and landing among their decoys. Chris would fire first, while the birds were on the water; then Larry would fire when the survivors took flight. Their volley usually consisted of five shots—Chris firing twice with his double-barreled Remington, Larry three times with his pump-action Winchester—and it provided them, on the average, with three dead ducks. In the late morning Larry shoved off from shore in his flimsy duckboat and retrieved the kill; then they left the blind and crossed the pasture and climbed the hill of willows and pines and said goodbye to Amos Peterson, who came and stood in the doorway of his barn and remarked either about the weather or about the leisurely life of teachers (the only two topics that seemed to interest him; both filled him with wonder), and they got into the car and drove home.

Home by noon, as Larry had promised. But not early enough to suit Rachel, his jealous bride. Rachel never mentioned her displeasure when Chris was present, but he sensed it whenever it was his turn to drive and he stopped in at the Quinns' apartment to pick up Larry. He could tell by the quick glances they exchanged that they had had an argument about Chris's interference in their married life, Rachel probably having said something like, "You're not married to Chris, Larry, you're married to me," and Larry having said something like "It's you I love with all my heart, my little autumn prairie flower" —his pet names for her were extravagant and seasonal —"but every man is entitled to a little time in the duck blind," and she having come back with something like "But it's *every* Saturday and Sunday, Larry, and it's all *day* every Saturday and Sunday," and he reminding her that it wasn't all day, it was only mornings, and she insisting that it *seemed* like all day, and he promising that once the duck season ended he would be constantly at her side.

But she couldn't wait. Halfway through the season Rachel got herself fitted out in hunting clothes and she took Chris's place in the blind. For the next three weeks the Quinns asked Chris to join them, but he went with them only once, and when he did, he was struck by two things: Rachel struck him as stunning, wearing her brown poplin hunting jacket with the leather belt and the leather patch at the shoulder and looking out from under the brown cap that sat lightly on her wavy red hair; and three in the blind struck him as overcrowding, if not unnatural. The next time Chris was invited he said no thanks; he said that Karen wanted him to stay home, which was not particularly true (Karen was totally absorbed in housekeeping and motherhood in those days and scarcely aware of what Chris did with his weekends), but it was an excuse the Quinns—especially Rachel—found easy to believe.

Chris and Larry hunted together once more that year. It was the final Sunday of the season and the weather was perilous. Snow and wind, but clearing in the forecast. Rachel stayed home. By the time Larry and Chris reached the farm they could hardly see to drive. They parked in the lee of the barn and walked down through the pines and willows. As they stepped out across the open pasture, they were plastered with sheets of wet snow. In the blind they uncorked a thermos and watched the snowflakes melt into their coffee and waited for the storm to let up and give the ducks enough visibility to fly and themselves enough visibility to shoot. In half an hour the snow diminished, though the wind did not, and flocks of mallards circled and landed and splashed about in the water and took off again in a dither. The ducks sensed that the time had come to move south to open water (the pond was turning to slush), but they were reluctant to go. They landed and flew away and came back and landed. Chris and Larry each fired off a full box of shells, and with a dozen mallards lying dead on the water they both got into the duckboat to retrieve them. They had never done this before. It didn't require two men to pick dead ducks off the water, and furthermore it was dangerous for both of them, heavily dressed and booted, to be floating about in the wind in a tiny boat. And of course they knew better: they had heard stories about hunters who had fallen out of overcrowded boats and drowned and, more horrifying than that, they were acquainted with a teacher in a nearby town—Staggerford —who last year had fired from a duckboat just as his partner stood up in the bow to see over a bed of tall reeds, and half the partner's head had been blown away. But Chris and Larry got into the boat together because the wind was turning bitterly cold and they wanted to take the shortest route to the car, which was along the driveway on the opposite shore.

Chris sat in the bow, Larry in the stern. They had picked up their birds and were paddling across the pond when Chris saw, out of the corner of his eye, a lone mallard sailing over the water behind him. He snatched up his gun and turned in his seat—awkwardly, bundled as he was in layers of wool and rubber—and he fired with his gun pointing back over his left shoulder and the duck dropped dead. It was the most spectacular shot of his short career and he shouted with delight before he realized that he had also shot Larry's cap off his head, the edge of his pellets having grazed the bill of the cap and driven it ten feet behind the boat and dropped it into the slush. Larry, staring at him in shock, sat hunched

forward, snowflakes melting in his hair; and Chris, terri-
fied by this near catastrophe, lost control of himself and
began to shriek with laughter, his eyes filling with tears,
his howls filling the saucer of land below the farmyard,
his movements wobbling the boat so that they were both
nearly spilled into the pond. Through his hysteria,
he saw that Larry's eyes, though still aimed in his direction, were unfocused, looking inward as though in self-
discovery, as though his finding that Chris could be a
killer was leading him to an even more astonishing prospect—that he himself could be killed.

Still laughing, but in silent spasms now, Chris turned
away from Larry and put down his gun and picked up his
paddle. He swung the boat around to retrieve the cap,
and when he picked it out of the water and handed it to
Larry and saw that the bill had been shot away, his
laughter dissolved into trembling. Larry examined the
cap, turning it over in his hands as though he were buying it, then dropped it into the water behind the boat.
"Let's go," he said, hoarsely, and they set off for shore,
paddling in silence, squinting into a fresh squall of grainy
snow.

When they bumped land, they got out and pulled the
boat up into the weeds and walked together up the
snowy driveway to the farmyard. Amos Peterson stood
in the doorway of his barn and spoke about the shortness
of the teacher's workweek and about the longness of the
coming winter. Larry and Chris told him good-bye and
got into the car. Larry drove down the hill. Chris trembled. They stopped at the edge of the pond and pulled
the boat up the slippery bank to the road and transferred
their guns and ducks into the trunk of the car. Then they
struggled to lift the boat—it was heavily glazed with ice
—onto the cartop carriers, for they intended to store it
for the winter in Chris's garage. Time after time it
slipped out of their grasp and fell to the road. Finally
Larry said, "The hell with it," and gave the boat a shove
with his foot. They watched it skid down the weedy
slope on its flat, icy keel and slip into the water, where it
rocked on the waves.

Driving back to Owl Brook, Larry spoke of his hunting plans for next year—a bigger blind, a new gun—in a voice unimpaired by shock or fright. His glimpse of his own mortality seemed to have interrupted the course of his thinking for only about twenty minutes and now he was back to normal, while Chris, who had fired the shot that initiated the glimpse, couldn't bring himself under control. His teeth chattered all the way to town, and when they stopped in front of his house and stood at the open trunk dividing the day's kill, Chris couldn't look Larry in the eye. He looked down at the snow in the street and said, "I'm never going hunting again."

Larry punched him hard in the shoulder and said, "Forget what happened, Chris, clean your gun and put it away for the winter. Next year we'll make a fresh start."

Chris nodded. He went into the house and spent an hour in the basement cleaning ducks and convincing himself that Larry was right, that he must put this morning's brush with disaster out of his mind. So awful were its implications—Larry's mortality, Chris's horrible clumsiness—that a man's mental health depended upon his ignoring them. He must turn his mind to something cheerful. And so, bloody-handed and whistling, Chris emerged from the basement with a panful of eviscerated ducks, which he rinsed at the kitchen sink, and he spent the rest of the day painting the bedroom which he and Karen were fixing up as a nursery. Their second baby was due in April.

The hunting season over, the Quinns and MacKensies became a foursome again, though the bond between the wives remained looser than the bond between the husbands. In those days—thought Chris, graying now, forty-five, driving northwest in his mint-green Chevrolet, passing in and out of sunshine as tattered clouds blew east . . . In Owl Brook—thought Chris, looking over at Larry tipping sideways in his seat, snoring, his corduroy cap having fallen into his lap . . . In those days in Owl Brook, wives were more totally married than now. A wife in those days thought of herself as half of a matched pair, seldom as an individual. Wifehood and motherhood

were all. Even if Rachel Quinn and Karen MacKensie
had had more in common than they did, even if they had
been deeply fond of one another, they would not have
allowed themselves, in 1961, the sort of friendship that
Larry and Chris enjoyed—as though any bond between
wives might be tantamount to betrayal of the marriage
vow.

In 1961 wives got busy and had babies. By some un-
written agreement couples of that era began their families without delay, and the Quinns—married now for six
months—were becoming alarmed that Rachel had not
conceived. Seven or eight of the Owl Brook faculty
wives (including Karen) were pregnant that year (mention the high school initials, OBHS, and everybody
laughed), and the Quinns were feeling unfruitful. So in
November they went somewhere for advice. They may
have gone to a clinic, but the advice they got sounded to
Chris as though it came from a pool hall. Larry was told
that his testicles were too warm. He was told to stop
wearing knit shorts because they nested his nuts in a
pouch and to stop taking warm baths before bedtime.
Larry obeyed. He wore boxer shorts by day and went to
bed every night with his equipment unwashed and cool,
and sure enough Rachel conceived. She went into labor
on the opening day of school the following September,
and Larry phoned Chris from the hospital. He sounded
frantic. "It's *hurting* her, Chris, what can I *do*?"

It was a rare occasion when Chris could speak with
more authority than Larry and he searched his mind for
something wise to tell him. The best he could do was
this: "Don't be surprised if the baby's head is shaped like
a catsup bottle, Larry. I was shocked when Billy was
born and his head was shaped like a catsup bottle, but in
just a few days it got round and nice."

Three hours later Larry called again. "It's a boy,
Chris, and sure as hell his head looks like a catsup bottle. God, if you hadn't warned me, I'd be in a state of
apoplexy. He weighs eight pounds and we're calling him
Bruce."

And this led, during the duck season of 1962, to an

even closer companionship between Larry and Chris, for so absorbed was Rachel in nursing her bonny boy that, when hunting opened in October, she cared not a tittle if Chris took her place in the blind. She hadn't wanted to be a hunter anyhow, she said, she had wanted to be a mother. And as a mother she had more in common with Karen, who had given birth, in April, to Kay. The two women spent a lot of time together with their babies, but still with a certain reserve between them, a reluctance to let their friendship deepen. If, earlier, they had thought of themselves not as friends so much as the wives of two men who were friends, now they seemed to see themselves not as friends so much as the mothers of three babies who were friends.

The duck blind was bigger in 1962, the boat new. The old boat, left all year in the pond, had developed a bad case of hull rot, and Larry and Chris bought a rubber raft for thirty-two dollars, each of them having put aside two dollars a week for two months. It was a season to remember, this second duck season, partly because of the plenitude of ducks (Chris made some spectacular wing shots and gave up blasting the birds out of the water) and partly because of the delicious duck dinners the Quinns and MacKensies ate together (while in the next room their babies dozed and belched and sucked rubber nipples), but mostly because of the beauty of those early autumn mornings, which began at five o'clock when they left Owl Brook and drove out to Amos Peterson's farm.

Larry and Chris would remember those mornings as long as they lived. When they parked beside the barn, there was a glimmer of light in the eastern sky and a faint cooing from beyond the open door of the hayloft, where pigeons were beginning to stir. The hunters walked down the slope through the woods and across the pasture, the frosty grass crunching under their boots, and they reached the blind about twenty minutes before the sun came up. They poured themselves a slug of coffee and sat on the edge of their hay bales with the expectancy of playgoers at curtain time. Did Chris's eye for the beauty of nature come into its maturity that year (he was twenty-eight) or why did his heart nearly stop when the sun came up? The east was a prism, its colors stupendously rich, and soon the whole landscape was colored like the sky—the sumac and saw grass, the meadows and maples. Across the sun was stretched the horizontal V of migrating geese; across the reflected sun was the V-shaped wake of a muskrat swimming totally submerged except for an eye and a nostril. A few minutes after sunrise a breeze sprang up and transformed the glassy pond into wrinkling ripples and small birds began to peep and dart among the cattails. Neither Larry nor Chris spoke of this display, but when Larry passed up an easy shot at a fat mallard and blamed the blinding eastern sky, Chris understood that, like himself, Larry was mesmerized, not blinded, by the unspeakable beauty of the morning.

6

LARRY—RIDING—SLEPT FOR an hour and a half. The mint-green Chevrolet emerged from the hilly forests and dropped down to the rich tableland of the Red River Valley, where the fertilizer factories and sugar refineries were visible for ten miles, their smokestacks for twenty, their smoke for thirty.

Seeing so far ahead made Chris sit up a little straighter behind the wheel. The sky was absolutely clear now, and he was glad, having been born with a craving for the openness, elbowroom, freedom. As nourishing to Chris as the oxygen in the air he breathed was the transparency of that air, its inexhaustible volume. What if air were opaque? Sometimes, in his nightmares, it was. In crowds, requiring latitude and the long view, Chris always strained to see over the tops of people's heads; reading novels, he started with the last chapter and only when he knew how the tale would end could he settle into its beginning. Two years ago he had given up a good job at Clement University because, among other reasons, his office had no window.

While looking ahead to Grand Forks on the Red River, he looked back to examine the murkier side of his Owl Brook days. The brilliant hunting days of 1962 were one thing; the darkness that fell over the MacKensies' domestic life was another. That was the year that Karen began to set aside certain portions of her day for brooding and drinking. Most often she treated brooding and drinking as separate activities (soberly brooding, happily drinking), but occasionally they were concurrent, which saved time. With the birth of Kay she had acquired a

46

nagging case of the postpartum blues, and while mothering her infants with a perfectionism bordering on neurosis, she had become deeply absorbed in the care and feeding of her own dejection.

Throughout his adult life Chris had been keeping a journal, in which he recorded events usually in the barest of terms—"October 7, 1962. Shot two mallards, flunked two sophomores"; "July 30, 1977. Divorced, finally"—but sometimes, when he was troubled, he went into detail:

October 8, 1962. Why is Karen so unhappy? Has she discovered too late that she doesn't want to be a mother? That she doesn't want to be a wife? That she doesn't want to be *my* wife? That she might have been happier in the nursing career she was training for when she dropped out to get married? Under the surface of her sadness is a strong current of anger.

Billy is two. His personality is forming. While I find this personality interesting and it draws me closer to the boy, Karen treats it like an annoyance. Maybe she loves Billy and Kay equally, but she dotes on Kay and speaks angrily to Billy. What she loves about Kay, who is six months old, is her absolute helplessness, her dependence. Kay's personality consists of an occasional smile and a lot of gurgling. At two years, Billy's consists of five million questions. What she dislikes about Billy, I guess, is his human nature. Her temper burns hot several times a day while her heart stays cold.

Today we strolled downtown, I pushing Billy in the stroller. Billy is the handsomest child in Owl Brook. He's practically the only non-Scandinavian in the county and thus the only little boy with dark hair and Celtic eyes. As we passed before the old Swedes chewing tobacco in front of Arnie's Pool Hall, they all stirred and murmured and chuckled softly. Karen, seeing their delight in Billy's cherubic face, cooed as well. She bent over him,

straightening his hair, straightening his collar and
generally fawning. Then at supper she screamed at
him for dribbling beet juice down his chin. He
wept. Karen grew more strident. I tried to shout
above her shouting. Alas and alack. Billy turned
purple with crying.

Yet outside the home Karen seemed happy. She
played the part of the faculty wife to perfection and was
honestly interested in the picnics and parties and fund-
raising teas by which teachers' wives marked their progress through the pages of the school calendar. Only the
Quinns understood how Chris's independent nature
caused him to bristle and sometimes rave against the in-
cessant advice that Karen handed out—or down—to
him. What had begun during the first year of their marriage as a sprinkling of wifely observations developed
later into a steady rain of motherly interdictions and after
a time Chris felt himself drowning in a torrent of repri-
mands and decrees. Wear your green tie and wipe your
nose and don't rustle the newspaper so loud, the children
are sleeping. Why is your salary so low and why can't
you be more civil to Superintendent Johansson? Chris,
losing faith in their marriage, did little to sustain it. Quite
the opposite, he longed for release, but when he said as
much to a colleague at the ragged end of a drunken
house party, he was thought to be out of his mind, for
Karen in the public eye was good for him.

"Karen is so good for you, Chris," he was often told.
Theirs was one of those marriages in which the wife is
thought to complement the husband but the husband for
some reason is never thought to complement the wife.
"She's just what MacKensie needs," Mrs. Johansson
was heard to say to the superintendent upon seeing Chris
and Karen enter the high school auditorium and take
their places for the second tedious act of *Death of a
Salesman* as performed by grade ten.

"She's so *good* for you, Chris," said the home ec
teacher as she stood in the MacKensies' dining room
with a small fork in one hand and a cup of shrimp

cocktail in the other and watched Karen circulate among the guests. Exactly what failings Chris brought to his marriage—in what way he was incomplete—were never made clear to him. He was neither an adulterer nor a wife-beater. He drank less than Karen. He never lied or cheated or missed a day of work or tried to be anything he was not. True, he was sometimes quick to anger, but no quicker than Karen, and he was just as quick to laugh. Maybe in a society as staid and humorless as that of Owl Brook his mildly mercurial behavior—his bold criticism of things that didn't please him (a fifteen-year-old playing Willy Loman, for example) and his explosive laughter at all the wrong things (the Bay of Pigs, for example)—needed refining. As thoroughly as he searched his conscience he came up with nothing more reprehensible than that.

Nor was he convinced that all those who claimed that Karen was good for him actually believed it. He was sure that half the people who said it were simply repeating what they had heard from the other half. In towns the size of Owl Brook—and particularly on faculties in such towns, where you associated with people you probably wouldn't have much to do with if the social possibilities were not so limited—your public image quickly hardened into permanence, like an acrylic portrait. Once the citizens of Owl Brook formed a mental picture of someone, they found it irksome to have to alter it. It was much easier to frame the picture and hang it at the back of their minds so that whenever your name came up in conversation—say, in the lumberyard or the beauty parlor—they could simply call up the portrait, and also its title. Who, upon seeing Renoir's lovely painting in the National Gallery, does not instantly think, "A Girl with a Watering Can," and who, upon hearing Chris's name mentioned in Owl Brook, did not think, "A Man with a Wife Who Is Good for Him"?

March 4, 1963. Well how good *is* Karen for me, anyhow? Actually quite good in some ways. She's good-looking—tall and dark. True, on her face are the lines you expect to see on a woman of thirty-seven, not twenty-seven, but they're easy to misinterpret as the lines of wisdom, not inner turmoil. Among the faculty wives she is respected, though considered a trifle too intense (Mrs. Johansson revealed this to Rachel, who told Larry), and they rely on her pies for their bake sales. She laughs as hard as she can at Mr. Johansson's moldy jokes. She gives as good as she gets in debating with the argumentative chairman of the village council, who lives next door and who can't put the fluoridation of drinking water out of his mind. When the school nurse is sick, Karen fills in as her substitute (though legally she isn't quite qualified), and last month when the home ec teacher lost all her cookie sheets to the boys of the senior class play (they were doing *Macbeth* and their cardboard shields sounded too much like cardboard), Karen rushed to her aid with our two cookie sheets. I guess all of this means that she *is* good for me in my line of work.

But today at hot lunch Superintendent Johansson said, "Having a wife like Karen does you a lot of good, MacKensie." Normally I can call up a meager show of deference toward this man who needs it so badly, but today I said nothing, not because I entirely disagreed with him but because I was so goddamn sick of hearing it. It makes me out to be the weaker partner of this marriage, in which, if the truth were known, it's Karen who has to have three drinks before supper and three drinks after if she's going to get through the evening. And another reason I'm so goddamn sick of hearing it is that I find it hard to tolerate people who can't think up anything new to say from one hot lunch to the next.

How did this fiction get started? I believe Mrs. Lester is to blame. Mrs. Lester has been our babysitter long enough to reveal her hatred of men. She avoids me like smallpox. She won't speak to me, even when I'm handing her money. She speaks only to Karen. She also sits for Larry and Rachel and the other day (according to Larry) she told them about the squabble she witnessed last week in our kitchen. I guess it was the day we were arguing about money. We don't have enough money. I want to go to graduate school this summer and Karen wants me to get a summer job. There are only two summer jobs in Owl Brook. The school hires extra hands to scrape old paint off the classroom walls and Karlin's Potato Farm needs potato pickers. Anyhow, Mrs. Lester (I can hear her say this through her thin, tight lips) told Larry and Rachel how I was slumped in the breakfast nook and giving Karen the cold shoulder as she tried to reason with me. Now it's true that I was silent. I had said my last word on the subject (I *would* go to graduate school) and I was watching the rain come down while Karen was standing at the sink, smoking, telling me how negligent of my family I was. In times like this Karen is always fluent while I, after a brief eruption, tend to clam up, and I suppose it was this more than the logic of Karen's argument that convinced Mrs. Lester that Karen was right and I was wrong and prompted her to say to the Quinns (to the endless amusement of Larry), "That dumb cluck, Mr. MacKensie—where would he be without that woman?"

In the fall of 1963, after two years together in Owl Brook, the Quinns and MacKensies parted company. A few weeks later the MacKensies themselves broke up.

The Quinns moved to Iowa City and enrolled at the university, Larry continuing his graduate studies in history, Rachel beginning work for a degree in theater. This left Chris alone in the frosty duck blind overlooking the ten-acre pond. On many October mornings he sat on a bale of hay and sipped his steaming cup of coffee as the sun came up, and as often as not without his gun. He went to get away from Karen and to savor the peace and beauty of Amos Peterson's corner of the world and to contemplate his discontent.

With Larry gone, Owl Brook seemed much smaller, the streets narrower, the atmosphere hazy. Larry had been more than a friend. He had been a model of the successful young teacher who was approaching thirty with ambition and self-confidence and a marriage that worked. In Chris's fondness for Larry there was a mixture of admiration and envy. Larry was destined to rise to the top of his profession. Tenure at a major university. Two or three important history books to his credit, scholarly yet readable. Chris felt an urgent need to keep pace. If he didn't get off the mark pretty soon, if he didn't resign at the end of this school year, he might molder forever in Owl Brook.

But where to go? What direction? Chris was weary of the classroom. His several years as an English teacher had left him impatient with the same prescribed poems at every grade level (why couldn't he change textbooks?) and the same five degrees of achievement (why couldn't he award his best students a double A plus and his worst a Z?) and the same eight parts of speech (why couldn't there be nine?). But more than all that, what really bothered him was the great number of students with whom he had no meaningful contact. He wanted to talk with them as individuals, not in groups of thirty-five. He felt certain that he belonged in education, but not as a classroom teacher locked into the fifty-minute period and the seven-hour day, and certainly not as an administrator puzzling over budgets and transcripts and attendance reports. What then? Librarian? Playground supervisor? Custodian? Bus driver?

By coincidence, at this time an entirely new position was created in Minnesota high schools and colleges that allowed for personal contact with students independent of classroom regimentation. Chris thought it over through the autumn and announced to Karen in December that he wanted to move to a university town and begin work on a degree in academic counseling. And after a few years had passed and Billy and Kay were in

school and not a full-time burden to their mother, he
wanted a divorce.

When he told this to Karen, she was sitting in the
breakfast nook, watching it snow, and Chris was standing at the sink. Because her face was turned away, he
couldn't make out her reaction. She said nothing for a
long time and he assumed that either she was waiting to
make sure her voice wouldn't shake (she detested weep-
iness; even during periods of great unhappiness she
might brood and bitch, but she never cried) or she was
sorting her questions into logical order (she was in the
habit of transforming discussions into inquisitions). Finally she turned from the window and, wearing her nar-
rowest, most critical look, said, "How much money do
counselors make?"

"Slightly more than teachers," he said. "Less than
principals. By the time I get my degree, I'll be worth
about six thousand a year."

"Billy and Kay and I will need three-fourths of that.
Can you live on fifteen hundred?"

"It isn't time yet to talk about child custody and
money."

"Oh, but it is. There's no time to lose. There's the
downstairs half of a duplex for rent on Iverson Street. It
has two bedrooms and a brand-new kitchen and a view
of the river. It's the perfect spot for a mother and her two
babies, at least for the time being. Later we can look for
something more elaborate, but for the next two or three
years we'll make do with the Iverson Street duplex. It
has a lot of things I've been wanting. It has a view of the
river and a dishwasher and a gas clothes dryer and best
of all it has no room for you! Now tell me, Kit, who's the
other woman?" Until he was twelve, his mother had
called him Kit, a name he liked as a boy but not as a
man.

"There is no other woman, there's only my need to be
free of you."

"But there has to be another woman, otherwise how
could you leave me?"

"I'm leaving because I want to learn how to live once

again without being harped at and nagged"—here his voice rose—"and interrogated and mothered! I intended to give you a few more years of my life so you could make plans for yourself, so the kids would be older, but if you're willing to separate here and now, I can hardly wait."

"Here and now it is, Kit." She sprang out of the breakfast nook with a vitality she hadn't displayed around the house for a long time. Her eyes shone the way they did at parties. "I'll engage P. B. Putterman to handle my end of things, he's said to be the best lawyer in town."

"Besides being the only one."

"But you will please initiate the divorce, I want it known that you left me. That way I can remain in Owl Brook and keep my self-respect. Nobody in Owl Brook initiates a divorce except bounders and fools. When people hear you've left me, they'll take you for one or the other. It's going to be hard for you to go through life without me, Kit. You may be capable of handling your schoolwork alone, but I'm the one who has made you what you are in the public eye. You don't understand your own failings. You've never appreciated my strength. You've never realized how *good* I am for you."

She mixed herself a gimlet.

By the following spring Karen and Chris were separated. When the school term ended, Chris went to Minneapolis and rented a room near the university and enrolled in graduate school. Once a week he drove the 175 miles to the duplex on Iverson Street to see his children and to drop into the office of P. B. Putterman, the nearsighted and palsied old lawyer who wore glasses as thick as a watchmaker's eyepiece and who was slowly, very slowly, setting in motion the stiff cogs of divorce.

When news of the separation reached Iowa City, Chris got a postcard written in Rachel's bold and upright hand, saying, "You dumb cluck, Mr. MacKensie, where will you be without that woman?"

7

THE DIVORCE TOOK THIRTEEN years
to become final. The delay, in the beginning was the fault
of P. B. Putterman. Paperwork took him forever. It took
him forever in 1963 because he didn't believe in divorce,
in 1964 because he was having strokes, in 1965 because
he was dead. Long before the death of their lawyer, however, the MacKensies had had a change of heart. In
southern Minnesota, in the pleasant town of Clement
Hill—where Chris with his master's in counseling took a
job at Clement University—he and Karen were reun-
ited, not out of love but out of Karen's interest in being a
professor's wife and living in a half-timbered bungalow
on faculty row, and out of Chris's interest in the upbringing of Billy and Kay.

For during his weekly visits to the duplex on Iverson
Street, Chris had seen Billy and Kay at the mercy of
their mother's mood swings. She went from high spirits
to low without stopping for long in between. One weekend she was civil and attractively groomed and the next
weekend she was drunk. One weekend he found his children spotlessly scrubbed and turned out in new clothes
and rejoicing over some new toy; the next weekend he
found them hollow-eyed and cranky and foraging for
nourishment in the messy kitchen. When he first sug-
gested a divorce to Karen, he had been reconciled to
losing Billy and Kay. He knew that no judge in the history of Minnesota had ever awarded a father custody of
his children. There had been the woman in Owl Brook
who ran off with the cocaine-sniffing drummer in a four-
piece band, and she was awarded custody. There was the

celebrated case of the woman in St. Paul who was awarded custody while serving time for prostitution. To the legal mind, a mother was better than a father every time. So be it, thought Chris in 1963—maybe there was something about family chemistry he didn't understand and the courts were right, and anyhow, he hankered to be free. But by 1965, when Billy was five and Kay was three and both of them jumpy as crickets, he decided they needed a sense of stability, a second adult presence in the house, a father. Ten years later, when Kay was on drugs and Billy wasn't speaking to him, he would question the wisdom of this decision (how could these kids be living a less satisfactory adolescence, even as orphans?), but if it was a decision with bad results, at least he had made it in good faith and he tried not to regret it. For there were plenty of other things to regret in those dozen years between 1965 (the year of their reunion) and 1977 (the year of their divorce), including the regret a man feels when he turns forty and discovers that among the investments that are lost when a bankrupt marriage takes a long time to dissolve are vitality and hope, the precious metals of youth.

And hadn't Karen lost even more than he? Yes, Chris couldn't deny it. Poor Karen had lost her looks and the treble tones of her voice. At forty she appeared fifty-five and at parties her croak was the voice you mistook for a man's. Gradually she lost the resolution that had kept her off the bottle for three or four months every year, and she lost all interest in the affairs of her children, though not her determination to possess them. She lost her driver's license. And then one day it occurred to Karen that everything she had lost in Minnesota might surely be recovered in California, whence her mother and her divorced sister wrote her letters about sunshine and grapes.

But one thing Karen never lost was her prominent place in the social scene. She had a lifelong talent for entertaining. Rooms full of people in their best clothes and their cups were her natural habitat. For her knowledge of who liked to be seated next to whom and her predilection for imagining exciting menus and her nimble way with table talk, Karen was an indispensable partner to all the hostesses along faculty row. And if she was that efficient and engaging and reliable at parties, mustn't she also be that way at home? That's what all the neighbors thought, even the senile Professor Hyde, who lived next door. Professor Hyde was the oldest member of the philosophy department, a nihilist who believed in nothing but tenure and who never trimmed the hair on his face (his eyebrows hung in his eyes, his mustache in whatever he drank) and who was therefore considered the sage of Clement University. It was this old man in all his wisdom who said to Chris (nudging him in the ribs with the point of his cane) on the day Karen and the children left for California:

"Jesus Christ Almighty, MacKensie, that woman was good for you."

During the MacKensies' dozen years in Clement Hill, Chris and Larry had gone hunting together once each autumn and had met on three other occasions. The first of these was the occasion of Karen's disappearance in the summer of 1965. She was gone three days before she called from Salt Lake City to say she was en route by bus to Fresno; she needed a breather; she'd be home in a couple weeks; love to the children. Later that day, when Larry—deep in his dissertation—called from Iowa City with questions about his writing style, Chris told him of Karen's disappearance, his alerting the police, her phone call.

"What the hell's in Fresno?"

"Her mother and sister. I should have guessed that's where she was headed. They've been phoning each other a lot lately."

"Chris, is your wife a mental case?"

Chris's answer was a sigh.

"So who's looking after the kids?"

"The neighbors and I. But day after tomorrow I'm supposed to be in Kansas City for the Midwest Counselors' Symposium, and I'm trying to find a live-in sitter for two days and two nights. My secretary's mother agreed to come in, but today she came down with the flu."

"Rachel and I will come in. What time tomorrow?"

"Nonsense. You're four hours away."

"Not the way I drive. What time do you leave?"

"Ten in the morning."

"We'll be there, the three of us. I can write scholarly prose in Clement Hill as well as Iowa City, and Rachel will enjoy the change of scene—our Quonset looks out on a gravel pit. Bruce can teach your kids how to eat paste."

"You're serious?"

"Go to Kansas City. Take three or four days. Take a vacation."

"I'm tempted."

"Do it."

The Quinns arrived at nine in the morning, delivered Chris to the plane and stayed two days beyond his return. Rachel devoting herself to the children and leaving the men to long walks and talks—Larry providing the counselor's ear for Chris's recital of marital conundrums.

Karen returned home in ten days—refreshed, she claimed, but looking bus-weary and hung-over.

Later that year, while spending a weekend with the Quinns in their Iowa City Quonset in order to proofread and discuss a late draft of Larry's dissertation, Chris was introduced to what remained of Larry's major adviser, Dr. Bresnahan, who was dying of lung and liver cancer. He was a highly esteemed man of such incredibly high spirits that the many friends and students who came calling at his hospital bed did so as much out of pleasure as out of duty. On the previous Wednesday, in fact, Larry had spent an hour at the professor's bedside, and his talk, though touched with melancholy, was cogent and wise; and so on Sunday afternoon, when Larry led Chris into the hospital and up to Room 400, neither of them was prepared to find Dr. Bresnahan delirious with pain and painkillers, and Mrs. Bresnahan weeping in a chair and covering her ears against the mysterious words he chanted:

"Laura, Laura, Laura, don't leave me, Laura, I love you." He strained against the straps holding him in bed. Open or closed, his eyes conveyed unspeakable anguish. This had been going on since yesterday noon, said Mrs. Bresnahan, and she had no idea who Laura was. Never in the forty years of their marriage had he spoken of anyone named Laura.

"Laura, Laura, I can't live without you, Laura."

Larry and Chris bowed out of the room.

Dr. Bresnahan raved and writhed for nearly a week before he died. After the funeral Larry wrote Chris an eight-page letter on the foolishness of prolonging life when the flesh was ravaged and the mind was gone. His tone was uncharacteristically strident. He had instructed Rachel to shut down all life-support apparatus if he himself should ever be brought that low; and if Rachel was incapable of seeing to it, then Chris must fly in from wherever he lived and pull the plug.

Farfetched, thought Chris, throwing the letter away, and he put it out of his mind for fourteen years.

In 1966 the Quinns stopped to see the MacKensies on their way through Clement Hill. Rachel was driving their station wagon full of books and clothes, and Larry and Bruce were following in a rented truck. They were moving from Iowa to Rookery State College in northern Minnesota, where Larry would join the history department and Rachel would finish her B.A. in theater. Larry had been offered jobs at Northwestern and Tulane, but Rookery lay at the center of the forestland which he intended would be the setting of his first book, a history of Minnesota logging. During this visit Larry casually announced that his nervous system was giving him a few problems and the most pessimistic of the three doctors he had consulted had feared that they might be the early signs of multiple sclerosis. But to Chris, Larry was the picture of health. His spirits had never been higher. He admitted to some eye trouble and a headache now and then and a nagging crick in his spine, but what was all that compared to his elation over the doctorate he was carrying away from Iowa City? It was Rachel who looked a bit worn, as the wives of doctoral candidates usually do when they emerge from three years of managing a family on the paltry pay of a graduate assistant, of making the best of campus housing, of typing long papers with footnotes. Bruce, who was four, was the same size as Billy, who was six. The Quinns hoped to reach Rookery by nightfall, so they stayed only long enough to empty a pitcher of lemonade, and when they left, everyone said they must visit each other soon.

But this was one of those cases, not uncommon, in which the wives keep the families apart while keeping them in touch. Karen and Rachel exchanged three or four letters a year (Karen's stationery was engraved with her initials; Rachel's was torn from a spiral notebook), but neither was eager to spend time in the other's house and so never instigated a family visit.

Once every autumn, however, Larry drove south and Chris drove north and they met in Owl Brook for a weekend of hunting. Because Amos Peterson's ten-acre pond had been taken over by other hunters, they drove out to the big swamp south of town and stood in the water, their guns on their shoulders, their conversations warm and amusing but year by year harder to sustain as their common experience in Owl Brook faded further into the past and the symptoms of Larry's disease became harder to ignore. Larry's eyesight was unpredictable and his aim got shaky, and Chris's fondness for him was complicated and deepened by conflicting emotions. One moment he felt himself drawn to Larry in a surge of sympathy and the next he was overcome with abhorrence at the slow death the man was destined to die. Chris always took the lead in arranging the Owl Brook hunt, yet when the meeting was at hand, it was all he could do to get out of his car and face Larry, who each October showed some new evidence of his degeneration. Most noticeable at first was his loss of coordination. Next he lost the color from his face and the lilt from his voice. Later Chris detected changes beyond the physical. The man fretted about small matters. He quit caring what he looked like. He never combed his hair. Though his research was nearly completed, he quit talking about his book on Minnesota logging. He allowed his suffering to show in his deep, cheerless eyes.

Their hunting petered out in 1975, Larry's last shot being a near miss at a tin can lying on the ground.

Then in 1977 Chris lost his wife and children and through a reassignment of rooms at Clement University he lost his office window. He missed his window a great deal and his children more than he had expected, and sometimes, in bed, he missed Karen. He craved a change of scene. He moved to Rookery State College, where he was named chairman of the counseling department.

Chris had a strong reputation among counselors. He had written a handbook for counselors which had become widely adopted as a text in graduate programs in education. Certain corporations distributed the book among their executives at human-relations seminars. Each October when he and Larry met in Owl Brook, Chris had been conscious of the contrasting developments in their lives. Professionally Chris was moving ahead while Larry, in his illness, was losing ground. Though Chris didn't say so because Larry would have called him sentimental, he was certain that it had been Larry's example years ago that got him off dead center and into counseling; and subsequently Larry's disease was a large part of Chris's need to excel in his work, as if he were somehow obliged to fill the gap in education left by his friend's diminishing abilities. In family matters, however, Larry was clearly the winner; Chris couldn't hope to compete. Each October everything Larry said about Rachel and Bruce indicated harmony, while Chris had less and less to say about Karen and Billy and Kay.

A Rookery realtor showed Chris six condominiums and one small apartment and was disappointed when Chris chose the apartment, which had nothing to recommend it except its view of the valley, two walls of built-in bookcases and its location near the Quinns, who welcomed him warmly.

During his first autumn and winter in Rookery, Chris ate two or three meals each week in the Quinn dining room and spent many evenings before the Quinn fireplace. He had not intended to be so often in their company and he protested, unconvincingly, that they went to too much trouble for him. But he couldn't resist what they offered him, a family feeling. The departure of Karen and Billy and Kay had left him empty. He had supposed that when you dissolved a joyless marriage, you opened yourself to the return of joy, but he discovered himself open instead to loneliness.

In matters of loneliness, Chris was a novice. He had never in his life been lonely. Indeed, during the last and most trying years of his marriage, when Karen was in treatment for alcoholism and Kay was in treatment for drugs and Billy's rock group was practicing in the basement, he thought of himself as suffering from the opposite of loneliness—which, he was amazed to discover, didn't have a name. Why, of the 600,000 words in the language, was there no word for the opposite of loneliness? Had no one else ever been spiritually crushed by an overabundance of troubled people in his life? There was a three-month stretch during his latter days in Clement Hill when every week he was expected to accompany Karen and Kay to group therapy, where he did his best to be helpful to the several drug counselors and alcohol counselors who took a scarcely concealed delight in counseling a counselor. These counselors (or moderators, as they were called) as well as the addicts themselves (immoderators?) probed Chris's psyche for the flaw that must certainly be responsible for his wife's drinking and his daughter's shooting up.

"Your daughter tells us you think too much, Mr. MacKensie."

"Your wife tells us you don't show her enough love."

"Your wife says you spend too much time at your work."

"Your wife says you aren't as sympathetic toward her as you are toward your students."

"Your daughter says you're an unfeeling clod."

"Your wife tells us she has given you the best years of her life and now you love somebody else and she doesn't know who it is."

"Your wife says you keep secrets from her. She doesn't know how much money's in the bank."

"Your daughter wants to love you, Mr. MacKensie, but you won't let her."

It was exhausting to take up these accusations one after the other and try to thresh the seeds of truth from the clouds of chaff (he had no lover; he did keep a small savings account hidden from Karen, for when she drank, she threw money away; he did work overtime at the college). Gradually Chris realized that what these people sought wasn't truth at all but emotional release. How often had he sat through an interminable session—one hour, two hours—and begun to wonder if the moderator had lost track of time, and then seen everyone brighten and the meeting end as soon as one of the participants—never Chris—broke into tears? He came to understand the orchestration of these encounter groups: first a long prelude of small talk from everyone, then a few measures of complaint from each of the four or five most troubled addicts, followed by an astonishing cadenza of anger or grief from an unexpected quarter (say, the man in the cowboy hat who had been looking so cool), then several bars of earlier themes (an interweaving of small talk and complaint) and finally an all-voice crescendo trailing off in a wail uttered by the weeper of the evening, whoever it might be. From the moderator's viewpoint there were mediocre sessions when the weeping amounted to merely a few sniffles and there were stupendous times when everyone but Chris broke down and cried.

Chris never cried, and this may have been part of the reason for the hostility he aroused. Quite often, in order to bring a deadly meeting to an end, he would have been more than willing to shed a few tears, but he couldn't remember how. He hadn't cried since he was thirteen and the mechanism for pumping water into his eyes had evidently atrophied from disuse. To compensate for this impediment, during cadenzas and crescendos, he did his best to look either hopeful, which required a false face, or melancholy, which didn't.

Dumfounded by weariness, Chris went home from each of these sessions only to hear the accusations reiterated, this time not filtered through a moderator or another addict but firsthand from Karen or Kay. And when he retired for the night, his sleep was usually delayed by the electric guitars and drums and screaming lyrics that blared up through the heat registers from the family room in the basement—Billy and his rock group, practicing. Billy was both the lead guitarist and vocalist. Between Chris and Billy the thread of communication had become badly frayed when the boy turned sixteen and began earning money with his music. Even-tempered and soft-spoken and mustachioed, Billy never defied his father; he simply ignored him. The boy had no time for dope or booze; punk rock was his needle, his bottle. "Aaaaaaaaaaaarrrrrrrrrrrrr," he screamed up through the heat vents as Chris, trying to sleep, asked himself how, in God's name, he had ever become boxed in like this; why, as a husband and father, he seemed to be growing more ineffectual by the day.

Chris had attended only one performance of Billy's group. This had been in a dive in North Minneapolis, where the crowd was unclean and glassy-eyed and the drinks were watered and the two bouncers got in a fight with each other. During the first number Billy spotted his father in the crowd and clamped his noncommittal gaze on him for about five minutes while he screamed, "Aaaaaaaaaaaaarrrrrrrrrrrrr." Chris didn't stay for the second number. He drove straight home and found six or eight of Kay's friends from therapy holding hands and singing a hymn about changing the things they could and accepting the things they couldn't. He found Karen in the bedroom passed out.

No wonder Chris longed to be lonely.

"But not *this* lonely," he said on one of his first evenings in front of the Quinns' fireplace, whereupon Rachel gave him a little hug and Larry chuckled and Bruce picked up his unamplified guitar and played him a quiet melody.

The benefits of this renewed old friendship were by no means one-sided. Upon moving to Rookery, Chris sensed Larry's despondency in its early stages, and three afternoons a week he went directly from his job to sit with him until Rachel got home from work and Bruce got home from football or swimming or whatever sport the season called for. This was Larry's first year of idleness, and it made him brood. Never mind the sun, the colors of autumn, the cheer that Rachel was certain to bring home at suppertime: these were very gloomy afternoons. Around four Chris would let himself in the front door and go through the house to Larry's den, where the two of them would sit drinking tea and listening to Mahler, who was Larry's god that year. They didn't say very much, for Chris was well trained in the futility of trying to extract speech from someone whose hope had been lost and whose self-esteem had been shattered. Because Larry had developed an aversion to artificial light, they let darkness creep into the room while below them in the valley the lights of the carnival came up and the graveyard disappeared in the shadows and only the river retained whatever color the sunset had left behind. From that time forward Chris would always see in his mind's eye—or rather he would feel in his breast—those oppressive moments of autumn sunset. Even worse were the sunsets of winter, for in winter the amusement park was boarded up and the river was frozen and the cemetery was covered with snow. Then the entire valley vanished at once as night clamped itself over the city in midafternoon, leaving the two men in darkness, impaled on the shafts of Mahler's dissonance and facing the black window and seeing nothing but the two points of red light that burned year round—the beacon atop the radio tower across the valley, the coal of Larry's cigarette reflected in the glass.

December 30, 1977. I'm a Beethoven man myself, and when Mahler begins to weigh too heavily on my soul, I insist on a Beethoven overture or concerto. At such times Larry allows me to indulge in what he considers my unschooled taste but not without screwing his face into a supercilious expression and making me understand my immaturity. Today, as I put the record of my choice on the turntable, he called me a goddamn romantic.

Why does Larry keep the stereo in his den? Why doesn't he put it in the living room, where Rachel might more easily listen to her show tunes; Bruce, his gospel rock? I suppose it's because he doesn't want to trouble Rachel and Bruce with the despondent picture he presents when he listens to music. When Larry listens to music, he sits on his spine in a deep chair and presses his chin on his chest and tears come into his eyes. *He's* the goddamn romantic.

Hard to say how this eerie companionship will affect the two of us in the long run. Some days I sense that I'm holding Larry back from absolute despair; other days I'm just keeping him awake— which might amount to the same thing. As for myself, I think I'm acquiring from Larry a more serious cast of mind. Gloom or bitterness might be closer to what I'm talking about, but where it applies to myself I'd rather call it seriousness. There's something about all these afternoons of cacophony and strong tea and encroaching darkness and seeing the tears of a forty-five-year-old man that leaves me serious.

In these dismal circumstances, Rachel is our ray of light. God, what would we do without Rachel? With Larry out of work, she has taken a full-time job as a social worker. Her degree is in drama and her heart is on the stage of the Rookery Civic Playhouse, where she's scheduled to open in *Desire Under the Elms* next month, but there's no living to be made as an actress in Rookery, and so she has taken a few courses in sociology and become qualified, as she describes it, "to bribe losers into telling me their secrets." She tries out for one play each year and is invariably cast in the lead. She says that one year of social work will be her limit. She can face misery either on the job or at home, but she can't face it both places. She says this in passing without a trace of self-pity, and then gets busy with supper, filling the kitchen with her delightful rendition of "Mack the Knife." Oh, Rachel, when you were eighteen and took my place in the duck blind, who could have foreseen the prominent place you would take in my heart?

Larry threw off his depression in the spring. On the day the hawks came back, there was a sudden flash of ardor in his eyes. Chris was sitting with him when he saw the first hawk. It was April and daylight lingered until after six o'clock and Rachel had just come home and looked into the den and said hello and gone into the kitchen to start dinner when a hawk came swooping down through the bare trees of the hillside behind the house and dipped and flapped and soared out over the river where the ice was turning black as it melted. Larry saw it and shouted, "The hawks are back!" and he went to the phone and called somebody he knew in Iowa City and said the hawks were back.

A day or two later he phoned Chris at the college and said he had seen two crows and a flock of ducks. He said there were grackles all over the place. He said he was going to get started on his history of Minnesota.

8

L ARRY — RIDING — AWOKE WITH a
start, as though from a nightmare. He removed a cigarette from his pocket and stared at it, unlit.

"Did you forget I've got to piss?"

Chris had forgotten. He had driven eighty miles since
Larry mentioned it. "Can you wait five minutes? We're
coming to Grand Forks."

"No." Larry dropped the cigarette beside him on the
seat.

"Well, how about two minutes? The first gas station."

"No."

"So what do you want—stop right here in the open?"

Larry pointed to his lap, his pants turning wet.

Chris braked and pulled over on the shoulder. Larry
opened his door and swung his legs to the ground and
finished from the edge of the seat. He drew his legs back
inside and pulled the door shut. They drove on.

"My doctor is always right, Chris. He told me the
incontinent stage was next." Larry fumbled with his zipper. "I'll need a catheter pretty soon. Sometimes I piss
when I don't know it, and sometimes I can't piss at all.
When I first got sick, it took the medical profession a
year and a half to figure out what was wrong with me,
but once they called it by its proper name every one of
their predictions has been on the money. They predict
depression, I get depressed. They tell me double vision,
I get double vision. They tell me crutches and canes, I
start using crutches and canes." He took out another cigarette and lit it. "They tell me piss my pants, I piss my
pants."

Chris turned off the freeway and they entered Grand Forks. They passed a brown golf course and a red-brick campus before pulling into a supermarket parking lot.

"We get breakfast and dinner at the camp, but we provide our own lunches in the field. So let's go shopping."

Larry looked at his lap. "I've got a raincoat in my bag. Would you dig it out for me?"

"Sure." Chris opened his door.

"Wait, let me tell you something." Larry looked out his side window, showing Chris the back of his home haircut. Rachel had trimmed a little higher on the right than on the left.

"Chris, I don't want to wear a catheter. I don't want to go around with a bottle of piss hanging from my leg."

Chris resettled himself behind the wheel and closed the door. "You didn't want a walker either, but you got one."

"But I never hated the idea of a walker as much as I hate the idea of a catheter. Haven't I got the right to hate some things more than others? Haven't I got the right to decide where I'll draw the line in my decline from a human being into a blob? Can't you understand that I'm telling you here and now that I won't allow myself to be pushed any further?" He looked at his lap and then raised his eyes, holding Chris in a deep, steady gaze until Chris had to look away.

"Let's go shopping," said Larry.

In the supermarket Chris grew impatient. Larry's confinement, his two years of thinking long thoughts and going nowhere and doing nothing had made him over-cautious when it came to buying cookies. Covered by his raincoat and supported by his walker, he stood at the cookie shelves and examined package after package, reading the details not only of weights and measures but of ingredients as well. Then at the produce display he stood for five minutes trying to decide if he wanted a banana or an orange. Next he called Chris into consultation over sacks of candy bars.

"Do you like Mounds or Nutty Rolls?"

"Mounds."

"I like Mounds too, but I'm also very fond of Nutty Rolls."

"Actually I like both," said Chris. "Take your pick."

"But you said you like Mounds."

"I *do* like Mounds. But I also like Nutty Rolls."

"Then why did you say Mounds?"

Chris was reminded of Karen, her inquisitions. He spoke to Larry in the tone he had often used on her: "Listen, Larry, the truth is that I really prefer the Nutty Roll, but I said Mounds because I bear a grudge against the Cooper Candy Company. They make the Cashew Creme Bar, too, you know. The last time I ate a Cashew Creme Bar I told myself I would never buy another product made by Cooper. The bar was nothing but a shadow of its old self. Never has a product been so eviscerated by its maker as the Cashew Creme Bar has been by Cooper. Have you had a Cashew Creme Bar lately? Back in the forties not even the harm worked on Butterfinger by the Great War was the equal of the harm now worked on the Cashew Creme Bar by inflation. Buy Mounds!"

A young woman wearing a red sweater stopped her cart to listen.

"Buy Mounds!" Chris told her.

She nodded seriously, stirred by his conviction.

He laughed. He didn't want her to think he was involved heart and soul in this question of candy bars. But she said, "My sentiments exactly," and selected a bag of Mounds.

Chris turned to Larry and laughed, but Larry was no less earnest than the young woman. "Now Hersheys," said Larry, leaning over his walker to examine a low shelf. "I think we should have some Hersheys."

"Definitely," said Chris.

"Semisweet or almond or Krackel or Mr. Goodbar? Or plain?"

"I like almond," said Chris.

"So do I," said the woman in red.

Chris walked off down the aisle of shoppers, leaving

his end of the discussion in the woman's hands. "And I also like Mr. Goodbar," he heard her tell Larry.

Ten minutes later, having picked up cheese and bread, Chris extricated Larry from the soda-pop section (Coke or 7-Up?—they took six cans of each) and steered him to the checkout counter.

"I need Rolaids," Larry told the cashier. "When I get away from my wife's cooking, I get gas."

"Over there," said the cashier, a girl in a green uniform and a hurry. With one hand she punched the cash register and with the other she pointed to a rack of razor blades and lozenges and *TV Guides*.

Larry squinted. "No, those are something else."

"But they *work* like Rolaids." The cashier glared at him.

"Not nearly so well. I need Rolaids."

"Then maybe over there." She pointed to another rack, far off. Chris went to investigate and came back and reported. No Rolaids.

The girl snorted. "Then maybe over there!" She pointed again.

Chris went and looked. No Rolaids. "Never mind," he told her. She punched the total button.

"Really, these work just as well as Rolaids"—spoken by the woman in the red sweater. She was standing near the *TV Guides* and holding up a roll of something wrapped in green foil.

"No, no, we need Rolaids," said Chris.

"Yes, Rolaids work best," said an elderly lady waiting in the checkout line.

"Thank you," said Chris, bowing low in her direction.

"I can't believe they don't have Rolaids in a store like this," said Larry. "Do me a favor, Chris, and look around, will you?"

"We've got to be moving on." Chris paid for the groceries.

"But what if I get gas?" Larry turned to the woman in red and the elderly woman. *"What if I get gas?"* This was a shout and both women turned away. He held his hands out, beseeching the cashier: "What if I get gas?"

"Fart," said the cashier.

In the car Larry sulked and muttered. He wanted Ro-laids. He didn't want a catheter. He wanted Nutty Rolls rather than Mounds. He had wanted Chris to eat breakfast with him, not just toast. He wanted to be home with Rachel. He wished he were dead.

Was this the same man Chris had known in Owl Brook? The man he had laughed with? The man who used to pick apart the fussiness of Superintendent Johansson? When had Larry and Chris last shared a full-hearted laugh? The candy bar discussion in the supermarket was the sort of thing that would have made them teary-eyed with laughter in the old days.

Larry sulked until they reached the border, where they stopped at customs. A Canadian official stepped up to the car and wanted to know how many guns they were carrying into his country.

Two.

How many shells?

Twelve boxes, twenty-five per box.

The officer cast his eye into the back seat. How long were they planning to stay?

Until Sunday.

How much liquor?

"I brought a quart of brandy," said Chris. He looked at Larry, who shook his head.

Destination?

Delta Marsh.

A hunting camp?

Yes, Blackie LaVoi's, near the town of Hill.

The officer stepped back from the car and saluted. "Good hunting."

Chris drove forward on foreign asphalt over foreign soil. Chris had entered Canada perhaps two dozen times in his life (several autumns he had driven up with men from Clement Hill to hunt grouse along the border; a few springs he had fished near Kenora), but never without tightening up inside. He had been three times to the British Isles and twice to Mexico, but neither of those places felt as distant to him as Canada. Crossing this frontier, he was invariably gripped by a sensation similar to that of having missed a deadline or called a wrong number or misread a map. He recalled how it felt to arrive at the Convention Center in Minneapolis last spring, where he was to address the Association of School and College Counselors (of which he was president), and suddenly realize that his speech was home on his desk. The knot his stomach tied itself into at that moment, though tighter, was much like the knot he felt upon entering the portals of Canada. What had he left behind?

It might have been daylight. All his trips into Canada had been in the fall or spring, around the times of equinox, when the Canadian sun hung alarmingly low in the southern sky. Driving north in the autumn, he saw the shadows lengthen and the towns grow smaller and the hardwoods, which at home were turning scarlet and gold, standing bare and birdless against the sharp horizon. Like flowers, like old men on park benches, Chris's natural inclination was toward the sunlight, away from the dark, and it made him uncomfortable to be speeding across the Canadian prairie with daylight at his back, and dying.

Or it may have been corn. Chris had been born in a town surrounded by cornfields. He'd seen the stalks bend and rustle in the wind, and he had heard them grow on hot nights. This hearing corn grow was assumed by many to be a legend or a lie, but more than once he had stood beside cornfields on sweltering, windless nights in August and had heard the stalks creaking as they grew. There was corn in Britain; there was a lot of corn in Mexico, but because of the short growing season, there wasn't much corn in Manitoba. Strange that the absence of corn should affect him like the absence of daylight. Strange that he should have come to think of corn— though he seldom ate it—as an elemental condition of life on this planet. Air, earth, fire and corn.

"Chris, what's it like at this Blackie's place?"

"It's pretty crude but closer to ducks than anyplace else. That's what I'm told by Perkins and Feitel and the rest of that bunch of hunters from the college. They go to Blackie LaVoi's every year. They drew me a map showing how to get from Winnipeg to Hill and from Hill to the camp."

"And you talked to Blackie LaVoi himself?"

"Yep. He roared so loud I had to hold the phone away from my ear. He promised us the best hunting of our lives."

"Then why isn't the place booked up a year ahead? It must be a dump."

"Maybe there were cancellations."

"Maybe there's no running water or food or beds. Maybe there's no roof. Maybe we sleep on the grass."

"There's running water—I asked. There's breakfast and supper and an indoor toilet and bunks for ten men."

"We'll see."

They were crossing a prairie of harvested wheatfields. Five miles ahead a single tree stood on the plain.

"I'm going back to sleep," Larry stubbed out a cigarette. He lay his head back, closed his eyes. "I wish I were home with Rachel."

9

So DID CHRIS.

Sailing along the flat road at fifty-five, sun and corn
behind him, Chris saw Rachel step out from the corner
of his mind where she had taken up permanent lodging.
In the course of his work, his reading, his sleeping, she
came forth like this, between thoughts, between dreams,
and edged into his awareness, sometimes standing in her
blue dress with the wide white belt and the top two buttons open at her throat, her eyebrows raised, her head
tipped slightly back, her smile animated. This was her
expression of high feeling—leading with her chin, her
eyes intense—and it gave her the aspect of eagerness
and yearning, the aspect of movement even when she
was standing still.

Or sometimes he pictured her in sweater and jeans
sitting in the rocking chair by the fire and reading aloud
from a script she was memorizing, or from a book of old
poems, or she might be talking about something that had
happened at the Rookery Civic Playhouse, where last
winter—Larry's second winter of idleness—she had
been appointed director. No more social work. No more
misery on the job as well as at home. And as for the
misery at home, it was less severe than the year before,
Larry's state of mind having become somewhat more
stable, not pleasant by any means but not so frightening.
This second winter came to be called the Doldrums
Minor, as opposed to the first winter after his layoff,
which they remembered as the Doldrums Major.

Sweater and jeans. Rocking chair and fireplace. The
birch-log fire, which Bruce had set, crackling high and

warm. Their tea cooling as Rachel read or recited or told her story. She liked to play with her voice, which could, if necessary, stir hearts in the balconies of theaters far larger than the Rookery Civic Playhouse. She was capable of bringing all the force of Lady Macbeth to bear on the question of whether you took cream in your tea. Poems she read quietly, under her breath, with long pauses. Larry and Chris were fond of the English poets, the older the better, and during their first winter together—the Doldrums Major—the three of them had begun taking turns reading from a thick anthology with a cracked spine, starting with Hopkins and working backwards. Rachel reading softly was something to behold. Chris remembered the night they had brought their tea in from the dining room, where Larry had been calling himself clumsy and worthless and unlovable, and Rachel told him she loved him more and more as time went by. Picking up the old book, she found Thomas Moore and softly, slowly, she read:

> It is not while beauty and youth are thine own,
> And thy cheeks unprofaned by a tear,
> That the fervor and faith of a soul can be known,
> To which time will but make thee more dear.

Chris was stirred by the conviction in her tone. Obviously she and Larry had plumbed love to a depth he himself had never known. He held his breath, jealous, as she read on:

> No, the heart that has truly lov'd never forgets,
> But as truly loves on to the close;
> As the sunflower turns on her god, when he sets,
> The same look which she turn'd when he rose.

Or sometimes, as now—2:00 P.M. on the Canadian prairie—he saw her in the sweatsuit she wore last November—could it be nearly a year already?—when she came jogging toward him as he strolled in the valley. November 1978. He was seeing much less of the Quinns

than he had the winter before. He had been elected president of the State Association of School and College
Counselors, and he was spending most of his spare time
on the road as a kind of missionary. With school enrollments falling and taxpayers looking for positions to cut,
counselors were becoming an endangered species, and
so he went around to various school districts and addressed the boards of education on the importance of
academic counseling. He consulted with administrators.
He sought out the counselors themselves and gave them
pep talks. Chris had never been one to climb on band-
wagons or attend rallies or join write-in campaigns (the
tiger, the whale, the snail darter would have to make it
without his intercession), but here was a cause that
swept him up, and he was surprised and pleased at how
zealous he could be. "Schools: Keep your Counsel,"
said the rear bumper of his Chevrolet.

So he had very little time this second year to visit the
Quinns. Moreover, he had very little inclination. He
didn't see how he could live through another winter in
Larry's dark den. During the Doldrums Major he had
served as Larry's companion and sounding board and
wailing wall, and to what end? Had he eased Larry's
suffering? Improved his temperament? Diverted him?
No, Larry was completely self-absorbed. If Larry were
underground, Chris sometimes thought, he couldn't have
been farther out of earshot. Despite the best efforts of
Rachel and Bruce and Chris to lift him up, he just kept
burrowing toward some undiscovered level of despair.
One winter of that was enough. When the hawks came
back that April and Larry climbed out of his tunnel,
Chris was determined to disengage himself from the
Quinns. The presidency of the State Association served
as a timely excuse.

But this was before he fell in love with Rachel. This
was before that cold November twilight when, as he
walked the footpath beside the river, Rachel materialized
in the gloaming. They stopped and talked.

"His mood grows darker as the days grow shorter,"
she said about Larry, panting, emitting small puffs of

steam. "But it's not like last year. It's too early to say, but I think this winter will be easier. Still, he broods."

"They've done a lot with medication lately, Rachel. There's medication for every mood. Ask his doctor."

"Oh, come now, Chris, you can't be serious. A dope addict is all I need. I *know* people on tranquilizers. You can't tell if you're talking to the person or to the medicine. Some of them are zombies."

She was right, of course, but hadn't the Quinns reached the point where Larry the happy zombie was preferable to Larry the brooding monster? He asked her, after a moment's hesitation, "What about my coming to see him when I can spare the time—when you and Bruce are gone? Would that help?" He spoke with only half his heart and with all his willpower.

"No, come as our guest whenever you please, Chris, but don't come anymore as our nursemaid. This year I have a different job—did you know?"

"I saw it in the paper. Congratulations."

"Thanks. It's marvelous. We rehearse mostly in the evenings, and Bruce is home with Larry then. How were we lucky enough to have a son so steady and good-natured?"

Surely she knew. She wasn't so ingenuous as to be truly puzzled by her son's charm. It was her gift to him. Was she asking Chris to point this out to her? Did her self-esteem need a boost? If so, it was the first time in Chris's memory. Before he could phrase a reply, she said, "Come home with me, Chris. We're having something good for dinner."

"Well, actually I've already eaten."

"I'll bet you haven't, not properly. I know how you eat. Tell me what you had."

"Popcorn."

"*Popcorn!* And last night for dinner, what did you have?"

"Sardines and crackers."

"*Sardines!* Chris, you're going to get rickets."

"Sardines are very nutritious. I ate a lot of them, and I had a cup of hot chocolate."

"And the night before last? No, don't tell me, I don't want to hear." She laughed and took his arm, and as they went up over the footbridge, he felt the beat of his heart keeping pace with the bounce in her step.

Dinner was something Italian that had been browning and bubbling in the oven for most of the afternoon. Bruce chatted happily about football, and Larry made an effort at companionability, but it was Rachel who commanded Chris's attention.

This meal marked the turning point in his relationship with the Quinns. Now Rachel came forward and Larry stepped back. Chris was fond of them both, but how could the twisted, sorrowful love he felt for Larry outshine this splendid new emotion he felt for Rachel? Was it love? No, he decided, not yet. But it was close. Later, in reviewing the course of his love for her, he would trace not love itself but the delight that led to love back to his first forkful of this delicious mixture of cheese and ground meat and spices. The cheese wasn't extraordinary, the spices were those to be found in little boxes in everybody's kitchen and the meat was probably hamburger, yet the finished product tasted so exotic and healthful and the entire meal was staged with such skill —the seating, the lighting, the lines of conversation— that Chris wanted to applaud. When they finished eating, Rachel went off to the Playhouse to rehearse *Harvey* and Larry and Chris moved into the living room, where Bruce built a fire and the three of them watched football on TV.

The following evening Chris again met Rachel on the footpath, not by accident.

He said he was still savoring whatever she had fed him for dinner last night, and he wondered if it had a name. She said it was lasagna with variations and asked how it compared to popcorn. They talked for a few minutes and he sensed a heightened enthusiasm in what they said, a vibration. Something between them had obviously shifted like tumblers in a lock; they were seeing each other with an interest altogether new to their friendship.

November 16, 1978. How to account for two old friends suddenly looking at each other in a new way? How does love begin? What brought Juliet out onto her balcony and Romeo into the garden? What gave Adam and Eve the notion that they were the interlocking parts of a plan? Surely something more cosmic, and less tangible, than a plate of lasagna.

Yet we're both reluctant to acknowledge the attraction we feel. Having known each other for nearly two decades, but only in relation to Larry, we're awkward without Larry between us. When, before yesterday on the footpath, were we ever alone together? I can't remember a single time. Seeing Rachel at home has meant seeing Larry as well, and usually Bruce. Seeing her at the Playhouse has meant applauding her with four hundred other playgoers or greeting her backstage with dozens of other well-wishers.

Facing her on this second night beside the cold river, Chris wondered if their delight was exactly mutual. He looked for the answer in her eyes, for it seemed that their faces—his as well as hers—were unmasked only around the eyes. They did with their eyes what they wouldn't do by word or gesture. His findings were inconclusive. First he thought he saw a look of deep affection but then, as though she had discovered him searching, her look turned noncommittal. He let his eyes drop to the shape of her breasts under her sweatshirt— not a stolen glance but a survey, deliberate as a touch— and at this she hopped twice, said goodbye and ran up over the footbridge. He turned and walked farther downstream, happy they had met, sorry they were so discreet, and aware that from now on he would take this walk with a sense of expectancy, hoping to see Rachel come pumping around the next turn in the path.

But this was their last meeting in the valley, for overnight Rookery was buried in a heavy snowfall and the paths along the river became unwalkable, unjoggable. Their next meeting took place outside Chris's apartment building on the day that he had decided never to seek her out again, never to build on the delight she had inspired. Never to see her again would have been impossible; in a city of only fifty thousand they were bound to meet on the street, and her stage performances were too accomplished to resist attending. Besides, there was always Larry. But let it die as delight before it turned into love. She was Larry's wife, after all. Forget her. Drive around the state and save counselors instead.

Such was his resolution on a snowy Saturday afternoon, dark and cold. During a pause in the snowfall he put on his overshoes, scarf, jacket, mittens and fur hat and went out to shovel the front sidewalk. The building superintendent had had heart attacks and his doctor forbade him to shovel snow or mop floors. The superintendent's wife mopped the hallways; Chris did the shoveling. He went to the superintendent's apartment to pick up the shovel and he took the superintendent's dog outside as well. The dog, a spaniel pup, scooted around in the snow like a Fisher-Price pull toy, its nose to the ground, its rump high in the air. Chris was cleaning off the front steps when he heard his name called and turned to see Rachel standing in the street, wearing a white stocking cap and a blue jacket over her sweatsuit. She bent to the pup, which stood on its hind feet and nuzzled between her legs.

"You're a jogger for all seasons," said Chris, joining her in the street where the snow had been plowed and the running was smooth, if icy.

"I ran to the library"—she held up a book for him to see—"but it's treacherous. I took a spill and thought for a minute I busted my ass."

He saw that the book was poetry by Berryman. "Him again," he said, recalling her reading Berryman aloud one evening a year ago.

"Yes, him again. His last book."

"I have difficulty understanding him."

"He's very appealing—spontaneous, flaky sometimes."

"It's my age. No new tricks for old dogs, I'm afraid. You were educated to different rhythms than I was, Rachel. You're nine years younger."

"That many?"

"I'm forty-five."

She nodded. "Nine it is. But there's hope for you, Chris. Come over tonight and we'll sit by the fire. We'll try to teach you some new tricks. Larry was saying this morning that he misses seeing you. . . . "

She had more to say, but Chris wasn't listening. He was distracted by her frosty hair. Hanging over her ears were curls of white in contrast with the rest of her red hair which flowed loosely from under her stocking cap. This was the frost of her breath—jogger's breath— caught at mouth level as it passed behind her, the wind of her pumping lungs trapped in her hair and turned to ice. He had an overpowering urge to melt it with his own breath.

"Tonight, Chris? Will you come over tonight?"

"Tonight? Yes. Definitely."

"Come early, we'll save dessert." She was off now, hopping backward down the snowy street, her book, her smile, her frosty breath bobbing away in the snowflakes that had begun once more to fall.

"Seven?" he called, holding the pup, who strained to follow her.

"Seven's fine." She turned and headed for home, running in earnest.

It was not yet seven when Chris knocked eagerly at the Quinns' front door. Bruce led him into the living room and deposited him with Larry, then went into the kitchen to tell his mother that he had arrived. Chris had brought one of his new albums for Larry to hear. Beethoven's *Triple Concerto*. Larry held the album on his lap and pondered the musicians pictured on the jacket. Rostropovich looked happy; Serkin, worried.

"I played the violin until I was eleven," said Larry. "After that I concentrated on the piano. I forget, did you hear me play in the days when I was good?"

"You sometimes played at faculty parties in Owl Brook," said Chris. "I remember your playing the Happy Birthday song."

"Whenever I listen to music, I wonder if I could have made it as a performer. If I hadn't got MS, who's to say I couldn't have made it as a concert pianist?"

"You never know—but from the little I heard you play, I'd say your repertoire was too limited. I mean, your touch was superb, but if you're going on tour, you need more than the Happy Birthday song."

"Be *serious*, for God's sake, stop being clever. Can't you see I'm being serious?"

"I *know* you're serious, Larry, and so am I. I seriously believe that when Rudolf Serkin went on the road, he knew how to play more than the Happy Birthday song."

Larry flung the record across the living room; it sailed like a Frisbee and struck a china pitcher on the bookcase, knocking it to the floor and shattering its handle and spout. Rachel, in the kitchen, apparently didn't hear the crash, for her singing went uninterrupted as she rattled pans in the sink.

Chris retrieved the album. As he picked up the pitcher in a dozen pieces—it was an heirloom from Rachel's mother—and set them on the bookcase, he regretted not humoring Larry. Yet he knew that humoring him seldom worked. Let his doctor humor him, let Bruce humor him, Chris could not. During the Doldrums Major Chris had run the gamut of responses to Larry and had found that the hard-boiled attitude was the only one that paid off.

A few minutes later Rachel, wearing a woolly tan sweater, brought in a tray of dessert. Tea and cheesecake. As they ate before the crackling fire, Chris waited for her to notice the broken pitcher, waited for her reaction. But of course he could predict her reaction. Seeing the pitcher, she wouldn't say or do anything about it until later, when she would try to glue the pieces together, or if that that was impossible, she would throw it away. Where Larry was concerned, she seemed to Chris imperturbable.

"I was telling Chris about my music training, Rachel." Larry was eating with his face low, close to his TV tray. "If I had full use of my fingers and my eyes, I could be a damn good pianist right now. I could be at the height of my career."

"It's true," she said.

"But Chris doesn't believe me."

"That's because Chris never heard you play."

"Oh but I did," said Chris, his mouth full of cake. "In 1962 I heard him play the Happy Birthday song."

"Don't be flip," she scolded. "Larry was serious about the piano, and very accomplished." She sat in the rocker with one leg folded under her, and she reached for Larry's hand.

Chris said, "How serious can you be and keep it a secret? I never knew him to practice."

"Margaret Mitchell kept *Gone with the Wind* hidden under her bed," said Rachel. "Hardly any of her friends knew she was writing it."

Chris nodded, acceding to the pretense—Larry the Great Artist.

They ate quietly for a few minutes; then Larry said, "Read us something, Rachel."

She put down her teacup and took the old anthology off the mantel, opening it to a page she had marked. Slowly, softly, she read the Thomas Moore poem, the last four lines of which never failed to pacify Larry. They aroused Chris.

> *The heart that has truly lov'd never forgets,*
> *But as truly loves on to the close;*
> *As the sunflower turns on her god, when he sets,*
> *The same look which she turn'd when he rose.*

She held Larry's hand as she read, stroking his knuckles with her thumb. If Larry were a cat, thought Chris in his envy, he would be purring.

* * *

Later that night, as he lay in bed reading, Chris's phone rang.

"Chris, I want you to hear this." It was Larry. "Chris, are you there? I want you to hear this. . . . Rachel, come on now, I want Chris to hear what you sound like when you blow your cork. . . . Come on, let him hear you, Rachel. I want him to hear that god-awful screech of yours. . . ."

There was no screech, no sound but Larry's breathing.

"Rachel, come back here and do that screech again for Chris, and say what you said when you saw the pitcher. He thinks you're so damn perfect, he should know what you're like when you blow your cork. Come on now. . . ."

Silence.

"Larry, I'm hanging up. Goodnight."

"No, wait a minute, Chris. You think Rachel's so damn perfect all the time. You sit around here looking at her as if you were venerating some kind of saint. Well, she's no saint, not by any means. She just found the pitcher and I told her what happened to it and she blew her cork. . . . Rachel, will you come back in here and run through that screech again for Chris?"

Silence.

"Goodnight, Larry."

10

*I*T WAS MIDAFTERNOON WHEN Win-
nipeg sprouted on the flat horizon. Chris was always
astonished to come upon this metropolis in the wheatfields. Just as the endless prairie was dulling him into
thinking that he had outdistanced the modern age, he
found himself at the edge of Winnipeg with its street of
London-like banks, its self-congratulatory billboards
("Friendly Manitoba") and its industrial haze.

Larry was awake. "Let's go into Winnipeg and get a
hotel room."

Chris said, "Blackie waits."

Northwest of the city they left the freeway and followed a crooked line that crisscrossed a crease in the
road map. The crease extended as far as the Yukon, but
the road stopped in the village of Hill, a town apparently
named by someone with a sense of humor, the only rise
in view being the bump where Main Street crossed the
railroad tracks. Above the cluster of one-story buildings
stood a grain elevator and a Ukrainian church. The white
elevator was weathering to gray and leaving slightly east.
The gold church steeple—an onion steeple surmounted
by a spike—was tarnishing to green; the spike bent
west.

Reading the hand-drawn map given to him by Perkins
and Feitel, Chris took a dirt road leading north from Hill.
They passed four farms at mile intervals: a large farm,
a small farm, an abandoned farm and finally the ruins of a
farm. Then, where the road turned right as though to
dodge oblivion, he drove the Chevrolet straight ahead
into a bumpy pasture (the barbed-wire gate was stand-

ing, or rather lying, open) and he followed a grassy trail along a fallen fence line and pulled up at the door of Blackie LaVoi's hunting camp.

"God, would you look at this dump." Larry was three hundred miles from his fireplace.

The camp was a series of sheds attached end to end, and if they didn't collapse in the first gale of winter, it would be a wonder. Thirty years earlier they might have been built square with the flat earth, the walls parallel with the rain, but three decades of sun and frost and hail and neglect had cracked the shiplap siding and shingles, separated the windows from their lintels and tipped the foundations. Beyond the buildings was the tall grass of Delta Marsh, a watery bog as big as the state of Delaware, a maze of waterways and islands which were the breeding grounds for most of the ducks that migrated up and down the Mississippi flyway. Beyond the Marsh, according to the map, was the vastness of Lake Manitoba.

"Do you want to wait here while I get our room lined up?"

"I need the toilet."

"Okay, I'll get your walker."

"I can't walk into a houseful of hunters with a walker. Let's try it without."

"Right."

Supporting him under the right shoulder and bearing half his weight, Chris helped him up the walk (a plank) to the doorstep (a packing crate). He pushed open the warped door. The floor inside was warped as well, and the door opened only wide enough to let a man through sideways. They entered a room containing ten bunks— five uppers, five lowers—and a wood-burning stove with a pile of wood and an empty pail standing beside it. A plastic basin stood on a chest of drawers, and behind the basin a mirror leaned against the wall. The ceiling was four inches above their heads. Whoever slept in the top bunks had scarcely a foot of clearance. The room had three windows, two of which were covered with cardboard while the unwashed panes of the third filtered half the light out of the afternoon sun.

Two women wearing jeans and blouses came into the room by another door. The woman in the lead was about fifty.

"Hi, who are you?" She had a broad smile and a tic in her right cheek. Her hair was gray and long.

"MacKensie and Quinn."

"We got a MacKensie and Quinn?" she asked the other woman.

"Yeah, from Minnesota." This other woman was shorter and younger, perhaps twenty-five; she had breasts of remarkable size, which on someone taller might have been attractive but on her were largely awesome.

"Okay then, my name is Gladdy," said the older woman. "You need anything, you just call Gladdy. Them two bunks on the end are yours." She pointed to the upper and lower next to the warped door. "You want water, there's a hose in the next room. You want hot water, you put water from the hose into that pail and you put the pail on the stove...What's the matter with you?" She was looking at Larry, whose knees were buckling. He was clutching an upper bunk.

"He's had too much to drink," said the younger woman. She smiled coyly.

"No, it isn't drink," said Chris. "He's always like this."

"Except when I'm worse," Larry said.

"Well, anyway, whatever it is, he don't look none too healthy," said Gladdy. "What he needs is some good home cooking." She laughed, her cheek twitching.

"Yeah, a goose," said the other, her smile turning sly.

"I need a bathroom is what I need," said Larry.

"Sure, come on, we'll show you around."

Before leaving the bunkhouse, Gladdy paused to say, "See there, you've got nails on the wall to hang up your clothes. And here's a chest of drawers if you need it." She opened a drawer to demonstrate that it was indeed a chest of drawers. They all looked in. At one time the drawer had been lined with newspaper (*Winnipeg Senti-*

nel, Chris made out), but the paper was chewed to shreds and mixed with mouse turds.

They went into the passageway connecting the bunkhouse with the next room. In the passageway was a toilet stool with no tank. A coil of hose lay on the floor.

"See here," said Gladdy, "you want to flush it, you squirt this hose in it. The faucet's there on the wall."

Larry said, "You folks go on ahead, I'll try it out."

Gladdy laughed. The younger one giggled.

"Looks like he's seen better days," said Gladdy as they entered the next room and she shut the door on Larry.

"Looks like he's come through the wringer," said the other. When she giggled, her front bounced.

This was the dining room, a narrow room. A trestle table down the middle left little space on either side. On the walls were newspaper clippings—photos of hunters, news of dead ducks. Chris saw that the room beyond was the kitchen, and at the far end of the kitchen was a curtained doorway, leading no doubt to the living quarters of Blackie LaVoi and these women.

He heard Larry turn on the faucet; he heard a stream of water; he heard the toilet gurgle. Gladdy opened the door on Larry and said, "Atta boy." Turning to Chris, she said, "You're too late for the afternoon duck hunt, but you've got an hour of daylight if you want to go out for chickens."

"Chickens?"

"Yeah, what you Yanks call partridges. You know, chickens."

"We'll see. First I think we'll bring in our gear and get settled."

"You got your hunting licenses yet?"

"No, I was told we could buy them here."

Gladdy nodded, smiling broadly. "From her." She indicated her partner.

"Fine, but first give us a chance to settle in." He led Larry back into the bunkhouse.

Clutching at the wall of beds, Larry made his way to their assigned places. He sat on the bottom bunk and sighed. "What the hell are we getting ourselves into, Chris? A hose to flush the toilet, for Christ's sake."

"This is duck hunting, remember? This isn't one of your MS Society ice cream socials. Hell, in the army you slept in a pup tent at twenty degrees and never complained."

"A guy grows up."

"I grant you it isn't the Biltmore, but for three nights it's plenty good and we've got the best hunting in Canada right outside the door."

"Then how come we're the only ones here?"

"Because the rest are out hunting. Look there— somebody's gear. And there, somebody else's." Four sleeping bags were spread out on four bunks. "There seem to be six of us in all, and probably more coming in for the weekend."

Beyond the dirty window, daylight was failing. Chris stepped to the center of the room and pulled the light cord—a forty-watt bulb in the ceiling.

Larry took off his pants, wet since Grand Forks. "Did you see the knockers on that woman, Chris? What did she say her name was?"

"I saw them. She didn't say."

"They have to be the biggest knockers in the North."

Chris made four trips to the car, squeezing through the door with their sleeping bags, duffel bags, guns, boots, shells. Hersheys and Mounds. On the back seat he found Rachel's sack of ham sandwiches and apples. He left it in the car for tomorrow's lunch; the night air would refrigerate the ham.

Gladdy came into the bunkhouse and watched Larry pull on his canvas hunting pants. When his shirt was tucked in and his belt buckled, she said, "Come on, she's ready for you now."

The men followed her past the toilet again. At the trestle table Knockers of the North was seated with government booklets arranged in front of her. She had changed her clothes. She wore a tight brown T-shirt and across her steep contours glittered a message in silver letters. The men were lifelong scholars and their eyes were drawn to the printed word: "THIS IS MY BODY BUT I SHARE."

"Get the message, Larry? Or should I read it to you?"

"Don't bother. I'm seeing double, but I get the message."

"I can take you guys one at a time," she said.

"Me first." Larry sat down on her left and she began to work on his license. It took a long time. While she pored over her booklets like someone writing a thesis, Chris read the news on the walls. Gary Cooper, he saw, had once hunted here. So had Ernest Hemingway. And here was an inscribed photo of Clark Gable: "Blackie: Thanks for a great shoot—Clark."

Moving along the wall, Chris came upon two pages from a 1955 issue of *Sports Afield*—framed, under glass. It was an article entitled "Blackie Saves the Day." It told of the time Blackie LaVoi rescued four hunters caught in a sudden late-autumn storm. The illustration, which occupied most of the left-hand page, showed Blackie LaVoi larger than life. He was walking knee-deep in icy water and towing, with a rope over his shoulder, a boat containing the four hunters. He wore a black mustache and he had a happy glint in his eye. The four hunters, cowering in the boat, were puny by comparison. The illustration was bold and colorful and it indicated that while the North was too much for the hunters, Blackie was too much for the North, the invincible conqueror all men supposedly dreamed of being. Did women have a corresponding dream? Chris wondered. And, if so, was it this conqueror they dreamed of conquering? In the picture Blackie was part reptile, impervious to the icy water; part goat, surefooted on the slippery stones. The wind parted Blackie's long black hair as Blackie parted the wind, delivering the frightened hunters safely to shore.

Chris heard voices in the kitchen—Gladdy's, and then a man's. The latter was the wheezy but commanding voice he had heard on the phone. "Why in the goddamn hell does the sun have to shine right in the middle of duck season? Them four Vermonters will be coming in pretty soon with their tails between their legs. Lucky to shoot a stray blackbird on a day this nice."

Chris looked into the kitchen and saw Gladdy peering into an ovenful of duck. It was a cast-iron oven in a range fired by wood and it held three shelves of sizzling purple duck breasts. On top of the range were a steaming kettle of potatoes and a steaming pot of coffee. Then he saw the man—Blackie LaVoi—step into the kitchen through the curtained doorway. He was tall, an inch or two taller than Chris, and he was dressed in dirty gray— a gray flannel shirt and baggy gray pants. His hair was thin and gray. His face was purplish, the color of duck meat. His mouth was sunken for lack of teeth. His mustache was white.

"Who's that?" he shouted, pointing a long finger at Chris in the doorway. One of his eyes was cocked. The other was angry.

"Quinn and MacKensie from Minnesota," said Gladdy, straightening up, closing the oven, smiling at Chris.

"I'm MacKensie."

"You got a reservation?"

Chris nodded. "I arranged it with you by phone."

"That's fine then. That's good. Good, good." He advanced upon Chris, put his long arm around his shoulders. "It isn't always easy getting into my camp, but once you're in, you're taken care of. Ducks, guides, women, meals, boats, decoys—you name it, I'll get it for you. Gladdy cleans your birds. You never have to pick a feather when you stay with Blackie LaVoi. I know it doesn't look like good duck weather today, but I smell moisture and sure as hell we'll get rain and wind before the weekend is over, mark my words." His words smelled of whiskey. "This here your partner?" He went in and stood beside Larry's chair.

"Yes, Larry Quinn. Larry, this is Blackie LaVoi."

Larry half rose and offered his hand, which Blackie took and examined in disbelief. It was so soft and pale. He felt Larry's thin right arm, elbow to shoulder. Larry sat down. Blackie, smoothing his mustache, scowling, turned to Chris and said quietly, "Holy Christ, what's the matter with him? You won't find a hand like that on any man in Canada, except maybe some faggot in Winnipeg."

"I have multiple sclerosis," said Larry.

Blackie spun around and pinned Larry with his good eye. "What's that?"

Larry glanced away for a moment, as though deliberating whether to confront this boor with his boorishness or demand that Chris take him home. Deciding to stay, he stood and delivered a brief lecture:

"I have a degenerative disease of the nerves. At the rate it's progressing, it will kill me long before my time. It has nothing to do with faggots." His voice rose and cracked. "I have come to your camp expecting the same ducks, boats, decoys, and meals—if not the women— that you promise all your hunters."

"That's fine then," said Blackie. "Fine and good. Good, good. Yessir, you're my friend just like MacKensie here is my friend." He patted Chris on the shoulder and he reached out to embrace Larry, but before he could do so, Larry sat down. "We're all friends here, right, Poo Poo?" He moved around behind Knockers of the North, put his hand on her hair and bent down to see what she was writing. "Quinn, eh? Born in 1932. Do you studs know what I was doing in 1932?"

"What?" said Larry.

"I was up in the Northwest Territories trapping beaver. You know what I was doing in 1933?"

"No."

"I was up in Hudson Bay, killing whales. You know what I was doing in 1934?"

"No."

"I was in Ontario teaching a bunch of government mapmakers how to survive in the wilderness. In 1934 I was twenty-four years old. Those city boys didn't know the first thing about the wilderness. I had to teach them how to paddle and portage a canoe and how to skin out a rabbit and how to wipe their ass with linden leaves. They were practically dead of thirst before they gave up and drank crick water. You know what I was doing in 1935?"

"You were trying to figure out how toilets flush."

"Larry," Chris cautioned.

Knockers of the north—Poo Poo—giggled.

Blackie overlooked the remark. "Rookery, Minnesota. That's where one of my wives came from. She was born there and she's buried there. She never liked it up here. She always said this country would be the death of her, and sure as hell, it was. She died of typhoid. We lived over east of here, in the woods. She always wanted to be buried back in Rookery, so that's where I shipped the body. Took care of the whole thing by telephone. She died during the deer season and I couldn't get away, and that was the first time I realized you can take care of everything in life by telephone. So a couple of days later, hell, I called up the Prime Minister of Canada, but some dink in his office said I couldn't speak to him, he was busy. I said I was Blackie LaVoi—there's nobody in the western provinces with a bigger name than Blackie LaVoi—and quick as a wink he put me right through to the Prime Minister. I said, 'Fella, this here's Blackie LaVoi in Manitoba and I say the highway you're trying to put through Delta Marsh is a goddamn boondoggle,' and I hung up before he had a chance to come back at me. I forget just who the Prime Minister was, but he was somebody I didn't have any respect for, not a bit." Blackie spoke with great force. His dark face was animated, his good eye hooded like a hawk's, his bad eye wide, fixed on the ceiling. "And that was the last we ever heard of a highway going through Delta Marsh. It was never built."

Chris stepped to the wall for another look at the illustration from *Sports Afield,* wherein Blackie appeared to be forty or forty-five. His chest was a barrel and his forearms rippled with muscle. Chris turned from the picture and looked at Blackie himself, the remnant, the husk. He stood behind the young woman, peering down, reading what she wrote, his large hand capping her head. And Larry: sitting on their left, his arms resting on the table, his shoulders stiffly hunched. Two men in the last stage of life, thought Chris, one about seventy, the other forty-seven. Blackie, depleted, was not so depleted as Larry. Time didn't ravage as ruthlessly as disease. In Blackie were vestiges of his former self. Although Time had sunk his chest and wrinkled his face and cocked his eye and bleached his mustache, he was still a commanding presence. He was tall and his voice was loud. His cocked eye gave him the distracted, intense look of an Old Testament prophet; his good eye was unmuddied. What did Larry have left of *his* former self? His muscle and color were gone. He had headaches and fits of depression and his bladder opened against his will. He had hung onto his wit, but it had turned cruel. His dark eyes were as deep as ever, but they scared people. Blackie would outlive Larry, Chris realized with a shiver, a pang of fear. Blackie had maybe eight or ten years left to him. Larry had forty-eight hours.

Larry slid over to the next chair and Chris took his place, thinking, Forty-eight hours—Saturday afternoon. As he sat on the young woman's left and answered her questions, his eyes pointed straight ahead, held by the map hanging on the opposite wall.

"Christopher MacKensie. MacKensie with a capital *K*." It was a large map of Delta Marsh, the waterways white, the solid ground black, the sinking bog gray. The Marsh was a maze. The waterways twisted like pretzels around small pieces of land. Each point of land was named after a species of duck. He saw Pintail Point, Teal Point, Butterball Point, Widgeon Point, Can Point, Redhead Point.

"Your eyes are brown, aren't they, Christopher?"

"Yes, brown." How many men would hunt on each point? Were these points all under Blackie's jurisdiction, or were they hunted by men from other camps?

"And your hair is sort of brown, isn't it, Christopher?"

"Sort of." The waterways, he saw, were named for men. Chuck's Channel, Duane's Channel, David's Bay. Famous hunters? Drowned hunters? Were the channels hidden from each other by swamp grass? How tall was the swamp grass? How deep was the water?

"How tall, Christopher?".

"Five eleven."

"And how much do you weigh?"

"One eighty."

"Is that without clothes on?" She giggled.

"Yes." He would have to find a channel or bay out of sight of everyone. This might be difficult, considering that hunters habitually scanned the water and sky with binoculars. The actual drowning would be easy (except in his forearms, Larry hadn't a healthy muscle left in his body), but it would have to be done in some remote estuary behind a high screen of swamp grass.

"And now your place of birth and the date."

"Haymarket, Minnesota. February 15, 1934."

"Oh, you're not as old as you look."

He would devote tomorrow, while seeming to hunt, to exploring the Marsh. He would see that Larry was comfortably situated in a blind; then he would paddle about the lagoons, looking for the right place for him to die. The act must not be rushed. Save the act for Saturday. Devote tomorrow to strategy.

"And your present address?"

"Seven hundred South Eighth Avenue, Rookery, Minnesota." Was there a current running through the waterways? When he left the body to go for help, he had to count on the body's being there when he returned. He didn't want any delays between Larry's death in the bog and his burial in Rookery. He wanted the body brought quickly to land, not by himself but by others, and the coroner called. It would appear that Larry had accidentally fallen into the water while Chris wasn't looking—while he was tramping around in the muck trying to retrieve a bird, and Larry, in his weakness, couldn't save himself. These steps then: first, the drowning. Second, help from other hunters. Third, the coroner. Fourth, notify Rachel. Fifth, arrange to have the body transported from the bog to the camp, from the camp to Winnipeg, from Winnipeg to Rookery. Dead on Saturday: would Rachel want the funeral on Monday or Tuesday? Tuesday at the latest. A four-day upheaval in their lives. An upheaval long overdue.

"Sign your name here, Christopher."

He signed, wondering if the weather would change by Saturday. Waves and high wind and sleet would be nice, would make the accident more plausible, though, as for that, Larry in his present state appeared so helpless, so death-prone that no one would be surprised if he drowned in his own bathtub. Everyone in the camp must get to know him and understand his frailty. They must not be incredulous when they heard of his death.

Poo Poo said, "That's forty-six dollars apiece." Chris gave her two fifties, which she handed over her shoulder to Blackie.

"I'll apply the change to your room and board," said Blackie. "Now git outside and git yourselves a few chickens before the sun goes down. You came through Hill, didn't you? Between here and Hill is some good chicken shooting. Look for a woods on your right about a mile this side of Hill. There's always chickens in there. Just make sure you're back here by seven. Grub's at seven. We're having breast of duck."

Chris looked at Larry, who said, "Not me." He'd been awake long enough to be weary again.

"No, we're here for ducks," said Chris.

"Suit yourself. I'm just trying to git you your money's worth out of your license." He folded the money into his shirt pocket.

They heard, beyond the dining room wall, the chugging of a tractor. It grew louder as it approached the camp, very loud; then a sudden silence as the tractor stopped near the door to the bunkhouse.

"That would be my Vermonters," said Blackie. "They're in before sundown, which means they got their limit. You fellows git in the bunkhouse and meet your bunkmates. I'll see you at supper." Blackie went into the kitchen.

The young woman gathered up her paperwork, giggled and followed him.

The men sat side by side, Larry smoking, Chris studying the map. In a few minutes Larry put out his cigarette and said, "Let's go meet our bunkmates."

The red sun, level with the dirty windows, filled the bunkhouse with a warm, rusty light, accentuating the sunburns the four Vermonters had brought in from the Marsh. Two of them were boys in their late teens, lying on upper bunks. Another was a short, heavy man opening a bottle of Scotch. The fourth was a tall man, shaving over the basin on the chest of drawers. All four watched Larry make his way across the room, drop onto his bunk and light a cigarette.

Their spokesman, the shaver, spoke: "We're from Vermont. We've been here two days and we've had the best hunting of our lives and we've got one day to go on our licenses. We shot our limit of mallards each day, which may surprise you, seeing as how the weather has been clear and sunny, but we always get our birds early in the morning. Hell of a lot of mallards moving around the marsh between sunup and ten o'clock. After that, nothing. We shot some smaller ducks too, but when we get our limit of mallards each day, then we throw the smaller ones away. No use carrying home a bluebill when you can carry home a fat mallard." He stood at the chest of drawers, bending close to the mirror in the dimming daylight. He was tall and thin. He had a prominent breastbone, like a barnyard fowl's, and a big bony nose. "We've been coming here for many years. Blackie and I are old friends from way back. We've got one more day of hunting, and then on Saturday morning, instead of getting up at four thirty—Blackie routs everybody out at four thirty—we'll sleep in and eat a late breakfast with Gladdy and Poo Poo and we'll take our time packing and we'll drive into Winnipeg and stay the night at a Holiday Inn—hot bath, steak dinner, luxury living—and then on Sunday we'll get on a plane and fly to Boston with our fifty-six ducks." Holding his straight-edge razor high in the air, he turned and said, "I didn't catch your names."

"I'm MacKensie and this is Quinn." Chris, sitting beside Larry on the bottom bunk, dug into his duffel bag for his brandy. "And I didn't catch yours."

"Sanderson H. Bleekman, but you can just call me Sanderson. I'm from Middlevale, Vermont, as is my friend here." He pointed his razor at the heavy man, who was sitting on his bunk pouring himself a glass of Scotch. He was a cheery-looking man; his smile was broad.

"And up there on the top bunks you have the man's sons." One of the boys, about eighteen, read a paperback. The other, somewhat younger, was softly playing a harmonica—Stephen Foster melodies.

The cheery man capped his bottle. Standing it beside him on the floor, he smiled at Chris and Larry and said, "Excuse the way I smell, I've been here three days."

"Is this your first time at Blackie's?" asked Bleekman. He had turned back to the mirror, through which he was keeping an eye on Chris.

"Yes," said Chris. Somehow the tone of the question made this a shameful answer.

"Too bad. You'll probably have fair hunting, but you've got to be old-timers around here to get the best points of land. Blackie himself will be your guide. That's too bad, too. Blackie's past his prime, and by afternoon he's always pretty well liquored up. He guides newcomers—partly to keep them away from the better points of land and partly because newcomers don't make the demands on a guide that we veterans do. Oh, you'll get some shooting all right, but you'll hear a whole lot more shooting from other points of land. Now the point of land *we're* hunting—Pintail Point—is without a doubt the best point of land in Delta Marsh, and there's a guy coming in late tonight who'll probably get Bluebill Point tomorrow because he's been here many years himself, though probably not as many years as *I've* been here. I've never met the guy, but I'm told he's from Wisconsin and he's bringing his kid along. I understand the kid's eleven. Jesus, can you imagine bringing an eleven-year-old into a hunting camp? The guy ought to have his head examined. There's rough talk in a hunting camp. There's stories not meant for kids to hear. This is a place for men and men only, and it's a hell of an imposition on the rest of us to bring in a kid."

Chris opened his brandy bottle and offered Larry a swig.

"Here, wait a minute," said the cheery man. He got to his feet and waddled through the bathroom and into the dining room and kitchen. He returned with two glasses filled with ice.

"Thanks," said Chris.

"Excuse the way I smell, I've been here three days and three nights. Day after tomorrow I'm going to soak for two hours in a tub at the Holiday Inn." The man was half-tight. His speech was thick. He backed up to his bunk and sat heavily, smiling. After picking his glass off the floor, he raised it to the forty-watt bulb and said, "Cheers, guys."

Sanderson Bleekman carried the basin to the outside door and threw his dirty water at the sunset. He filled the basin with warm water from the pail on the wood-stove and he set to work scrubbing his arms and narrow chest. "If you can't get Pintail Point—which you can't because we've got it—you might ask Blackie for Widgeon Point. It's on David's Bay and it's usually not all that crowded. There's hunters from other camps in the Marsh, you understand, but for some reason they shy away from Widgeon Point. On my first trip up here to the Marsh, when I was starting from scratch the way you guys are, I hunted Widgeon Point and did just fine. But whatever you do, be sure you don't lose sight of Blackie. Get lost in the Marsh and you'll never find your way out. Everything looks the same—no landmarks, nothing but swamp grass, or I should say swamp *cane*; you know what I mean, it's a canelike plant that stands an inch or two taller than your head and no matter where you're looking you're looking at cane. One channel looks like another. Isn't that right?" He turned to his three friends.

The reading boy ignored him; the other boy, playing "Old Black Joe," nodded. The cheery man raised his glass: "Cheers." He drained his glass and refilled it.

Sanderson Bleekman washed his armpits. "So the

first thing to remember is don't lose sight of your guide. Blackie and his guides are the only ones who know their way around the Marsh. Too bad you can't have *our* guide. He's everything you want in a guide. His name's Bob. He carries all our gear and he sets out the decoys and he shows us a little respect. Keeps his mouth shut unless we ask him to open it. Hell of a good shot, too. He only shoots when we want him to shoot, because if he shot whenever he felt like it, he'd shoot everybody's limit before they fired a round. Drop a duck in the cane, he knows right where to find it. Bob's a better retriever than a lot of dogs I've seen. If you guys ever come up here when we're not here, be sure to ask for Bob."

Chris crawled into the bunk above Larry's and lay on his back with his drink on his chest. The ceiling was six inches from his forehead, the mattress was thin, the bed was a board; he felt as though he were lying in a box with the lid shut. Fighting off a spell of claustrophobia, he closed his eyes and pondered, with alarm, the problem of the guide. He hadn't foreseen going out with a guide. He had imagined being alone with Larry in the Marsh. For their kind of hunting—Larry stalking death, Chris stalking Larry—the last thing they wanted was a guide. Somehow they would have to elude him.

Sanderson Bleekman dropped his pants and washed his crotch. "I've been to camps where the guides were an insult to the hunter. They showed you no respect. They took all the best shots. They bragged. They spent all their money each night on booze and were hung-over in the morning. Blackie's guides are handpicked, and the best of them is Bob. Bob's better than Blackie himself. Blackie's too old, too fond of the bottle. But Blackie's better than some. And he's a great host. He never forgets who his friends are. He's never been anything but generous with me. In time you guys will work your way up in this camp and find you haven't a better friend in the world than Blackie LaVoi."

What did Sanderson Bleekman lack in life (thought Chris) that made him such a pain in the ass? As newcomers Larry and Chris were obviously doing wonders for his self-esteem, making him feel like an insider, a welcome old veteran, a privileged guest. Chris leaned over the edge of his bunk to see Larry's reaction to all this drivel. Larry was on his back with his mouth open, sleeping.

Sanderson Bleekman ranged on, extolling Blackie—his hospitality, his sense of direction, his wisdom. Chris finished his drink and wedged his glass between the mattress and the wall. He closed his eyes, fell abruptly into an uneasy sleep and dreamed that he and Larry, locked in a desperate embrace, were sinking into a sea of mud.

11

*A*T THE TABLE FOR ten, they were six—
Sanderson Bleekman at the head, no one at the foot,
Chris and Larry on one side, across from the cheery man
and his two sons. As Gladdy served plates of duck breast
and mashed potatoes, Chris caught sight of the curtain
parting at the far end of the kitchen and Poo Poo emerging from behind it, leading an old woman by the hand.
The old woman was blind. She walked very erect past
the stove and sink, her free hand feeling the air. There
was majesty in her posture and in the flare of her nostrils. From where he sat in the dining room, Chris
couldn't see the table where she joined Blackie, but he
heard what they said.

"How many tonight?" Her voice was husky.

"Six now. Two more coming in round midnight or so.
The plumber from Milwaukee and his boy. You remember the plumber from Milwaukee?"

"He's an awful man. Who's here besides the men
from Vermont?"

"Two Minnesotans, from Rookery. One's got something wrong with him."

"What is it?"

"Cancer or lumbago or something, I can't remember."

"What am I eating?"

"Veal."

Chris's duck was underdone, but he ate it anyway, in
small bites, listening to Sanderson Bleekman, who said
he was glad that he wasn't a newcomer in this camp
because some of the points of land newcomers were assigned to didn't have any solid footing. You stood up to
your knees in mud all day. It was hard to shoot when you

were up to your knees in mud. Bleekman's advice was becoming malicious rather than helpful, designed not to put newcomers wise but to make them apprehensive. Meanwhile, his chubby friend chewed duck and cast a benign smile up and down the table, his whiskery cheeks growing redder from the Scotch he sipped between bites. Chris could tell that these were two very satisfied men; they had come a long way for good hunting and they had been successful, and now each in his way displayed his pleasure. Sanderson Bleekman ran at the mouth; he warned; he bragged; he instructed; he cautioned; he held his fork in the air and sometimes shook it at his listeners, an abbot dispensing holy water on novices. The cheery man said nothing; he ate; he drank; he stoked the inner fire that made his flesh glow. He had brought his two sons to these fabulous hunting grounds where they had shot perhaps twice their limit and kept as their allotted share only the mallards and left the rest of their kill—the puddlers, the whistlers, the dives, the scaup—as food for the swamp turtles. Chris could read the cheery man's tranquil mind. He was thinking about Saturday night at a Holiday Inn and about the flight from Winnipeg to Boston. He was thinking about packing the ducks in his freezer at home, mallards for Thanksgiving, mallards for Christmas. His sons were seated silently at his left and right. The older boy held his paperback open beside his plate. The younger one, finding the duck no more savory than Chris did, was having trouble swallowing. He ate with his mouth crimped, as though chewing a balloon.

The cheery man was the first to finish. With a crust of bread he mopped duck juice from his plate and popped it into his mouth. Standing up, he raised his glass and said thickly, "Excuse me, guys, I'm sleepy."

Chris, Larry and Sanderson Bleekman bade him goodnight. So did his sons.

Twenty minutes later, opening the door to leave the dining room, the three men and two boys found the cheery man sitting on the toilet. As they filed past him into the bunkhouse, he raised his glass with a smile. "Cheers, guys."

12

MIDNIGHT. THE BUNKHOUSE chilly and dark, the others asleep, Chris zippered into his sleeping bag, bristling with apprehension, horrified at the thought of murder yet eager to get it over with.

To ease his nerves, he forced his mind away from Larry and thought of Rachel, recalled the day last winter—February 1979—when she came to him in distress. It was late in the morning and Chris, in his office, had just been buried under a load of complaints by a twenty-year-old student named Lorna Boone, who visited him almost daily with reports of bad sex and bad grades. Despite Lorna Boone's discontent, her voice was soft and flat, a passionless voice that seemed to deny the passion she spoke of—a tiresome voice, to be frank, and it left Chris feeling frigid. (This wasn't unique with Lorna Boone, this habit of describing intense emotion with an absolute lack of emotion. This low-key delivery was common to at least half the students who monopolized his appointment calendar—Chris had written about it in his *Handbook for Counselors*; he called it the Monotone of Trouble—and whenever he had to listen to it for longer than thirty minutes, he felt his blood icing up.) Now on this cold winter morning (snow flurries, wind) Lorna Boone had slouched into his office and sunk into a chair and switched on her Monotone of Trouble—a slow, steady unfolding of how her life had taken this shitty turn (she used "shitty" where her mother might have said "vile," her grandmother "odious")—and when her monologue ended, she seemed not the least upset.

She unloaded enough misery to render Chris cold and melancholy through lunch, yet she rose from her chair so lightly and made such a smooth departure that he wondered if this, for her, had been a serious talk or simply a performance, an exercise in grace.

And then, by contrast, Rachel appeared—the actress, the jogger, the woman who warmed his ventricles left and right. Sweeping into his office in her long navy-blue coat and her long flame-red scarf, she dispelled every trace of Lorna Boone.

He stood in surprise, delight. He offered her tea, which she declined, and a chair, which she accepted, hanging her purse strap on the back of it.

"I'm here with Bernard Beckwith, Chris, to see about borrowing some props from the college theater." She pronounced the name Bern*ard*. At the Rookery Civic Playhouse, Bernard Beckwith was producer, house manager, publicist and ticket seller. He and Rachel (she was stage and lighting designer, as well as artistic director) were the only two full-time employees of this civic theater where the lean budget was derived from ticket sales, corporate grants and a trickle of tax money. Larry and Chris were agreed that Bernard Beckwith—to use a term from their boyhood—was a drip.

Chris looked at his watch. "Let's have lunch."

"No, no, I left Bernard on the way to the car. He's waiting for me. But I wanted to have a minute with you alone."

Rachel had come to the college needing more than props and costumes. Chris sensed that she needed a fresh look at the response her femaleness aroused in him, fresh evidence, in the unspoken signals he sent her, of the grip she had on his heart. For he knew that Rachel measured her self-worth not only by the rules of hard work, amiability and artistic taste (the qualities for which she was admired at the Playhouse and around her neighborhood); she measured it as well by her good looks, her sexuality. She had a sensitive ear for the strings she set vibrating in men. Every now and then she wiggled her tail in Bernard Beckwith's direction in order to solidify her position at the Playhouse. Every now and then she flirted with certain handsome young actors who gave her meaningful glances and invitational winks, staying out of their reach, however, because while she enjoyed eyeplay and valued some of the things these actors seemed to be offering her (a strong shoulder to lean on, amusing companionship, a good time in bed), none of them came close to tempting her into infidelity, lacking, as they did, the thing she valued most in a man, which currently (the result most likely of Larry's condition) was staying power. Handsome young actors were as flashy and vagrant as gypsies, as soon gone as wild flowers. They never took root in Rookery; they showed up for a season, bloomed and disappeared. As for Bernard Beckwith, the fondness he felt for Rachel, she knew, was that of a fan for an actress as well as that of a boss for a reliable employee. She got on well with him. He was helpful and courteous and easy to please (a wiggle every week or so was sufficient); they worked on a wavelength almost entirely uncluttered by the interference of sexual overtones, Beckwith's true love being the CB radio he kept in his office at the Playhouse, where you would find him at odd hours of the day and night conversing excitedly with truckers on the freeway, ten four.

Because she looked warm with her coat buttoned, her scarf around her neck, the long end thrown back over her shoulder, and because the shape of her body interested Chris as much as her mind, her good nature, her vivaciousness, her cheekbones, he said, "Take off your coat."

"Yes, you've got a hot office." She slipped out of her coat without standing up.

He swiveled to his desk to freshen his tea, pouring tepid water from his dented electric coffeepot.

"The college has a remarkable inventory of throneroom trappings," she said. "Most of which we'll borrow for *Twelfth Night*."

He swiveled to face her. Over his tea, he drank in her beauty. Rachel, he thought, nothing is so remarkable as the inventory you are, from your long feet in scuffed loafers to your red hair in fetching disarray. Today she wore her tan woolly sweater and plaid slacks. On a chain around her neck and resting between her breasts was a silver medallion.

"Really, I wish you'd ditch Beckwith," he said. "I have no appointments for an hour, we could have lunch in the college cafeteria. It would do my image a lot of good to be seen around campus with the foremost actress in Rookery."

"My acting is rusty, Chris. I take only bit parts now that I'm directing."

"If you mean your chumminess with Beckwith isn't acting, I'm grieved."

She laughed.

"I mean it, Rachel, Beckwith is a drip."

"Please, Chris, I wish you and Larry would pick on someone else for a change. Bernard is a good man in his job. The Playhouse was never solvent before he took over."

"Before *you* took over."

"All right, before *we* took over."

"Rachel, do you know what bothers me about Beckwith? He uses so much grease on his hair."

"But it smells so nice."

"It looks like lard."

"And his hair isn't as greasy as you think, Chris. If you'll just run your hand through it sometime, you'll see." She threw her head back, her thin eyebrows arched in amusement. "Bernard's hair is actually quite dry to the touch."

"It's lard."

She cast an eye at his cluttered desk, at the curling memos pinned to his bulletin board. "So how's counseling these days?"

"I can't say. The results aren't in."

"When will they be?"

"Never. I thought by going into counseling I might see the results of my efforts, but it hasn't worked out that way. It's no different from the classroom. Students go out into the world and I never see them again, never

know what they become, never know if they're happy.
Or less unhappy. There's not a job in all of education
where success is measurable."

"I couldn't survive in a job like that. I need somebody's judgment after opening night. A good review, a
bad review, I have to know whether I succeeded or failed
in the public eye. That's why I had to get out of social
work. I need applause." She took a deep breath, as
though bracing herself against the heaviness of what she
was about to say—a ponderous declaration leaning, tipping, about to fall—but then she seemed to change her
mind and kept to the subject at hand. "Of course, by
taking a curtain call, we almost force the audience to
applaud. Odd to think how much importance we put on a
bunch of people clapping their hands. What you educa-
tors should do, Chris, is take curtain calls. At com-
mencement you should all stand up and bow."

This was a conversation they had had before. In front
of the Quinn fireplace they had spoken of these things,
Larry joining in with his accounts of the small rewards of
teaching, the inconclusive results. This was typical of
the way Rachel and Chris talked to each other—steering
their ideas into areas of smooth sailing, keeping close to
the lee shore of platitudes rather than risk the peaks and
troughs of what was really on their minds. Rachel had
never revealed to Chris exactly what it was like to live
with a man who was dying by inches. Except for an offhand remark now and then, Chris had never mentioned
to Rachel the lingering regrets left over from his marriage, the guilt left over from his divorce.

"The reception we got with *Harvey* was marvelous,
every review ecstatic, every performance a sellout. I believe I could survive half a dozen flops on the strength of
that alone. Now we're starting work on *Twelfth Night*.
We have a strong cast lined up. I don't remember when
I've had so much talent to choose from at tryouts."

Sipping tea and nodding, Chris detected in her voice a
slightly higher pitch than normal. Usually her voice was
robust, at once spontaneous yet slightly theatrical, but
now—her head still thrown back a little, her eyes nar-

rowed so that she was looking down at him from under her lashes—her voice was strained, tight. She had more to say about the Playhouse season; then she stopped abruptly and looked down at her medallion, fingered it, looked up and said, "Chris, I think I'm on the verge of losing control for a while."

She put out her hand to him. Her eyes filled.

He set down his tea and rolled his chair close to hers, took her hand.

"Last night we were reading Hopkins, or rather I was reading and Larry was reciting from memory. And he blurted out the line about the mind having mountains. And just like that I broke down." There was a tremor in her lips, a flutter in her wet lashes.

Chris remembered the line. He spoke it: "'O the mind, mind has mountains; cliffs of fall/Frightful, sheer, no-man fathomed.'"

"That's it." She pursed her lips, ducked her head twice, swallowing a sob. "Larry recited it, and all of a sudden I felt as though I were at the edge of a cliff or chasm, and about to fall. And I am, Chris."

"You've been over that ground for years, Rachel. You've never fallen. You've always been in control."

"But not now." She gave him her other hand. She turned her head away and blotted her tears on her shoulder. A deep breath. Another. "God knows why that line should have set me off any more than a hundred others we've read lately. I mean we've been reading Eliot and Lowell and Berryman and we've been bearing up very nicely, but last night Larry came out with that business about 'cliffs of fall' and I just went to pieces. The mind does have mountains, Chris."

"I know."

"Do you? I don't think you do. At least I don't think you know how *high* they are—and *steep*."

"I know how high and steep they are, for God's sake. Karen and I spent seventeen years in those mountains, climbing and falling."

She let go of his hands. She wiggled into the sleeves of her coat. "Bernard's wondering where I am. I'll have to stop in the rest room and do something about my eyes. Where's the rest room, Chris?"

"Wait one minute." He was scanning his bookcase for Hopkins. "You read Hopkins the way Larry does. You don't consider the whole poem. You read a line that feeds your unhappiness and you forget the rest."

"That's what Bruce says. Bruce is very high on Hopkins these days. Both he and Hopkins like God a lot."

He found Hopkins on the bottom shelf with the texts from his teaching days. "Bruce is right. Hopkins always turns despair into hope."

"Not in this poem he doesn't. This one is anguish right through to the end."

"No, it can't be. I'll point out the hope." He searched the index.

"I dare you." She was sitting on the edge of her chair, her coat buttoned, her hands folded on her knees.

He found the page. "Listen to this. Here's the line that follows the one about 'cliffs of fall': 'Nor does long our small durance deal with that steep or deep.' See, Rachel, the steeps and deeps don't last long." He read it again: "'Nor does long our small durance deal with that steep or deep.'"

"Who taught you to read? That means the steeps and deeps are more than our small endurance can stand. Read on."

"And the next line mentions comfort . . ."

"Read on. Read the last line."

He skipped to the last line: "'All life death does end and each day dies with sleep.'"

"You find that comforting?"

"Well . . . sleep restores us."

"And death? Death restores us?"

"In Hopkins's view."

"And in Bruce's. But not in yours and mine and Larry's."

"I've never been sure, Rachel. I've never ruled out the possibility of another life after this one."

She stood and draped her red scarf over her sleeve. Lifting her purse strap off the back of the chair, she twirled to face him, her smile troubled, her eyes nearly dry. "I didn't come here for literary criticism. I didn't come for counsel either. I just came to say I was feeling empty. I'll be fine. I keep telling myself it's a better winter than last year, Larry's not quite so low. It's the Doldrums Minor, not Major. And now, the rest room."

He took her by the arm and they passed through the outer office. There, chatting with the secretary, was Lorna Boone, who clamped her sloe-eyed gaze on Rachel and said, "Mr. MacKensie, are you free for one more minute? There's something I forgot to tell you."

"I'll be back shortly."

He showed Rachel to the rest room, and as he waited for her in the hallway, he looked out the window over the snowy parking lot. He spotted Bernard Beckwith's black Oldsmobile, its stream of exhaust whipped by the wind, half its windows frosted. Beckwith was hunched over the steering wheel, glancing every few seconds at the door below Chris, waiting impatiently for Rachel.

Chris felt an ache close up under his ribs. It occurred to him that he had never before seen Rachel cry real tears. What was it—eighteen years since they had met in Owl Brook? Onstage she was a wonderful weeper. He'd seen her weep on cue, playing Ibsen and O'Neill and Tennessee Williams, and he'd felt the audience secretly weeping along with her, but only now, this noon, had he seen her weep as Rachel. To tell the truth, it was reassuring. She'd been so steady for so long that he'd begun to wonder where her feelings were. She claimed that her acting served as her release and of course that made sense (a year ago she had seemed most at peace with herself during the three-week run of *Streetcar*, when, as Blanche, she threw a fit every night), but how could the stage drain off all the emotion that must surely be building up as Larry came apart?

She stepped from the rest room tearless and smiling— the skilled actress.

"Beckwith looks cold," he said.

"The poor dear."

On the stairs she said, "I'm sorry for interrupting your day."

"Please, anytime." He wanted to turn her around and lead her back to his office. He wanted her to *be* his day; let his students be interruptions.

"Be strong," he told her downstairs, at the door to the parking lot.

"Say it again." Her smile intensified his ache.

"Be strong."

"And once more." She laughed a short laugh to cover her need.

"Be strong."

"I know it sounds dumb, but it helps to hear that. Your voice has a healing effect. I may come back again to hear you say, 'Be strong.'"

Then she was out the door, running along the snow-packed sidewalk and across the icy parking lot, throwing her scarf around her neck, the long end flying behind her.

Chris watched her get into the car, and he watched the black Oldsmobile move along behind a line of parked cars, out into the street and out of sight in the flow of traffic.

He let the door swing shut and climbed the stairs, deciding—insofar as one can decide such a thing—that he was in love. What he felt for this woman was more than delight. Delight was fleeting and fun. This was a throbbing that warmed his brow and breast like a fever, a wound.

In the outer office, Lorna Boone rose slump-shoul-dered and word-weary from the chair by the secretary's desk and followed Chris into his office, where she dropped into Rachel's place. She said, "There's this creep in my sociology class, Mr. MacKensie. He's got these real big eyes and he wears this big pair of glasses, and he's always trying to get me to go out with him and drink beer. Now I drink beer with practically anybody that asks me, I'm not fussy, but everybody I talk to says this guy is a real creep, a fairy. Now that's his business, of course, but what I want to know is, what's this creep

of a fairy asking *me* to drink beer with him for? I mean
what kind of unnatural acts has he got in mind? *Me*, one
of the most heterosexual people you'll ever come across.
What does it all *mean*, Mr. MacKensie?"

Chris wasn't listening. He was sitting with his arms
folded on his desk, his eyes on the open book of poetry.
Hopkins had pulled a fast one. Hopkins had written a
poem without his characteristic twist of hope at the end.
Chris read the poem through, twice. Rachel was right.
Where was the solace? It was a frightening poem.

"Mr. MacKensie, are you listening?" said Lorna
Boone.

"No, but go ahead anyhow."

And she did. She droned on in her Monotone of Trouble, which Chris was only vaguely conscious of as he
read and reread the closing line:

All life death does end and each day dies with sleep.

PART TWO

— ❖ —

1

THE PLUMBER FROM MILWAUKEE, arriving at two in the morning, slammed the door, jolting Chris awake and causing another of the sleepers (it sounded like the cheery Vermonter) to clear his throat and utter a coughing word or two. Just as Chris opened his eyes, the forty-watt bulb came on, blinding him.

"Well, this is it, son. How do you like it? These are all hunters here, lying along this wall, and over here—see —here's some more. They come from all over the U.S. and Canada to hunt Delta Marsh because it's got the best goddamn duck hunting in the Western Hemisphere. They've all probably been coming here for years and years, but none of them as long as your dad." This was a resonant voice, deep and uncivilly loud; it flooded the bunkhouse. "The last time I went skeet shooting, I shot ninety-seven skeet out of a hundred and took home the trophy. Did I ever tell you about the time I shot a mountain goat through the left eye from a hundred and twenty yards away? And don't forget the time I killed that entire family of deer—buck, doe and two fawns—in just four shots. Now put your sleeping bag on that top bunk and get yourself up there and go to sleep."

Another cough from the Vermonter, and a groan.

"I'm glad to meet you," said the plumber. "Me and my boy just pulled in from Milwaukee—made it in under fifteen hours—and now we're hopping in the sack so we can be sharp when Blackie gets us up. I didn't catch your name."

The cheery Vermonter mumbled cheerlessly.

The boy squeaked, "Daddy—"

117

"Don't call me Daddy, for Christ's sake, call me Dad.
And keep your mouth shut so you don't wake up the rest
of these hunters. Don't you realize it's the middle of the
night? This here's my son."

The Vermonter groaned.

"This is his first trip to Blackie's and so he isn't used
to the ways of hunters, but it's high time he learned, he's
going on twelve. Saturday's his birthday. He's got his
own Ithaca Automatic twelve-gauge, besides a thirty-
ought-six deer rifle, and he's been hunting with me for
many years, but never before in a camp. How you guys
been doing? You been getting your limits every day?"

Silence.

"Last year I shot more ducks in Delta Marsh than I
could take home. I gave half of them to Blackie to feed
his hunters with. It was the same two years ago. I've
given Blackie dozens of ducks."

Chris said, "The one I ate tonight must have been
from two years ago."

"Hey, who said that?"

Chris lay still, looking at the wall.

The plumber shook him. "Was that you?"

Chris rolled over on his back, pointed to his watch.

"Yeah, yeah, we'll be settled in a minute. How'd you
guys do today?"

"Just got here," Chris told him. "Haven't hunted
yet."

"You been here before?"

"No."

"Never? Well, you just better be ready for the best
goddamn hunting of your life. Three years ago when I
was up here, I not only shot my limit of ducks, I shot
four *geese*. I couldn't take four geese across the border,
so I gave one to Blackie to feed to his hunters."

"Maybe *that's* what I had for supper."

"Tell him about the time you took Uncle Jeff ice fishing, Daddy."

The plumber laughed, glad to be reminded. "If *that*
wasn't the funniest ice fishing trip *I* was ever on. My
wife's brother Jeff is from Texas, see. The whole family,

my wife included, was born and raised in Texas, where they never saw ice on lakes thick enough to walk on, let alone drive on. Well, this brother of hers, Jeff, he came to Wisconsin for a visit last January and he's nothing but a puny-assed pantywaist, you know what I mean, a mama's boy even though he's twenty-five years old, maybe twenty-six. I asked him along ice fishing with me and my fishing buddy Fred. You ought to meet Fred, he's a gas. So we got into my pickup, see, me driving and my wife's brother Jeff sitting in the middle and my buddy Fred on the other side, and as soon as we drove out onto the ice, I could see Jeff was scared shitless. Well, I thought to myself, there's no time like the present to put the fear of the Lord into this cowardly son of a bitch, so ever few yards I stopped the truck and I said to Fred, 'What do you think, Fred, do you think it's safe to go any farther?' and Fred caught on right away, and he said, 'Gee, I don't know, what do *you* think?' and I said, 'Maybe I better get out and walk on ahead a ways and check how thick the ice is because we're over the deepest part of the lake right here and I'd hate like hell to bust through,' and I got out and walked on ahead a ways and came back and said, 'I think she's safe for a little ways yet,' and I put the pickup in gear and we went ahead twenty, thirty yards, and then I stopped and said, 'What do you think, Fred, think it's safe to go ahead some more?' and Fred said, 'Gee, I don't know, what do you think?' and this time Fred got out and checked the ice. Of course there was two feet of ice on that lake— safer than driving on a city street, but we kept up that routine all the way out to our fishing spot, and by the time we got there Jeff was so goddamn scared he didn't know whether to shit or sharpen his pencil!"

The boy laughed a high pitched, hiccupping laugh. The plumber roared. The cheery Vermonter coughed. Chris put his arm across his eyes.

This was followed by a minute or so of unpacking— snaps and zippers opening, sleeping bags unrolling, then: "How come you're getting into bed without your long underpants on? It'll be cold in here by morning. Where in the hell's your longjohns?"

"I don't know," said the boy. "They aren't in my bag."

"What? A hunting trip to Canada in October, and no longjohns?"

"I guess Mother forgot to pack them."

"Mother! You mean you let your *mother* pack your bag for a hunting trip? Listen here, this is the last time your mother packs your bag, see? You're the one that's going hunting, not your mother. You think your mother's going hunting?"

No reply.

"Answer me, do you see your mother along on this hunting trip?"

Meekly: "No."

"All right then, what business has she got packing your bag? What are you, almost twelve? And not old enough to pack your own bag? Christ, I give up."

The boy crawled into the upper bunk adjacent to Chris's. The plumber turned out the light and got into the lower bunk adjacent to Larry's. The bunks were connected end to end by a framework of two-by-fours, and they all swayed, upsetting Chris's stomach (he tasted again the underdone duck) as the father and son shifted and bounced and settled into sleep.

Chris recalled meeting other men like this. Fathers who tried to hasten their sons' maturity. When the boy was seven, the father wanted his son to be eleven. When he was eleven, the father wanted him to be seventeen. But when the boy turned seventeen, the father would want him to be eleven again—or—seven—because by that time the son would have pushed on past any need or regard for his father, as the sons of pushy fathers so often did. This boy, this plumber's son, if he had mettle enough to endure his crude upbringing over the next four or five years, would be independent at an early age. Chris wanted to warn the plumber, to tell him about his own son's indifference toward him. Chris had not been a pushy father, yet Billy throughout his teen years had been utterly—grievously—independent of him. Chris had never understood why. As a counselor he had known a good many boys with the opposite problem, delayed maturity, but that seemed no worse to him than abnormally early independence. Lying in the dark, listening to the faint huffing and popping in the stove where the fire was dying. Chris considered telling the plumber, tomorrow, about his Father's Day card.

2

AT *FOUR THIRTY* C H R I S awoke again, his unsavory supper surging up his esophagus. He stopped it short of his throat and sent it back down to his churning stomach. He lay in the cold darkness, listening to the scuttling noise in the bureau, mice rummaging through a drawer, further shredding and chewing the *Winnipeg Sentinel*, transforming the old headlines into tiny black pellets. He heard breathing from the three bunks—the sighing sleep of Larry below him, bubbly snoring from the plumber, light whistling from the plumber's son. One of the four Vermonters wheezed. He dozed and woke again with a start—today he must plan a killing; tomorrow he must kill. For a few moments he had forgotten and he had felt relaxed. Now he was tense and wide-eyed.

"Git in there and wake up them hunters! What the hell they come here for—hunting or lying in the sack all day?" The voice of Blackie LaVoi from beyond two or three walls.

Poo Poo burst into the bunkhouse. "Come on, you studs, get out of the sack." She turned on the light and stood under it, grinning at the horizontal men. "Come on, the boss says it's time to get out of the sack." She wore a different T-shirt this morning, a white V-neck shirt with no message, her bralessness speaking for itself. She watched with interest as the hunters climbed out of their bunks in their underwear.

"Oh, there you are, Jimmy," she squealed. "I thought for a minute you didn't come."

Jimmy was the plumber. He peered out from his bot-

122

tom bunk, a gray-bearded man of about fifty-five. "Ah, you goddamn wench!" He wrapped a hairy arm around Poo Poo's thighs and pulled her, screeching, in on top of him. They wrestled. The plumber's son watched from the bunk above, laughing, shivering, hiccupping. The boy was blond and scrawny. His face had a refined look, the lips thin, the brow high, the lashes long. He bounced on his mattress in delight as the thrashing in the bunk below him caused the framework of beds to crack.

Along the opposite wall, the cheery Vermonter, watery-eyed and not so cheery, got to his feet and pulled on his hunting pants and plodded barefoot toward the toilet. A fat gray cat sprang into his warm bunk and curled up on his pillow. The two younger Vermonters yawned as they dressed. Sanderson Bleekman pulled on his pants, pulled up his suspenders, poured water from the bucket into the basin (cold water, the fire out) and went to the mirror and washed his ears.

Chris let himself down to the cold floor and sat on the bottom bunk beside Larry, who was huddled over his shaving kit, looking for his morning pill.

Poo Poo screamed, "Don't *bite* me, Jimmy." The bunks swayed.

"Better take all your pills along with you," said Chris. "We probably won't be back here before dark."

Larry nodded, tearing off his afternoon pill and putting it into his shirt pocket.

"And how about your headache pills?"

Larry nodded, tearing off a headache pill.

"And an extra Ayrozil?"

"No, I'm not going to get depressed today."

"Well, *I* might." Chris tore off an Ayrozil capsule and stuffed it into the pocket of his pants, which hung from the bedpost.

The plumber released Poo Poo. She got to her feet, panting, giggling, straightening her T-shirt, straightening her black hair. "Hurry up, you studs, breakfast in ten minutes." She reached up to the plumber's son and squeezed his cheek. "Better get dressed, Jimmy junior."

Passing the young Vermonters, she ran her hand through their hair.

At the bureau, she snapped Sanderson Bleekman's suspenders from behind. He turned and scowled at her.

On her way through the bathroom she goosed the cheery Vermonter as he stood dribbling over the toilet.

At the table for ten, they were eight, the plumber and Sanderson Bleekman sitting at the ends, each believing that the other sat at the foot. Toast, grapefruit sections, rubbery fried eggs. Once again the blind woman was led across the kitchen, this time by Gladdy. Again she sat where Chris couldn't see her, but he heard her ask, "How many hunters?"

"Eight," he heard Blackie say. "The plumber and his boy showed up."

"A good day. Two hundred forty dollars."

"Plus another thirty per hunter for guides. That's four eighty."

"Maybe if the weather holds and hunting is poor, the Vermonters will stay an extra day."

"Their licenses run out today."

"When has that ever stopped them?"

The sleepy silence at the trestle table was broken by Sanderson Bleekman, who, as he ate, had been keeping a wary eye on the plumber. "Did I hear you say last night that you've been coming here for many years?"

The grizzled plumber had snappy eyes. He cleared his throat and said, deeply, "I've been hunting Blackie's camps since I got out of the army in '49, that's exactly thirty years. I hunted with Blackie when he had a place in Ontario, near Kenora, and I fished with Blackie when he had a fishing camp above the Arctic Circle. Hell, when hunting season comes, Blackie and I are like brothers." He raised his voice. "Am I right, Blackie?"

From the kitchen, gruffly: "You tell 'em."

"See?" said the plumber.

"Well," said Sanderson Bleekman, pulling in his little chin and puffing out his narrow chest. "I've been coming here for many years myself, and because I'm an old hand

around here, my friends and I have been assigned to Pintail Point."

The plumber jumped slightly in his chair. "What do
you mean, you've been assigned to Pintail Point?"

"Just so it's understood."

"But Pintail Point is *my* point!"

"I just thought I should mention it before we set out.
Pintail Point's already taken."

"Blackie, what *is* this?" The plumber spat grapefruit.
"Blackie, what's this guy telling me about Pintail Point?"

Sanderson Bleekman continued, glancing behind him
at the kitchen, looking for Blackie to come to his aid.
"Yessir, we've had excellent shooting for two days on
Pintail Point, and we have one more day to go. Tomorrow Pintail Point is up for grabs, but today it's spoken
for."

"Blackie, what the fuck!" The plumber pounded the
table with both fists, rattling the silver. "Blackie, come in
here!"

Blackie came in from the kitchen, brushing crumbs
from his mustache. He wore a pair of hip boots buckled
to his belt. Over his gray shirt was an old brown jacket
with an elbow-length rip in the right sleeve. On his head,
a black stocking cap. He stood halfway down the table,
halfway between the feuding hunters, and quelled the
altercation by boring into the plumber with his hooded
good eye, then into Bleekman—no words, merely a
chastening glower, a king subduing his two princes. Then
he went around the table to the map on the wall and
pointed to Pintail Point with a long finger, his sleeve
hanging from the elbow. "Listen here, Milwaukee,
maybe you fished with me above the Arctic Circle, but
you're sure in hell not hunting Pintail Point if I've already given it to somebody else. Tomorrow it's yours if
you want it, but for today you take Bluebill Point. It's off
here to the east. Last weekend there was good shooting
on Bluebill Point."

The plumber nodded.

"And let's not have any more of your uppity talk. Remember what happened last year. I kicked your ass out

the door for starting a fight in the bunkhouse.''

The plumber was silent, his eyes on his plate.

"Now eat your eggs."

The plumber ate his eggs.

"And you guys from Rookery." Blackie bent to Larry to verify that he had lived through the night. "You guys I'm taking to Widgeon Point. It's in David's Bay, across from Teal Point. Now get a move on, the guides'll be here any minute."

Blackie retired to the kitchen.

Vindicated, gloating, Sanderson Bleekman said, "Bluebill Point isn't at all bad. I hunted Bluebill Point myself, before I had seniority here, and I recall above average shooting. Of course, it's nothing like Pintail Point, but there's not a thing wrong with it." He turned to his friend. "Were you ever here with me when we hunted Bluebill Point?"

"Hmmmmmmmmmmmm?" The cheery man's vision was entirely inward this morning, and bloodshot. Either he was a naturally slow starter or he had drunk too much Scotch before bedtime. Last night's color had left his cheeks and moved into the whites of his eyes. His breakfast was a cup of black coffee; he blew into it, warmed his hands on it, tasted it, stared at it.

The plumber's boy, sitting on Chris's right and twitching with excitement, was spreading jam on his toast and hand and sleeve. The two young Vermonters, across from Chris, ate hungrily, one on either side of their father, the older one reading, the younger one watching Larry, who was shaking.

Chris had been trying not to notice as Larry, on his left, sloshed his coffee and then spilled egg on his shirt. He was having a spasm. He laid down his fork and sat back in his chair, rigid.

The plumber muttered. "Thirty years I pay the son of a bitch an outrageous fee to hunt land he doesn't even own, and what do I get? I get Bluebill fucking Point!"

"Come on, the guides are here." Blackie charged through the dining room, trailing his ripped sleeve. "Git going, git outside, the guides are here." The Vermonters stood up and followed him through the bathroom.

"I don't have to take this kind of shit," the plumber said to Chris. "Next year I'll find myself another camp, that's all. Let Blackie keep his goddamn Delta Marsh, I'll go to Alaska. Son, next year we're going to Alaska and we'll get hunting like you've never seen. I hunted Alaska before you were born, and I'm going back. We'll fly up there for a week and I'll show you what real hunting is. No more of this Bluebill Point bullshit."

Chris watched the plumber lead his boy into the bunkhouse; then he turned to Larry, who looked at him out of the corner of his eye, half-smiling, nodding, seeming to say, "Don't worry, I'll just be a minute." He sat low in his chair, stiff, his right leg twitching. In a minute it was over. He raised his eyebrows and stretched his mouth wide, a swimmer emerging from water. He sat up straighter.

"What was that all about?"

"Nerves," said Larry.

"Something new?"

"Fairly new. It's happened a few times. My right leg goes kind of crazy, my right side tingles. Let's wait a minute, while I settle down." He lit a cigarette with a trembling match.

Gladdy came in and sat across from them. "You guys going hunting?" Her long gray hair was pulled back and noosed at the nape of her neck with a rubber band.

"In a minute," said Chris. "We want to finish our coffee."

"You ain't got time. Blackie's starting up the tractor." Through the wall they heard the popping and coughing of a stiff gasoline engine.

The blind woman spoke from the kitchen: "You men, when you're out with Blackie, please don't take liquor along. Blackie's got no resistance to liquor."

"Or maybe you guys'd rather spend the day here with us girls," said Gladdy. Her smile was sleepy. Her check twitched.

Poo Poo appeared in the kitchen doorway, alert for their decision. Her smile was impish.

"Thanks anyway, we're going hunting," blurted Chris, hurt by the thought of Larry's betraying Rachel.

Larry said, "I'll speak for myself if you don't mind."

The blind woman's voice: "Blackie's trouble enough without liquor. Liquor makes him irritable."

Larry held his cigarette before him, studying the wet end. Lately the mouth end of his cigarette was always wet.

"Same price in the blind or in bed," said Gladdy. "Thirty bucks for girls, thirty bucks for guides."

Climbing out of his chair, Larry said, "Let's go hunting."

Standing, he swayed for a moment, scanning the wall of pictures; then, when he sensed that his eyes and legs would do what he wanted them to, he linked elbows with Chris and, using his free hand to grasp the wall, moved along the room toward the door, brushing—perhaps accidentally—the *Sports Afield* article off its nail, the glass shattering as it hit the floor Chris stooped to pick it up, but Larry, with a headlong stumble, pulled him through the doorway, through the bathroom and into the bunkhouse.

3

S *ITTING HIGH ON HIS* chugging, stutteri
tractor, Blackie LaVoi drove out of his yard, pulling
flatbed wagon loaded with his eight hunters and tw
guides. The men sat in a rectangle, their feet hanging
the sides of the wagon, their guns standing up betwe
their legs. There was no light yet, only an absence
stars in the east, where the blackness was growi
slightly less black.

The light over the bunkhouse door receded as th
lurched over hummocks of earth and through puddle
the light disappeared as they passed into the mars
lowlands and followed a winding trail through the t
cane. They rode for ten minutes in the fumes of the tra
tor; then they jerked to a stop and Blackie shoute
"Clear off! Clear off before we all sink out of sight
From the tractor seat he swept the wagon with his flas
light and as soon as it was empty of men and backpac
and boxes of shells, he let out the clutch and drove in
circle and back along the way he had come. Quite su
denly it was quiet, the engine noise baffled by the cane.

The men moved aimlessly in the dark, uncerta
where they were, where to go. The ground quivere
where they stepped, sank where they stood. The tw
guides, with the help of their blinding flashlights, sort
out the faces of their hunters.

"You the one from Milwaukee?"

"Yep, and this is my boy."

The guide's flashlight disclosed the boy, head to fo
to head.

"How old?"

129

"Going on twelve. Been hunting with me since he was five."

"Keep him close by you. This Marsh is no place to lose anybody." The guide had the voice of a very young man.

"You don't need to tell me about Delta Marsh. I've been hunting with Blackie LaVoi since before you were born."

"Well, your boy hasn't, so keep him close."

Having parked the tractor on high ground, Blackie came down through the cane, shouting, "Okay, you studs, let's go hunting." He was spotlighted by one of the guides and handed something in a small paper sack. He quickly stuffed the parcel into his pocket and called, "Where's my two hunters from Rookery?"

"Here." Chris spoke into the beam of Blackie's light.

"Okay then, follow me."

"Wait a minute." Christ harnessed himself with the backpack containing shells and lunch; then he took both shotguns from Larry and held them barrel-up, one in each hand, while Larry put his right arm around Chris's waist, his left on Chris's near shoulder, and they shuffled forward a few steps, testing the footing. They did this in three beams of light, everyone having paused to watch.

"Ready?" said Blackie, chuckling. "You look like a couple lovers."

"Lead on," said Chris.

"Further on, the trail gets narrow. You'll have to walk single file."

"Lead on."

Carrying a gun on his shoulder (barrel pointing forward, his right hand around the muzzle), Blackie followed his flashlight between two high stands of swamp grass, walking slowly so Chris and Larry could stay at his heels. The other two lights moved off in two directions and vanished, with the other men, into the cane.

Larry murmured in Chris's ear, "God, I never thought I'd feel bog under my feet again. It takes me back to my good years."

"Mine too," said Chris, thinking: It will take you

much further back than that—it will take you back to nonexistence.

"Do you think Blackie knows where he's going?"

"Of course he knows."

Larry stumbled and clung, kneeling, to Chris.

Blackie stopped and watched Chris lay down one of the guns and help Larry to his feet. "This is where it gets narrow," he said, casting his light ahead.

"Better get behind me," said Chris. "You can hold onto the pack straps."

They set off, Larry hanging so heavily from the straps that Chris had to hunch forward to keep his balance. The farther they trudged, the springier the ground became. Their footsteps made sucking noises in the dark.

"He's leading us into the underworld, isn't he?"

Chris half turned in astonishment—he had been thinking this very thought. "What are you talking about?"

Larry's voice, close to Chris's ear, was a breathy whisper. "He's leading us down to the river of forgetfulness."

"That's news to me." Did Larry know what he was saying, sense its truth?

"He is, Chris. He's leading us into the underworld."

Every few steps their footwork became tangled, and Chris used his two guns as staffs to keep from falling, plunging their stocks into the soft earth. On their right was water now, on their left the wall of cane. Dawn was breaking in the water as well as in the sky—a faint glimmer the color of flesh. No clouds. The day would be bright and warm, a day for dozing in the blind, surely not a day for shooting ducks.

"Forgetfulness, Chris. Help me down to the river of forgetfulness." Larry's breathing was labored. "Please ...please...please."

Chris felt suddenly very powerful. He was overcome by a mighty urge to stop right here and drown Larry on the spot. Surely he was asking to die. Nothing easier than to swing around and topple him face-down into this wet pathway and press his nose into his own watery bootprint, holding it there until the twitching stopped. Nothing easier, that is, if they were alone. Damn Blackie's heart for interfering. If it weren't for Blackie, it might be accomplished here and now, before the sun came up: Larry face-down and dead in the Marsh, released from his misery; Chris calling for help; the coroner summoned; an undertaker; Chris returning to camp, leaving camp, driving home; Larry shipped to Rookery and put on brief display; or not, as Rachel wished; then into the earth with him, into the underworld; forgetfulness. If it weren't for Blackie.

"Please," said Larry, stumbling, and then again: "Please." Or was it a wheeze? Chris couldn't tell if Larry was speaking or wheezing, and along with this uncertainty he felt his resolution, his power, drain away. Up until a moment ago he could have killed Larry without a qualm, but now, six or eight steps farther into the Marsh, his will was evaporating and being replaced by revulsion —jitteriness—at the thought of murder. He was alarmed by this abrupt change of heart. For weeks the act had been settled in his mind. His plan had not been a matter of emotion only. That Larry must die was a matter of logic. Larry himself wanted to die. He had said so more than once. How many times during the Doldrums Major? Ten? Twelve? And how many times again last winter? Less often, but still he had spoken of oblivion. It was so reasonable. Larry's life was worth nothing to him anymore. And his wife was worth everything to Chris.

Would I kill for her if Larry were happy and hale? Chris asked himself as he struggled forward, pulling, balancing, puffing. Of course not. I would win Rachel in other ways. But Larry's unhappy and dying. His death will right a wrong. A moment ago I had the strength to do it. From that moment forward Blackie became the air Larry breathes. Blackie is now the blood running in Larry's veins.

Blackie stopped. "Here's our boats." With his flashlight—its beam gone, absorbed now by daylight—he pointed to the edge of the water where two duckboats stood side by side, their bows resting on the mud, their sterns afloat. They were short, shallow boats, each with two seats and two paddles.

"You guys take the one on the right. I'll take the other one—it's full of decoys."

Leaving the path and approaching the boats, the men sank mid-calf into the mud. Larry got stuck. Chris laid the two guns and the backpack in the boat, then took Larry's hand and pulled. Larry, muttering, tried to step forward, but, rooted in the bog, he began to tip over. Chris braced him upright and called to Blackie. Both men gripped him under the arms and lifted him clear, sinking deeper themselves; they slogged forward to the boat and dropped him into the stern seat. Larry lit a cigarette, blew smoke straight up and said, "Whose crazy idea was this anyhow?"

They shoved off, the two boats sending dark concentric ridges across the bright orange water. Chris looked over the side and plunged his paddle down as far as he could reach, testing the depth. Though the water was shallow, the bottom was bottomless; it looked grainy, like solid ground, but as he probed it with his paddle, the mud parted like syrup.

Blackie set off down a channel between cane and cattails, pausing now and then to see that his hunters were following. His paddling was quick and smooth—three splashes on the right, three on the left, three right, three left. Chris, in the bow of the second boat, paddled strenuously to keep up. Behind him he heard the clumsy splashing of Larry's paddle. The channel narrowed, then widened into a lagoon. Chris rested—his shoulders ached—and he expected that this would bring the boat to a standstill, but Larry was actually moving them along.

Larry drew his paddle out of the water and said to Chris's back, "What's our hurry?"

"Right, what *is* our hurry?" Chris shouted, "Wait!" to Blackie far ahead, and his shout flushed a pair of squawking mallards out of the rushes nearby. He reached for his gun, but the ducks circled behind the boat—Larry's shot. Larry made no move for his gun, aware that he wasn't quick enough; he hadn't fired a gun in four years.

"That was your shot," said Chris.

"I know, but I remember the time you took it and blew my cap off." Since the day it happened this was their first mention of the near-fatal shot on Amos Peterson's pond. Chris watched the ducks swing east, swoop low and disappear in the blinding tip of the sun blazing on the water.

When they caught up with Blackie's boat, Chris said, "We're in no hurry." The two boats bumped and parted.

"Whatever you say." Blackie scratched his head through his black cap. "With newcomers I never know what I'm getting. Most of the time it's meat hunters and they really put the pressure on me. They like to be set up by sunrise, ready to shoot. Then sometimes I'll get the no-pressure type. So far this year I've had only one bunch of no-pressure types." Blackie paddled slowly and smiled at the memory. "We never fired a shot all day. They brought along a bottle and we just sat in the weeds and got loaded." The smile transformed his face, erased ten years from around his eyes, made the good one sparkle.

"We're the no-pressure type," said Larry.

"But we didn't bring a bottle," said Chris. "We left our brandy back at camp."

"Good thing you're not meat hunters—a day like this." The sun was high enough now to warm the air; soft breezes moved back and forth over the water. Along the far shore of the lagoon each wavelet was a chip of silver, each blade of swamp grass a stalk of gold.

"I still say it'll turn rainy and windy by tomorrow," said Blackie. "Today you can concentrate on your suntans."

Leisurely, silently, they paddled down corridors of cane, the sun first ahead of them, then behind. Chris began to sweat.

"Is there current running in these channels?" he asked. The drowning pool of his dreams was perfectly still—no danger of the body floating away while Chris went off in search of help.

"Not here. This is mostly backwater. Up ahead, beyond David's Bay, there's some moving water. That's where the Marsh drains into Lake Manitoba. Here's David's Bay, just ahead."

The channel opened into a lagoon the size of a city block. There were two tongues of land extending into the water, one from the right, the other—the more distant one—from the left.

"That's where we hunt," said Blackie, pointing with his paddle to the nearer peninsula. "That's Widgeon Point. Up there on the left you see Teal Point. There's some hunters there already—see them decoys?" There were a hundred decoys floating at the tip of Teal Point. "You guys get yourself ashore and I'll set out ours."

Chris paddled up to Widgeon Point and stepped out. Here the footing was somewhat more solid. He helped Larry out. Larry sat down in a clump of swamp grass and laid his gun carefully beside him. Chris pulled the boat into the weeds.

From his boat Blackie plopped two dozen rubber decoys on the water. They were old decoys, shot at and stepped on, bleached and leaky; they listed like a flock of cripples.

"How do they look?" Blackie called into the grass.

"Like hell," said Larry, getting to his knees, then, after a moment's rest, to his feet. He felt the seat of his pants. He turned to Chris. "I'm wet." He turned to Blackie. "Say, Blackie, before you come ashore, would you go back to camp and get me a chair?"

Blackie laughed. These jokers were a lot of fun.

"I'm serious."

Blackie laughed again.

"How much are we paying you? Thirty bucks a day apiece for lodging? And another thirty for guiding? For my sixty dollars you can go back to camp and get me a chair."

"Don't be tiresome," said Chris, loading his gun, scanning the horizon.

Larry picked up his gun and inserted a shell. Through the screen of grass he aimed it at the water near Blackie's boat. "Go and get me a chair."

"What the hell's going on?" said Blackie, holding his gun upright beside his knee, his smile gone, his eye on Larry, his boat turning slowly in the breeze.

Chris called, "Come ashore, Blackie. The chair's a joke."

"Like hell it is," said Larry, swinging abruptly toward him, the muzzle of his gun passing over Chris's foot. "There's no place to sit down, Chris. I can't stand up all day. Tell Blackie to go back to camp and get me a chair." Larry swung around to face Blackie and again the gun pointed at Chris's foot. Enraged, Chris wrenched it away from him and pumped out the two shells—they flew up over the swamp grass and sank in the water.

Larry looked at him in wonder. "You didn't think I was going to shoot him, did you?"

"You were aiming at my foot!" Chris handed him the gun. "Here, now load it again, and this time watch where it points."

Larry handed it back. "Load it for me, would you, Chris? And then point it for me, would you? And when a duck flies over, would you pull the trigger for me? That will save me a lot of trouble." He was smiling bitterly, his eyes intense with anger.

Chris broke into a shivering sweat of frustration. He didn't want to be standing on Widgeon Point holding two shot guns and sinking imperceptibly into the Marsh. He didn't want to be responsible for this diseased and demented man he had brought from Rookery—this contentious, feeble son of a bitch whom he loved and hated by turns. He wanted to kill him and go home. He wanted to be rid of guns and hunting and Larry forever. He wanted peace. He wanted Rachel in his arms.

He took a deep breath and turned away. Carrying both guns, he followed a circular path beaten through the cane by other hunters. His head cleared as he walked. He felt his frustration ebb. The path took him along the spine of the peninsula and in three or four minutes it brought him back to Larry. Though he was calmer now, he still didn't want to look at Larry's taunting, angry expression. He turned his head away as he handed him his gun.

Larry took it.

Chris set off on the circular path again. He stopped where the path lifted him above the six-foot cane. He set his gun down and raised his binoculars to scan the bay. He saw the hundred decoys on the glistening water around Teal Point. They were new rubber decoys, too flashy and buoyant to look like waterfowl; surely no duck would be fooled if Chris wasn't. Above the decoys, in the weeds, were three figures in tan hunting clothes, the jackets and caps too new and starchy to blend into the swamp grass. Before the faces of these three hunters, glinting in the sunlight, he saw three binoculars aimed at his own. He returned to Larry's side and they watched Blackie paddle to land.

Blackie pulled his boat across the grass and left it next to the other one. Carrying his gun yokelike across his shoulders, he stepped up to Larry and peered closely into his eyes. "Are you crazy enough to kill somebody over a chair?"

Larry laughed.

"I didn't think so. Now if you want to sit on something dry, sit in your boat."

Larry regarded the boat, its muddy bottom, its hard seat. He reached out to Blackie for support. "All right, give me a hand."

Blackie gave him more than a hand. He laid down his gun and put out his arms to receive him in what looked to Chris like an embrace—a fatherly hug, gentle yet eager. Blackie guided him to the boat and helped him in, and when he saw that Larry was settled, he pulled the paper sack from his pocket and drew from it a pint bottle of whiskey. He held it up to the sun. It was one swallow short of full.

Larry sat looking out across the bay, his gun across his knees, his back humped, his head pulled down into his shoulders—the neckless posture Chris recognized as

Larry's sign of fatigue. It was seven in the morning and Larry was ready for a nap.

Blackie opened his bottle. "Care for a drink?"

Larry roused himself, looked up. He took the pint, drank, sighed. He drank again, sighed again. He gave back the bottle and lay down, his feet up on the stern seat, his shoulders braced on the small deck over the bow, his head pillowed on the backpack. He pulled his cap down over his eyes, twisted a bit for comfort and lay still, his fingers laced on his stomach. The boat fit him like a coffin.

Blackie turned and handed the pint to Chris.

"Thanks." Chris swallowed and immediately broke out in another sweat, not the rising tide of frustration this time, but last night's duck. He stumbled off into a thick clump of cane to vomit.

Blackie enjoyed this. "Not your brand?"

Chris, returning, shook his head. "Gladdy's cooking."

Once more Blackie held his bottle against the sun. It glowed like honey. He took a deep swallow and capped it before returning it to his game pocket.

"You guys are quite the hunters. One crippled and going to sleep and the other sick as a dog."

"I feel fine now."

"After guiding meat hunters all season, you guys are like comic relief."

"Comic relief?" said Larry from under his cap. "Where did you pick that up?"

"My wife. Whenever something funny happens, she says, 'Comic relief.' She used to be a schoolteacher."

"The blind woman?" asked Chris.

"Yep. She was a teacher. She taught high school in Hill until the high school burned down in '39 and they never built another one. After that she went and taught freshman English at the University of Manitoba. That was during the war, when they were short of teachers. We were married, but we didn't live together very much in those years. I was always off hunting or fishing or trapping. Then she went blind. Been blind for thirty

years. When her father died and left her the grain elevator in Hill, I decided to quit roaming and settle down. I
came back to Hill and ran the elevator for two years.
Couldn't stand it. Felt like roaming again. Roamed east
to Kenora. Roamed northwest to the Yukon. Trapping,
hunting, fishing—it's all I cared to do. But she followed
me, blind as a bat, but tracking me down all the time.
Always riding the train to the nearest town, then getting
somebody to drive her out to wherever I was camping.
She found out about my other two wives that way. See,
over the years I had picked up a wife in Kenora and
another one in the Yukon. Upset her to find me married
to two other women. She raised some hell. But not
much, really. She seemed to know that someday she'd
have me all to herself, which is the way it turned out. Of
my three wives she was the oldest and least horny, to say
nothing of the only blind one, and yet she's the one I end
up with. Funny how things work out, isn't it?"

"Comic relief," said Larry.

"Comic relief is right. The best wife of the bunch was
the one in Kenora. She could run a trapline like nobody I
ever saw. Skin out a beaver in no time flat. She's the one
that's buried in Rookery. She died the day John Glenn
went up in the first spaceship. Died of typhoid. Drank
some dirty crick water."

Larry said, "Were these women really wives, or girl-
friends?" His voice was muffled by his corduroy cap.

"No, they were wives all right. I married all three of
them fair and square. Vows and all that. I don't believe
in shacking up over the long haul. I believe in marriage."

The sound of shots. Over Teal Point, out of a tight
flock of mallards, one dropped to the water. The flock
came whistling toward Widgeon Point. Blackie crouched
and fired, killing the lead duck. He fired again and killed
another. He jumped to his feet and watched where they
fell; then he saw that neither of his hunters had raised a
gun. Larry hadn't even raised the cap off his face.

"What's the matter with you guys? You in a trance?"

"I'm sleeping," murmured Larry. "I wish you'd keep
the noise down."

Blackie turned to Chris. "What's your excuse? We aren't going to get many shots like that today."

"I'm in a trance."

It was true. He felt disoriented. Had Chris been standing on a street corner in Rookery he couldn't have felt less prepared for hunting. The sight of those mallards flying within range of his pellets and powder had triggered none of the old reflexes—gun up, swing, fire. Had his lust for game, which had been in gradual decline for several years, finally deserted him? Or had his obsession with killing Larry made him indifferent to killing of a lesser sort? He shouldered his gun and walked, for the third time, the circular path through the cane. At his back he heard Larry ask, "What happened to your Yukon wife?"

"I don't know." Blackie slid his boat into the water. "Last I heard, she ran off with a salesman that used to travel the Alcan Highway selling jewelry." He hopped into his boat. "He drove a red Lincoln." He stabbed a clump of earth with his paddle and pushed himself off, turned the boat and paddled toward the two dead ducks, calling back. "He promised her rubies."

I must fire at the next flock of ducks, Chris told himself, I must make a pretense of hunting so that after Larry's death no one can accuse me of suspicious behavior. I must act like a hunter, not a killer.

He circled back to the boat and stood over Larry. He looked out at Blackie, who was reaching for a dead duck with his paddle—slipping the paddle under the bird like a spatula, then lifting it, dripping, into the boat. He felt a movement of warm wind at his back. He saw it sweep out across the bay. Wavelets shone. The decoys rocked. A pair of small birds hopped at the water's edge, pecking among the roots of cane for seeds and bugs. They were slate-colored birds, pointed at both ends, their tails as sharp as their beaks.

Chris was sinking. Wherever he stood, it took only a minute for him to sink to his ankles. He kept extricating himself and placing his feet on hummocks of mud, but they all sank slowly under his weight. He strained to look beyond the vegetation—the head-high swamp grass, the cattails, the cane—but wherever he parted it with his gun barrel or his arm, it opened on a deeper curtain of vegetation. He felt stifled, desperate for open air and a long view. He wanted firm footing, a promontory, room to breathe and think and plan.

Through his binoculars he scanned the Marsh for high ground. Miles away, to the south, was Hill, its onion steeple and its grain elevator, the treeline that marked the road from Hill to Blackie's camp. East and west were nothing but swamp grass, the Marsh was too watery for trees to take root. North, toward Lake Manitoba, just as his vision sank below the top of the grass, he saw a line of trees against a vast sea of blue. He stepped into the boat and up onto the stern seat, his feet between Larry's ankles.

Larry raised his cap, lifted his head. "What's going on?"

"I'm exploring. Go back to sleep." The trees were bare of leaves; their branches and twigs formed a gauzy curtain behind which the lake reached to the horizon and beyond. He felt he must go to those trees and stand under them, where his vision north would be unrestricted. Only there could he properly plan. Along the way, he would come across the perfectly hidden place for drowning Larry.

Stepping out of the boat, he heard Blackie shout, then shoot. He looked up in time to see a duck plummet to the water. Its mate, a mallard, was coming straight toward Chris. He raised his gun, fired, missed. The bird whizzed overhead. He fired at it going away and lodged a few pellets in its tail and wing. It faltered, swooped and splashed down near the far shore, a hundred yards from Teal Point.

"Too bad," said Larry, sitting up and shading his eyes, following the movements of the wounded bird at the edge of the distant weeds.

"I'll paddle over and get it," said Chris.

"No use, you'll never find it. It'll dive and drown itself rather than be caught by a hunter. Wounded mallards do that, you know."

"Sometimes."

"They choose which way they want to die, Chris. They're very proud."

Chris's gun was jammed. He couldn't eject his second shell.

"Doesn't that strike you as an honorable way to end your life, Chris? To drown yourself rather than let yourself be caught by a turtle or a hunter or freeze to death when winter comes?"

"It makes sense, I guess." Chris was busy with his gun.

"Rather than die the slow death of lead poisoning? That's what you've done, Chris, you've given that duck a case of lead poisoning."

With his jackknife Chris pried out the empty shell. He replaced it with a fresh one. "Larry, I'm going to leave you with Blackie. I'm going out in his boat for a while. I want to explore. I'll be back later." He reached into the backpack and brought out two ham sandwiches, an apple, a can of 7-Up.

Larry lay flat again, covering his face, lacing his fingers. His wedding band glinted in the sun.

"Rachel always fixes me something in the morning. Juice and Jell-O usually."

"That so?"

"Chris, are you in love with her?"

Chris shot a glance at Larry, but his face and voice were masked by the brown cap.

"Tell me, Chris, are you in love with Rachel?" His voice was steady, casual, muffled.

"I've always thought a lot of Rachel. She's..." Chris looked out at Blackie in the boat, wishing he would hurry. He felt stranded. "She's an extraordinary person."

"Are you in love with her?"

"Well." Reaching behind his back, he dropped the sandwiches and 7-Up and apple into the game pocket of his hunting coat. "Yes and no."

"Explain the yes." On the "yes," Larry's voice broke. There was a quaking in his shoulders.

"Yes means I've always loved her in a way, Larry. Like an old friend."

Silence from under the cap. Then: "Explain the no."

"No is obvious. No means no." Chris peered out through the cane at Blackie, willing him to hurry ashore.

"No is a lie. You love her."

"Like an old friend."

"Like a lover. If I were dead you'd live with her. Don't lie to me, Chris. If I were dead you'd be her lover and she'd have you, I know she would. Or has she had you already? Have you two had each other, Chris?"

"You're talking nonsense."

"Have you had her?"

"No," he lied.

"No is a lie. You've had her."

"Like hell I have!" Chris bent over Larry, speaking to his corduroy cap. "Don't you know Rachel well enough to realize she'd never be unfaithful to you? She's yours and yours alone, even when you act like such an asshole that any ordinary woman would leave you. For a man who picked his wife out of a high school history class, you sure as hell hit the jackpot. Did you know all this about her when you married her? Did you know you were getting the most steadfast woman in the world? No, how could you have known? It was blind luck! Look at me, Larry!" He swept Larry's cap off into the mud and for an instant saw tears in Larry's eyes before Larry brought his trembling arm up and laid it across his face, his eyes tight in the crook of his canvas sleeve.

Chris pressed on: "You looked over your history class and you picked out the likeliest teenager and you married her, and then you discovered that out of sheer blind luck you'd got yourself the strongest, kindest, most beautiful woman in the whole damn *world*!"

Larry uttered a noise deep in his throat, a noise like a laugh, though it may have been a sob.

Chris turned away and saw Blackie paddling toward shore. Across the bay the wounded mallard was strug-

gling toward Teal Point. As it swam, it beat the water
with its good wing, trying to fly.

"You're a scream." Larry removed his arm from over
his face. He *was* laughing. With wet eyes he was laughing up at Chris. "You can't lie worth a damn. You're in
love with Rachel and all you can do is stand there and
tell me yes and no. Yes, she's an old friend and no, you
don't love her. Like hell you don't love her. You've been
in love with Rachel for a long time and there's not a thing
you can do about it because she loves *me*. She's faithful
to *me*. I know you've never had her, Chris. I know you
want her, but I know you never had her because she's
the way she is. She likes to flirt, I know that. I've seen
her do it. I've seen her get guys hot for her and it doesn't
bother me in the least because it's always an act. She
tries out different lines and different expressions on men
to see how they work. I've seen her do it to you, work
you like putty in her hands, and I just sit back and enjoy
it because it's an act and you think it's real." He paused
to chuckle, to wipe his mouth and eyes. "For two years
now you've been hanging around our house like a lost
tomcat and she's been feeding you and petting you and
saying nice things to you, and you're not one step closer
to being her lover than you were in Owl Brook. Did you
want her in Owl Brook, too, Chris? Does your desire go
all the way back to the year we met, all the way back to
1961?"

Chris took a step toward the water's edge to meet
Blackie.

"You know what you are, Chris?" Larry sat up.
"You're not a tomcat, you're a chicken. Remember that
woman in Owl Brook that called you a dumb cluck?
Well, she was right. In any flock of chickens there's
always a dumb cluck rooster and that's what you are, the
runt rooster that hangs around the edge of the barnyard
and lives out his scrawny life in misery because he's too
timid and too unlucky to ever get in on the good stuff.
You never get any of the better slop they throw out for
the rest of the chickens. You never get close to a hen.
You never fertilize an egg. You hang around and you eat

dirt and grass and on the first hot day in summer you get sunstroke and fall over dead and the farmer comes along and throws you on the manure heap." Having put all his strength into this cracked spiel, he lay down to rest.

Standing over him, Chris eyed the paddle beside the boat and imagined the damage he could do to Larry's skull by bringing it down with all his might flat on his forehead. Or he could bring it down edge-first on the bridge of his nose. All the suppressed and secret jealousy he had ever felt toward Larry engulfed him now in waves of rage.

Larry continued, smiling, speaking more slowly: "All it takes is one look and it's clear you're a loser, Chris. That woman in Owl Brook, she saw it right off, remember? She said"—here Larry shifted to falsetto— 'What *will* he do without that woman—that dumb cluck Mr. MacKensie?' Larry's voice gave out. He closed his eyes and whispered, "Fetch me my cap, will you?"

Chris stepped around the boat and picked up the cap. Wiping off the mud with his sleeve, he looked down at Larry, trying to see Larry's outburst as an expression of despair, not hate. Larry's abandon was that of a man who fears no reprisal, for no reprisal could be worse than his present agony. Chris placed the cap over Larry's face and imagined how it must feel to have lost your job and your power of locomotion and the use of your sphincter. How painful it must be to know that the anger you can't help causes pain in those who can't help but love you. How forsaken you must feel to view your only friend as a tomcat and a chicken by turns, a dumb cluck waiting to win your wife. Chris was torn between pity and rage. Closing his eyes, he stooped and gripped Larry's wrist tightly. "I'll be back later."

"I'll be here."

At the water's edge, Chris steadied the boat as Blackie stepped out. He said, "Nice shot."

Blackie nodded. "I left one for you."

"I botched it."

"So I saw."

"I want to take your boat out and paddle around for a while."

"No use trying to retrieve it. It's swimming toward Teal Point and in about two minutes that bunch of hunters will blast it to hell."

"They can have the duck. I want to explore. I want to paddle as far as the big lake."

Blackie raised his heavy eyebrows. "I don't know. Between here and the lake the Marsh is hard to navigate. The channels twist and turn. You'll get lost."

"Listen, I might shoot like a beginner, but I know my directions."

Blackie moved his good eye back and forth between Chris's eyes. His immovable eye was raised to the sun. "Okay." He pointed, his torn sleeve hanging. "Over there, about where your duck landed, is the outlet. Take the outlet and follow the channel and keep bearing right and it will take you to moving water. That'll be the deep channel that empties into the lake. The lake's a mile and a half from here. Even if you don't make any wrong turns, it'll take you a couple hours to get there and more than that coming back, against the current. Whatever you got in mind isn't worth it. There's hunters already on the lakeshore. They'll kick your ass if you try to hunt there."

Chris looked at his watch. "I'll be back by three." No need to tell Blackie about his desire to get out from behind this endless hedge of cane, his urge to flee this quivering spit of mud poking into David's Bay, his need to sit down on a piece of solid earth and rest his eyes on the hazy distance, his need to cool his temper, to scheme, to draw away from Larry as Larry's death drew near. "There's pop and food in our pack. Help yourself." He laid his gun in Blackie's boat.

"Now wait a minute, getting there's the easy part. It's finding your way back that's tricky. On your way out, watch where you enter the deep channel so you know where to leave it on your way back. When you're paddling, you can't see over the grass unless you stand up, and when you stand up in a tub like this, you fall in and

get wet. So what you want to do is notice things at eye
level that you'll remember."

"See you later." Chris put his right foot into the boat,
shoved off, brought in his left as he floated free.

"One more thing." Blackie held up his gun. "At three
o'clock I'm going to fire three shots real quick, and I'm
going to do that every five minutes till I see you paddling
into this bay. That's in case you lose your bearings. It
might cloud up, and then how would you know north
from south? I've never lost a hunter in this Marsh yet,
and I'm damned if you're going to be the first."

"Save your shells."

Free of land, Chris felt suddenly calm, almost care-
free. He sat in the stern, floating, at rest. For a minute or
more he peered into the water and watched a crayfish
treading the slime. Then he began to paddle. As he
moved around the point, he heard Larry call, "Bon
voyage," and he looked into the weeds and saw him sitting in the beached boat, raising a can of Coke in farewell. Blackie was standing beside him also holding a
Coke, into which he was carefully pouring a dose of
whiskey. It was clear to Chris that the old guide and the
hopeless hunter would pass the day in a kind of abrasive
harmony. Alcohol worked on Blackie, said his wife, as
an irritant. It worked on Larry, Chris knew, like a knock
on the head, immediately depressing him. Rachel seldom
allowed him even a glass of wine; a mere sip made him
sad and a few swallows dropped him into a restless
sleep. Nipping on Blackie's bottle, he was likely to spend
most of the day muttering and snoozing.

Paddling away from Larry—the sun in his face—
Chris felt like a sleeper waking from a hideous dream.
Boats always made him glad like this. Something at the
bottom of his psyche responded to sailing, drifting, row-
ing, paddling. Bobbing across the bay, he recalled how
he had felt as a boy reading the *Horatio Hornblower*
books. At the age of ten he had found them in the village
library and read them over and over for several years.
This was a village in the Corn Belt where the nearest
body of water was a backed-up creek twenty miles away,

yet how fond he had been of all the salt spray on those pages. It may be been that C. S. Forester made him a would-be sailor through his tales, but Chris suspected that it had worked the other way around, that he had had his predilection for the sea long before he picked up *Hornblower*, a buoyancy handed down perhaps from his seafaring ancestors—say, the O'Gradys of Cork or the Zellners of Bremen, who were said to have shipped before the mast. And his forebears in Scotland, he had been told, were fishermen. The forebears of everyone, he had been told, were fish.

He passed within fifty feet of Teal Point and caught the glint of three binoculars—six lenses—aimed his way. He skirted the vast flotilla of decoys and called into the weeds, "Nice day."

"Hell of a day for ducks," was the reply.

Off to his right the wounded mallard swam within range of the three hunters. The binoculars dropped and three gun barrels came up. Simultaneous with the swirl of shot on the water, Chris felt in his ears the concussion of three explosions, then three more as the hunters fired a second round, three more as they fired a third. The duck, absorbing the nine shots, spun and sank and came up again, dead. Its downy gray underside lay stonelike on the roiling water; one of its feet stood up like a flower on a short stalk—a flat, webbed foot slowly contracting like a blossom going shut.

4

CHRIS FOUND THE OUTLET and paddled along a narrow estuary, water bugs skating the surface ahead of him. Here and there the boat went aground. He tried to pole his way along, but this proved impossible, the bottom of the channel being too soft to offer resistance, the mud swallowing his paddle. He had to pull himself across the shallows by clutching at the swamp grass on his left and right, and as he did so, he set in motion a family of frogs that leaped and plopped from clod to clod. Perspiring, he took off his hunting coat and laid it across the bow seat.

In something under an hour he came to the wider channel where, but for the underwater vegetation bending north, the current was imperceptible. Here his progress was impeded not by shallow water but by a series of choices. At a dozen points this waterway opened into two waterways, the wider of which was not always obvious. Twice, taking a course he judged to be correct, he came to a dead end and had to go back. It was hard work. He took off his wool sweater and laid it on the bow seat.

At several points along the way, the green water resembled the pool of his dream, the site for drowning Larry. In the dream, however, he and Larry were always alone, while here in the channel he could never be sure hunters weren't peering out from the weeds. An hour and a half from David's Bay—and hour and a half from what he thought was the northernmost trace of humanity—a voice spoke to him from the cattails, a voice so close to his ear that he jerked his head aside and lost his cap: "Pardon me, do you have the correct time?"

Picking his cap off the water on his left, Chris peered into the weeds on his right. There, sitting on a small overturned boat and eating lunch, was a hunter, a pinch-faced man with a quick, squirrelike way of chewing. His meal, spread out beside him on the keel of the boat, was a two-pound package of Hydrox cookies and five or six carrots.

Christ looked at his watch. "Five minutes to ten."

The man nodded. "Thank you."

"Any luck?" said Chris.

"I shot one at sunrise. Lost him in the cane. Need a dog in cane this thick. Had a dog last year. Died."

"Did you paddle all this way before sunrise? You must have started at midnight."

"It ain't far. I came in from the lake. See them trees?" The hunter stood and pointed north. "The trees are on the lakeshore. There's a dirt road leading into the trees from the west. I came in on the road and paddled from there. Ain't far."

"Why not hunt the lakeshore? You could see where you dropped your ducks."

"That's all private land. Lawler's Resort. No hunting."

"But I'm told it's hunted."

"Sure, by the owner and his friends. They're hunting there this morning. I've been hearing a few shots."

Chris's boat was moving slowly downstream, sideways. He sat and dipped his paddle, straightening his course. "See you later."

"Right. Want a carrot?"

"No thanks, I brought lunch."

"Okay then. You said ten o'clock?"

"Yes."

"That means the Pope's saying mass in Chicago."

Chris paddled on. The channel was hot and still. He took off his wool shirt, and as he laid it over the bow seat, he was startled by two voices on his left:

"Jesus, no wonder we aren't getting any shooting, here's a guy in a boat."

"I be damned, a boatful of clothes. And he's wearing a white T-shirt. Hey, fella, ducks see you forty miles off."

Two hunters stood in the weeds, both with binoculars hanging from their necks, both with red meaty faces.

"Just passing through," he told them, dismayed to realize how close you can be to someone in the Marsh without knowing it; the tall grass, concealing a murder, might also conceal a witness.

"Well, I hope you don't stop till you get to Hudson Bay."

"Yeah, I hope you don't stop till you get to the North Pole."

They grinned at each other, pleased by their wit.

"Yeah, I hope you don't stop till you get to China."

"Yeah, I hope you don't stop till you get to hell."

Chris moved on, then stopped to unlace his boots and slip them off. He pulled off his wool socks and draped them over the bow seat. Giving the boat up to the current, he leaned over the stern and looked past the blue of the reflected sky to study the rich brown bottom, furrowed by crayfish and studded by the colorful casings of spent shotgun shells. The water looked pure enough to drink. He imagined it flowing into Larry's lungs.

When he sat up, the current had quickened; he was floating around the final bend in the stream; from here on, the channel ran straight to the lake, the trees dead ahead. Beyond, blue water stretched farther than the eye could see—Lake Manitoba blending horizonless into the sky.

He sighed aloud. At last the broad lake, the long view. To hurry himself forward, he raised his binoculars and rested his eyes on the various shades of blue-gray that never failed to soothe him, the muted color of hazy distance, the hazy color of Rachel's eyes. At the mouth of the stream, where the water swirled and caught the sun, the lake was silver. In the middle distance, under a small flock of ducks that wheeled in and out of his line of vi-

sion, the water held a tinge of green. Drifting faster down
the broad channel, he held the lenses to his eyes for a
minute or more—his elbows out like wings, his loose
T-shirt fluttering in the breeze—and he felt himself in
accord with the universe, as though he were being borne
along not on a Canadian stream, but on the current of his
destiny—a course leading him out of all perplexity and
into realms of peace.

A stretch of fast water carried him under the trees and
out into the lake and left him becalmed a hundred feet
from shore. Ahead lay an island. That's where he belonged. What better place to plot a killing, to ponder his
future—tomorrow and beyond—than an island?

He looked back at the mouth of the stream, marking
where the rippling water poured forth from the grassy
bank beneath the trees. Among the trees (mostly willows, a few aspen) two hunters were watching him with
binoculars. With his own, Chris swept the grassy bank
where it curved around to the west. He saw a point
where the bank flattened into the stony beach of a resort
—boats and buildings and cars. Evidently this was
where the road met the lake—Lawler's Resort. He
counted five large fishing boats, overturned and lined up
on the beach. Near them was a hunter, a young man
sitting under a willow tree, his gun leaning against the
trunk. Beyond the boats, five small cabins; beyond the
cabins, a two-story house. Parked in the yard were four
cars with license plates of four different colors.

The island, separated from the mainland by twenty
minutes of steady paddling, was shaped like an overturned bowl, its rocky middle high and dry and about
forty yards across, its shoreline veiled by reeds. With the
last of the strength in his numb shoulders and arms,
Chris paddled around to the north side and ran his boat
into the bank. He stepped out, pulled the boat up from
the water and put on his wool shirt and his boots. Leaving his gun behind, he climbed the slope to the crest,
heartened by the feel of rock through his boot soles—a
red-brown rock, sharply fissured and emblematic to
Chris of the stability he sought in life, the uneven yet

solid foundation upon which man might build an endur-
ing sense of happiness.

As he stood on the rock, facing the void of the watery
horizon, the plan he had been straining to develop instantly unfolded in his mind. Tomorrow he would insist
that Larry and Blackie come with him to this island to
hunt. He would bring along with him an ample supply of
booze, and as soon as Blackie was safely drunk, he
would drown Larry at the base of this north slope, out of
sight of the mainland. So simple was this plan, so easy to
accomplish, that he laughed aloud and ran across the
crest of the island, his shirttail and bootlaces flying. He
looked down the south slope into the reeds at the edge of
the water. There, in a cove, Blackie would be stationed,
facing the Marsh. He hurried back to the north side, took
a few steps down the slope, and noticed, off to his right,
a steplike formation of rock—a natural seat. There was a
flatrock bench for him to sit on, a slanting wall for his
back, a boulder for his feet. He stepped through a patch
of dead thistles, sat, leaned back and felt like a visionary
king of an indestructible throne at a turning point in history. The arduous years of his life were behind him,
years as miry as the Marsh; below him were the ripples
where Larry's life would end; before him lay his hope, as
vast as the hazy line where he imagined the horizon to
be.

He brought up the glasses and held them on the plane
of the world's edge and saw the color he loved—gray
veiled by the blue of airy distance: precisely the color he
saw in Rachel's eyes when she was wistful. Or weary. Or
gorging herself on his love.

5

H I S   L O V E.   R E S T I N G   O N his seat of stone, the sun warming the back of his neck, his hands moving absently over the warm, rough rock, Chris pondered his love. After Rachel's visit to his office in February (the day she found royal costumes in the college theater and he found himself in love), Chris had seen nothing of her for several weeks, except in his mind—and there he saw her constantly. In weak moments he longed to be with her (she had made a deep incursion into his loneliness); in strong moments he promised himself he would forget her (she was married to his closest friend); in spare moments he occupied himself with the duties of his presidency of the School and College Counselors (he made weekly trips to St. Paul, half of them necessary). Spring was a busy time for him at the college, and he succeeded in moving Rachel from the front to the back of his mind; he succeeded (he thought) in burying his love. But around Easter it came to life again.

Easter 1979 was late, and so were the runoff of snow and the first robin in Rookery. Not until Easter Monday did Chris open his seventh-floor window on a late-afternoon breeze that smelled of spring—a delicious puff of air from the south in which he thought he detected the essence of the Ozarks, perhaps even a salty whiff of the Gulf of Mexico. Standing at his window and holding a Martini, he inhaled deeply and tried to put from his mind the stress of his job.

He had spent the early part of the afternoon presiding over a department meeting at which the main business was self-preservation: how to protect his seven-member

154

counseling staff from the layoffs resulting from next year's predicted drop in enrollment. Chris had been eloquent. Hearing his assurances (he hoped they weren't altogether false), at least five of his counselors left the meeting with renewed confidence.

Upon adjournment, he had spent the middle part of the afternoon sipping Martinis with Vickie and Steve, two young counselors without tenure. The setting was Harry's Campus Bar and the subject was again self-preservation: how to protect these two in particular. Chris made an elaborate case for their indispensability. He sent them home reassured and looped.

Then, alone in his apartment, he had spent an hour sipping another drink and asking himself why he himself should want to keep his job. Why not resign from Rookery State at the end of spring term? By sacrificing himself, he could see to it that the assurances he had given his staff were neither bluff nor blind hope. One position was threatened in each department, campus wide. If he eliminated his position, the college could afford to keep Vickie and Steve and the five others.

For what, beside the Quinns, was holding him in Rookery? Surely there were other directions his life could take. Jobs were dwindling in education, but he had connections in other fields. In Minneapolis, General Mills had offered him a consultancy in its personnel department. In Washington, Senator Sorenson, a former student of Chris's, needed a speech writer and researcher. In Fargo his aunt Geraldine was looking for a manager for her ice-cream parlor.

Standing, or rather swaying, at his window and pouring himself another Martini, Chris saw Rachel descend the opposite hillside and set off on her two-mile course. He put down his glass and his bottle of gin. He fumbled into his windbreaker, catching his tie in the zipper, and took the elevator to the ground floor. He greeted the building superintendent's wife as he passed her open apartment and he staggered out the back door. Rachel was half a mile downstream on the opposite bank. She was emerging from the cemetery and running along Badbattle Drive. Another half mile and she would leave the roadway and cross the river on the footbridge and return along the near bank.

Waiting, timing his descent so that they would meet below his apartment, Chris stood under the bare birches and felt, by turns, light-headed and heavy-hearted, light-hearted and hard-headed, heavy-headed and hard-hearted—in other words, drunk. He lost sight of Rachel among the willows at the far end of the valley, where the treetops were becoming opaque as they swelled with buds. Then he saw her on the near bank, running upstream. He started down.

Here the hillside was steep and without steps or walkways. He took a path beaten through the brush by children and melting snow. It was a gravelly path with a number of exposed roots, one of which tripped him and sent him rolling for ten feet and sliding the rest of the way on the seat of his pants and the heel of his hands. When Rachel came upon him, he was standing, stooped, against a tree and pressing his hands, cut and burning, between his thighs.

"Chris, what's wrong?"

"Fell down. Cut myself." He laughed, light-hearted at the sight of her. The sky was still bright, but the valley was in shadow. Against the fading colors of the hillside, her face was an amber light.

She looked at his hands. The right one was bloody. She kissed it. "Are you drunk?" she asked, smelling gin.

"I think so."

They walked the path upstream. Beside them a dozen mallards floated among the weeds, quacking, preening, diving for food.

"I'm feeling sentimental today, Chris. As you know, we're doing *Twelfth Night* at the Playhouse. When I was in high school, we read *Twelfth Night* in English class, so today I got out my old high school diary to see what I might have thought about the play when I was seventeen. Well, there wasn't anything in the diary about *Twelfth Night*, but I came across my earliest entries about Larry. How handsome he was. How blond. How

at least seven girls fell in love with him on the first day of
school. Everything I wrote about him has an exclamation point after it. The more passionate remarks have
several. 'He eats with his right hand' has an exclamation
point. 'He touched me' has five."

Chris chuckled because Rachel did.

"In June Larry and I will have been married eighteen
years, Chris. Think of it—that's exactly half my life."

Chris cradled his right hand in his left, lightly pressing
his thumb on his abrasions. "Which half was better?"

She didn't answer. She walked between Chris and the
water, her eyes on the ducks that swam abreast of her,
hoping for crumbs.

After a while she said, "We've done you one better,
Chris. Wasn't it seventeen years for you and Karen?"

"Yes, seventeen. Two of them happy."

She touched his arm. "More than two, surely."

"Maybe two and a half."

"I don't believe you. Nobody but a masochist lives in
misery for fifteen years, not if there's a way out."

"I'm not saying they were fifteen years of misery.
They were neutral years, mostly. Years of nothing. Some
suffering and some nonsuffering, and after it was all
over, it balanced out to neutral." This, as he spoke it,
sounded false; the nonsuffering had not balanced the suffering, but never mind.

"So what's wrong with neutral? Neutral can be happy,
can't it?"

Chris's ears buzzed; his head throbbed. "Neutral's the
wrong word. I mean vacant. Empty. A lack of happiness."

"Happiness is what you make it," she said.

"Hey, that's clever."

"Thank you."

They came to a bend in the river. Here the path was
squeezed tight between the water and the steep hillside.
The shadows were deep.

"Rachel, tell me honestly how much of your marriage
has been happy since Larry got sick."

"Happiness is what you make it."

"Be serious." He bumped her shoulder, not as lightly as he intended.

Jolted, she said, "I don't feel like being serious. I've been serious all day."

"I mean, damn it, Rachel, just admit for once that you and I got ourselves into a pair of disappointing marriages."

"I won't admit that." She left the path and stepped down to a narrow opening between two thorny bushes. The ducks swam close, like pets.

He followed and stood behind her. "You've been nothing but happy?"

She shrugged, then nodded. "Happy enough." She was looking across the water at the cemetery on the opposite hillside, at her house above it. Her kitchen window mirrored the purple sunset.

"I don't believe you."

She turned to face him. "Listen, Chris, Larry and I have had more arguments and tears than I like to remember, and we've had to worry about his job and about house payments and about Bruce—though not many worries about Bruce, thank God—and looming over all of it has been this awful, awful disease. But is that supposed to make me wish I lived like my neighbors? Is that supposed to make me wish I could attend the sappy parties the housewives on my block go to—the kitchenware parties? The cosmetics parties? The dinner parties where the swingers swap wives and the nonswingers get their kicks out of watching the swapping and then telling me about it the next day on the phone? Is that the kind of life I'd be expected to live if my marriage were ordinary?"

She turned to the river again. She took a handful of dried corn from the pocket of her sweatshirt and scattered it around her feet. The dozen ducks crowded ashore and ate busily, each bird, while it pecked, claiming as much more corn for itself as it could cover with its wide, leathery feet. When the food was gone, all but one of the ducks returned to the water. The one that remained pecked at Rachel's shoe, begging. She drew an-

other handful of corn out of her sweatshirt. She squat-
ted, holding the corn over the water; the flock stretched
and leaped and splashed around her hand as she let the
corn drop, kernel by kernel.

"Is the fact that Larry got sick supposed to make me
think I didn't mean it when I vowed to love him in sickness and health?" Squatting, her head down, she seemed
to be asking the ducks. "I vowed to love him in sickness
and health, and to start with, I fulfilled the health part—
and now I'm fulfilling the other part."

"But if you had known ahead of time..." He stood at
her back, looking down at her narrow shoulders.

She brushed the chaff from her hands and rose, her
back to him. "What difference would *knowing* have
made?" She continued to face away. "When I was a senior in high school, if somebody told me that this man—
this dream—I was going to marry would keep his health
for only a certain number of years and then he would get
MS, do you suppose I could have changed my mind
about him? Do you suppose I would have said, 'No
thanks, I guess I'll shop around'?" She turned. "I would
have married him with the promise of only a *week* of
good health. I was that much in love with him. Don't you
remember what love is like in its early stages, Chris?
Don't you remember the intensity? How much you'd
risk? How much you'd give up in order to possess the
one you love?"

"I remember." His head swam. "I don't have to remember. I feel it now."

"Then he got MS. So what do you mean, has our marriage been happy? That doesn't strike me as a very intel-
ligent question. I'm not sure it even applies. I think the
first thing you ought to ask about a marriage is whether
it's working, and whether it *has* been working right
along—functioning—man and wife moving as smoothly
as possible through the days and nights. I don't think
you understand the word 'happiness,' Chris. I think by
'happy' you mean 'easy.'"

"By happy I mean...happy."

She pushed up past him to the path, extending her

hand for him to follow. As they walked, she carried his bloody hand in both of her own.

"It hasn't been an *easy* marriage, if that's what you mean. It's been difficult, arduous. Sometimes I drop into bed at night feeling the way I used to in high school gym class after our teacher made us climb ropes. That was the hardest and dumbest exercise ever devised—climbing those big long ropes that hung from the ceiling of the gym. 'Go climb the ropes, girls,' and there we'd be, struggling like monkeys up vines—except we were a lot slower, a lot ungainlier—and when we didn't have an ounce of strength left, we'd come sliding down and end up with abrasions on our hands and between our thighs."

They walked for a while in silence. The path veered away from the water. The ducks, giving up hopes for more corn, let themselves be carried downstream.

"Interesting, isn't it, to think that my high school gym class was my preparation for marriage, in a way. You might say it got me ready for the days when Larry's really down. Like last Friday, when he got out of bed gloomy and stayed gloomy all day. It wasn't one of his *silent* gloomy days. This was gloom articulated. He wanted to talk incessantly, mostly about himself, his state of mind. He didn't like himself and he couldn't stop examining himself for flaws. All I could do was steer the conversation away from his flaws. And my flaws too— he wanted to tell me about mine as well. He called me a scalp collector and said my main interest in life was seeing how many men I could cast a spell over. He said I was that way even as a high school girl. Well, he'd know if anybody would."

The path led them to the bridge at the upper end of the valley. The boards creaked underfoot. They stopped midway and peered over the rail at their reflections— black forms on the purple surface.

"A day like that is hard work, Chris. Then at seven I went off to rehearsal and the moment I stepped outside I felt as though a great yoke had been lifted from my shoulders. We had an absolutely brilliant rehearsal. I put the cast three times through Act Five of *Twelfth Night*—

Bruce is in it, did I tell you?—and each time it was twice as good as the time before. I lectured the cast about the play. You should have heard how wise I was. I told them things about *Twelfth Night* that Shakespeare didn't even know." She laughed. "It was that night toward the end of rehearsals when everything finally comes together, and you feel that if they'd give you a chance, you could direct the affairs of *nations*. You could bring the entire *world* into harmony—you're that good a director. Of course a night like that is usually followed by a dress rehearsal where absolutely everything goes to hell— there'll be a short circuit in the lighting and your stage manager will come down with the mumps and your leading lady will trip on the hem of her costume and fall into the orchestra pit—but knowing that doesn't make a speck of difference. For the moment, you're on top of the world. So picture me, Chris, coming home like the wise woman of the Western world and walking into the living room and finding my two men having a fight. Bruce had gone home ahead of me—he got a ride with one of the actresses. There in the living room was Larry lecturing Bruce—badgering him—on the subject of God. Fate was blind and the world was a trap and God, if he existed, wore an executioner's hood. He was *saying* that, standing in front of the fireplace shaking his finger at Bruce, and Bruce was sitting in the rocking chair looking into the fire with his eyes wet. This man I married—this dream—scolding this dear, all-conference tackle because he's friendly with a crowd of teenage evangelists. Are you picturing it, Chris? Me walking up to the front door convinced I'm the greatest director since Guthrie and then stepping inside and finding that I can't even keep my own household together—do you see it?"

"I see it. I'm sorry."

"I'm not telling you this to make you sorry, Chris. My point is that some nights I go to bed feeling as though I've been climbing ropes."

After stepping off the bridge, they crossed the roadway and came to the cemetery gate. They entered and followed a lane that ran flat for a way, then bent uphill. They were out of step. Rachel was gradually speeding up, perhaps because of the chill that had come with the twilight, perhaps because of dinner. Chris wanted to slow down and prolong his time with her.

"Climbing ropes, Chris. After that long, long day with Larry in pain and complaining, I had that little respite at the Playhouse and then it was right back to the pain— made worse by Bruce being involved. The living room was full of sorrow and I couldn't possibly let the evening end that way. I had to set things right."

"And did you?"

"Of course." She gave him a quick shrug and tossed his hand away. "You shouldn't have to ask. It's the sort of thing I *do*. I settled them down."

"How?"

She thought. "I made popcorn."

"And?"

"And? And I don't know. How should I know what else I did? I just got them settled down. In a case like that you go on instinct and you don't remember the details. All I remember is we ate big bowls of popcorn."

Chris panted as they made their way up the steep lane of the cemetery. His head ached on two levels, a steady pain beneath the throbbing. "I've got to cut down my drinking. Exercise more."

She smiled, took his hand and swung it in great arcs as they climbed between the lettered stones. They came to the wroughtiron gate where a path led uphill to her house. She squeezed the hand and let it go. "Forgive my lecture, Chris." She laughed. "You look like a man who's been severely lectured."

"I've never minded lectures. But I'm not convinced that just because a marriage survives year after year it's necessarily happy."

"Well, ours *has* survived. *Is* happy."

He looked closely into her eyes. "Honestly?"

"Yes."

"In spite of last Friday?"

"Yes, in spite of last Friday. Maybe *because* of last

Friday. Last Friday I went to bed feeling like a good wife. I had affected the state of mind of my husband and my son. I had brought peace to the living room. I had that as my reward, even if it left me feeling as though I'd been climbing ropes."

He bored more deeply into her eyes, his own not quite in focus. "But with no abrasions between your thighs." Larry was losing his virility. He had confided in Chris.

Rachel stepped back, assumed a formal stance—chin up, shoulder back. "If it were any of your business, I would tell you that my thighs are bruised more often than you might think."

"By Larry?" Instantly he knew this to be the most idiotic question of his life, but when she spoke of her thighs, he saw in his mind—no doubt a short circuit caused by the Maritinis—the leering face of Bernard Beckwith: an intolerable conjunction of images to be exorcised by the quickest means possible, and the stupidest: "Or by Beckwith?"

Rachel's laugh was full-hearted and lasted about three seconds. Then, appearing to have squeezed all the enjoyment possible out of his question, she let him have it across the mouth and nose—a slap of such force that he stumbled back against the iron gate and covered his stinging face with both his hands.

6

THE NEXT EVENING. RAIN in Rookery. A musty smell in the Playhouse. Chris dropped in on rehearsal and took, unnoticed, a seat in the back row of the dark auditorium. In the past he had done this a few times with Larry, to pass a dull evening, but now he was alone. At midnight, rehearsals ended, the cast departed, the stagelights dimmed. Two or three voices were heard in the wings. Filtered through the backdrop was the sound of hammering backstage. The lights went further down, leaving a single small spot highlighting the grit on the empty stage. Against this light, Chris saw Rachel slowly rise from her director's seat in row eight. She stretched, then picked up her papers and empty coffee cup from the seat beside her.

"Rachel..."

She turned, peering into the darkness.

"It's me. Chris." He sat forward in his seat but did not rise from it, did not go down to join her in row eight. He was here to apologize for yesterday's idiotic remark, yet the devastating force of her slap was fresh in his mind and he wanted her to atone for that. He wanted a sign of reconciliation. He wanted her at least to come and sit with him.

She did. She climbed the sloping aisle—wearily, it seemed to Chris—and she sat down at the end of the last row, leaving an empty seat between them. She set her papers and cup on the floor. Here in the dark she was barely visible, her face a faint moon. Beside it an earring glinted.

"This is an apology, Rachel. I'm sorry I said what I did."

She nodded. "Good."

He sat back.

So did she.

For a long time they were silent, facing forward as though the drama were onstage, not between themselves. The voices in the wings droned on. The carpenter hammered.

"A good rehearsal?" he asked.

"A dumb rehearsal."

The spotlight moved upstage and half the circle stood upright against the backdrop, a bent coin.

"A good day of counseling?" she asked.

"A dumb day of counseling."

She slid low in her seat and laid her head back. "Chris, there's something you have to know. And there's something *I* have to know. What you have to know is that I sleep with nobody but Larry."

"I know it. I knew it."

"So that's settled. Now what I have to know is—" She giggled. "Did I hurt your nose?"

"It bled."

"No!" She popped over a seat, to look at his nose. Close up, he saw that she wore jeans and a dark turtleneck with floppy sleeves.

"You slugged me and it bled a little," he said. "And this morning it still hurt."

"I'm sorry, I meant it to be a stage slap."

"No, you didn't. You slugged me."

"But entirely on impulse. If I had given it any thought, it would have been a stage slap."

"You meant no harm?"

"Of course not."

"It was totally unpremeditated?"

"Right."

His turn now to slump in his seat, lay his head back. He said, happily, "I'm not consoled."

She leaned on the seat in front of her, arms folded under her chin. "Tough."

He laid his palm on the slant of her back and spread his fingers. They sat silent for a long time. This was not at all the uneasy confrontation he had expected. It was a meeting of minds—and moods—in placid repose. Back-stage the hammering gave way to sawing—the labored, uneven strokes of a dull saw through hard wood. The actors in the wings said goodbye to one another; one of them stepped onstage, hopped off and came up the aisle, murmuring lines to himself in the dark. As he went out the door, light fell in from the lobby and lit for a moment the flame of Rachel's red hair. The light narrowed and went out.

"Do you mind if we go over some of last night's ground again, Rachel? Talk a little more about you and me and Larry?"

"We'll leave out the rope-climbing metaphor."

"I want to tell you something about Larry that you don't know. It's something even Larry doesn't know."

"Yes?"

"Larry is the only man in my life I've ever envied."

She said nothing.

"I'm not the type who falls in love very often, Rachel. In college I was in love with a girl named Helen, and then a girl named Betty, and later I was in love with Karen for a while, and now I'm in love with you."

Under his hand he felt her arch like a cat, inhaling deeply.

He said no more. He wanted his declaration to stand alone, unobscured by explanation. *I'm in love with you.* It struck him as one of the purest statements he had ever made, a perfect reflection of what he felt—or rather not a reflection at all but a direct exposure, as though at the sound of these words the door to his soul had been re-placed by a window, the words a pane of clear glass.

"I'm in love with you." He said it a second time, softly, and at once there was an involuntary hitch in his breathing, as though the slightest change in atmosphere —a breath—might fog his meaning.

And then there was light. Having turned up the house-lights, Bernard Beckwith strode out from the wings, calling, "Everybody out, we're locking up, everybody out, it's time..." His thin voice trailed off as he noticed the two figures in the back row, saw that it was Rachel with Chris, saw how well planted they were in their seats, Rachel leaning forward, her chin on her arms, Chris slouched back. Was he touching her? Bernard Beckwith came forward to the edge of the stage and saw, squinting, that Chris's right hand indeed caressed her back.

"Rachel dear? Are you needing a ride?" His tone was overcourteous.

"Thanks, Bernard, I've got my car."

"Well, Bruce asked me to tell you he caught a ride with Viola, so I thought perhaps you didn't have your car. Now be sure to get your rest, Rachel. It's midnight and tomorrow's Wednesday and we'll need all afternoon and evening if we're ever going to get this show ready by Friday. Scary, when you think of it—only one more rehearsal, then dress, then opening."

"Relax, Bernard, we're right on schedule." This was one of her stage voices—full, commanding. It seemed to make Beckwith thoughtful. He stood at the edge of the stage with his head tilted, putting Chris in mind of a player whose soliloquy has slipped his mind, whose cue has come and gone. Beckwith had this habit of staring at people while sorting through his thoughts. Tonight he wore a tan raincoat and dark pants. His slick black hair shone in the overhead lights. What was he pondering? He said, finally, "Hello, Christopher."

A curt nod: "Hi, Bernie."

Rachel turned quickly to Chris with a glare and a "Tsk"—a reprimand for baiting her boss, who insisted on Bern*ard*.

"Charles is still working in the scene shop, Rachel; otherwise everybody's out. Don't forget—lights and lock."

"Right. Thanks, Bernard. See you in the morning."

"Ten four." Exit left with a wave.

I'm in love with you. Were these words intended only for the dark, Chris wondered, or why did they seem inappropriate, thin, almost half-baked in all this light? He said, "Rachel, let's go have a drink somewhere."

"No." She rose, stood for a moment, massaging her forehead with two fingers, and said, "Wait here." She picked up her papers and her cup, and as she went forward to the stage, he watched the motions of her downhill stride, the medium-high heels of her boots causing her seat to swing and her hair to bounce. She went into the wings. The sawing stopped.

All day Chris had been in turmoil. With his students he had not been able to concentrate, troubled by the fear of a permanent rift between himself and Rachel, and so tonight he had driven across the city in a downpour to close the gap. And to do more than that. Tonight, he decided, was the time for declaring his love. Until now he had spoken only in hints which she had either missed or chosen to ignore. But now he could no longer hold back. Nearly as strong as his desire for the woman was his desire to make his desire known. Too long he had kept it secret, partly out of regard for Larry and partly because he couldn't be sure how Rachel might respond. Sometimes, before the Quinn fireplace, he thought he saw behind her brisk smile and her breeziness an appeal to be rescued, to be loved by someone other than Larry, an appeal to Chris to console her, soothe her, save her. Imagined or not, it was a rousing signal which set Chris to planning how he might claim her. But the signal was fleeting. With Chris on the brink of declaring himself, she would turn to Larry with a tender, wifely gesture; she would hold his hand to her cheek or she would kiss him quickly on the temple, as though to indicate that it hadn't been Chris's signal after all; it hadn't been his cue.

Or had it? Maybe she was teasing him, encouraging him one moment and retreating the next—playing with him. Entirely possible—Rachel of the Playhouse.

April 17, 1979. The trouble with loving an actress is that once you figure out the meaning of her lines, then you have to figure out if they're being spoken from a script or from the heart. From the heart, you first suppose. Rachel brings such skill to her acting—to her living—that you naturally think "heart" first and "script" second. Every word, movement, and glance strike you as genuine. But suddenly you notice in her eyes a flicker of guile or irony or amusement and you begin to wonder; and you go to a play and you see her display some of these same words, movements and glances with the same offhand authenticity, and you wonder further. You wonder where she ever learned that lightness, that deftness, that grace. Did she learn them in life and were they therefore part of her real nature? Or did she learn them in the theater and were they therefore art? In which of her houses— the Quinn house or the Playhouse—does she train for the other?

Well, tonight it no longer mattered. Chris was beyond puzzling it out. He was obsessed—hamstrung—by his love for her and there was nothing to do but proclaim it and see what she made of it. *I'm in love with you.* It was urgent news, but now, as he waited for Rachel (what was taking her so long?), he lamented speaking of it here in the Playhouse. *I'm in love with you*—the lights had come up and his words seemed lost. How many times over the years had that message, in its various phrasings, been delivered inside these walls? Surely hundreds of times. Thousands, counting rehearsals. No wonder his single utterance, though heartfelt, sounded like rhetoric and seemed to float up and evaporate into the tiny holes of the acoustical ceiling, leaving no trace.

Backstage a man said goodbye. A door opened and closed. All the lights went off. A minute passed. Two minutes. Just as it occurred to Chris that she might have given him the slip, gone home, the lobby door on his right opened and Rachel was beside him, handing him a styrofoam cup of coffee. He took it from her as the door shut and left them in total darkness.

She sat beside him. She sipped and swallowed. She said nothing.

Was she purely a listener tonight? Was she waiting to hear more? If so, he would oblige her, for he had secrets to tell. He felt her floppy sleeve beside his own. He put out his hand and she touched, gently, his lacerations.

"Rachel, I'm in love with you," he began, and he went on to say that there was currently no one in his life who lifted his spirits the way she did and that he loved her good nature and her vigor and her freckles. He said that if she wanted him to pinpoint the day this love began he could do it; his love began the day she came to his office quoting Hopkins. He said he hadn't loved her when she was Larry's bride in Owl Brook and he hadn't loved her—though he admired her—during the Doldrums Major, when he spent so much time at her house, nor had he loved her this past winter—the Doldrums Minor—until the day she came to campus to see about costumes and props. He said that however you accounted for the first stirrings of love—whether you traced it to the chemistry of the brain or the conjunction of stars—they began for him the moment she showed up in his office and quoted Hopkins and wept.

He told her that during the last years of his marriage and during the first year or so of his divorce he had been afraid that he had lost his capacity for love. He had become so cynical where love was concerned that when he moved to Rookery, he anticipated living out his life as a mean old bastard, and liking it. To illustrate this, he told her the story of the death of Ms. Rover.

Ms. Rover had been a stub-tailed mongrel with the dark and light markings of a Jersey cow. The MacKensies had owned her during the last two or three years of their marriage, and the dog had developed a great fondness for Karen, who fed her. Around the time of the divorce, when Karen and Billy and Kay made their first scouting trip to California, they left the dog with Chris. One day he took her out for a long walk. He didn't use a leash because Ms. Rover, despite her name, was very deliberate, not easily sidetracked by noises and smells.

Well, they came to a highway and Chris held Ms. Rover's collar while he waited for an opening in the traffic. Down in the wide ditch near the intersection a telephone truck was parked with its door open. Near it, a man stood before a metal cabinet—one of those junction boxes where underground cables come to the surface to have their filaments braided or soldered or whatever is done by those telephone men you so often see standing in ditches. Suddenly a woman's voice—loud and scratchy—came over the truck intercom. Something in the voice sounded like Karen's, though Chris wouldn't have noticed this if the dog hadn't stiffened at the first syllable and then strained to get away and run to the truck. Chris tightened his grip on the dog's collar, and when he saw his chance, he hurried her across the highway. They walked for an hour around a wooded hilltop and then turned back. Approaching the highway from the other side, the dog heard the voice on the intercom again, and before Chris could restrain her, she ran headlong toward what she thought was the woman she loved —and was destroyed under the wheels of a bread truck. The bread truck stopped and the driver, apologizing, halted traffic while Chris picked up the body. Ms. Rover was heavy, and carrying her was hard work; her bones hung in her loose skin like rocks in a sack. He lugged her home and buried her in the backyard. When Karen returned and he told her what had happened, she railed at him for being a negligent fool. He didn't tell her that Ms. Rover had been drawn into the traffic by the voice of her dear mistress; he sensed that instead of consoling Karen, this would compound the tragedy. Nor did he tell her that Ms. Rover's last act corresponded to his own jaded definition of love. Love, according to Chris, was that heedless dash toward what we believe is the source of our happiness, never mind if the source proves, when we get there, to be nothing but a squawk box.

That's how cynical he had been, he told Rachel in the back row of the dark theater. He had moved to Rookery in an advanced state of sourness. And spending all those winter afternoons with Larry during the Doldrums Major had done nothing to change him. True, the many good meals at the Quinn table and the many warm evenings before the fire had helped to allay his loneliness, but had done nothing to correct his distorted view of love. The Quinn's marriage, like his own, seemed to have been twisted into a grotesque mockery of its earlier self. Love was a trap. If you loved, you doubled your chances of sorrow. Better to go it alone. When he remembered the Quinns as he first knew them (that Sunday in the Owl Brook park, happily drinking beer and Hula-Hooping) and he compared that to their present state (adapting their lives to disease and depression), he felt that he understood all there was to know about the set trap of love, the sprung trap of marriage.

He told Rachel (shifting now in his seat, setting his half-empty cup on the floor, taking her hand firmly in his own) that for a while he had savored his cynicism. It was nourishing. It made him strong. Cynicism was the perfect prescription for his first year at Rookery State College, making him gruff and impulsive and something of a bully. He had been hired to rebuild a department that had fallen into disarray under the previous chairman (who had resigned to become a free-lance tree surgeon), and Chris's unorthodox moves took the campus by surprise. He sized up his seven counselors and saw that as individuals they were competent but as a group they were like geese in a barnyard, moving through their working day in a flock. Between appointments they were forever office-hopping and clucking over the secrets they had learned from their interviews with students. They had become inbred. They shared a single philosophy of counseling (the non-directive approach), a single opinion of their former chairman (a nonentity) and a single view of the world at large (no nukes).

First, Chris relocated their offices, scattering them across the campus in seven different buildings. He told them to quit thinking of themselves as a coterie and to start thinking of themselves as missionaries to the confused, the troubled, the misfits. Instead of sitting back and waiting for students to come to them, they should

snoop about campus and become versed in the require-
ments and eccentricities of the faculty and keep track of
the students they advised throughout their four years of
college, from freshman orientation to job placement.

He called frequent meetings of his staff at which he
presided, at first, with a heavy hand. Then, as his department began to take a renewed pride in itself, his hand
became lighter and looser, until now, late in his second
year, the counseling operation was pretty well running
itself. His seven counselors, working harder and seeing
less of each other, had grown to have a greater respect
for one another and what they were doing. Gradually (a
couple of them grudgingly) they were even growing to
like their boss.

And now, looking back at his first year at the college,
he was struck by the great quantity of bitterness he had
taken to work with him every day—acerbity enough to
divide up and dole out to his seven counselors; and it
didn't do them a bit of harm. He handled them roughly
because he didn't give a damn if he was liked or not.
Although at first they resented his harsh manner, they
later came to see that while the nondirectional approach
might be all right in counseling students, it was a disaster
in counseling counselors. The end result was that he and
his staff of seven were, to quote a recent report from the
college Selfstudy Committee, "operating optimumly."

And then (he leaned closer to Rachel's ear, spoke
softly), during this second year at Rookery State, he had
begun to lose his bitterness. He had been chewing on it
for quite a while and he didn't like its taste anymore. His
crust began to crumble and underneath he uncovered an
old layer of tenderness. Softness attracted him; harshness repelled him. His taste in movies took a sentimental
turn. Certain melodies by Liszt moved the heavy furniture at the bottom of his heart. He drove to Minneapolis
to see a traveling exhibit of Renoir and couldn't take his
eyes from the canvases in which Renoir's people wore
expressions of peace. They stood and sat in postures of
ease. They fit with obvious tranquility into their land-
scapes, into their rooms, into each other's company. No-

where a severe line or a hint of pain. He moved through the galleries, enchanted by the works themselves and by his mental picture of Renoir himself in his old age, painting with fingers so arthritic that he couldn't hold a brush. It was a matter of record that the artist had finally bandaged his knuckles and stuck the hilt of his brush into the bandages, and (though this was not a matter of record, it was nonetheless true) he had done so in order that Chris—two generations later—might understand how agreeable life could be when you shed your shell and learned to be easy with others. When you lost your suspicions and learned to trust. When you lost your severity and learned to love.

He told Rachel ("Be patient," he said, "I'm almost done") that, with the passing of time and a little help from his books and Liszt and Renoir and a great deal of help from his loneliness, he had come to see that there wasn't anything in life more important than love. The best thing human beings could do was to love one another. Others had said it before him. Believed it before him. But nobody believed it as intensely as Chris did now. Not that he was good at loving. He wasn't sure he even knew *how* to love any longer. Or how to be lovable. But that didn't weaken his wholehearted belief in the power of love. In its value and rightness. In its necessity.

What he didn't know about love, he asked Rachel to teach him. Loving was her talent, her gift. Never in his life had he seen anyone with such an inexhaustible fund of love. He was speaking now about Rachel the wife. She took a lot of shit from Larry—Chris had been witness—and yet her love was unshakable. In his two and a half years in Rookery he had never known her to waver. And except for the day she came to his office quoting Hopkins, he had never known her to weaken. How was she able to sustain her grace year after year, her weightlessness, her ability to skim along slightly above the surface of life? How had her touch remained so light while her heart had grown so stout? And how could a man help loving her?

He couldn't help it, he said.

He loved her.

There was fatigue and surrender in the way Rachel rested her head on his shoulder, yet when he stirred to kiss her on the forehead, she got quickly to her feet and said, "I have to go." Suppressing his urge to hold her back, he followed her across the lobby to Bernard Beckwith's office, where she had left her raincoat and purse.

Outside, the rain had stopped. The air was heavy with fog and coalsmoke. It felt cold enough to snow. Cars passed, their tires whistling on the wet street. Chris and Rachel walked down the block to the Quinns' blue Opel. She unlocked it, but before getting in, she had two things to say, one thing to do.

She said she was appalled to think that Chris envied Larry—it was a horrible thing for him to say or even to think.

She said she was exhausted beyond words tonight— she would call him soon.

She put her arms around him and pressed her face tightly into his shoulder and neck. He nudged her with his lips, but she buried her face in the collar of his jacket, resisting his kiss. He ran his healing hand up her back and slipped it into her hair and they stood for a long time in the rising and falling light of passing cars, clutching one another with all their might.

7

*T*HE NEXT AFTERNOON, WEDNES-
day, Rachel phoned from the Playhouse.

"Chris, I'm sorry to bother you at work, but I want to
talk about my footprints. Do you have a minute?"

"Yes, I'm between visitors."

"Do you want to hear about my footprints?"

"By all means." He closed the book he had been
reading—the poetry of Wyatt: *Her wily looks my wits
did blind . . .*

"My footprints, when I run, aren't very big, Chris."

"I see . . . Have you been drinking, Rachel?" He
meant this to be amusing, but having asked it so ear-
nestly and often of Karen, he was unable to make it
sound funny.

"Only coffee. We've been rehearsing like mad since
ten this morning. I've given everybody a half hour off,
and I'm sitting in Bernard's office drinking coffee."

"Is Beckwith there?"

"Bernard is in St. Paul today, lobbying for grant
money."

"Is the play coming together?"

"Like nothing I've ever done. It may just be the best
production of anything Rookery has ever seen, Chris.
I'm holding my breath."

"Who's minding Larry?"

"Nobody."

"Do you want me to drop in on him?"

"Not necessarily. I don't want him to feel any more
watched over than he already is. I'm here day and night
now—we open Friday—but I'm sure he'll be fine. Now

176

about my footprints. An inch of snow fell in the valley
last night and I made two laps this morning and on my
second lap I noticed what a small part of my foot touches
the ground when I run. Just the ball, nothing of the
heel." She spilled this out in a rush, then stopped.

He waited for her to continue. He prompted her:
"And?"

"And it reminded me of what you said about the way
I'm living my life these days, Chris. You said I was living
it lightly. I guess 'weightless' was the word. Just skim-
ming along, never coming down hard. Do you recall saying that, Chris?"

"Of course."

"I guess you meant it as a compliment."

He extended his foot and set his office door swinging
shut. When the latch clicked, he said, "It's one of the
things I love about you, Rachel. Your ability to skim."

"Oh, yes—love. Well, I'm not ready to discuss that
now."

"I am."

"No, give me more time on that."

"You've had since last night."

"I'm not ready to say what I think about"—she lowered her voice—"about your alleged love for me."

"What do you mean, 'alleged'?"

She laughed.

"What do you mean, 'alleged,' Rachel?"

Her laugh blended smoothly into what followed:
"This is about my footprints, Chris. My footprints when
I run are hardly anything more than puffs in the snow.
When I slow down and walk, my footprints are four
times as big as when I run. My whole big sneaker makes
this big flat print in the snow. I have big feet, Chris."

"Ah."

"Is there some scientific formula about speed making
things lighter, Chris? Did Einstein say anything about
that?"

"I'll ask somebody in physics."

"I wish you would, because I'm going about my life at
high speed these days and I have the feeling that I'm

barely touching the ground. I'm directing *Twelfth Night* and I'm cooking and washing and ironing and cleaning the basement and helping Bruce rehearse his gospel songs and cheering up Larry, and in spice of it all—or because of it all—I'm feeling very light, as though I could take on even more duties if I had to."

"Take on my alleged love for you, Rachel."

"But here's what I wonder—what will happen when I slow down?"

"You mean when the play is over?"

"No, when this one's over, we're going right into rehearsal with the next one. No, what I mean is, what will happen next year when Larry dies?"

A shocking thing to hear—not "if," but "when." A moment ago she had been laughing.

"What are you telling me, Rachel?"

"Larry hasn't long to live."

"Who says?"

"Doctor Flanders."

"When did he say that?"

"About three years ago, 1976."

Chris the counselor had a repertoire of replies. "We're all dying, Rachel."

"Not as fast as Larry. In the early years of his MS we were given all kinds of things to hope for. The disease might be arrested. He might live a normal lifetime. He might not have much pain. But it wasn't long before his decline became too obvious to justify that sort of Pollyanna attitude, and his doctor admitted that his case was advancing faster than he had hoped. Still, there was a good chance he would come to a period of remission, or at least a plateau—a long time before further deterioration took place. But there's been no such plateau for Larry. By 1976 he could hardly walk and he was having trouble standing and he was tired all the time. He lost his job. Did he ever tell you about the incident that lost him his job, Chris?"

"No."

"He fell down in the classroom."

"They fired him for that?"

"They fired him for incompetence. You know as well as anyone what a superb teacher he was—yet the goons at Rookery State charged him with incompetence. He was brought before the Personnel Committee three times to answer charges of incompetence, so you see he was in trouble long before he fell down. His falling down only clinched it. First they accused him of being unable to read and grade papers fairly. Then they charged him with being unable to serve usefully on college committees. And then they charged him with delivering incoherent lectures. Each time students came to his defence. He's always had strong supporters among his students. But nothing came of their defense. And after he fell down, the committee charged him with being unable to stand up. He hit his head on the chalk tray as he fell, and he had to be taken to the hospital for stitches."

"I never heard any of this."

"Because we don't talk about it. But you can see, can't you, why he was so low when you came to Rookery? The college had put him through this awful series of meetings where they examined his shortcomings, and they pronounced him officially a failure and threw him out."

"The administration here has a heavy hand."

"They're butchers. That was the year the administration announced that they wanted someone to write the history of the college. Rookery State was turning fifty years old and America was turning two hundred, and they were asking for a volunteer to write this book. Well, you know about Larry's interest in local history, and you know he's been living all these years with a book in mind. So he made the college a proposal. This wasn't long before they fired him. He knew his days in the classroom were numbered—he was getting lame and shaky—but he was still capable of research, so he proposed that in return for a reduced teaching load—reduced by half, I think he said—he would write the history of Rookery State College, and any profit he realized from the sale of the book, over and above his expenses, would go into a scholarship fund."

"Generous."

"Generous is right. He saw the book as a way to hang onto his job, at least for another year or two. He couldn't stand the thought of being cut from the faculty."

"And they turned him down?"

"Not only did they turn him down, they threw him out."

He heard her inhale. It was the long breath with which she customarily faced conundrums. He imagined her nostrils flaring slightly, her eyebrows lifting. Whenever she was offended or puzzled or saddened in the course of an evening with Larry, in the course of a poor rehearsal, she responded with this wide-eyed intake of air.

"Rachel, why are you telling me this on the phone?"

"Are you busy?"

"No, no, but why don't we meet somewhere?"

"I don't talk about this stuff very well except on the spur of the moment. Bear with me, Chris, I'll be quick about it."

He looked at his appointment book and lied, "I've got all afternoon." He swiveled his chair to face the window. The campus walkways were snowy in the shade, wet in the sun. A tall old man in a black coat was making his way to the library, a man who had been introduced to Chris as Professor Emeritus Simon Shea, a revered veteran of the Division of Arts and Letters. The old man tipped his hat to a young woman wearing cowboy boots and a ski jacket—Lorna Boone slouching this way for her three o'clock appointment.

"So where was I, Chris?"

"They threw him out."

"Yes, they threw him out. They gave him nine months' notice, it's a state regulation, and sent him his dismissal letter in the fall of '76. He taught his last class the following June, just before you appeared on the scene. And that's not the half of it. We've never told you about the other disaster of '76. You see, on top of losing his job, Larry also learned that he had only about four years to live."

"Rachel, with MS there's no predicting."

"That's what *I* thought. That's what I told Larry, but the doctor has Larry believing that by next summer his four years will be up and he'll be dead. And Larry has *me* believing it—though I pretend not to. See, when Larry got his dismissal notice, he went to Doctor Flanders over my objections and asked how much longer he had to live. He said it was something he needed to know because he was facing a change of career. He was losing his job and he wanted to know if it was worth his time to get involved in a rehabilitation program. Of course the doctor told him that by all means he should get into such a program, but Larry said that he himself would be the judge of that; all he wanted the doctor to tell him was how long he would live. The best the doctor could give him was a guess, but Larry said a guess would be fine as long as it was an *educated* guess. The doctor told him to come back in a week; in the meantime he would study Larry's file and the case histories of other MS victims, especially the dead ones, and he would read the latest studies in journals and consult with his colleagues. A week later Larry went back and the doctor told him at the rate the disease was progressing, and barring plateaus, he'd likely be dead in four years. That was in September of '76, now it's April of '79. He's got till the summer of '80."

"That's barring remission."

"Then Larry asked him what he could expect in the way of further symptoms. He wanted a list of things that would go wrong with him in those four years and in what order they'd go wrong. Here the doctor balked, but Larry insisted. He wanted to know the worst because the worst the doctor could imagine probably wasn't nearly as bad as the worst he himself imagined whenever he woke up in the middle of the night. So the doctor laid it on the line. He'd have slower reflexes, first to physical stimuli, then to mental. His arms and legs would quit doing what they were supposed to. He might have spasms—muscle spasms, twitching. Toward the end he'd become incontinent and his speaking and thinking

would be impaired and his muscles would go rigid for
longer and longer periods until finally he would stiffen up
like a board. It sounded like four years of unspeakable
agony, Chris. It was far worse than the worst Larry had
imagined when he woke up in the middle of the night."

"Plateaus, Rachel. That's barring plateaus."

"Who wants plateaus when you're in the spasm
stage? Or when you're stiff as a board?"

"But don't you see, he's obviously on a plateau right
now? Three years, and he hasn't become incontinent.
His thinking isn't impaired, we know that. Nor his
speaking."

"The doctor says it all piles up fast at the end."

Chris searched for an anodyne, something more
soothing than his earlier one: we're all dying, Rachel.
But he had none at hand. He said, "Get back to your
footprints."

A knock on Chris's door. He coasted across the carpet on his ball-bearing casters, the phone to his ear. He
opened the door on Lorna Boone—sad, black-rimmed
eyes; jeans tucked into boots; jacket soiled around the
pockets. "Mr. MacKensie, I'm a minute or two early, but
I just have to tell you about the stupid poetry course I'm
taking."

"Chris, I look at those footprints and I think how
lovely it would be if I never had to slow down and walk.
How lovely if I could handle the rest of my life the way
I've handled it so far. Chris, you called it grace, remember?"

He covered the mouthpiece. "Will you wait, Lorna?"
I'm on the phone."

"Remember, Chris? You called it grace."

"Yes, of course."

"Mr. MacKensie. I haven't got all afternoon. I'm in a
kind of a hurry you know and stuff."

"Well, I don't know if 'grace' is exactly the word,
Chris, though I *like* the word. My word for it is 'momen-
tum.' But whatever you call it, I can't keep it up forever.
If Larry should die next year, I'm afraid I'll drop in a
heap. I know you're not a runner, Chris, but you must

remember how it was when you were a kid and you'd go
running down some hill and you seemed to be moving
forward and downward faster than your legs could carry
you. You could hardly keep up with yourself. It's that
very same thing I'm talking about. I have the feeling I'm
overextending myself and . . ."

"Mr. MacKensie, how much longer will you *be*?"

He covered the mouthpiece again. He said, "Out!"

Lorna Boone didn't budge. He stood and took her by
the shoulder and twirled her around and shut the door
and locked it.

". . . Chris?"

"I'm here. Somebody distracted me for a second."

"And it's time for me to get back to work. I'm not
sure I'm making sense, Chris, that I've told you what I
called to tell you."

"I'm not sure either. That's why we should meet
somewhere. Tonight, when you finish rehearsing."

"No, just let me sum up, and then we can both forget
it. All I want to say is that going by the doctor's prognosis, we're looking at Larry's possible death in the
summer of 1980."

A long pause. Her long intake of air.

"We don't talk about it, you understand. We haven't
mentioned it since the doctor first told us. But we're
looking at his death separately, Larry and I, and his reaction is pretty obvious—what with his temper and moods
and all—and my reaction is this headlong dash I seem to
be making toward God knows what. I just wonder if I'll
go all to pieces when he dies. Now, Chris, dear, it's time
for both of us to get back to work. Please forgive this
crazy call."

"Nothing to forgive."

"And don't worry, I'm taking your alleged love under
advisement. You'll be getting a ruling from me on that."

"Soon, I hope."

"Right now the play's the thing. Goodbye, Chris,
dear."

"Goodbye, Rachel."

He hung up, opened the book to reread a line of

Wyatt ("Her wily looks my wits did blind") and then went to the door to summon Lorna Boone. But he changed his mind. He turned and stood by his window. Resting his eyes on the stand of scrawny pine trees at the edge of the campus, he imagined Larry dead in a year or so, the flat earth covering him in the cemetery below his house. He saw the stone and the chiseled number, 1932–1980. This vision was replaced by another; he saw the day of the burial, the open grave, the mourners— Bruce and some people from the college and Beckwith. Surely that wasn't Rachel in the black dress and veil— she was too old. No, that would be Rachel's mother, flown in from Arizona.

To dispel this vivid tableau, he cranked open his office window and inhaled the chill spring air. He focused on the scrawny pines again and reproached himself for being so ready to believe in Larry's imminent death. Had Larry's death been under the surface of his thinking all along, so that the mere mention of a season and a year made it a certainty? Why not add the month and day as well? June 1, 1980, he thought—the sooner Larry dead, the sooner Rachel free—and here his mind made the leap from imagining Larry dead to wishing Larry dead. Though he had yet to conceive of *causing* Larry's death, this was the awesome moment when he first desired it: 3:06 P.M. on the 23rd of April, 1979—the seminal moment from which would grow weeks and months of yearning for Larry's death and Rachel's love—a longing so intense that at certain times, witnessing Larry at his deadliest, Rachel at her loveliest, he would shudder in the rough clutch of his desire.

8

CHRIS WAS OUT OF town on Thursday, visiting high schools in Fosston, Park Rapids and Melrose. On Friday, Rachel phoned him in the late afternoon, inviting him to join her at the Concord Street Coffee Shop.

"By all means," he said, and ten minutes later he entered, shaking the rain out of his cap, and saw her in the booth at the front window. Even as he slipped in opposite her, he sensed her excitement.

"I can't wait for curtain time, Chris. You won't believe how perfectly the leads fit their roles. And not just the leads—the whole cast, right down to the servants and sailors. And I guess I've told you that Bruce plays Feste with great feeling. He's a serious clown, Feste is, Bruce is. Well, it's going to bowl everybody over, including the *Morning Call* reviewer. Is it sheer luck, or do you suppose it's true what Bernard says—that I have this knack for casting people in the roles they secretly play in their dreams?"

"Surely it's your knack. The luck is all Beckwith's."

"You're a flatterer. And I'm on pins and needles. I stay away from the theater on the day of opening night. I told Bernard I wouldn't show up till six. I spent the morning baking and cleaning house and making poor Larry a nervous wreck because he was trying to concentrate on a talking book. About noon I went out running, but the rains came and I had to give up. Now all afternoon I've felt this great need to talk, but Larry is napping and after school Bruce went directly to the Playhouse. So I thought, why not coffee with Chris? Surely you'll see me through a half hour of my opening-

185

day jitters." Her smile widened, her eyes danced. "Did I call you away from something important?"

"Yes, luckily. Another meeting about falling enrollment. Important and awfully discouraging." He admired whatever novel thing she had done with her hair to make it frame her face so fluffily. She wore layers of wool today—a dark V-neck sweater over a darker turtleneck.

She took his hand and turned it over on its back to examine the mending lacerations. "Could I interest you in taking Larry to the play tonight?"

"Of course."

"And afterwards will you come with us to the Cellar? The cast will go there for drinks after the show."

"Of course."

"Good. If you could pick up Larry about seven thirty..."

The waitress came. They ordered coffee.

"You know what's so fascinating about plays, Chris? It's making harmony out of chaos. You start with a bunch of mismatched actors and an empty stage and an auditorium with five hundred empty seats and a mess of threadbare props and costumes and this impossible deadline and you go to work—and suddenly it's opening night, and if you've done your job, everything comes together, including the audience. I mean if the play works, it draws the audience into it. Onstage you can feel the five hundred people breathing with you. You feel this great sense of order and understanding. You feel this..." She searched for the word, looking deep into Chris's eyes, as though it might be there. She settled for her original word. "You feel this harmony."

"Obviously dress rehearsal went well."

"It was superb. Nobody down with the mumps. Nobody falling into the orchestra pit. We had a few guests in—a couple of college classes that Bernard rounded up for the sake of public relations, and for the sake of making the cast a little nervous, and they actually cheered. Oh, nothing's as lovely as the theater, Chris. And to think it took me all these years to really plunge into it full time."

Their coffee came.

"And of course it doesn't last. In three weeks *Twelfth Night* will be over and the set will be struck and then chaos again. And then the next production. Which is the way of the world, isn't it, Chris? Building, then losing. Then building again."

"All the world's a stage."

She laughed. "How original." She tossed her head and tilted her face to the daylight, which, though rainy, was strangely bright and pervasive as it fell through the wide window and highlighted every crease on her face, every blemish and lash. He studied her lips and imagined kissing them, knew he must kiss them.

"At home it's that way, too. We have chaos and harmony by turns, but at home it's different. We know we're going to lose in the end. In the theater you never run out of plays, you never run out of seasons, but with Larry..." She covered her face with her hands, the tips of her fingers in her hair. She was silent for a time; then she dropped one hand, looked at him with one eye. "At home I'm foredefeated. Isn't that a grand word—foredefeated? I read it in a poem. Robinson Jeffers, I think." She dropped the other hand. "I'm glad I told you about the doctor's prognosis. All this time I've needed somebody to tell it to, but I didn't think I should. I thought it would be a kind of betrayal to talk behind Larry's back about something as private as his death. I thought I should suppress it. I pushed it way in the background of my thinking. I kept putting plays on in front of it. But the other day, after spilling it all out to you on the phone, I felt very relieved. You're a lovely listener, Chris."

"It's my profession." He held her wrists, loosely. "With you, it's my pleasure."

"Well, now that I've unloaded the dismal truth on you, you're probably in for a lot more of the same—are you up to it?"

"Anytime."

"Do you think *Rookery* is up to it?" This in reference to an elderly woman, a neighbor of Rachel's, who had come into the coffee shop and was making her way to-

ward their booth. She wore a small ceramic bunny—an
Easter leftover—at the collar of her wet fur coat. She
spied Rachel ("Well, Rachel, how very nice to see you")
and then, as she turned to greet the man she assumed
was Larry, there was an obvious hitch in her formality
when she found him to be a stranger. But it took her only
a second to recover her decorum; her eyes slid over
Chris as though he were invisible and she proceeded se-
dately past them. She chose a booth for herself in a
corner where her view of the couple would be unob-
structed.

"I try to be objective about Larry's death, and some
days I can do it. Today, for example, I feel very clear-
headed about it. I don't think about falling in a heap; I
think about money. Say Larry dies next year, in early
summer. His disability check will stop, of course, but
another check will start—a Social Security check for
Bruce as Larry's minor child. So where will that leave
us? It'll be September of 1980 and Bruce will be ready to
start college and our only income will be my Playhouse
salary and Bruce's Social Security. Have I ever told you
what my salary is, Chris?"

"It isn't much."

"It's five thousand dollars a year."

"The Board ought to be ashamed."

She shrugged. "You can see the Board's viewpoint.
We put on only eight productions a year. I punch no
clock."

"But the hours, Rachel. If you computed the hours—
most of them by the light of the moon—"

"Yes, I've done that. Or rather Bernard has done it
for me. He goes to the Board every so often and presents
the budget and pleads my case. He divided my salary by
my hours of work, but it came to around six dollars an
hour and he decided he couldn't use that as an argument.
You see, in Rookery six dollars an hour still sounds like
a fortune."

"The carpenters of Rookery make fifteen."

"I know it, and the plumbers make twenty-five, but
the average salary in Rookery—citywide—is something

like four ninety-five. And my job, after all, is in the arts.
Public support of the arts is a new idea here, and when
you consider that half the Board was appointed by the
mayor, whose favorite vocalist, I'm told, is Dolly Par-
ton, you have to admit they do pretty well. So Bernard
pleaded my case not on the basis of hourly wage, but on
the basis of quality and audience support. He reminded
them of the good reviews we've been getting my whole
first year as director—reviews from papers in the Twin
Cities, mind you—and our audiences are running to
eighty-eight percent of capacity—serious plays as well
as light ones. The Board squirmed and strained and had
to admit that the Playhouse was paying its way and the
director was probably one reason for it, and they hinted
at a raise for next year."

"They still ought to be ashamed."

"I can't complain, really. It's heavenly work—though
a hell of a *lot* of work—and do you know how many
directors in the Twin Cities make five thousand dollars
or more?"

"How many *are* there in the Twin Cities?"

"Too many—there's fierce competition for jobs. And
of all those directors there are exactly four who make as
much as I do. Down there, hardly anybody's on a yearly
salary. They free-lance. Not that I wouldn't like to try
my wings at it sometime. Rookery, after all, is the bush
leagues. But instead of that, I probably should go back to
social work."

"That's not right for you."

"I'd hate it, but I'd be able to make the house payments and put Bruce through college."

"Bruce is taken care of. Even without a football
scholarship, he'll qualify for more financial aid than he
can use. Grants, workstudy. Leave that to me, I'm a
whiz at financial aid."

"So you've told us, but what if he doesn't want to go
to Rookery State? At our house we're not exactly in love
with Rookery State." She sipped her cooling coffee.

"Send him wherever—I'll get him the money."

Now close upon the entrance of Rachel's elderly

neighbor with the Easter bunny at her throat, Chris witnessed, through the window, another interesting bit of eyeplay. There at the curb, umbrellaed and waiting for a bus, was Eloise Hanson, who worked at the college as the registrar's second secretary, an earnest, guileless drudge. Her eyes were caught, and held, by Rachel's profile in the window. Eloise Hanson was perhaps forty years old, hardly five years older than Rachel, but in this case they were the five years between plainness and beauty, between indolence and vigor, between age and youth. She stood in the rain, enchanted. On her open face Chris saw indolence admiring vigor, age admiring youth. She gazed without a trace of envy in her eyes, the way absolute plainness can sometimes admire absolute beauty. And then her eyes fell upon Chris, and her eyebrows lifted in amazement. The chairman of the counseling department (said her eyes) is carrying on with a woman of striking cheekbones and lustrous red hair; I mustn't forget to report this Monday morning at the office. Chris nodded at Eloise Hanson and gave her a big smile, which she returned with a puzzled smile of her own. Then her bus pulled up and took her away.

Rachel said, into her cup, "Once in a while I get stern with myself, Chris, and say that playacting is for children; that it's time I grew up and took my place among the other women of the great American work force, dressed in a business suit, and carried a shoulder bag and took a job in the real world. What do you think?"

"I see no harm in a shoulder bag."

"Don't laugh. This is something I think about—how if I stay in theater I'll never grow up."

"That's crazy. You have to do what you love to do; otherwise life is pure crap."

"But what if all I ever amount to is an old and wrinkled Tinker Bell?"

"How long would Tinker Bell have survived as the wife of Larry Quinn?"

"Please, Larry is *not* all that difficult." She said this quickly, nervously.

"Except when he's awake. I wish you'd get over that

reflex of defending Larry to me. Don't forget I'm the guy who held his hand one whole winter. I was in your house the night he broke your mother's antique pitcher. A week ago you spent a day climbing ropes, remember? I'm the guy you told that to."

She looked out the window. She stared beyond the traffic, beyond the rain, at the fourteen years of Larry's disease. "You're right, he is difficult. But not all the time. On his good days he's still the Larry I knew, you knew, years ago. He's still considerate...more often than not. He still has good judgment...a lot of the time." She fingered the handle of her cup. Her nails were painted deep red. She wore a thin gold bracelet over the cuff of her dark sweater. "He's still the man I love."

Chris was moved. He knew she spoke the truth, that her love for Larry was thoroughgoing, uninterrupted, absolute; that it beat on through the years as relentlessly as time itself. He was glad for Larry, for although his own love for Larry had become tainted with pity and envy, it was still the attachment that a man feels for his best friend. In loving Larry, Chris wanted nothing but the best for him, and what was better than Rachel? Looking at Rachel now, her face turned toward the rain, her hair in the gray light the color of dark plums, her eyes far off, Chris wished that he himself did not love her. He wished this for Larry's sake. And only for a moment.

"You do believe me, don't you, Chris? That he's still the man I love?" She spoke more slowly now, more thoughtfully, *Twelfth Night* upstaged by her husband.

"Yes, it's obvious." If his own love for the man, though harshly tested, had not diminished, why should Rachel's? Chris was not so innocent as to believe that perfectly requited love was the only kind that lasted. As counselor he had listened to a hundred tales of one-way love, unilateral love, hopeless love. Of course there were love stories with happy endings and there were love stories that seemed never to end at all (for years after Chris's mother died, his father went on loving her memory), but Chris knew that love for some was a continual giving without getting, love spilling from the heart like water from a hillside spring, love bubbling up from a vast reservoir and coursing off as unrestrained as a river to the sea. Such was Rachel's love for Larry. And Chris's for Larry. And Chris's for Rachel.

How long (thought Chris) am I fated to feel this one-sided love for this woman, how deep is my reservoir? It occurred to him once again that he ought to leave town. Why not extract himself from the Quinns before he became any more tightly knotted in the bonds that held the three of them together? He reviewed his alternatives: General Mills. Capitol Hill. Aunt Geraldine's ice-cream parlor. And in the college placement office he would doubtless find a dozen more directions his life could go.

But they would be twelve ways to loneliness. Leaving Rookery, he would be straining against what he had come to think of as his destiny, which, for the present, was to sit here in the window booth of the Concord Street Coffee Shop and gaze at the face of Rachel Quinn.

He said, "While you're on the subject of love, let's get around to—"

"Yes, I'm coming to that." She bent closer to him, over her coffee. "I know love when I see it. It's in my kitchen these days. It always used to be in my bedroom and sometimes it still is, but not very often anymore. But it's in my kitchen—I feel it among the three of us at mealtime, Bruce and Larry and I. A bond. And of course the other night I felt it between you and me in the back row of the Playhouse. That was a convincing declaration of love if I ever heard one, Chris. It has to rank right up there with the most stirring addresses of American history."

"I wrote it on the back of an envelope." How many times, to his regret, had their talk slipped a cog like this, shifting from earnest to clever?

She recovered the earnestness. "How could any woman not be moved by what you said? I was moved."

"How far?"

She pondered the question, decided to evade it. "A woman likes to be told she's loved."

"So does a man."

She put four fingers to her lips and looked thoughtful. She breathed deeply.

"How far were you moved, Rachel? Far enough to imagine what it would be like if you loved me?"

"I've been imagining that since you came to Rookery. You see, with me you're not starting from square one."

"Oh?" He sat forward. "Tell me—what square?"

"Square two. Larry's on four and you're on two."

"And who's in between?" He felt the cog slipping again.

"Nobody. All the rest of the men of the world are on square one."

He imagined himself on a game board, two squares from the goal, two billion men breathing down his neck. He described this to Rachel—men from all lands at his heels, men of all races.

"Yes"—she nodded, her eyes keen—"and with a bad roll of the dice you could be lost in a pack of Hottentots."

Their laughter was sudden and sharp, causing the Easter-bunny lady to pause at her pie.

Rachel took a small mirror from her purse, looked into it. "It's five o'clock, Chris. Would you have time to come with me to Prinn's Department Store?"

"I'm idle till seven thirty."

"It will take about half an hour for what I have in mind."

9

*P*RINN'S DEPARTMENT STORE OC-
cupied five floors and the basement of an old building on
the busiest corner of Division Street. Rachel and Chris
went directly to the fifth floor, and as they stepped off
the elevator, Rachel said, "I'll tell you right at the start
what I'm up to, so you know what you're in for. Starting
here on five, I'd like for you and me to stroll a few aisles
of each floor in this building, right down to the bargain
basement. See, one result of having a husband like Larry
is that I have these fantasies, sexual and otherwise, and
one of my fantasies has me out in public with a good-
looking, able-bodied man on my arm. I imagine people
looking at us and thinking, Well, now, there's a nice-
looking couple, and whenever I have this fantasy, it's
you I imagine, Chris, because you're the only man on
square two. My, look at all that glassware, isn't that
stunning?

"Fourteen years ago Larry was strong and good-looking and I remember the pleasure it was to go places with
him and feel the approving glances we got, and this is
surely unforgivable of me—it's entirely selfish: my large
ego, you know—but more and more I long to be looked
at like that again. I'm talking about the satisfaction that
comes over a woman when people glance from her to her
escort and they try to imagine how in the world she ever
snared such a knockout. It's a nice sensation, Chris, it
appeals to a woman's pride, some animal instinct she
probably shares with the doe that attracts the biggest
stag in the herd or the hen that snares the cock of the

194

walk. Well, I hadn't given this much thought until Larry's problems became so obvious that people stared at us when they saw us on the street or at the theater or sitting in the park. You see what I mean—I get stared at for being in the company of this weak-looking man. Obviously it's a look I've learned to live with, but it's given rise to this fantasy where you and I are seen in public places like airports and Orchestra Hall. And, for some reason, Prinn's Department Store. Look here, Chris, a sale on air pots for coffee. Seventeen ninety-five. Rugs are on this floor—I'm thinking of a new rug for the front entryway."

They found their way to rugs.

"Another reason I've brought you here to Prinn's is so that I can tell you how I feel about you. I do my best thinking when I'm jogging in the valley or in the middle of a busy place like Prinn's. I feel more spontaneous. You're obviously the kind of person who can spill out his heart in the back row of an empty theater, but in order for *me* to spill out *my* heart I have to pretend I'm not spilling out my heart. I have to pretend that what I'm saying is a casual observation and my real business is running two miles or selecting a scatter rug from this display. Don't these scatter rugs look flimsy? Surely Prinn's has better rugs than these. Maybe on four."

Chris pressed her against the shoulder-high stack of scatter rugs, cupped her cheeks in his hands and kissed her.

"Oh, don't." She looked about. Apparently no one had seen. "My God, Chris, not here in Prinn's."

On four, she said, "I'm always amused when *Redbook* or one of those magazines runs an article on women's fantasies. Usually it's the result of a questionnaire in which they want to know how many times a week a woman dreams of being pleasantly raped or who she imagines is lying beside her when she's in bed with her husband. Well, what would they think if I wrote in and said that I have this recurring fantasy where I take this college counselor for a walk through a department store

—what would they make of that? Naturally I have more interesting fantasies than that—erotic, some would astonish you—but it's good to have one or two harmless ones as well, because we can hardly indulge in the more interesting ones—you and I—but we *can* stop here and have a look at these nice backgammon sets in these exquisite cases of inlaid wood. The only trouble with backgammon is that everybody's playing it these days, have you noticed?"

On three, she said, "You can be sure that I've imagined what it will be like to be a widow, Chris. I mean, I've thought about a lot more than the problem of Bruce's college tuition and making house payments. I've imagined being alone and wanting a man. I'm good at imagining things. I wouldn't be an actress if I weren't. Years ago I didn't see my widowhood so clearly, I guess because I didn't know how old I'd be when Larry died. Would I be forty? Fifty? I couldn't tell. But the picture's quite clear now, isn't it? In all these scenes that I'm rehearsing it's 1980 and I'm a widow at thirty-seven. I've been reading these books about widowhood on the sly—I keep them in the bookcase in Bernard's office—and I've been trying to figure out if my responses will be like other women's. I realize there'll be grief and regret and self-pity and all that, but I can't get over this feeling that my sense of release will be greater than everything else. Where is men's? Have they moved the men's department to another floor? Larry needs underwear.

"I mean, why shouldn't I feel this tremendous sense of release along with the rest of it? I'll only be thirty-seven. Maybe at forty-seven I'd want to feel sorry for myself, but thirty-seven doesn't strike me as a hopeless age to start a new life. There's even life after forty—right?"

"At forty-five I'm being reborn," he whispered into her hair.

"Oh, Chris, please. People are looking."

On two, she said, "And another thing I can predict about being single again is that I'll want to be courted.

None of this bouncing out of one marriage and into another. I was never properly courted, Chris. I fell in love with my history teacher at eighteen, we got married, and what kind of a courtship was that? It was mostly seeing each other on the sly, and then it was leaving town because Larry got fired for marrying me. Not that there's anything I would have done differently, but now, as long as I'm going to get a second chance at this business, I'm not going to be easy to get. Of the women I've played, I've always thought the coy ones were the most interesting. I'd like to see what I can do with a coy role in real life. Maybe that's why I worry about money. I don't want to be backed into a corner financially and feel I have to grab the first guy I meet with money in the bank, like my mother did. If it's true, as you say, that Bruce can get through college on grants and loans and work-study, then I can probably handle the house payment and live quite independently and make choices. Oh, there's men's over there. Let's see what they have in underwear, Larry likes the boxer style.

"And even if I do go through all those stages of sorrow that the books predict, I'm sure I'll survive. I've seen others survive, including my mother. She was fifty-two when my dad died, and although she was never the most stable person in the world, she really came through it quite well. In fact, she considers herself on top of the world right now, sunning herself down there in Tempe with her new husband. Along came this guy with stock in Standard Oil and gone was her sorrow. Nothing coy about Mother."

Waiting for Rachel to make her purchase, Chris saw the Easter-bunny lady step off the down elevator and turn quickly in several directions, looking for someone.

On the main floor, Rachel said, "But of course the main thing is this: what do I do about your love for me? I'm serious about this business of independence, Chris. After being at Larry's beck and call for all these years, I love the thought of being elusive, beyond anybody's call. . . . Look at these crowds, would you? Why aren't these people home preparing dinner? Larry's broiling himself a steak. I told him I was going out for coffee with you, and then I'd go directly to the theater. I told him that either you would pick him up for the play or Bruce would drive home for him after he's through in the makeup room. I'll call from the theater and let him know you'll pick him up. He'll be glad. He doesn't like to sit through a play alone. There's a lunch counter down-stairs—how about a snack before I go off to the Play-house? They have good homemade soup.... I love the way you go charging through crowds, Chris. With Larry I'm always waiting for him to catch up."

In the basement, on stools, they had soup and they shared a tuna sandwich. "I'll bet I sound awfully sure of myself, running on like that about my independence and playing hard to get. Well, at least half of it's bluff. How do I know if independence will suit me? Sometimes I wonder if I'm already too independent for my own good. One of the worst things about Larry's MS is how inde-pendent I've *had* to be. We're both subservient to the disease, Larry and I, but Larry is also subservient to me. I'm the one who runs things. I control his diet. I tell him when it's pill time. I move him around so the sun shines on him. I'm independent the way the captain of a ship is independent—free to make decisions, but they damn well better be the right decisions or the ship will sink. Sometimes it's nice to depend on somebody else. Maybe after Larry dies, instead of wanting to be free, I'll want to be more dependent, more secure.... Chris, don't tell Larry that you kissed me. I know you tell each other everything but don't tell him that."

Oh his swiveling stool he made a move to kiss her.

"No!"

She stood and slipped into her raincoat. She looked distraught. Her brow was furrowed.

Chris rose from his stool. She put her hand on his arm—a plea to stay where he was.

"I love hearing that you love me," she said, and she hurried away. She found a clear aisle through ready-to-wear and broke into a run. Chris watched her take a sharp right turn at the corner of slips and robes. Behind a table heaped with flesh-colored fabric and roofed by an awning ("Flawed Foundations," said the awning), she boarded an escalator and rose and disappeared.

10

A WET DUSK. CHRIS knocked on the Quinns' front door. The house was dark. He knocked again, then let himself in and found Larry sitting at the kitchen table, smoking. The oven, too, was smoking. Chris switched on the ceiling light, opened the broiler drawer and saw the remains of a steak cooked to blackness. He stabbed it with a fork and held it up for Larry to see.

Larry's eyes darted between the steak and Chris's face, between the window and the stove, darted about the kitchen in a jerky manner that Chris had never seen before—a wild-eyed look. Chris was alarmed. Larry drew deeply on his cigarette and put it out and lit another. Before him on the table, the smoldering ashtray was full of carelessly stubbed-out butts.

"Larry, what the hell's going on? You've wasted a four-dollar steak."

"I'm not hungry. Is it time for the play? Let's go." He got to his feet and gripped the cane that stood beside his chair, a free-standing cane with four metal feet.

"Wait, you haven't turned off your stereo." Drifting into the kitchen was a plaintive strain of Mahler, high-pitched and discordant. Chris dropped the burnt meat in the sink and went into the den. Here another full ashtray sent up a thin column of acrid smoke.

In the car Larry said, "Rachel tries to be clean, but she can never be clean. She cleans house all the time. That's her way of trying to be clean. I think she knows she can never be clean, but she won't admit it."

"Larry, what's wrong?" They were stopped at a traffic

light. Larry's darting eyes were following the lights of the cars that passed before them.

"I'm fine, but you know it gets ridiculous after while, trying to be clean. I mean, you're either clean or you're not clean and Rachel isn't clean. I'm not saying I'm clean necessarily. But that isn't the question, whether I'm clean or not."

Chris's ears pounded with dread. Could this be insanity? Larry, for all his moods, for all his neurotic fumbling, for all his angry dejection, had always maintained his grip on the handles of the real world. It was his nature to fight off craziness with the only weapons left to him—the aggressive arms of defiance and anger, the defensive arms of somnolence and silence. Gloom was Larry's hiding place when the battle turned against him —nothing wrong with that. But what was this talk about Rachel, her uncleanness? Had some war been waged inside Larry's head today, and had he come away the loser? Had he surrendered to lunacy?

Chris was on the point of taking Larry home and calling Doctor Flanders when the traffic light changed, and, with it, Larry's train of thought. Chris, accelerating, was vastly relieved to hear him say, "*Twelfth Night* is a play I've never seen. From what Rachel tells me, it's got a lot to do with mistaken identity...disguises...that sort of thing. Chris, you taught English. How come Shakespeare couldn't write comedies about anything but disguises and mistaken identity? Did he have an impoverished imagination after all?"

"It was a convention of his time. He knew what made people laugh."

"Do you think he'll make me laugh tonight?"

"Toby Belch will make you laugh."

Twelfth Night was a dazzle of color and light. Aside from the customary missed cue and hurried lines of opening night, it was a joyous success, an exuberant blending of the grand and the slaphappy. Orsino was amusingly moonstruck, Malvolio perfectly silly, Olivia fetching. Sir Toby Belch, in red pantaloons, and Sir Andrew Aguecheek, in bright green tights, made everyone laugh, most of all Larry, who sat with Chris in row four, on the aisle, and whose unrestrained roars caused heads to turn.

But in the scenes where Bruce appeared as Feste the Clown Larry became intensely serious, leaning forward, his head trembling as he strained not to miss a word. Bruce wore red and black, his shirt checkered, the toes of his slippers rising to a curly point. When he strummed his lute and sang, Larry grew agitated. In Act II Bruce sang:

> *What is love? 'Tis not hereafter;*
> *Present mirth hath present laughter;*
> *What's to come is still unsure:*
> *In delay there lies no plenty;*
> *Then come kiss me, sweet and twenty,*
> *Youth's a stuff will not endure.*

"Yes, what is love?" said Larry aloud. "What is love? Rachel cleans and cleans, but what's the use?"

The woman in the seat ahead turned and glanced at him, raising her shoulder slightly, as though to ward off his words.

"Sex isn't clean," Larry told her.

"Shhh," said Chris. He looked about for Rachel and saw her standing at the doorway to the lobby.

In Act IV Bruce said he doubted Malvolio's sanity: "'Nay, I'll ne'er believe a madman till I see his brains.'" Then he stepped downstage, strummed his lute, and the audience (having learned in Act II how pleasing was his voice, how pure his pitch) collected its collective breath and hung on his words. He surprised them with something snappy:

> *I'll be with you again,*
> *In a trice,*
> *Like to the old vice,*
> *Your need to sustain;*
> *Who, with dagger of lath,*

In his rage and his wrath,
Cries aha! to the devil,
Like a mad lad.
Pare thy nails, Dad.
Adieu. . . .

"What, what?" said Larry. "What did he tell me? Pare my nails? What's he telling me, Chris? Who's mad, who's crazy? He saw me sitting here, Chris. Why is he up there and I'm down here? He's my son." Larry nudged the woman ahead of him. "He's my son but he's up there and I'm down here." Larry rose, his hands tight on the grip of his cane, but as soon as Chris touched his arm, he allowed himself to be drawn back into his seat.

Chris, tense, now, convinced of Larry's derangement, heard scarcely a line of Act V. He held himself alert to Larry's sudden gestures and the remarks he mumbled, subdued him three or four times by gripping his arm. He could tell by the turning heads and whispers that word of Larry's behavior was spreading down the row.

The final lines of the play were Bruce's; the stage was left to him alone. By this time he had established a warm bond with the audience and he had only to turn his eyes in their direction for them to sit hushed, ready to be enchanted. His words—Feste's words—were mostly devoid of sense, but he delivered them with a clear voice, a sweet melody:

When that I was and a little tiny boy,
With hey, ho, the wind and the rain,
A foolish thing was but a toy,
For the rain it raineth every day.

Larry said, "He's my little boy." He tried to stand; Chris restrained him.

But when I came, alas! to wive,
With hey, ho, the wind and the rain,
By swaggering could I never thrive,
For the rain it raineth every day.

"Unclean!" Larry spoke to the row ahead. "Unclean."

> *But when I came unto my beds,*
> *With hey, ho, the wind and the rain,*
> *With toss-pots still had drunken heads,*
> *For the rain it raineth every day.*

Larry stood and leaned forward. He groaned. Several people got to their feet. The woman ahead stepped into the aisle, out of his reach. The entire house was on its feet now, most of the audience having misinterpreted the movement around Larry as a standing ovation; Bruce's final stanza was lost in a great wave of applause. The curtain came down and went up immediately for a curtain call. Rachel appeared beside Larry, took him firmly by the arm and led him out. Chris followed them across the lobby to Beckwith's office. Rachel knocked on the door, opened it and found the room empty (Beckwith was standing outside under the marquee, prepared to bid farewell to his pleased patrons).

"Sit down," she told Larry, steering him to the desk chair.

Chris remained in the lobby.

Larry sat, his eyes darting among the photos and plaques on the walls, among the CB equipment on the desk—mike, transmitter, coils of wire.

Chris heard her say, "Damn, Larry, damn!" as she closed the door. Her tone continued shrill, but Chris couldn't make out the words over the chatter of the audience as they came spilling into the lobby.

In half a minute she stepped out, pulling the door nearly shut, and said to Chris, "What's the matter with him, for God's sake? Is he going out of his mind? And why is he doing it on the biggest night of my career?" Her eyes were intensely wide, her face tight and pink. She was alarmed and angry: now at the final curtain of her most ambitious production, Larry was going crazy. It occurred to Chris that the unfortunate timing might be due not to sheer rotten luck, but rather to Larry's resentment of Rachel's success.

"I'm afraid it's serious," was all that Chris had time to say before Rachel was surrounded and carried off by a swirl of people telling her they loved the play and they loved her son as Feste and the only thing wrong with the entire evening was her not being in the cast. From the office doorway, Chris watched her react, left and right, to her fans, rewarding each with a word of thanks and the fondest of smiles, squeezing the hand of the drama critic of the *Morning Call*, throwing her head back and laughing at something said by Professor Emeritus Simon Shea, accepting a kiss on the cheek from Bernard Beckwith, who had been blown indoors by a squall of rain.

Chris stepped into the office and took a chair facing Larry across the desk. He said, "How are you feeling?"

"Tops." Larry was smoking. He seemed less agitated. His eyes had slowed down.

"You were acting strange."

"Was I?" He didn't look surprised. "What's strange about laughing? Do I laugh so seldom these days that you think it's strange?"

"Maybe that's it."

When the lobby cleared, Rachel returned to the office and stood before Larry with her arms crossed, reading his state of mind, reading her own. Then she reached out and nervously straightened his collar, smoothed his hair. "I want to go to the Cellar with the cast and crew. Chris, could I possibly ask you to take Larry home? I won't stay long."

"By all means. Stay as long as you want."

"Now wait a minute," said Larry. "You blow your cork at me and you stash me in this office while you go out and talk pretty to your fans—tease the men—and then you send me home with Chris. Sitting home with Chris isn't my idea of a good time. Listen, Rachel—" Larry slumped in his chair and lowered his eyes. A change came over his face. "I'm sorry, Rachel, you're right. This is your night to enjoy. But how about if Chris and I stopped in at the Cellar too?" He took Rachel's hand and gave her a rare, honest smile. "Just for a minute so we can bask a little in your glory."

Bernard Beckwith skipped into their midst. "Let's go, everyone. Hello, Larry. Hello, Christopher. My, my, my, my, what a colossal triumph this evening has been." He gave Rachel the same kiss he had given her in the lobby —a sisterly peck. "Hurry, hurry, let's go to the Cellar. Do you have your car, Christopher? I'm without mine tonight, I came in a taxi."

Beckwith held Rachel's coat for her; then he handed his own to Chris to hold for him.

The Cellar, a saloon in the basement of a warehouse near the railroad yards, was favored by the acting crowd, perhaps because it was twice removed from reality— first, when it had been stripped and scrubbed and fumigated and carpeted and every last trace of the warehouse had been banished, and second, when it had been meticulously decorated to resemble a warehouse, every detail convincing and artificial: the Formica tables designed like packing crates, rubber rats peering out from the bottle shelves behind the bar. There were two exits—a stone stairway leading to the street and a freight elevator opening onto the alley.

The Quinns and Chris and Bernard Beckwith sat at a round table against a brick wall and tried to converse over the twang and thump of the stereo system. Every few seconds a revolving pink light in the ceiling lit up Beckwith's slick hair. Something worrisome was furrowing Larry's brow.

Rachel said she would close the season with *A Doll's House*, though she hadn't yet found a young actress with talent enough to play Nora.

Beckwith said that Rachel herself must play Nora. Breathlessly he repeated that she must, she simply must.

Larry looked askance at Beckwith.

Rachel said she didn't feel young enough to play Nora.

Chris objected, said she could pass for twenty.

Larry looked askance at Chris.

Beckwith said he had half a mind to try out for the part of Nora's husband. He was thinking of reviving his stage career. He had starred in something by O'Neill in college.

Larry said something to Chris—Chris didn't catch it —about soap.

They were joined by a young woman carrying a long-stemmed rose and accompanied by a middle-aged man with a merry eye and hair to his shoulders. Rachel introduced them to Chris. They hugged and kissed Rachel and chatted for a minute or more before Chris recognized them—Olivia and Malvolio without their makeup, and wearing jeans. Rachel asked if they would try out for Ibsen. They agreed in unison: "Christ, yes."

Larry looked askance at Olivia.

Next, by stair and elevator, came the rest of the troupe, all of them gathering around Rachel's chair to pay her homage—to kiss her, to shake her hand, to touch her on the shoulder, to demonstrate in any number of ways that she was more than their brilliant director; she was their brilliant friend. She received each tribute graciously and paid for it in kind. "You make a marvelous imbecile, Sir Andrew." "I knew you could do wonderful things with your face, Sir Toby, but developing dimples overnight?"

Larry excused himself and limped toward the rest room. Rachel caught Chris's eye. Chris stood up to follow him. He was hemmed in by the cast and crew and by the time he stepped free Rachel was calling to him, "Bruce will go." She turned to greet her son and Viola— a dark-eyed blonde—who were coming down the stairs with their hair wet, Bruce declaring—expansively, his arms wide, his voice low and loud—"The rain it raineth every night."

Bruce bent to receive his mother's message in his ear, found a chair for Viola, then went to the rest room. In a few seconds he was back, whispering to his mother. She looked up, startled.

"Chris," she called across the table, "Larry isn't in the rest room."

Chris stood again and surveyed the Cellar. He made his way to the rest room and called to the man sitting in the closed compartment, "What's your name? Who's in there?"

"I am Antonio, sea captain, friend to Sebastian." Not Larry's voice.

From the rest room Chris went to the elevator. Waiting for it to descend, he was joined by Bruce.

"What was the matter with Dad at the play, Chris? What was he saying at the end?"

"Nothing that made sense. I'm afraid he's having a nervous breakdown. Has he been acting strange all day?"

"I don't know, I went right to the Playhouse after school."

They got aboard and were lifted slowly up the cold shaft.

"He said some incoherent things while I was driving him to the play. I should have called his doctor from the Playhouse."

"Of all nights for him to go bananas. It's not fair to Mother."

The elevator stopped. The door groaned open on a ramp leading to the alley. As Chris and Bruce stepped out into the rain, they heard the screeching of brakes, the impact of crunching metal, the tinkling of glass. Then curses. Then horns. They ran to the end of the alley and saw several cars stopped in the street, the drivers getting out. The driver of a station wagon was shouting, "This crazy klutz walked out in front of me!" He was hurrying down the middle of the street toward a phone booth in the next block and pointing back at Larry, who stood in the beam of the station wagon's left headlight. The right headlight was buried in the door of a parked pickup. Larry, illuminated, glistening wet, leaned on his cane and turned jerkily about—apparently unscathed by the accident he had caused.

"Get your mother," said Chris, "we'll have to explain to the police when they come. We'll wait in my car." He led Larry to his mint-green Chevrolet, which was parked under a streetlamp.

Bruce, returning to the Cellar, met his mother coming out. She rushed through the rain to Larry and reached him as he bent to get into the back seat.

"Larry," she said.

He turned and brought up his cane to hold her at bay.

"Acid rain!" he said. His eyes weren't wild exactly, his cracked voice wasn't abnormally loud or strained, yet his face seemed altered—an expression of intense concentration—and his words were clipped and quick. "I hope you're satisfied."

Rachel swept the cane from his hand, threw her arms around him, pinning his arms at his sides. He was suddenly docile. She helped him into the car and got in after him. They settled into the back seat, her hand on his knee. The peach light of the streetlamp fell through the wet windows, and she saw his eyes turn on her suspiciously. They were narrow, more intense than before. He seemed to be focusing on something hanging between them, something infinitely small. An atom. A germ.

Chris went to the phone booth, waited for the angry driver of the station wagon to finish his call, then stepped in and asked the operator for Mercy Hospital.

Traffic resumed, winding around the disabled station wagon and its driver, who stood steaming in the wet street and waiting for the squad car he had been promised over the phone. The moving headlights flashed across the faces of Rachel and Larry in the back seat of the Chevrolet, across Bruce's face in the front.

Mercy Hospital reported to Chris that Doctor Flanders was not on call this evening, but in a case like this he might possibly be reached at home.

Chris dialed the doctor's house and was thanked, by a recording, for calling.

He dialed Mercy Hospital again and talked to an emergency room nurse. She said Mercy wasn't equipped for mental cases. He must take Larry to the State Hospital.

He called the State Hospital. Yes, they were prepared to handle walk-in cases. No, there was no doctor on duty tonight, but there was a counselor. Was this alcohol? Or drugs?

"Neither. This is psychosis in its pure form."

"Fine. Come to admitting, building three."

The light over the phone went off when Chris opened the door. He stood for a while in the dark booth, looking through the glass. The rain was beating down harder. The angry driver moved to shelter himself under the marquee of an abandoned movie house, where he paced in a small circle. Still no squad car. A man crossed the street from the Cellar and suddenly threw his hands in the air—the owner of the pickup. The other driver stepped out from under the marquee and explained. Chris saw both of them gesturing wildly, making fists, tossing their heads.

Chris ran to his car. Getting in, he glanced back to make sure the two men were still preoccupied with their creased metal and shattered glass. He started the car and pulled away, lights off, speeding around the nearest corner.

"What about the police?" said Bruce.

"Hell with the police."

Larry mumbled, "Acid rain."

Rachel said, "Did you talk to Doctor Flanders?"

"I couldn't reach him. And Mercy won't take a mental case."

Larry said, "Let's the four of us kill ourselves."

"So where are we going?" said Bruce.

"The State Hospital."

"Oh, God," Rachel said.

Rookery State Hospital was out in the country— seven brick buildings on a rocky hill. Chris had heard that in accordance with the residents' distorted view of things (surely not as an aid to rationality) the hospital grounds were called a campus, the officer in charge of each building was addressed as the dean and the admitting clerk's nameplate said "Registrar." Maybe not so foolish, thought Chris, recalling certain mad days at Rookery State College.

He followed a crooked drive past four or five dark buildings and stopped at the end of a sidewalk leading to a lighted doorway. He switched on the dome light and turned to look into the back seat. So did Bruce. Larry's eyes were darting; his breath was loud and fast through his nose. Rachel sat with her eyes shut.

Silence. Indecision. Rain on the roof.

Rachel opened her eyes on the wet walk, the amber light over the alcove and doorway. She sighed. "Must we go in here?"

"At least for some advice," said Chris. "And maybe some medication."

"Larry," she said. "Do you know where we are?"

"The funny farm," he said quickly, scowling. "Let's go in, I need a drink of water."

"Larry, we're going in to see about your state of mind. Do you understand?"

"I'm thirsty."

"Bruce, would you go to the door?" said Rachel. "See if it's open?"

Bruce ran up the walk, tried the door, pressed a button, waited.

Rachel asked Chris, "What do you know about this place?"

"Not much. I'm not even sure this is the right building, but it's the only one with a light over the door."

Light fell out from the building as the door opened. Bruce turned and waved and the three of them got out of the car.

"Toby Belch made me laugh, Rachel."

"Yes, he was wonderful."

Inside they were met by a young woman who wore a white smock over her jeans. "Follow me," she said, leading them down a hallway. They came to a sliding glass door, which she pushed open. They stepped into a large brightly lit room that smelled bad. "Sit," said the woman, indicating a worn-out couch, the only piece of furniture. She crossed the room and went down another hallway.

Rachel and Larry sat. Chris stood at the sliding door. Bruce went to a window. The room had green walls and red woodwork; the floor tiles were loose in some places, missing in others. The ceiling was white with dark brown spots.

"What did you tell her?" Rachel asked. Her voice echoed off the walls.

"Nothing," said Bruce. "She seemed to know what we came for."

They waited five minutes. A door opened down the hallway. A woman in a nightgown shuffled barefoot into the room. She wore a happy, distracted expression. She must have been forty, she might have been seventy. She sat on the couch next to Larry and played with his ear. Rachel reached around Larry and restrained her, gripping her wrist, but when she released her hold, the woman went for Larry's ear again. Larry held himself very stiff as she squeezed the lobe. He looked at Rachel out of the corner of his eye. He said, "Life on the funny farm."

Chris came over and offered the woman his hand. She took it (her blanched skin felt powdery dry, like birch bark) and he led her away from the couch.

A young man in his stocking feet came down the hallway and entered the room. He wore black pants and a gray sportcoat. His chest was bare. He carried the unlit stub of a cigar in his cupped hand. At the center of the room he cast his eyes straight up, moved about, studying the brown spots overhead; then he thrust the cigar at the ceiling, where it stuck for a moment, then sagged and fell to the floor. It wasn't a cigar. It was a gob of shit.

"Oh, God," said Rachel.

Chris slid open the glass door and fled with the Quinns.

One A.M. Rachel took Larry upstairs, where he fell asleep almost before he was flat on the bed; then she went down to the kitchen, where Chris and Bruce sat in the breakfast nook. She served them hot chocolate.

"All he needs is a good night's rest," she said. "He hasn't slept well for a week or more."

"Right," said Chris, not believing it.

"Was he acting funny all day?" said Bruce.

She shook her head slowly. "It's just a passing thing. Sleep will cure it." Her gray eyes were weary.

Bruce said, "I think a doctor should see him."

"In the morning. If need be. Chances are sleep will set him straight."

"Right," said Chris. With no place to go for help, they would put their trust in sleep.

"Rachel!" Larry called down the stairs. "Rachel!"

She dashed from the kitchen, climbed the stairs.

"Chris," she called. "Chris, Bruce!"

At the top of the stairway Larry leaned over the banister gagging. His tongue was thickly lathered and hanging out of his mouth as far as he could stretch it. He held in his hand part of a bar of soap—the part he hadn't eaten. He vomited over the rail and down the wall.

Chris, Rachel and Larry left for Minneapolis at two in the morning, an intern at Mercy Hospital having rinsed the suds from Larry's system and relieved his choking fit and stomach cramps, Bruce having reassured his mother that Saturday night's performance would go on without her and Chris having phoned a Minneapolis psychiatrist and arranged for Larry's admittance into a mental hospital.

Before reaching the open highway, they stopped for three red lights in Rookery and each time they did so Larry tried to open his door and get out; Rachel, sitting behind him, held down the lock. Thwarted for the third time, Larry turned quickly, bringing his arm up over the back of the seat. His elbow struck her in the mouth—by accident, she decided as the car moved forward and she fell back, her eyes stinging with tears. Her lip was cut, she could taste the blood. She rode silently in the dark, her handkerchief to her mouth, to her eyes.

No one spoke for fifty miles. At three o'clock Chris

saw an occasional snowflake shooting into the headlights and he switched on the radio for weather news. At the sound of music, Larry began to jabber. "Tell me, Chris, are we making this trip because you think I'm out of my mind? You may think I'm loony because of what Rachel tells you about me, but I'm really very stable." He spoke fast and precisely. "You've got a mistaken notion of what MS does to a man. You think MS is driving me out of my mind, but you're wrong. Doctor Flanders says there's no reason to think MS makes people crazy. It just makes them depressed and the medicine sometimes makes them forgetful and dull-witted and—I don't know—other things like that, but it doesn't make people crazy and it hasn't made *me* crazy. So if we're going to the city for my sake, we're wasting time. Who's this doctor you called?"

"His name is Anderson. I met him when Karen was in treatment, and I've referred people to him from time to time. He's good with depression."

"Waste of time. There's nothing wrong with me. Turn around and take me home. Jesus, when you and Rachel get an idea into your heads, you get stubborn. Have you ever known me to go out of my mind? How many years have we known each other, Chris—eighteen, right? In all that time have you ever known me to go out of my mind? Listen, turn around and take me home. I'm not in the mood to see a shrink. I'm no crazier than you are, I'm depressed and forgetful and dull-witted and whatever else I'm supposed to be, but I'm not crazy."

Chris said nothing. The radio said clearing and warmer.

"I'm not crazy."

"You ate soap."

"I did? Well, I'm concerned about cleanness, Chris. Everybody and everything is so dirty, and it's worse every day. Everything you read tells you about dirt, it's just ridiculous. What's the use?"

Chris turned off the radio and Larry fell silent.

Miles of straight highway. A few snowflakes. A shower of rain. Farms beside the road, the buildings huddled in the cold white glow of yardlights, blackness lurking behind the barns, blackness lying in the fields. Chris, longing for dawn, strained to see beyond his headlights; he looked in vain for the glow of the city reflected in the cloudy sky.

At four o'clock he turned on the radio again. Larry spoke. "One of the reasons I never wrote the history of Minnesota was the impossible job it would have been to research all the dirt. All the dirty dealing that went into the building of the railroads and acquiring land grants and things like that. How can a person research all that dirt and keep his good name? You have no idea the kind of filth you get into when it comes to writing a history book. Everything is basically dirty. Every person. You and I and Rachel and everybody in the world. Rachel, are you awake?"

From the back: silence.

"When I was young, I never believed everybody was basically dirty. I thought most people were clean." He turned and directed his words back over his shoulder. "I thought dirt was the exception and goodness was the rule, but after what happened at Rookery State I saw that everybody was basically dirty. It took me two years to lose my job once they started out after me, and during all that time nobody came forward to defend me except students. Students signed petitions to keep me teaching, but nobody in the department came forward with a good word for me, except one or two junior members, newcomers. I think the old guard was downright dirty jealous of my success with students. Dirt is the nature of man, that's what life has taught me. It's all around us. Watch TV and what do you see? Dirt. Crime and lewdness and plain dirty stupidity, it's all around. You're dirty, Chris, and so is Rachel, and so am I. Let's face it. But when I say we're dirty, I'm not saying we're any worse than other people, so don't get me wrong. You hear me, Rachel?"

From the back: a sigh.

"Rachel, I'm not saying you're any worse than anybody else."

From the back, the voice small: "Thanks, Larry."

"Have you ever thought about your motives, you two? Really thought about them?" He leaned toward Chris, his complexion green, reflecting the dash lights. "Has it occurred to you that your motives probably aren't as pure as you'd like them to seem? I'm talking about the way you're handling my MS. You're both being very noble about it. You're both long-suffering." He straightened up and spoke straight ahead. "You're both peachy. But why? Isn't it for the rewards? Rewards such as being well thought of by the neighbors—isn't that your true motive? Rewards such as pumping up your self-esteem—that's another reward. To others your long-suffering looks pure, but I see it up close and I see what it does for your pride. I wouldn't be telling you this if I didn't love you, but I have to tell you that you're both a couple of toadies. Toadies to your pride."

From the back: "Shut up, Larry."

"But don't worry about it, nobody's pure. If I've learned nothing else in life, I've learned that."

Chris turned off the radio and Larry shut up.

At five o'clock Chris stopped for gas at a self-service station at a junction of highways. Filling his tank under a bank of harsh neon lights, he hunched against the raw wind sweeping over the land. When he went into the station to wake the dozing cashier and pay, Larry got out of the car and pumped five gallons onto the ground. Chris, coming outside, found him standing in the puddle and holding his cigarette lighter at the ready. He was grinning. Above him, strings of plastic triangular flags whipped and clicked in the wind.

"Get in the car," Chris ordered.

Larry did so, his lighter unflicked, his shoes smelling of gas. Rachel snatched the lighter away from him. Chris went back into the station and paid for the five gallons on the ground.

At five thirty, Minneapolis materialized in the cloudy dawn. The hospital—the Fawn River Health Center—was located on the near edge of the city and resembled an apartment complex for the well-to-do: two-story brick buildings with pillared porches, groves of evergreens, ducks circling a pond. Here Chris knew his way around. He led the Quinns into the admitting office, a richly furnished living room: easy chairs, a chandelier. From hidden speakers a violin sonata. The night-shift attendant, a long-faced woman dressed in blue serge, interviewed the Quinns and explained the system—Larry would share a double room in a dormitory; he would leave his valuables here at the desk; he would sign his name on this page assenting to whatever procedures the staff deemed necessary for the safety of himself and others; he would sign his name on this other page indicating that his health insurance was massive and in force. The music swelled. The overheated room filled with the stench of gasoline.

The blue-serge woman said, "Now we must take you into the next room and X-ray your lungs." She pressed a buzzer.

An orderly dressed in white came and steered Larry through a doorway. Chris and Rachel slumped in their chairs, exhausted. When Larry reappeared, he was wide-eyed with delusion.

"Rachel, you proud whore!"

The blue-serge woman said a car was coming to take Larry to his dormitory; Doctor Anderson would see him early Monday morning; Rachel could go with Larry if she wished, to see him settled in his room; have a good day.

The car came. Rachel got in with Larry and his suitcase.

While she was gone, Chris phoned a downtown hotel and booked two rooms.

Chris slept until noon in 704. When he awoke and opened the drapes, he found Seventh Street full of sunshine. He dressed and went out and bought a shirt and a newspaper and returned to his room and showered. Dressed again, he went out into the hall and listened at the door of 706. Here at seven o'clock this morning, with the bellhop standing between them, Rachel had said, "Goodnight, Chris, what would I do without you?" and she had closed the door. No sound now from within. He went back to his room and absently read and watched TV, his thinking divided between Larry in the hospital and Rachel next door. Larry was proving to Chris that a man could be driven crazy. In studying to be a counselor, Chris had been led to believe that mental aberration stemmed either from bad genes or a troubled childhood, but here was a case of a man gone mad at forty-seven, a man of sturdy stock whose considerable powers of mind had been worn down and dismantled by suffering—the screws loosened, the balances tipped.

And Rachel. He considered the irony of having the woman he loved in the next room yet out of reach. Here they were, far from the prying eyes of Rookery and far from Larry, yet separated by Larry's grave condition. He pondered the impropriety, the baseness inherent in a man's pressing his love on a woman in her time of sorrow. But what if Rachel, in her extremity, reached out to Chris for solace, led him on—would his compliance then be any more proper, any less base? Yes, he decided happily. He went out in the hall again and listened at her door. She was stirring.

Twenty minutes later she came to his room. She wore a blue skirt, a white blouse, a blue sweater. "Let's eat, Chris, I'm starved." Although she looked refreshed, her gray eyes seemed withdrawn, filmed over, as though her attention were elsewhere. Her cut lip was swollen a little. "Then we'll go and see how Larry's doing."

He took her hand and drew her further into the room. She looked about. She took away her hand and improved on his careless bed straightening. She went to the window.

"Thank you for seeing me through this awful time," she said softly. "We're in for a lot of trouble with Larry, aren't we." It wasn't a question.

He stood at her side looking out. "He isn't Larry right now, Rachel. The man we left at the hospital is somebody else." Across the street a building lay in a heap under a wrecking ball.

She threw her head back and inhaled. She turned and

put her arms loosely around his neck, her eyes glistening, edged with tears. He was shaken by the sweet touch of her body against his own. He kissed her.

"I love you," he said.

Her vigorous nod encouraged him. Her words, "I believe you," disappointed him.

He kissed her again, hard. Her lips tasted faintly of blood.

"I'll get my coat," she said, hurrying from the room.

They stopped to eat on the way to the hospital; they both ordered a lot and ate little.

At the Fawn River Health Center they found that Larry, further removed from himself, had been removed from his dormitory room. A nurse told them that after being left alone this morning, he had tried to set fire to his bed. He had asked for cigarettes and matches and burned a corner of a blanket before the smoke alarm went off. She gave them directions to the Intensive Treatment building.

On the second floor of Intensive Treatment Larry was standing behind a glass wall with four dozen deeply disturbed men and women, most of them young, half of them smoking, two or three only partially dressed, several pausing in their pacing and talking to gaze stupidly at Chris and Rachel through the glass; their unblinking, heavy-lidded stares reminding Chris of animals he had seen in zoos. Caged ostriches. Dispirited yaks. Larry was standing at a distance and looking at his wife out of the corner of his eye. The room had thick blue carpet and soft furniture. A nurse appeared on the near side of the glass. "Yes?"

"I'm Larry Quinn's wife."

"Ah, excellent. Larry's much better this afternoon. We have him on some neat meds that seem to be agreeing with him just fine. He's much less agitated. This morning he was really out to lunch." She went to a screened opening in the wall. "Larry, honey, your wife is here."

Larry advanced to the screen in slow stages, grasping at those standing near him for support—he was without his cane. His eyes were half-closed, his pupils greatly dilated. He lowered his head to the opening, which was below mouth level.

"It bothers me to see you two together," he said, his tongue thick. "Chris ... why don't you disappear ... and let me talk to my wife? Why don't you ... get lost?"

Chris retreated. Rachel stepped forward.

"Rachel, would you do me a favor? Would you have the doctor ... when you see the doctor would you have him put me out of my misery? Would you have him ... you know ... give me something fatal? Tell him I'd like it to be something quick ... and tell him I'd like it to taste good. And I'd like it to be painless, of course." His eyelids fluttered as he tried to smile. "And then, after you've told that to the doctor, you can go and screw Chris for all I care."

Chris heard this from a distance. When Rachel turned (after placing her hand for a moment flat against the screen) and came to his side (her eyes cast down), it was all he could do not to take her up in a consoling embrace. He led her away, feeling the weight of Larry's eyes on his back.

"That man isn't really Larry," he said on the way downstairs.

"I believe you, Chris."

"That man is a stranger."

"I believe you."

They left the hospital and headed back into the city. Now in the late afternoon the colors of spring were stunning. They drove through a neighborhood of chartreuse elms and emerald aspens. Lawns gleamed so green they might have been outdoor carpet or the artificial grass that covers the dirt of open graves. Darting across the street, inches from their windshield, were a pair of finches so golden they seemed lit from within. In a park children cavorted under a kite.

"I'm feeling cramped, Chris." She looked at him with stress in her eyes, which were still withdrawn, filmy. "All boxed in," she added.

"I know what you mean. When I used to bring Karen

to the hospital, I felt the same way. It leaves you feeling off-balance and ineffectual."

"I need to run."

"I remember feeling that in order to get my balance back I had to get away from things for a time—put some distance between me and the life I was leading."

"I should have packed my sweatsuit."

"I developed a couple of tricks that sometimes helped."

"Tell me."

"Well, leaving the hospital, I would go straight to the IDS Tower and look down on the city from the fifty-third floor. Sometimes that worked. Being that far above everything and seeing so far beyond the suburbs was helpful. I'd spend a long time watching the movement on the freeways, the swirls of cars on the cloverleafs. Life looks like it has a pattern when you see it from the fifty-third floor."

"Maybe we should try it."

"Or there's the Institute of Arts. It has certain paintings that open up and let me in. There's a Van Dyck, for instance, 'Christ Taken in the Garden.' It's full of faces —apostles, soldiers—and if my mood is just right, I can lose myself in those faces for about twenty minutes at a time."

"Show me."

He looked at his watch. "We have just enough time before they close."

They stood holding hands before the Van Dyck. The soldiers led by Judas, rush in from the left and are caught in paint the instant before the first hand is laid upon Christ. A rope to bind him is flung up overhead. Soldiers and apostles struggle, wrestle, tumble underfoot. Peter severs somebody's ear. All is turmoil and sharp edges. Except at the center, where Christ has turned toward his attackers without a trace of alarm in his eyes, without a flinch. Though he faces the lips of Judas and the violence of brigands, his eyes are sadly unperturbed—the eyes of a man who knows that struggle is futile, defeat certain.

But so is triumph certain. He sees beyond present peril and beyond future peril. Imprisonment, torture, death—then life. Not happy days—there is sorrow behind them—but in this mad dance of catastrophe the eyes are two pools of peace.

"He has distance," said Chris, nodding toward Christ.

"Yes," said Rachel, "but I haven't." She turned in a circle. "What's this?" She led Chris across the large gallery, her heels echoing, and came to a stop before Goya's "Self-Portrait with Doctor Arrieta"—Goya propped up by his doctor, his head tipped back against the doctor's breast, the doctor reaching around in front of Goya, offering him a concoction in a cup; and this lettered low on the canvas: "Goya, grateful to his friend Arrieta for his expert care, who saved his life during a painful and dangerous illness endured at the end of the year 1819 in the 73rd year of his life."

Chris contemplated the two old men, both wearing the pallor of age; then he backed away and contemplated Rachel. This was her domain—the care of the sick. In the century and a half since the artist painted it, who had come to this canvas better prepared than Rachel to understand it? Standing close to the painting, her hands clasped behind her, she had intercepted the beam of light intended for the canvas; light was caught in the sheen of her russet hair and was mirrored in the patent leather of her black shoes; she looked slight and vulnerable and beautiful in this vast, high-ceilinged gallery along whose walls were dozens of treasures but nothing as precious to Chris as this full-length profile of the woman he loved contemplating Goya.

"No distance in that," she said suddenly, pulling her eyes away. "It's too much like home."

A bell chimed, a voice announced closing time.

"But I did pack my sneakers, Chris. Let's go back to the hotel for my sneakers. I'll run in my skirt."

Twenty minutes later Chris was standing on the corner of Seventh and Nicollet watching her run away. It was early evening and the stores were closed and she had the sidewalk to herself. When she reached the public library several blocks north, she turned around and headed back; at each corner she burst from shadow into the red sunlight that filled the cross streets; with her chin up, her skirt aswirl about her knees, she swept past Chris with a smile but without a pause in her bobbing stride; off she ran south—Ninth Street, Tenth, Eleventh —and she curved with Nicollet out of his line of sight. For half an hour he stood on the corner and waited. He began to worry. Nicollet led through a pocket of seediness. She was mugged or raped. Sweating with alarm, he rushed off down the street—Ninth Street, Tenth, Eleventh—and he met her coming back.

"I've been through Loring Park," she said, panting, taking his arm, throwing her hair back.

"That far?"

"And I went around the track in Parade Stadium." She stopped and put her hands on her knees for a moment, catching her breath.

"Did it help?"

"No." They resumed their walk. "Not enough distance."

At the door of 706 she said, "I'll see you after I shower, maybe *you* can give me some distance." She said this with her eyes averted and she quickly closed the door.

It was dark when she came to his room. She wore her blue robe tightly buttoned at the throat and reaching to her bare toes. She wore no makeup. Her swollen eyes told him she had been weeping.

"I talked to Bernard on the phone. He said the *Morning Call* praised us to the skies. Tonight the cast had a meeting right before curtain time and Viola gave everybody a pep talk. They all agreed to give the performance of their lives—in honor of me and Larry."

"You have good friends in that cast." Chris led her to the chair by the window. He sat and drew her onto his lap.

"They're dear, dear people." She laid her head on his shoulder. She was light in his lap. Through her robe he felt her smoothness. Suddenly she quaked with weeping and he tightened his hold.

"Chris, I've never had such a sense of doom. It's worse than that time in your office. 'Cliffs of fall,' remember? Tonight at the Playhouse that wonderful cast is playing its heart out for me and Larry, and do you know what I felt when Bernard told me about it?"

"Honored."

"I felt nothing. I'm conscious of nothing but Larry in that glass cage. I can't move my thinking off that horrible sight." She ground her eyes into his shoulder, wetting his shirt. "I'm suffocating, Chris. I want distance. I want to go far away."

They moved to the bed. He pressed himself upon her, kissing her eyes, her cheekbones, her throat above the tight collar. They lingered over buttons, and after breathing had grown stormy he said, "Does this give you distance?" and she said, "Yes, but not enough, but yes," and she enfolded and tightened herself around the great thrust and release of his pent-up yearning, and later, when he felt the joy of his passion dying into the joy of peace—an emotion more sublime than any he could remember—he whispered, "Distance enough?" Her head was tipped back over his arm, her chin high; it took her a long time to answer from deep in her throat: "From what?"

They lay in a loose embrace, brow to brow, and only after Rachel fell asleep did Chris realize that the tears wetting the pillow were his own.

Chris returned to Rookery on Sunday evening.

Rachel took the bus home on Wednesday, went about her business at the Playhouse for four days and returned to Minneapolis after the Sunday matinee. Each of her four days in Rookery she spoke to Chris by phone, but she didn't see him.

"No, don't come over," she insisted.

"But let me at least drive you to the bus depot."

"No, I'm taking the car to the city this time. Bruce

doesn't need it. He has his bike and a number of friends with cars."

"How about a walk along the river?"

"No."

"A walk through Prinn's Department Store."

"Chris, I don't want to see you."

"Why?"

Sternly: "Because I love you." She hung up.

11

WHEN RACHEL ARRIVED HOME the following week, she called Chris to say that Larry had been taken out of Intensive Treatment and put back into the dormitory. He was sleepy most of the time but coherent when he spoke. Doctor Anderson foresaw his return home in about two weeks.

"Has he said anything more about our being together?"

"No, Chris, your name doesn't come up. As a conversation piece you're a little too hot for us to handle right now."

Chris shut his office door. "Rachel, I can't go much longer without seeing you. Will you be home tonight?"

"I'll be home, but please don't come."

"Just for a few minutes. I miss you."

"No, don't you understand? One man at a time is my limit. Please don't come."

He dropped the subject for fear she would hang up. Searching for another, he swiveled to face his window. The campus was turning a brilliant green. The leafing-out stage of spring, which they had seen ten days ago in Minneapolis, had moved north. Warblers chirped, robins warbled. Dozens of pale students, as though gassed between classes, lay sunning themselves on the grass. It was May Day.

"How's Bruce doing without you?"

"Fine. Half the time he's been staying at a friend's house. The friend's mother, it seems, cooks nothing he doesn't like and a great deal of what he does. Swiss steak, for instance, and sugared doughnuts. Tomorrow after school I expect him back home to stay. After this, I'll go to the city for only a day at a time."

They talked about Bruce's college entrance exams (90th percentile in science, 82nd in language), about faculty layoffs (Chris was preparing a stirring address to the Personnel Committee in behalf of his department), about *Twelfth Night*, which had one more weekend to run.

"I have to go now, Chris. I'm meeting Bernard to make plans for Ibsen."

"I'll see you tonight."

"No!"

From Chris's seven o'clock class—Academic Adjustment for evening students—half the students were missing and he understood why. Between home and campus they had obviously lost their way (as though in a blizzard) in the magic of the soft, heavenly weather. This May Day evening was the apotheosis of May evenings. The campus rang with birdsong. Nest-building orioles swooped down from high boughs and flashed, bright as beer cans, in the classroom window.

When Chris interrupted his lecture to open the window, his train of thought was derailed by the aroma of lilacs. He turned to his small, distracted class and said, "Let's go home."

In the blink of an eye the room was empty, his students gone outside to bathe their winterbound sensibilities in the coral and benevolent sunset, Chris gone in his Chevrolet to Rachel's house.

She met him at the door with an eager smile. She wore a dress he hadn't seen before (plaid, light blue and light gray) and a scent he hadn't smelled.

She wore a lipstick he hadn't tasted.

She led him by the hand into the kitchen, saying, "I asked you please not to come."

There on the table, by the window overlooking the valley, were plates of cheese and fruit and two wineglasses. She handed him a chilled bottle. He poured.

They talked through sundown and dusk until Rachel said that her neighbors would be wondering about the

Chevrolet at her curb. She said a lot of people were taking an interest in her case now that word was out about
her kissing somebody in Prinn's Department Store.
Some said it happened in glassware. Some said the basement lunch counter.

"I'll drive the car home."

"Yes, I think you should." She cupped her chin in her
hands and gazed at him across the table, across the orange peels and cracker crumbs. The wine was nearly
gone.

"And I'll come back through the valley. Look for me
at the back door."

He tried to read yes or no in her steady gray gaze. He
settled on yes, and left.

It was black night when he started down the steep
hillside below his apartment. He lost his way and slid
into a spiky bush and was reminded how crooked and
various were the ways men took to other men's wives.
While the approach to marriage was clearly marked by
conventions (dates, dances, diamonds), the route to infidelity was always new; every adulterer blazed a trail.

He reached the river without falling. He followed the
bike path upstream to the footbridge. He crossed over to
Badbattle Drive and at the main gate of the cemetery he
took a bearing on the light in Rachel's kitchen window.
He climbed the narrow paved lane to the high gate and
the narrow dirt path to her yard.

The kitchen light was off when he reached the house.
The back door was locked. He called to her.

She spoke from an upstairs window. She said she was
sorry but he couldn't come in.

He stepped back and looked up at the window. He
couldn't see her behind the dark screen. He could only
hear her. She said she was sorry.

Rachel brought Larry home in the middle of May. He
had spent ten days behind glass and fourteen days in the
dormitory. During these later two weeks he had passed
most of his waking hours (which were few) in group ther-

apy, where he squirmed and yawned and said little; in physical therapy, where he strengthened his wrists by squeezing a soft rubber ball; and in vocational therapy, where he made a small ceramic ashtray. He came home shrunken and docile and drugged to the eyeballs.

In June Rachel phoned Doctor Anderson and said she wanted Larry's dose of medication reduced. Her husband was a zombie. Doctor Anderson said he wouldn't advise it.

A week later she reduced it herself by fifty milligrams. After a few days of the shakes, Larry seemed brighter.

In July she reduced it by another fifty. After a few days of dark emotion, he seemed brighter still.

In August, she reduced it by fifty more. After a few hours of muttering, he called her a slut and took a big bite from a bar of Palmolive and said he wanted to die.

From that day forward she kept Larry on the dosage prescribed. And Chris began to inquire about Delta Marsh.

12

*D*UCK FOR SUPPER. NOT breast of duck this time, but duck whole and entire on Chris's plate, duck dying on its back with its knees up, its abdominal cavity stuffed with something stringy. Chris's appetite for duck was not great. He sliced the flesh from the bones, nibbled, then stashed the rest inside with the stuffing. He looked at his tablemates. The Vermonters and the plumber were consuming their ducks down to the last gristly tendon and all the while glancing about, looking for the telltale signs of squeamishness left on their neighbors' plates. They talked as they chewed, reviewing the day's hunt. On Chris's left Larry was eating slowly, his head low to his plate, his hands trembling. On Chris's right the plumber's son evidently felt the way Chris did about duck; he had flensed the bones, piled the meat off to the side and was studying the skeleton. Breathing noisily through his nose, absorbed, the boy moved the wing joints, probed along the breastbone, disassembled the rib cage.

At the foot of the table, the plumber said, "I fired seven shots today and killed three ducks and our guide retrieved them all." He described the seven shots—the flying-away shot, the left-to-right shot, the overhead shot, the point-blank shot, the right-to-left shot, the veering-away shot, and the skimming-over-the-water shot. "But I've had enough of Delta Marsh. I've had my *fill* of Delta Marsh. After this weekend Blackie La Voi will be damn lucky if he ever sees me again. This isn't duck hunting, this is the tropics. If you're going to enjoy yourself, you've got to be where it's cold and windy and

230

snowy, none of this goddamn sunshine. Next year I'm hunting Alaska, and unless my kid learns to act more like a hunter than he did today, I'm leaving him home. My kid was sleeping when he should have been scanning the sky, he was looking east when he should have been looking west and he was picking his nose when a flock of twelve flew over."

The boy, if he was listening, seemed not to mind. He was dismantling a wing.

Sanderson Bleekman, from the head of the table: "I shot well today myself, but we didn't get our limit, which means we'll be staying on another day. The few shots I took, however, were marvelous shots. I shot *four* birds with only *five* shots."

There was a moment of silence while the plumber found a way to top that. He found it in the past. "I'll never forget the time I was hunting in Upper Michigan and I fired three times into a flock of mallards and dropped five birds. I dropped the two lead ducks with the first shot and I dropped a single with my second shot and I dropped two more with my third shot. Five ducks in *three* shots. That was up near Escanaba."

"Now speaking of multiple kills..." Sanderson Bleekman raised his fork in the air, held it there until he had everyone's attention. He was dark around the eyes tonight and his cheeks were sallow—the wear and tear of a five-day hunt. "Now speaking of multiple kills, I have been hunting the coast of Maine for close to forty years and there is a certain small bay up there where the ducks used to be so plentiful that you always held your fire unless you stood a good chance of dropping two birds. The bay has a name, but most of the adjoining land is owned by a family who would prefer that you people not know its name, and therefore, I do not call it by name except in the company of the few hunters who go there by invitation of the family. I first went there many years ago with my father. My father suspended his law practice for a month every autumn and off we went to shoot ducks and geese. We hunted Hudson Bay and we hunted Mexico and we hunted Maine. Sometimes we hunted with Blackie LaVoi. My father knew Blackie as early as 1940."

The plumber stuck out his lower lip and exhaled wetly with disgust. This was tough competition. Hudson Bay. A cape in Maine. Five ducks in three shots. Like Bleekman, he did what all little boys do in tight places; he called upon his father: "My father knew Blackie in 1938. Am I right, Blackie?"

From the kitchen: "Did he?"

"You damn right he did!" The plumber slapped the table as though trumping a trick.

From the kitchen: "Okay."

The plumber continued: "My father was not only the foremost marksman in Wisconsin, he was also the foremost sewer man in the city of Milwaukee. He carried all the sewers of Milwaukee around in his head. That was because there was no map of certain sewers that had been installed in the early years, and my father was the only man in the city who knew just where they were and where they led. During the years I was growing up, there was a square mile at the center of the city where if somebody's sewer was plugged or a water main broke, the city had to call in my father to explain the layout of pipes. In some places the sewers ran down the middle of streets and in other places they cut through private property. Before he died, he drew a map of all those sewers and for a good long time that was the only map of sewers in the center of the city. I'm talking about your grandfather, boy." He looked down the table at his son, who was flexing the duck's neck. "Your grandfather was the skeet-shooting champion of North Milwaukee for nine straight years."

Silence for a while. Sanderson Bleekman evidently wasn't going to return this serve.

Then Larry spoke up, startling Chris. "Your father was indeed a great man."

The plumber suspected no guile and replied, "You damn right he was a great man."

"Incredible," said Larry. "Imagine all those sewers in one man's brain." Larry had pushed his plate away, his duck barely eaten. He looked half-asleep. When Chris had returned to Widgeon Point late in the afternoon (without the guiding reports from Blackie's shotgun he never would have found his way), he discovered Larry in a high state of excitement over a duck he had shot. Now, exhausted, Larry sat with his right arm hooked over the back of his chair; this may have struck the others as a casual pose, but Chris understood it was Larry's way of keeping himself from sliding off onto the floor.

"And where is that map now?" asked Larry.

"In the main office of the Milwaukee waterworks. Of course they've made a new map since then. They've got a whole book of fancy sewer maps put together by engineers and draftsmen, but they've kept my father's map in their files. I've seen it there."

"When I'm in Milwaukee next, I'd like to see it," said Larry.

Chris cleared his throat and cast about for something to say, sensing what was coming. He called, "Where's dessert?"

"Because I'd hate to take a shit in Milwaukee and not know where it was going to end up."

The plumber's eyes flashed in surprise, then anger.

"When I'm next in Milwaukee, I'm going to the main office of the waterworks and read that map and see where my shit ends up."

Tense silence. Gladdy and Poo Poo came in from the kitchen carrying dishes of grapefruit sections. They stopped, sensing the electricity in the room.

"Because when I take a shit in Milwaukee—"

"I'll tell you where it goes," squeaked the plumber's son, his eyes riveted on his bone-strewn plate. "It goes into Lake Michigan. Dad says it *all* goes into Lake Michigan."

A moment more of silence, then laughter. The Vermonters laughed, even the boys. Gladdy laughed. Poo Poo laughed and stepped up behind the plumber and kissed him on the ear and the plumber chuckled. Blackie looked in to see what was so funny. With laughter, harmony. Sanderson Bleekman spoke across the table to the plumber's son, told him he could expect the best shooting of his young life if he went to Alaska. Poo Poo sat down next to the plumber and tickled his belly. Gladdy pulled a chair up next to Chris and said, "I hope you're enjoying yourself." Chris smiled and said yes, he was having a grand time. The table talk was high-spirited for a while, and then, one by one, the group became conscious of a story being told by the cheery man. They all fell silent to hear what he was saying:

"... and I believe I was fourteen when my father took me hunting for the first time..." It was a long dull story and it was followed by another from Bleekman, but Chris didn't listen. He was lost in his own earliest memory of hunting. A dark Sunday morning. He was six. His father took him out in the country to a small pond, where they met a friend of his father's, a lanky farmer who said that if they stood very still in the tall weeds they would see some ducks. There was no sunrise that day, for the sky was heavily clouded; day advanced in imperceptible stages of gray light. They stood for a long time in grass much higher than Chris's head, and at least once a minute the tall farmer bent over to emit a long brown string of tobacco juice. Then suddenly Chris's father shot a duck. It fell to the pond and floated out of reach. They had no dog or boat. The farmer said he would wade out and get it. Chris's father protested; the water was icy cold, the duck wasn't worth it. No trouble at all, said the friend, and before their very eyes the man took off his boots and socks and pants and revealed that he wore no underwear. He stepped carefully into the cold dark water, went in up to his knees, up to his hips, and drawing his shirt and jacket up under his arms, he went in up to his ribs. He picked the duck off the water and he came ashore, water dripping from his hairy scrotum. He handed the duck to Chris, smiling, expecting Chris to be pleased, but the duck flapped a wing—a dying spasm— and Chris screamed and dropped it. Shivering, the farmer grabbed handfuls of swamp grass to wipe himself. His feet were covered with a black sludge that was difficult to wipe away, and he put his socks on over it. So this was hunting. It struck Chris as an extraordinary business indeed—the dark day, the dead bird, the farmer's genitals, the blind enclosure of grass. There was more to it than a child could understand, but he carried away (and he had kept it all these years) the notion that entangled in the urge to hunt was a sexual impulse vying with the desire to kill. So it had been when he was six.

And so it was today.

Or, to be precise, tomorrow.

Chris shook off his past and went to work on his future. He got up from the table and went into the kitchen. There, sitting at a cardtable, Blackie and his blind wife were eating cheeseburgers and drinking beer from bottles.

"Can I have a word with you?"

"Sit down," Blackie pointed his cheeseburger at the woman. "This is the wife."

She looked up at Chris as though she could see.

"This guy's from Rookery, Minnesota, where Lollie's buried," Blackie explained. "He ain't much of a hunter, but he doesn't pretend to be—not like some other guys we know."

"How do you do," said Chris. He took a chair.

"Quite well, thank you." Mrs. LaVoi carefully wiped the corners of her mouth with a paper napkin; then she smiled. Her face had sharp, bony lines. Her eyelids were pink, her eyes dead. She wore her long white hair in two braids, which were thrown back over the shoulders of her faded dress.

Chris said, "Blackie, I think we ought to hunt the big lake tomorrow. That island near the mouth of the river. We can go by road and save ourselves all that paddling and tramping around in the muck. I spent hours on that island today, and I saw ducks all the while."

"How come you never shot any?"

"They were high. Out of range. But with clouds tomorrow and wind, they'll be flying low."

Blackie chewed, swigged beer. "I don't hunt the big lake."

"Why?"

"Rough water for duckboats."

"But that island isn't more than three hundred yards from shore."

"I ain't hunted the big lake since the time I damn near had four hunters drown on me. Did you see that article about me in the other room? That one from *Sports Afield*?

"Yes, I read it."

"Well, that was the time."

"Larry and I are willing to take our chances. We've come a long way for ducks and the island looks to me like—"

Blackie raised his hand to silence Chris while he stuffed his mouth full of cheeseburger. He chewed for a while, then washed it down with beer. He wiped his mustache and mouth with the back of his hand, belched and spoke:

"Four hunters from Fargo that didn't know north from south or up from down or their ass from a hole in the ground. I took them out in little boats to hunt that island. I led the way with my own boat, and while I was setting out the decoys and they were hiding themselves in the weeds, the damnedest wind came up you ever saw. Like to blown the fish out of the water. Colder than hell, too. Late in the season and freezing cold. I hollered at the guys, 'Git in your boats and head for land!' I said, and they got in their boats and they fell right out. They looked like my decoys, their heads bobbing around in the water, and I had to paddle out and pick up all four of them and haul them to shore in my tiny little boat. I had to make two trips between the island and the mainland. I lost two boats that day and I lost about two dozen good decoys, and besides, I lost my nerve. *Sports Afield* says I'm the bravest man in Manitoba, which is probably true, but on that day I was also the scaredest. So from that day to this I never send my hunters out on the big lake. I send them out in the Marsh, where the worst they can do is get lost and holler till I find them. None of this getting out in the whitecaps in a duckboat."

"We're willing to take our chances."

"Another thing, I ain't got any boats beached up there on the big lake. I used to keep boats up there, but I don't anymore."

"We'll rent boats. There's that place at the end of the road with boats on the beach. I saw at least five of them, good-sized, safer than duckboats."

"That's Lawler's Resort. I don't get along with Lawler."

The woman spoke: "Lawler's dead."

Blackie lowered his head and glared at her with his good eye. This put his stationary eye on Chris.

"His daughter's running the resort," said Mrs. LaVoi. "She'll rent you boats. I had her in school years ago."

Blackie said, "Since when are you running this camp?"

She said, "You may have had a grudge against her father, but you've got nothing against Kate. She'll be glad to rent out her boats. I had her in school. I haven't seen her for years and years."

Chris told Blackie, "I'll pay the boat rental and I'll drive my car and it won't cost you a cent to go to the island with us. I'll even pay you extra for guiding." He took a fifty from his billfold. "This is over and above. A tip. It's for coming along and guiding us on the big lake." Was fifty too much? In his overeagerness was he inviting suspicion? He probably should have offered twenty, but it was too late.

Blackie drank beer.

The woman said, "They've come a long way for ducks, Blackie. Take them up to the big lake."

"I've got hunters to take into the Marsh." But his eye was on the money.

"One of the guides can drive the tractor. Take these men to the big lake, where the good shooting is."

Blackie drained his bottle and reached into the refrigerator.

Chris held out the fifty-dollar bill. He was depending on Blackie to corroborate his story of accidental drowning. To kill Larry without Blackie along might cause the authorities to investigate. Not that anything criminal could be proved. Or could it?

Blackie twisted the cap off the beer bottle and handed it to Chris. He opened another for himself. He said, "Why not?" and took the money.

His wife said, "I'd like to go with you and spend the day with Kate."

Blackie glared at her again. However long she had been blind, Blackie seemed unconvinced that his expressions were lost on her.

"We'll take you along," said Chris. Would a murderer be so kind?

"How nice. I'll phone Kate. Gladdy. Gladdy."

Gladdy came in from the dining room. "Done eating?"

"Gladdy, would you dial Lawler's Resort? I'd like to talk to Kate."

The telephone hung beside the cardtable. Gladdy dialed, handed the phone to Mrs. LaVoi and went back to the hunters.

"Let me tell you a secret," said Blackie, moving his chair close to Chris, speaking low. "If I was really interested in ducks, I'd hunt the big lake all the time. You're right about the big lake. That's where the best shooting is, and when you drop a duck on the big lake, you can always find it. None of this hide-and-go-seek in the cane. But to tell the truth, I don't give one goddamn shit about shooting ducks. You can't imagine how sick I am of ducks."

"Kate, how wonderful to talk to you," said Mrs. LaVoi.

"See, I've been in this business for a lifetime and it wasn't so bad in the early years when I could move around and hunt the Yukon when I felt like it and hunt the Marsh when I felt like it and hunt over east in the woods, but now I've been living in this godforsaken Marsh for twenty duck seasons and I'm just plain sick of everything about it. And mostly I'm sick of hunters."

Mrs. LaVoi nodded, smiling over the phone to her neighbor across the Marsh. Chris heard Larry in the other room speaking of Bruce, his selection last year as all-conference tackle.

Blackie continued: "So what I do is take my hunters into the Marsh and save myself that long drive to the lake and the worry of having them out on open water. Let them stumble around in the swamp for four or five days and wear themselves out just putting one foot in front of the other, and whether or not they get their limit of birds, they go home feeling like they've come up against nature and conquered it. When all they've really done is stumble around in the swamp for four or five days. That's what they pay me for—that feeling that they've conquered nature. If they were smart, they'd find their own places to hunt. They'd sleep in a tent and cook their food over a fire and go home with more birds than I can show them and they'd save a pile of money besides. But they're not smart. They're dumb. Bleekman's bunch from Vermont—they're dumb. That pissant plumber from Milwaukee—he's dumb. They all pay me thirty dollars a day for the privilege of stumbling around in the muck—which is a privilege I'm in no position to offer them if the truth was known, because the swamp doesn't even belong to me. I just happen to have a tractor and a trailer for hauling them in. They pay me for the privilege of hearing the mice in the bunkhouse. Gladdy was going to set traps for mice and I said nothing doing, my hunters come up here expecting wild animals and that's what we'll give them. It's comic relief, my friend. And another thing—they come up here expecting to eat duck every day. Half of them don't like duck. It tastes gamy and it makes them sick the way it made you sick this morning, but it also makes them believe they're tough. There's a guy from Omaha comes up here opening weekend every year, and I swear he spends the whole time shitting. I swear he shits half his weight in liquefied duck. He goes home pale and shaky and convinced that he's had the time of his life."

Blackie pounded his chest and belched. "And me? When the season is over, me and the wife pack up and fly to Anaheim. I own an apartment house in Anaheim.

We usually get down there in time for the tail end of the
Los Angeles Rams' football season."

Mrs. LaVoi laughed, speaking of some schoolday
memory. She brought one of her long white braids
around in front of her and stroked it as she talked.

"But you're right," said Blackie. "Why the hell not
make a trip to the big lake and shoot a few ducks tomorrow? Looks to me like your friend in there will be dead
before another duck season comes around. He's quite a
case. Ornery asshole one minute and friendly the next.
You've got your hands full with him, I can see that. We
sat out there on Widgeon Point today and had a pretty
good time chewing the fat. He told me about his son—
plays football. And his wife—she acts out plays. He
says she's a good-looking redhead. I suppose you know
her. He told me about the hunting you guys used to do
when you were young. And of course I told him a few
stories from the Yukon and the woods around Kenora—
mostly true stories. He's really not a bad guy when you
get to know him. Is it true his wife's a good-looking redhead?"

"It's true. He's married to the most..." Chris
checked himself. "It's true."

"So you want to haul him up to the big lake—what
the hell, that's what we'll do. And we'll haul the wife
along and drop her at Lawler's."

Mrs. LaVoi said goodbye to her distant neighbor.
Chris stood and hung up the phone for her. Looking into
the dining room, he saw the hunters rise from their
places, all but Larry, who sat now with both arms
hooked over the back of his chair, his shoulders and
head hanging forward as though from a cross. One of the
cheery man's sons—the older one—stepped around the
table to help Larry up. He put his arm around Larry's
waist and guided him out of the room, nodding as Larry
told him about Bruce, his nine unassisted tackles in one
game, his four A's and two B's at midterm.

Blackie opened another beer. "I understand the Rams
might move to Anaheim next year. If they do, they'll be

playing their games just about a mile and a half from my apartment house."

Chris sat down again with the LaVois. As he sipped his beer, Blackie told him tales of the wild. Killing mule deer in the Sharktooth Mountains. Trapping beaver along the Peace River. Gladdy came and led Mrs. LaVoi away. Poo Poo came and took the cardtable. A long story about killing a whale in Hudson Bay. With the table gone, Chris and Blackie faced each other across empty space, holding their beer in their laps. Blackie, though sick of the hunt, wasn't sick of talking about it when he was full of alcohol. He spoke with force, shooting saliva. He spoke of bearhide and goosedown, moose meat and venison, racks of deerhorns, traplines, fisheye soup, tracking the blood of wounded elk in the snow. Chris listened politely but with only half his attention.

Land on the island. Get Blackie drunk. Drown Larry.

13

*S*TEPPING INTO THE BUNKHOUSE, Chris found a four-handed poker game in progress. Sanderson Bleekman, the cheery man, the plumber, Poo Poo. "Jugs," said tonight's pink T-shirt. The three boys had crawled into their bunks, the older Vermonter to read, the younger to play his harmonica, the plumber's son to watch the card game from above. Larry lay on top of his sleeping bag, snoring. Chris put on his jacket and said he was going out for a walk. No one looked up or replied.

The night was warm for October. A damp wind blew from the northeast. Chris walked away from the buildings, out from under the glow of the yardlight, and scanned the sky. High thin clouds, with a few of the brighter stars showing through. The city of Portage la Prairie was two red-lit radio towers in the southwest; Winnipeg was a faint rosy glow in the southeast. Huddled under its circle of light, Blackie's camp looked as forlorn by night as it did by day. The several rooms, attached end to end, leaned left and right; wispy smoke rose from the chimney of the endmost room. Light seeped through the chinks in the walls. A slat-sided cattle train, headed north, derailed.

Chris got into his car, drove along the ruts of the field, then followed the dirt road into Hill. He went into a tavern and was told he couldn't buy whiskey by the bottle, only by the drink. He drove twenty miles farther to Portage la Prairie, where he bought a quart and a pint of whiskey and a can of Pepsi. The quart he would press upon Blackie when they reached the island. The pint was for Larry, who, when he drank it on top of his medication, would become insentient and pliable. Before laying the bottles in the trunk of the car, Chris opened the quart and spiked his Pepsi; then he returned to camp, sipping from the can as he drove and listening to the radio—a nun complaining about the Pope; His Holiness was a male chauvinist.

In Blackie's yard he stood beside his car, finishing his drink, reluctant to go indoors. Another night in the bunkhouse would test his patience. Another meal at the trestle table would test his powers of digestion. Through the walls he heard the poker players, louder now, tipsier. The northeast wind was blowing in gusts, swinging the light over the bunkhouse door, whipping the smoke from the chimney. When he threw the can away, he heard it clinking off across the pebbly yard in the darkness, rolling with the wind.

The poker game continued into the night. Between twelve and one, Chris was able to sleep, but then he was awakened by shouting—the plumber in a drunken rage. Chris lay facing the wall and tried to make out the plumber's meaning, but except for curses, his words were slurred beyond recognition. He heard Sanderson Bleekman raise his voice: "Do that one more time, you son of a bitch, and I'll call Blackie in here!" He heard Poo Poo shriek with excited laughter. He heard a chair tip over on the wooden floor and he heard the sound of a pump-action shotgun, a shell being moved into the firing chamber. He heard the gun go off—oh, such a noise, a deafening concussion, the bunkhouse shook, the woman screamed. Had the plumber shot Bleekman? Had Bleekman shot the plumber? Chris, his ears ringing, was afraid to roll over and look at the carnage. Now there was silence. The room reeked of gunpowder. Then there was a great roar of laughter. Chris rolled over and looked. The laughing plumber stood under the light bulb, ejecting the spent shell from his gun. The door stood partway open and the others were looking at the plumber in drunken amazement. He had fired not at Bleekman but at the black night. He had opened the door—rain was coming in on the wind—and from the middle of the bunkhouse he had fired out the door. Now he felt better. He stood his gun against the wall, picked up his chair and sat down. He said, "Deal."

PART THREE

— ❖ —

1

D*ROWNING LARRY IS HARDER* than
Chris expected.

First he trips him so that he falls flat and face-down in
the shallow green water; then he presses his right knee
between Larry's shoulder blades and his right hand on
the back of Larry's head. But Larry struggles mightily
against death, and his head keeps slipping out of Chris's
grip; his face keeps turning up for air. With both hands
Chris could drown him, but in order to keep his balance
in the sinking muck, he has to clutch at cattail stalks with
his left hand. Mud rises in the water as they splash.
Larry's short hair becomes slippery with mud. Again and
again he snaps his head up to the right, to the left, for air.
Chris is astounded by his strength—Larry should be as
easy to drown as a cat.

With a single great breaststroke Larry moves himself
out from under Chris's knee. Chris tries to hop forward,
but his left foot is sunk thigh-deep in mud. He throws his
arms around Larry's legs as he falls. Larry, still face-
down, has moved himself within reach of a hummock of
dirt and swamp grass. With both hands he grips the grass
at the roots and churns his legs, struggling to bring them
forward under himself so he can stand, but Chris, lying
flat on Larry's legs, tightens his grip around his knees.
Chris crawls forward on top of Larry and embraces his
thighs. He inches farther along Larry's body, holding
him tight under him, his arms around his wet canvas
clothing; he embraces Larry's pelvis, his stomach, his
chest. Now Larry is sinking under Chris, but because he
still grips the swamp grass ahead of him, he is able to

hold his chin out of the water. Chris tries to press Larry's head down, but Larry holds his arms rigid, gripping the grass, and Chris can't force his head down between his elbows. Chris beats on Larry's arms, but they do not weaken. Larry's fingers are entwined in the grass; his grip is powerful. This is not the strength one derives from kneading a soft rubber ball. This is the rigidity of nerve spasms, the power of paralysis.

With one hand, Chris reaches farther forward and strains to pull the grass out by the roots, but the roots are like ropes and they are knotted around Larry's fingers. The grass is rooted deep in the marsh and Larry's life is rooted in the grass. He draws his life from this clump of dirt and marsh grass and shows no sign of weakening.

It is Chris who is weakening. He is short of breath. His wind is harsh in his throat. He can't get the oxygen he needs. Something covers his head and cuts off his breathing. It isn't water. It feels like fabric. Chris shakes his head sharply and gains relief, draws a deep breath, but then he feels himself suffocating again. To get air, he has to whip his head from side to side with each breath. This takes all his energy. His grip on Larry fails. Larry bucks and throws him off. Chris regains his hold, but in the instant of his freedom Larry has turned over on his back and they embrace chest to chest. Now Larry is helpless. It was a bad move for Larry. In turning over he has given up his grip on the grass. Sinking, face-up, he throws his arms up over his head, but the grass is out of his reach. Chris presses his forearm across Larry's throat and holds him under. He and Larry are face to face with the surface of the water between them. Submerged, Larry's face is transformed. His eyes are no longer so dark and piercing. They're no longer brown. They're gray. And his lips are red. His hair, too, looks red, and it seems longer and darker than Larry's. Darker with mud, no doubt. But how can it be longer? And how can the lips be so unnaturally red—lipstick red?

This isn't Larry. This is Rachel. Chris is drowning Rachel. She wears hunting clothes. Her eyes are smoky.

Her arms come up from the water and tighten around Chris's neck and she draws him under. Chris can't breathe. Who's killing who? He wants Rachel alive, not dead. Must he die to have her? Where is Larry? It's Larry's death their love requires—not Chris's, not Rachel's. Everything has gone wrong. Utterly wrong. Chris gathers his strength and thrusts himself up out of the water for an instant, straining to draw Rachel with him, but her grip, tight as a sprung trap, pulls him down. The water is deep. Down and down. He's surprised to feel what it's like to drown. It feels like suffocating under heavy layers of warm wool.

At the instant of his waking, Chris shrieked and took a swipe at the gray cat lying across his face. The cat leaped off the bunk into the dark. Chris lay on his back, drawing deep gulps of air, his chest pumping. His bunk wobbled as Larry stirred beneath him.

"What's the matter up there?"

Chris said nothing, panting.

"You all right?"

"A bad dream." He lay stiff, reliving it. The strength in Larry's arms. The feel of Rachel's body beneath him. Her drawing him under. His wish to remain upright but not without her. His head locked in her killing embrace. His giving up and drowning. The dream seemed to mean something, but he didn't want to figure it out. He sensed that the meaning wouldn't please him.

He listened to the rain on the roof, eight inches above his nose, and he tried to sleep. He was wide awake. He listened to the mice in the dresser. The rain diminished and he could hear the breathing of the unconscious men lying all about him. Larry's breathing was measured and wet. From the far wall came wheezes and soft whistles. For nearly two hours he lay awake, toying with the dream, approaching it and backing away from it, reliving it and modifying it. Finally he grew tired of it and gave all his attention to the slackening and recurring rain.

2

*B*REAKFAST WAS TOAST, JAM, eggs and grapefruit sections. Chris had no appetite. The other men ate fast, urged on by Blackie, who paced from the kitchen into the dining room and back again, speaking of ducks. For a man sick of ducks he put on a convincing performance:

"Git that food swallowed, you studs, this is the best hunting weather we've had since opening day. Rain and fifty-two degrees and a high wind from the northeast. Ducks flying all over hell. You'll shoot your limit before noon. Hurry up now, git yourselves out in the Marsh. Radio says rain and wind all day and the temperature dropping."

Two chairs stood at the foot of the table where last night there had been one. The plumber and Poo Poo sat side by side. The plumber was feeding her grapefruit with a spoon. She smiled blissfully, swallowing.

"Git that food in your bellies and pick up your guns. The guides'll take you Wisconsin and Vermont studs out with the tractor. Me, I'm taking these two guys from Rookery up to the big lake by way of the road. See if we can git some decent hunting up there. Like to see both these guys get their limit once, so they can go home and tell folks that when you hunt with Blackie LaVoi, you shoot ducks till your gun melts down." The plumber coughed and sneezed and gave his pipes a loud clearing. "I'm not going hunting today," he announced, wiping his nose.

Blackie raised his active eyebrow. "You staying in with Poo Poo?"

250

One quick nod. "This is my Poo Poo day." He explained to the other hunters, to his son, "When I hunt this camp, I like to have two days in the swamp and one day with Poo Poo. Right, Blackie?"

"You do for a fact."

"Besides, I've got a cold, haven't I, Poo Poo?"

She giggled. This morning she wore a flowered blouse and a pink ribbon in her hair. She fingered the plumber's gray beard, scratching him under the chin.

The plumber's day off was news to his son, who stopped eating and looked at his father. He seemed not dismayed, merely alert for instruction.

"It's all right, son," said the plumber, "you can go out with somebody else."

The boy glanced from one hunter to another. Who would have him? His eyes fell on the cheery Vermonter. The boy hoped he might hunt with him and his two sons. But this morning the Vermonter had eyes only for his black coffee. He bent over his mug, bathing his sickly face in the steam.

"If you wish to come with us," said Sanderson Bleekman, "you may."

Blackie said, "No, no! That would put three of you in a duckboat. That's suicide."

"Not in the Marsh it isn't," said Bleekman. "The water's shallow."

"But the bottom isn't."

"He can come with us," said Larry. "We'll be in lake boats."

Chris spilled his coffee, blurted, "No!"

"We'll take him with us," said Larry. "If we're going to have good shooting, he might as well get in on it."

"But I don't know, Larry..." He stopped before his voice revealed his panic.

"We'll take him with us," said Larry.

"I used to take Bruce hunting when he was that age. It's nice going hunting with a boy that age. You must have taken Billy."

"Billy wouldn't go."

Larry asked the boy, "What's your name?"

"Jim."

"It's settled, Jim. Come with us."

The boy looked at his father.

"Suit yourself," said the plumber. "Only today I hope you act like a hunter for a change—none of this day-dreaming and picking your nose."

Poo Poo pulled the plumber's face close and snickered into his beard. The boy looked back at Larry and nodded, a smile breaking across his fine, pale features. He said, "Yes, thank you."

Blackie said, "Come on, you studs, I hear the guides outside trying to start the tractor. You can't sit here stuffing your faces all day, it's already coming on dawn."

Chris followed the others out of the dining room, stunned, groping for a way to fit the boy into his plan.

Outside, mist and breeze—not rain and wind as Blackie had said. Nor was dawn breaking. The morning was black. Water dripped from the metal shade over the yardlight. The yard was mud.

Chris carried his backpack out to the car and then went back to the bunkhouse and brought out four shotguns—his own, Larry's, Jim's and Blackie's. He took from the trunk the quart and the pint of whiskey; he slipped the pint into the rubber poncho he wore, and he put the quart into the backpack. Then he returned for Larry, helped him out to the car. Around the corner of the building, from another door, Blackie led his wife with a stick—not a white cane, not a cane of any color, but a gnarled stick wrenched from a tree. The woman wore a scarf tied under her chin and a cloth coat with a brooch glinting at the lapel. Blackie settled her into the back seat while Chris settled Larry into the front; then both men went around the car and got in on the other side.

The plumber's boy dropped out of the bunkhouse and hopped into the front seat, Larry having moved to the middle to make room for him. The boy wore jeans and a light poplin jacket. "This is my birthday," he said.

"Where's your raincoat?" asked Larry. "You'll get drenched."

"I haven't got one." The boy sat on the edge of the seat, eager to go, his forehead against the windshield.

"Chris, have we got something he can wear?"

"Nothing waterproof!" he barked, feeling the day begin to slip from his control. What right had Larry to take command? How do you occupy a twelve-year-old while you kill a man?

"Go in and get your dad's raingear," said Larry.

"He doesn't have any either." The boy's words steamed the glass. "He never hunts in the rain."

Mrs. La Voi said, "Go in and ask Gladdy for something. We've got a closet full of clothes hunters have left behind."

The boy ran to the bunkhouse and in a few seconds came out wearing an eight-buckle coat of gray rubber with a large floppy hood—the coat of a fireman. It trailed on the ground as he walked.

The tractor and trailer chugged and rumbled out of the yard toward the dark Marsh, one of the guides driving, the other guide riding on the trailer with the four Vermonters.

Chris drove in the opposite direction, across the pasture and down the road to Hill. He felt eager and afraid. He gripped the steering wheel tight with both hands to keep from trembling.

At Hill's only intersection he turned right and traveled six miles west, the road narrowing and twisting where it led between swamps, widening and straightening where it ran between fields—six miles without passing a house or a crossroad.

Mrs. LaVoi said, "How long has it been since we were in a car, Blackie?"

"I was in a car last week. Those guys from Dakota took me into Hill to shoot pool."

"I believe the last time I was in a car was the day we buried my father. That was in '46. There was a procession of seven cars. Thirty-three years ago, think of it."

"I drove you into Hill just last month."

"That was in the pickup, Blackie. I'm talking about cars. It's over thirty years since I rode in a car."

"Pickups are the same as cars."

"Oh, Blackie, your pickup smells."

"We ride in taxis in Anaheim. Taxis are cars."

"No, they smell like buses."

Blackie directed Chris to turn right and they traveled north for six miles, fenceposts on their left, swamp grass on their right. Along the way a turtle in the road. A skunk. A rabbit. A cat.

"This is a lovely ride," said Mrs. LaVoi. "What sort of car are we riding in?"

"Chevrolet," said Chris.

"It smells so nice. Is this a leather seat?"

"Vinyl."

"A lovely ride. Smooth as a barge on the Nile."

"Jesus," said Blackie.

Larry, smoking, chuckled through his nose.

Mrs. LaVoi said, "Riding makes me light-headed. I'm the queen of Egypt, Blackie, who are you?"

"What the hell are you talking about?"

Larry said, "You married royalty, Blackie. Her name is Cleopatra."

"Yes, that's my name," she said. "And the driver, I believe, is Sextus Pompeius, and his friend is Mark Antony and the boy is my young servant and this is all comic relief."

"Jesus," said Blackie.

"And you are a clown."

Larry laughed.

"How I loved that play as a girl. There's heroic business going on in that play. Heroic fighting. Heroic love. I used to know pages and pages by heart, but I've lost it all, I can't remember a line."

The road curved right and grew bumpy with stones and narrowed to two ruts with a ridge of grass in the middle. It was raining.

She said, "You know, there aren't many heroes anymore. At least not in western Canada. I married one of the few. Right, Blackie?"

He agreed: "That's what it says in *Sports Afield*."

The road became the driveway into Lawler's Resort

and led to the back door of the two-story house.

Blackie said, "Let the wife out here and then drive on down to where the boats are."

Chris pulled up to the back stoop on his left, hoping the heavy rain would continue and retard the break of day, for it occurred to him that he might drown Larry within the next ten minutes—as they got into the boats in the dark. A light went on over the door and a woman —Kate Lawler—came outside with a newspaper over her head. She wore Levi's and a checkered red shirt. Blackie rolled down his window. "Get her out the other side."

The woman went around in front of the headlights (she looked forty; she was lean and wiry; she wore several large rings on the hand that held the newspaper) and she helped Mrs. LaVoi out of the back seat, both women exclaiming what pleasure this visit was sure to give them.

"Albert has your boats ready," the woman said to Blackie. She closed the door.

Albert? Who was Albert?

Hand in hand they passed in front of the car, Mrs. LaVoi poking her stick before her, and they stepped up on the stoop.

Larry told Chris to roll down his window and he leaned, or rather toppled, across the steering wheel and called, "Wait, Mrs. LaVoi, I want to tell you something."

Both women turned. Mrs. LaVoi clamped her stick under her arm and cupped her ear.

Larry said, "I'm *dying*, Egypt, *dying*!"

Mrs. LaVoi's eyes were aimed at a point above the car, as though the message had come from the sky.

Chris drove ahead, along the row of five cabins, all of which appeared deserted—no lights in the windows, none of yesterday's cars parked nearby. He stopped at the edge of the grass, where the land tipped down toward the water. He and Larry and the boy peered past the swinging windshield wipers at the wild lake, at the faint dawn. Here the wind was stronger; waves washed in from the northeast, splaying foam up the stony beach. The rain diminished. A dock, dismantled for the season, was piled in sections on the grass, beyond reach of next spring's crushing ice floes. At the edge of the water two boats stood ready. Into one of them a young man wearing rubber boots and a rubber parka was dumping an armload of decoys. Seeing the headlights, he walked uphill toward the car.

"That's Lawler's grandson, name's Albert," said Blackie. "They claim he's a nice enough kid, but I never could stomach his grandfather. He used to steal beavers from my traps."

Chris opened his window and the young man said, "This'll be the best day of shooting so far. Ducks'll be down from the north today." He thrust his hand in at the window. "Name's Albert."

"Chris here." He shook the hand. Albert had a blunt face, a wide blunt smile.

"I got you two boats ready with ten-horse motors and about a dozen decoys, but if you want to stay and hunt the shoreline with me, you're welcome. Today the shoreline ought to be as good as the island."

"No, we want to hunt the island."

The young man looked into the back seat. "Hi, Blackie, what kind of a season are you having down there in the Marsh?"

"Can't complain. Averaging six, eight hunters a week."

"We haven't been doing all that great here. Weather's been too nice. This week we had four cabins full of hunters, but they all took off last night. I told them to wait one more day and they'd see ducks, but after a week of sun they gave up and went home. If you want to hunt the shoreline with me, you're welcome."

"Makes me no difference," said Blackie. "It's up to these sharpshooters from Rookery. I'm just along for the ride."

"We'll hunt the island," said Chris. His voice was tight, impatient.

"You could save yourselves a bumpy ride out there and back. Waves are kicking up."

"Let's git," said Blackie, stepping out.

As they stood at the trunk uncasing the shotguns, the plumber's boy carelessly swung his gun in a circle and didn't understand why the four men flinched and Blackie shouted angrily.

Larry drew the boy around to the side of the car. While Chris slipped into his hip boots and buckled them to his belt and Blackie and Albert carried the backpack and guns to the boats, Larry instructed the boy in the handling of firearms.

The boy, an eager listener, looked up at him, nodding, intent on his words.

Chris and the boy helped Larry into his boots and then they helped him down the stony beach. The wet wind felt very cold.

The boats were sixteen-footers, three-seaters. They had high gunwales for riding out stormy weather. Each was equipped with two oars as well as an outboard motor. Blackie and the plumber's boy got into the boat with the decoys, and Albert shoved them afloat.

"Jesus, with service like this I ought to hunt here more often," said Blackie. He sat in the stern and pulled the starter rope and the motor sputtered to life. He opened the throttle, turned in a splashy arc and headed into the wind, climbing and dropping over the waves.

Standing beside the other boat, Larry said, "Let me run the motor."

"Okay, okay!" Of all days for Larry to assert himself!

Larry glanced at him with curiosity, surprised by his abrupt tone.

"Okay," Chris said softly, as he sat Larry down on the stern seat. Then with Albert's help Chris pushed the boat into the water and hopped in and sat on the middle seat. He pulled on the oars to keep the boat from washing back on the beach as Larry twisted around and studied the motor.

"Pull out the choke," Albert called. "Then pull the rope. Then push *in* the choke."

"I know," said Larry. He pulled out the choke. He pulled feebly on the starter rope. Four, five, six times he pulled, but without enough snap to ignite a spark.

The keel rasped on the stones and Chris strained harder at the oars, working against the waves and against the stiffness left in his muscles from yesterday's paddling in the Marsh. With the boat ten yards out and pointed toward the island, Chris stood up, stepped—or rather lurched—astern, reached over Larry's shoulder and gave the rope a sharp tug. The motor started and he sat back down. Larry pushed in the choke, accelerated and faced forward into the rain. Larry was stirred to excitement by the rough water, by the boat rearing up over the crest of each wave and thudding down into its trough. When Chris glanced at him, his rain-beaded face broke into a small, pure grin. Larry as helmsman looked like the Larry of old, hale and young, his left hand behind him on the throttle, his right elbow resting on his forward knee, his raincoat concealing the angles and hollows of his emaciated body, his wind squint replacing his aching stare. Chris recalled how effortless it had been to like Larry in the days when he had looked like that, in the days when he was likable. Now liking him was hard work (though loving him was not), and it was easy to forget the steady pleasure of their early friendship, the buoyancy they had felt in each other's company how satisfying—after all this time of supporting Larry, lifting him, guiding him—to be driven across this water by him, following in the foamy wake of Blackie's boat. For a moment he had almost forgotten he meant to murder him. Chris turned on his seat and faced forward. Ahead, beyond Blackie and the boy, beyond the rain-veiled island, gray daylight was enlarging like a blot.

3

I N   T H E   L E E   O F the island Blackie and the boy floated on the calm water and waited for the other boat.

"Does this island have a name?" the boy asked, looking out from the heap of his rubber coat.

"No." Blackie picked up a pair of decoys that were tangled by their weight strings.

"Does Poo Poo have a name?" The rain plopped loudly on the boy's stiff rubber hood. "I mean, a real name?"

Blackie shrugged. "I guess Poo Poo's her real name." He worked at unknotting the strings, holding the decoys at arm's length, which was as close as he could focus his eye.

"You guess? Aren't you her dad?"

"Naw." Blackie gave up and threw both decoys into the water; they floated side by side, one bottom-up. "At least not that I know of." He picked up another tangled cluster.

"I have a sister named Mary," said the boy. "She's fifteen."

At the approach of the second boat, Blackie pointed to a stand of reeds, into which Larry steered as he cut the motor. The reeds parted at the bow and closed at the stern as the boat drifted silently into a small cover—a natural blind.

Blackie left seven decoys floating at the edge of the reeds and then rowed in close. "Here's the plan," he said, turning his frayed collar up against the rain. "The four of us will hunt the four sides of the island. I'm leaving half the decoys here and I'll put the other half down on the south end, where there's another little bay like this. That's where I'll park this boat. No use putting decoys out on the north side, or the east. Water's too rough. Ducks'll want to land where it's calm."

"I'll hunt the north side," said Chris, thinking of his stone seat, his throne of vision.

Blackie frowned. "Don't you want the south—over the decoys?"

"You take the south."

"You'll get more shooting over the decoys."

"You're the best shot." From the backpack lying at his feet, Chris drew out the quart bottle.

Blackie shook his head. "You guys are quite the hunters."

"I want the boy here with me," said Larry, peering out from under the dripping bill of his corduroy cap.

Blackie said, "Then who covers the east?"

"Hell with the east, I want the boy here with me."

Chris said nothing, but he seethed with frustration. Larry was creating chaos.

"Suit yourself." Blackie poled his boat closer. The boy jumped out and crossed on submerged stones to the other boat and climbed in. He stood his gun up in the bow, its stock resting on coils of anchor rope, and he sat on the bow seat—all this with a noisy creaking of his stiff rubber coat.

"See you guys later," said Blackie, poling himself away.

Chris had to act. It was time to regain control of this day. "Wait," he said, holding up the bottle of whiskey.

Blackie poled back, took the quart, drank, grimaced, drank again. "Thanks." He handed over the bottle, departed again. Out beyond the reedbed he shipped his oar and turned to the motor. He pulled out the choke. With his hand poised on the starter rope he said, "Most of the bird's'll be flying in from the north, MacKensie, so holler when you see them coming."

"Will do."

Blackie pulled the rope and sped off in the rain, south, disappearing around the curve of the island.

Chris reached into his backpack for his thermos and three plastic cups. He poured coffee, then handed one cup to the boy, another to Larry. His own cup and Larry's he spiked with whiskey.

Larry sipped. "Strong."

"Keeps you warm."

"Where did that whiskey come from?"

"Portage la Prairie. Last night while you were sleeping."

The wind was growing stronger and the wet reeds bent over them, brushing their heads and shoulders as they drank. Rain made small ripples in their cups. It was fully daylight now, as light as this day would be.

Larry drained his coffee and handed the cup to Chris.

"Look!" said the boy, pointing at a pair of ducks flying toward them from the mainland, low, beating hard against the wind.

Larry twisted around to face out over the stern. He sat stockstill, uttered a long soft "Ohhh" and then performed an act of such virtuosity that Chris felt his heart skip. Bringing his gun up to his shoulder, Larry fired and killed the duck on the left, and before it hit the water, he was already swinging and firing at the second duck, which folded and somersaulted and fell near shore. His movements were sheer grace; not even in Owl Brook had he shot with more precision; he had drawn a perfect circle in the air, raising the muzzle of the gun not to the duck but to the point where duck and shot would intersect, and he had fired with the gun moving, swinging to the right to meet the second duck, fired again and lowered the gun to his lap

Chris said, "God, just like the old days."

"Ooohhhh." Larry drooped slump-shouldered and limp, as though his chest had caved in. "Christ Almighty, did that feel good."

The second duck lay in the reeds. Chris got out, waded over to the bird and picked it up—a thick-feathered hen mallard, a line of bloodspots beading across its breast. He returned to the boat, stood beside it. Larry was still hunched over.

"You all right, Larry?"

Larry didn't look up. He was shaking his head slowly from side to side and breathing heavily. "Sort of dizzy." His shoulders heaved. His wet hands, resting on the gun in his lap, trembled.

"What is it, Larry?"

No reply. To call up his old grace with gun and shell, Larry had reached far into the past. On this gray day of 1979 he had brought forth for about three seconds the Larry Quinn of 1961, and it had sapped him. Time warps didn't come cheap.

Chris dropped the duck between the bow and middle seat. The boy bent over to study it.

Larry straightened up. There was a flash of something in his eyes—an animation that reminded Chris for a moment of the *Twelfth Night* crisis, the darting eyes of lunacy. But this was different. This looked like hopeful excitement, eagerness.

"When's the last time I dropped two for two, Chris?"

"Not since Owl Brook, I guess."

"My heart's pounding like I'd been running."

"Let it pound, that was nice shooting." His own heart pounded with astonishment at the liveliness in Larry's face. Killing someone who wanted to live was not a mercy.

"Yes," the boy piped up, "that was nice shooting."

Larry turned and nodded at the boy, then looked back at Chris. "For a second there I had the damn best feeling I've had in years. I felt like there was nothing wrong with me."

"Do it again," Chris said halfheartedly, pointing at a flock of bluebills sailing over the reeds. He crouched beside the boat, water pouring into his right boot, chilling his thigh. Larry again raised his gun as though by habit, not willpower, and he fired and killed the lead duck. The others flew overhead, swift on the wind, and Chris fired at them going away, dropping one.

Larry groaned, "Oooohhh," then slumped, shaking his head. He drew labored breaths. Chris laid a hand on his shoulder, waiting for the trembling to subside. These two ducks and the one Larry had shot earlier were small dark lumps on the waves, floating away. Chris heard the sputter of Blackie's motor and in a few seconds he saw him heading out to retrieve the birds. The front end of Blackie's boat was weightless and high, waggling in the wind.

"Beautiful shot," said Chris. He reached into the boat for the whiskey.

"Yes, beautiful shot," said the boy. The boy's gun stood behind him in the bow. He had made no move to pick it up and fire at the flock. More interesting to the boy than hunting was the behavior of these two hunters, the crippled man killing ducks and then deflating with a groan and the other man acting nervous. The other man, he noticed, was attentive to the crippled man yet attentive in an awkward manner; there was something forced and false about the way he put his hand on the crippled man's shoulder, something less than joyous about his "Beautiful shot." And the healthy man's bottle of whiskey! One thing the plumber *had* taught his son was that you must never mix guns with booze. The crippled man's face looked different now. High emotion had turned his gray face rosy; suppressed tears had reddened the white of his eyes.

"I'm feeling two things at once, Chris"—he rolled his head and looked far off—"I feel good, and I feel like dying."

"Here, have a swig."

Larry pushed the bottle aside. "I have this sense of what it used to be like to be normal, and I have this sense of dying." He swung his intense brown eyes back at Chris—pained eyes, yet shining. "Normal and dying."

"Forget about dying." He would be dead soon enough.

"I *can't*, for Christ's sake!" Larry wrenched himself around on his seat and faced south, toward the spot where Blackie's boat bounced on the waves. I feel..." He took a deep breath. "Chris, when that last duck came down I felt like I was twenty-five again." His voice rose and broke.

Chris squeezed his shoulder but quickly drew back as though singed by a flame. He sloshed away and raised his binoculars. On the mainland Albert, as yesterday, crouched under the willow tree.

Larry turned to the boy. "For a second there I felt like I was *twelve!*"

The boy blinked and lowered his eyes as though from too much light. He picked up the dead duck at his feet and set it on his lap. He parted the beak. He opened an eyelid. He watched the beak go slowly shut. The shiny eye stayed open, a polished black marble.

Larry raised his voice: "Do you remember that first duck season, Chris? When Rachel went along?"

Chris, knee-deep in water, eyebrow-deep in reeds didn't answer. He dropped his binoculars and drank again. He capped the bottle and slipped it into his poncho. He returned to the boat. "I'll be back after a while. Help yourself to some lunch." He picked his gun out of the boat and climbed the rocky slope to think, to plan, to evade the net of confusion that Larry was casting over the day.

High at the center of the island Chris stopped and looked down at the boat and tried to convince himself that what he had seen in Larry's eyes was not a flash of joy or hope or a renewed urge to live. Let it be wild desperation, insanity, anything else. What if Larry wanted to go on living? What if this journey brought Larry to life instead of death? Down there, crouched in the reeds, Larry appeared to be coming further to life with each duck he dropped. Could Chris kill a man who wished to live? Could he kill a man in love with life in order to clear a path to love? No. The mercy of this killing depended on two conditions—Rachel's magnetism and Larry's death wish—the second as essential as the first.

Making his way down the slope toward Blackie's cove, Chris told himself that Larry's excitement was momentary. Surely his brief triumph over despondency and death would leave him weaker than ever, not

stronger. A few hours in the wet wind, straining to accomplish one fine shot after another, and Larry's spirit
would be worn down to its irreducible nub of despair.
Let him fire away. A fitting end to his life, actually—
making these expert shots during his last hours. Chris
would tell Bruce about them; he would tell Rachel. Let
him shoot. Let him groan with pleasure as the birds fell
to the water.

Dropping down to the water's edge, Chris conceived a
simple, foolproof plan. Here in the south cove the reeds
were sparse, but in Larry's cove they were thick enough
to block the view from the mainland. No need to drag
Larry around to the north side. At the end of the day's
hunt merely send the boy down here to the south cove to
join Blackie for the trip to shore. With Blackie stewed, it
would take them awhile to gather up the decoys and
motor around to the west cove—and there they would
find Chris pulling Larry's body from the water and calling for help.

When Blackie returned from retrieving the three
ducks and came slicing through his flotilla of decoys,
Chris was waiting for him. Standing on a flat rock at the
water's edge, he held out the quart of whiskey and
Blackie cut the motor and coasted to a perfect mooring,
his outstretched hand closing around the bottle as the
boat ran aground in the reeds.

"How many of these are yours?" asked Blackie. The
three ducks lay at his feet.

"One. I shot the last one."

"You mean Quinn dropped the first three?" Blackie's
good eye brightened like a proud father's. "Those first
two quick shots were his?" His cocked eye remained
dark and skeptical.

Chris nodded.

Blackie laughed. "I'll be a son of a whore." He drank
deeply.

Hearing distant shots, they turned toward Lawler's
Resort, which was momentarily obscured by a rain-
squall. A dozen mallards flew out of the squall toward

Larry's blind. Blackie and Chris watched the birds lift and split into two groups before they heard the shot that caused them to do so—a near miss by Larry. A moment later they saw one of the birds crumple and fall among the rocks at the center of the island and then they heard the shot that killed it—Larry's fourth direct hit.

Blackie laughed again. "I'll be a son of a whore." He drank again.

"I see where it came down." Chris moved up out of the reeds.

"Here, take your bottle before I drink it all."

"That's what it's for."

"No, take it. You'll need it to keep warm over there on the north side."

"I've got my own." Chris took out his pint and showed him.

Blackie reached into his jacket and took out a pint of his own, and laughed. He proudly displayed the label—Jack Daniel's.

"Well, I'll be a son of a whore," said Chris. He took the quart and climbed the hill.

He walked in circles, combing the crest for the fallen duck. In a few minutes the boy came up the west slope to help him search. Back and forth they walked until the boy shrieked, startling Chris and causing Larry to turn and look uphill. The boy was pointing to a patch of this-tles where the wounded mallard was lodged head-down in a stony crevice, its webbed feet swimming in the air. Chris snatched up the bird and quickly wrung its neck. He held it high for Larry to see and Larry nodded, then turned back to the water, drawing his raincoat tightly around him. Chris noticed that Blackie's attention, too, had been drawn by the boy's shriek. He held the duck up for Blackie to see. Blackie held up his Jack Daniel's.

"Tell Larry, 'Nice shot.'" He handed the duck to the boy, who took it delicately by one foot and skittered downhill to the boat.

4

SITTING ON HIS THRONE of rock, facing north, Chris knew that this would be the longest, most wretched day of his life. He adjusted his poncho to keep water from running in around his neck and to keep his gun dry across his lap. He pulled his cap low to keep the flying mist out of his eyes. The poncho was too short to prevent the seat of his pants from absorbing moisture from the rock, and the bill of his cap was too short to prevent water from dripping on his nose. He sighed and shivered. He squinted into the wind and tried to get a grip on yesterday's vision—the memories, the plans— but the sagging sky concealed most of the lake and he couldn't seem to budge his thinking forward or backward. There was only the soggy present and the absurdity of being led in pursuit of a dream to this miserable outcropping of rock in Lake Manitoba; the nonsense of sharing an island with a landlord from Anaheim who passed for a legendary woodsman; the stupid bad luck of babysitting a twelve-year-old who served, without knowing it, as Larry's bodyguard.

The morning passed slowly, slowly. Eight thirty. Nine. Over the rush of wind sounded the fitful popping of shotguns far away in the Marsh, and occasionally louder reports from Blackie's blind and Larry's. Half a dozen times Blackie's motor started with a sputter and its whine faded across the water and returned in a few minutes to the south cove.

Nine thirty. Ten. Gradually Chris's mind detached itself from the discomfort of the moment and began to wander. It went back to the Fawn River Health Center

—Larry behind glass—and forward to the killing—Larry underwater. The first image was incomplete without the second. Behind glass, Larry had begged Rachel for death, and today he would die. Chris wanted it to be now, this instant, for he had been up and down the scale of determination a thousand times, resolved one moment, uncertain the next, and while his determination this morning was as high as ever—not even in his dream had he felt so ready to kill—he was beginning to feel the strain of holding his will at this pitch. He feared that his resolution, like the muscles of his shoulders and arms, might be growing numb from overuse, and the longer he waited, the greater the chance of a disastrous hitch between thought and action.

But, no question, he must wait until the four of them made ready to leave the island, the day's hunt ending either because of a full limit or fading daylight. A full limit wasn't likely—they had yesterday's limit to fill as well—so surely it would be midafternoon or later before he could order the boy out of Larry's boat and into Blackie's for the trip home. The boy was smart, observant, not the type to be ordered about unreasonably. The boy, as well as Blackie, it seemed, had a high regard for Larry. Chris must do nothing to arouse their suspicions.

Suspicions and the risk of being arrested for murder —Chris had been skirting this topic for weeks, refusing to face it head-on, telling himself it was a prospect so unlikely as to be inconceivable. Well, wasn't it inconceivable? What possible evidence would he leave? On the back of Larry's head and neck any bruises where he placed his hands to hold him under could just as well be the traces left by a rescuer in mouth-to-mouth resuscitation. And what was improbable about Larry's tipping the boat as they picked up decoys, the two of them falling out opposite sides and Chris unable to reach Larry and pull him to shore before it was too late to revive him— though he tried?

"I tried mouth-to-mouth but it did no good," Chris rehearsed silently, rising from his seat of stone and pacing in a circle.

He sat down again and watched the waves break on the rocks below him. Eleven o'clock. Eleven thirty.

"Jesus, no wonder we aren't shooting hardly any ducks!" This was Blackie suddenly standing beside him on the stone seat and nudging him with the toe of his boot. "They're mostly coming over us from the north and you're sitting there with your cap over your eyes."

Chris, looking up, irritated, was chilled by a runnel of rain down his spine. He wished Blackie would stay in one place. Every unexpected movement on the island was somehow a potential flaw in the plan.

"There's been whole flocks coming over from the north and we been seeing them too late. You're supposed to holler when they come." Blackie's tongue was thick.

"Here, have a drink." Chris held up the bottle.

"Don't mind if I do. My pint's dead." Blackie stepped down to a lower level in order to talk face to face. Pickled, he stood stiffly at arms, his gun on his shoulder, his chest out, his fly unzipped, his good eye bleared by booze. He drank and handed back the bottle. He turned and looked north, shielding his eyes, his torn sleeve hanging loose from his elbow. His short canvas jacket, where it covered him, was greasy with age and keeping him dry. Water beaded across his shoulders and ran down his back. But his pants and black cap and sleeveless right arm were drenched. "I thought more ducks would be flying today."

"So did I." Chris searched the clouds, which were lower and darker than before.

"I picked a total of nine off the water so far. That's nowhere near our limit, if we count the boy."

A shot from Larry's blind. Blackie looked up and said, "Here they come." He crouched stiffly, not quickly. He took aim, his gun wavering, and fired into a flock of eight or ten bluebills. Nothing dropped. Squatting, swiveling on his right foot to fire again, he lost his balance, slipped off the rock and landed on a lower one with a squawk of pain. His gun clattered downhill and came to rest in weeds.

Chris sprang to his feet. Below him, Blackie got to his

knees and then collapsed face-down, his back bucking, the fall having knocked the wind out of him. Chris laid his gun on the stone seat and went to him, rolled him over on his back and sharply lifted his waist three or four times. With each lift, Blackie's mouth came open in a noisy suck of air—a backward cough—and soon he was nodding, his breathing free.

Chris went farther downhill to pick up the gun, and when he returned, Blackie was on his hands and knees, muttering. Chris tried to help him up, but Blackie shook his head, needing more time to settle his breathing and clear his brain. On all fours, swaybacked and hanging his head, he reminded Chris of Ms. Rover, who used to stand like that for minutes on end, her head down, her eyes on the rug or the grass, as though lost in a long thought. Blackie's hunting clothes were spotted in much the same design and colors as the dog's coat had been— indistinct splotches of dark and light.

"Get up." Chris wanted Blackie to return to his boat and stay put. He slipped his hand under Blackie's arms, but Blackie swatted him away and got to his feet un- aided—slowly, cringing with pain, his teeth on edge. He stood in a stiff crouch, favoring his right side. With his left hand he explored his ribs under his sleeveless right arm.

"Feels like I skinned myself good." He felt further, under his jacket. He grimaced at the sky. Though full of pain, his expression struck Chris as comic—good eye shut, dead one open, teeth bared, mustache dripping.

"Look here." Blackie opened his jacket and shirt and peered with Chris at a large bloody bruise close up under his armpit.

"Lucky you didn't break a rib," Chris told him.

"Might as well have. This'll stiffen me up for the rest of the season. Of all the shit-eating luck."

They climbed to the stone seat. Blackie said, "I'm hungry. I'm going down to Quinn's boat and have me a bite; then I'm coming back here to take your place."

"No, no, go back to your cove. The shooting's better over your decoys, and I'm a poor shot."

"My shoulder's too sore to shoot, so I'll sit here and be lookout while you sit in my boat and hit 'em or miss 'em. Probably all you need is practice."

A logical arrangement. Nothing to argue about. "All right, as long as we go back to Lawler's in the same boats we came out in. I'm responsible for Larry, after all."

"Right." Blackie started off toward Larry's cove.

"Here, take some painkiller with you." Chris held out the quart.

Blackie came back and grasped it by the neck and trudged away, listing to the right, his elbow tight to his wound.

Chris picked up his gun and went over the crest and down into the south cove.

5

A T TWO O'CLOCK THE sky brightened and
the wind blew dry. The clouds did not lift, but they
thinned, and as a glow of sunshine filtered through them
and spread over the lake, the plumber's son came down
the slope to the south cove and stood on a rock near the
boat. Chris facing the water, his ears full of wind, didn't
notice, and when the boy said, "Hi," Chris jumped.

"Blackie wants to know how many ducks you've
shot."

"Three." Since getting into Blackie's boat, Chris—
killing time—had killed three birds in eight shots and
had motored out to retrieve them. To ward off the chills,
he had been sipping whiskey, and to maintain his mur-
derous intentions, he had been calling up memories of
Larry at his most disconsolate.

"I shot one that was sitting on the water. My dad will
be glad to know I shot at least one."

"How many has Larry shot? How's he doing?"
Nearly five hours had passed since he left Larry's boat.
He didn't want to see Larry again until the fatal minute.

"I think he shot seven. He's having a real good time,
he says. He and Blackie have been telling stories."

Chris was surprised, troubled. "I thought Blackie was
over on the north side."

"No, he's been in the boat with us all the time, drinking. Once time way up north he killed a bear with a sharp
stick. Do you believe that?"

"Has Larry been drinking?"

"No, just coffee."

Chris looked the boy over. The hem of his rubber coat

272

hung over the rock and into the water. His floppy hood
hung over his brow. There was something intense and
unsettling in his eyes, as though he were reading things
in Chris's face, and so, fearing that his thoughts were
betrayed in his expresssion, Chris forced a smile and
said, "Are you having a good time?" He must appear
cool. It was important that the boy think well of him.

"My gun kicks real hard, so I don't like to shoot it,
but I always like to go hunting. My dad says it's the best
time of your life—going hunting."

"I'm giving up hunting."

"You are? How come?"

"It isn't the best time of my life anymore."

The boy drew his face into a serious squint. "I don't
think my dad will ever quit hunting. I know *I* never will."

"You can't tell, you might change your mind someday." Despite the killing that crowded his mind, or perhaps because of it, Chris was captivated by the boy's
open, innocent face, the way he listened, his look of ab-
sorption. You won the confidence of a boy like this—as
Larry and Blackie had apparently been doing—with
stories. "When I was your age, I loved to hunt. Pheasants mostly. There were a lot of pheasants around where
I lived."

"My dad says when you shoot a pheasant in the heart,
it flies toward the sun."

Chris nodded. "I've seen pheasants do that, fly
straight up toward the sun after they'd been hit. But I
don't know how you'd tell whether they were shot in the
heart. But yes, I've seen a lot of them do that. And then
all of a sudden they fold up and drop." Chris couldn't
take his eyes from the boy. Something about his sandy
eyelashes and pale cheeks struck him as familiar. Whom
did he resemble?

"My dad says next year we're going to hunt pheasants
in Nebraska."

Suddenly Chris thought: Peter! This boy reminded
him of Peter Ellis, one of his boyhood friends, his first
friend to die. Now *there* was a story.

"When I was your age, I had a friend who got very sick and died."

The boy put his hand to his mouth. "What of?" He appeared to be holding his breath in dread.

"Rheumatic fever. Ever heard of it?"

"Yes."

"It weakens the heart."

The boy leaned forward on his rock, fearful yet eager for details.

"I haven't thought of Peter Ellis for years and now I see him plain as day. I'll tell you about him."

The boy climbed into the boat and sat in the bow. He adjusted the hood around his face and then he drew his hands up into his rubber sleeves to keep them warm.

"It was 1944." Chris rummaged around in his memory, searching for the proper opening; he wanted the boy to be impressed. "In the summer of 1944, polio was the main crippler and killer of boys and girls." A good opening. Morbid enough to be gripping—he could tell by the boy's satisfied look. "But my friend Peter Ellis surprised everybody by getting rheumatic fever instead. He stayed home through the school year, growing thinner and weaker all the while, and in the spring, after he turned twelve, he died and was buried in a cloudburst."

"I'm twelve today."

A gust of wind rocked the boat.

"Although he never complained, it must have been a lonesome year for Peter. His doctor told him to stay home in bed and I don't think he had many visitors, except for relatives. I was the only friend who went to see him regularly—every Saturday morning."

Chris paused to think of himself at eleven, walking along the path behind the row of small houses at the edge of Haymarket, Minnesota. Between his own house and Peter's there were three others: the Grangers' (three apple trees in the backyard), the Tylers' (white cats sleeping on the sunny back stoop), and the Sorensons' (a yardful of rusty farm machinery). Peter's was the smallest house.

"Yes?" The plumber's son prodded.

"Peter's house faced the highway, which in those days was only a narrow gravel road, but it was our link with the outside world, and Peter's mother moved his bed into the living room where he could watch the traffic go by.... There wasn't much traffic, it was wartime.... Peter read a lot and worked with his stamp collection."

Chris recalled Peter's mother, a widow who cleaned houses for the well-to-do. She was the sort of person who smiled so easily you sometimes wondered if she was in her right mind. Though nursing a dying son, she always wore a bright look when she opened the kitchen door to let Chris in. She had two older daughters who were married to farmers; she saw a lot of them, probably drew strength from them.

"Yes, what else?"

"Peter's father was dead. I don't remember what he died of. Maybe he died in the war. There was a picture of him on Peter's dresser. He wore a suit and a tie in the picture, not a uniform. And he was bald." Images sealed away for thirty-five years came welling up and spilling across Chris's memory.

"The living room was small. Peter's bed was by the window. His dresser blocked the front door.... 'This seeing the sick endears them to us,' said Hopkins, the poet, and of course he was right." Chris paused to consider the horrible irony in what this endearment, in Larry's case, was leading to.

"Seeing Peter Ellis every week endeared him to me. As I approached his house, I always felt reluctant to go in, especially if my other friends in the neighborhood were outside calling to me, but as soon as I settled down in the chair beside his bed, I was content to stay for a while, sometimes on into the afternoon. We listened to the radio—*Grand Central Station* I liked best. We talked. We looked at stamps."

The diffused sunlight faded from the lake, upper layers of cloud having fit themselves together again. The day grew dark as twilight.

"Peter got me interested in stamp collecting. I was hooked the first time I walked into his room and saw his stamp books and stamp catalogues and packages of stamps and a saucer holding tiny paper hinges for gluing stamps in books. I can still see a stamp from some nation on the Baltic Sea—a sailboat with a billowing yellow sail. He held it with a tweezers. It was a hot drizzly day and Peter's window was open and the room smelled of rain and his bed was rumpled and all the trappings of his hobby were lying across his bunched-up blankets. 'Stamp collecting is a good hobby for rainy days,' he told me as he held up another stamp and studied it through a magnifying glass. It sounded like something you might hear from adults; it wasn't the sort of thing you expected a boy to say. I suppose he was repeating what he had been told by whoever gave him the stamp album—probably one of his sisters who had said it to cover up the truth of the matter, which was that stamp collecting was a good hobby for invalids. Which is true, of course: stamp collecting *is* a good hobby for invalids; but Peter lived by the principle that stamps were for rainy days, and he never looked at them when the sun was shining. He only worked with his stamps when it rained."

The plumber's son left the bow, stepped over the middle seat and sat down on the stern seat next to Chris. "What did you and Peter talk about?"

Chris pictured himself as a boy, sitting in the soft chair by Peter's bed, their conversation threading itself through the late morning and early afternoon and interrupted when Mrs. Ellis brought them sandwiches and milk. What did they talk about? From all those hours of conversation, only two statements survived these thirty-five years—Peter's declaration about stamps on rainy days, and Peter's saying, one morning as he pointed across the highway at the distant athletic field, "I can see you guys playing football over there after school." He meant Chris and several other of his classmates. There wasn't a trace of jealousy or bitterness in his voice; he seemed to speak entirely out of pleasure, glad to see his friends have fun. But what, after all, could he see? The athletic field was at least a quarter mile from his window and his friends couldn't have been more than a cluster of shapes moving up and down the field.

And, oh, yes, they talked about the weather. "We talked a lot about clouds. From Peter's window we had the best view in town of the weather approaching out of Dakota. You know how old people dwell on the weather, particularly old men who have been out in all kinds of weather all their lives. Old farmers, for instance. Well, Peter had this old man's knack of talking about the weather—maybe because he had two brothers-in-law who were farmers or maybe because he himself was old before his time. At the age of eleven he was about as old as he was going to get."

The plumber's boy looked at the weather, tipping his face to the low sky. He clenched the floppy hood tight under his chin. Chris, feeling him shiver, put his arm around his shoulders. The boy lowered his head and nestled into his side. He said, "What did Peter look like?"

Chris was about to say, "He looked something like you," but didn't. He said, "He was very pale. He kept shrinking as the months went by because his appetite weakened along with his heart. His brothers-in-law, the farmers, were very fond of Peter and they never came to town that they didn't stop in at the house to visit him. One of these men was upset by how thin Peter was getting, and he used to bring him things to eat, hoping to fatten him up. Rich feed fattened his livestock and he couldn't understand why rich food didn't fatten Peter. One day he brought him a quart of vanilla ice cream and he demanded that Peter eat it all at once. He did this early one Saturday morning—he had just been to the creamery—and when I showed up for my visit, the brother-in-law was gone and Peter was bloated and amused, patting his belly and laughing about how he had eaten that whole quart of ice cream while his brother-in-law sat beside his bed and wouldn't leave until he was finished. He liked both of his brothers-in-law. He was proud of them."

The boy said, "I have two uncles in Milwaukee.

They're very nice." He bent his head to the water. "But the ice cream didn't make him better?"

"No, it didn't. Peter just kept shrinking till he died. And that was that." The boy looked up, his face so vulnerable that Chris decided to stop the story, afraid that the rest of it might do him damage. Was the boy softening him up? Was he growing too sensitive to kill? No—he checked his determination; it still ran high—but his mood, his thinking, craved a balance; his dark motives, it seemed, required a counterpoint of light.

"Let's talk about something cheerful." He wanted to hear the boy laugh as he had when his father told of driving on the ice—a pure, full-hearted laugh.

"Tell me some more about Peter. Tell me about when he died."

Chris said, "I suppose you're right." This puzzled the boy. What Chris meant was that a story, once begun, had to be finished. Unfair to begin a tale and stop in the middle. The same with any act or gesture—the act of love, or murder. Once the course was set, there was no graceful way to stop undone. "Follow through," he told the boy. "Always follow through."

The boy nodded. This was shooting advice—the swing of the shotgun as you fired—he had heard it from his father. "But my gun kicks," he said.

Chris patted him lightly on the shoulder. "Peter turned twelve in April and died in May. I don't remember the details, whether he died peacefully or not, whether during the day or night. Maybe I never knew. All I know is that one day he was dead, and the last time I went to the Ellis house was with my parents to see his body. It was a warm sunny evening and after supper we walked along the path behind the houses, my dad first, my mother next, me behind. The apple trees were in blossom and smelled very sweet. My mother reached up and snapped off a blossom and put it in my buttonhole. We went into Mrs. Ellis's kitchen and there were her two daughters and the two farmers and their children. It was very crowded in the kitchen, but that's where we all stayed, except for maybe a minute when we went into the living room to take a look at Peter. The sun was low and red coming through the front window, and I positioned myself at the foot of the coffin so that whenever I glanced toward the body, I was blinded by the sun and didn't have to see him dead. After a minute—maybe it was half a minute—we went back to the kitchen, where one of the daughters served us ice cream. I'll never forget how we crowded together in that kitchen, as though we were afraid to leave each other's company, as though we who had loved Peter while he was dying had no time for him now that he was dead. He had the front room entirely to himself. He was in there with a few flowers."

"Did Mrs. Ellis cry?"

"I can't remember. I don't think she did. But I do remember she smiled at me when I left, and her smile moved me very deeply. I had this tremendous urge to do something for her, to give her something. As I said goodbye and passed outside through the kitchen door, I think I loved that woman more than I had ever loved Peter, more than I had ever loved even my own mother. It was a fleeting thing, it passed, but I'll never forget how urgently I wanted to show Mrs. Ellis that I loved her. I thought of giving her the apple blossom from my buttonhole, but it was too little to give. There was only one gift in the world that was good enough for her, and that was Peter restored to life."

"But how could you give her that?"

"I couldn't. I can't. Nobody can. And that's why I felt so frustrated walking home that night."

Chris and the boy watched the waves forming out beyond the lee of the island. The wind was stronger than before and some of the waves were ridged with white froth.

"What about the cloudburst? You said Peter was buried in a cloudburst."

Chris had thought he wouldn't tell this part. It was too dismal. But he *would* tell it. The boy was asking for it. And after all, what was there to talk about today but the death of friends?

"The day of the funeral the rain came down in sheets.

It rained so hard there was talk of postponing the funeral, but no, at the appointed time the whole sixth grade
was released from school and we ran down the street to
the Catholic church and sat through a long ceremony
with a lot of candles and incense and the choir singing
hymns. I remember the drumming of the rain and the
dimness of the light as it came through the stained-glass
windows. It was midday, but it was dark. Darker than it
is now. Well, we went from the church to the cemetery
and there was water standing in the bottom of the grave.
Everybody was horrified to think of lowering the coffin
into the water. But as reluctant as we were to see the
coffin go down, we saw that it had better go down quick
because as we stood there waiting for the priest to finish
his prayers, the grave was already beginning to fill itself
with mudslides. First little slides, then bigger ones.
Somebody nudged the priest and asked him to hurry, and
he did. He grabbed the holy water sprinkler from one
altar boy and mingled a few drops with the rain falling on
the coffin. Then he grabbed the censer from the other
altar boy and gave it a couple of swings, pretending it
still held fire, and then, while the crowd broke up and
splashed away to the cars, the undertaker and his helper
slipped the cogwheel that held the straps and dropped
the coffin down into the water before the cars had even
begun to move away."

The wind gusted violently, the waves peaked like pyr-
amids. The sky rolled and the boat rocked. Chris and the
boy held each other and swayed.

"It turned out all right. Peter was buried, probably not
as deep as most, but deep enough. The next day the sun
came out, and in a few weeks if you went to the cemetery, you could hardly see where the sod had been
moved. That's rich land around Haymarket. Everything
grows fast."

And now for a proper ending, a summing-up. Chris
assumed that his story was building like a poem to a final
line of wisdom or power or tenderness, an ending as impressive as its opening line about polio. But the ending
eluded him. He was suddenly bereft of words. "Every-

thing grows fast," he said again, regretting its poor fit.

The boy drew away from him. "My dad never tells stories like that." He stood up in the boat and, gathering his folds of rubber about him, stepped out onto the flat rock. His hood whipped in the wind as he regarded Chris with a serious frown. He said, "I like my dad's stories better."

Chris nodded and turned away and said to the wind, "So do I."

6

THE BOY WAS HALFWAY up the slope when Blackie appeared at the crest, shouting, "Git the hell back down there, kid, we're clearing off the island!"

The boy stopped.

Using his gun as a staff to steady himself, Blackie stood on a promontory and stretched out his free hand as though commanding the waters to part. "Git the hell out of that boat, MacKensie." His voice swept down the slope before him on the wind. "Git back to your friend Quinn and head for the mainland before we all drown."

Chris emptied his gun and stood up in the boat, his heart brimming with a wild mixture of relief (the waiting over), fervor (the call to action) and horror (Larry about to be pressed into the ooze).

Blackie started down, following the boy. His descent was careful and lurching by turns, his footwork both overcautious and reckless; he took longer steps with his right foot than with his left, and he lifted his knees higher than he needed to—a drunk's progress. "What the hell do you think this is, a picnic? Wind blowing like sixty, and if it catches your boat sideways, you'll be swamped. Whose idea was it to come out here on the big water? Sure's hell wasn't mine."

Chris stepped out of the boat as Blackie came forward on stones, steadying himself with a hand on the boy's head. "I've been sitting in that cove talking to Quinn and not paying attention to what the weather's doing. This here's a hell of a mean wind, MacKensie—like to drown us all. Git going now, git yourself and Quinn off the is-

land and make it quick. Me and the boy'll pick up the
decoys and follow you to land."

Chris nodded. Precisely his plan.

Throwing his leg over the side of the boat, Blackie
slipped; Chris caught him and nearly collapsed under his
drunk weight. He righted him and helped him into the
stern seat. The boy hopped into the bow.

"Keep your stern end into the wind no matter where it
wants to blow you, otherwise you're dead," said
Blackie, slurring his words. His cocked eye drilled
Chris; his good eye was the merest slit. "The wind's
swung a little to the north since we came out here, but
it'll still blow us pretty close to Lawler's. Now shove us
out and git going."

Chris turned the boat in the water, pointing it out, and
pushed hard on the stern. Immediately it was caught by a
gust of wind and swept through the flock of bouncing
decoys and out into rough water, and by the time Blackie
opened his good eye wide and discovered himself adrift,
the boat was rocking twenty yards from shore, twenty-
five, thirty.

Chris, standing on stones and watching the boat being
slapped over the side by the tall waves, felt the thrill of
fear compound the turmoil in his heart, fear for the
safety of the boy and the old man. He watched Blackie
pull the starter rope again and again.

"Pull out the choke," Chris shouted.

Blackie looked up and around, the wind in his ears,
his bearings lost, uncertain where the voice came from.
The boy sat hunched on the bow seat, gripping the gunwales, a strange twist in his face as though he were about
to cry out. He did cry out: "The choke!"

Blackie nodded and turned back to the motor. As he
tightened his fingers around the choke, a wave crashed
into the boat, spilling him into the bilge between the
stern and middle seat. He still clutched the choke button
in his fist; he had pulled it, stem and all, out of the
motor.

The boy stepped over him and tugged at the starter
rope three times before the next big wave nearly tossed

him into the lake. He crouched next to Blackie, who was lying on his back in the bilge, frightened now, but no less drunk, no more coordinated, no better able to sit up.

"Lie down flat," Blackie told him, but the boy, obeying an instinct more reliable than Blackie's, waited for the boat to level itself between waves. Then he leaped over the middle and bow seats and wedged himself tightly into the point of the bow, sitting on coils of anchor rope and extending his legs to brace himself against the seat. When the next wave struck, he held himself rigid and rocked with the boat. Thus he rode the waves, clutching tightly at the gunwales and sensing that he would not drown unless the boat turned bottom-up.

Chris was paralyzed with horror. The boat was out over deep water and rocking steeply. Climbing each wave, it stood on its starboard gunwale and showed Chris its keel. Dropping into each trough, it stood on its larboard gunwale and, though said to be unsinkable (flotation cubes of styrofoam were built into the struts under each seat), it seemed about to capsize. With each rise and fall Blackie slid across the smooth aluminum bottom, flailing and kicking. The boy was secure for the time being—he had fastened himself tightly into the framework—but Blackie was not. If the boat tipped any more steeply, Blackie would fall out; his oversupply of booze would be the death of him. His hip boots would fill with water and pull him down like a stone. Blackie dead instead of Larry. Chris to blame.

With a great effort of will, Chris broke out of his stupor of fear, lifting his gun overhead and dashing it into the water. He turned and scrambled uphill. His plan was coming undone. The day was out of control. Rain was falling again, and the climb was slippery. Under his heaving breath he cursed whenever he lost his footing and slipped back on the stones. Running across the rocky crest, he cursed the wind for blowing his scheme to tatters. He was momentarily blinded by a stinging sweep of rain. Shielding his eyes, he skidded down the west slope and splashed through the water and threw himself into Larry's boat.

Larry peered out from under his hood. "Ready to go?" Larry, as though pounded down by a day of exertion, was bent almost double on his seat. He was well wrapped in rubber, his only exposed parts being his knuckles and nose.

Chris dropped onto the middle seat and pulled on an oar, pointing the boat toward the open water. "Start the motor! The other boat's in trouble!" He was out of breath and his eyes were swimming. He felt an awful pressure in his head.

Larry drew his gun out from under his raincoat and carefully stood it up against the seat.

"Hurry up, they might be drowning!" Chris pulled on both oars, moving the boat out of the reeds where Larry was to have died. As they emerged from the cove, the north wind caught them, blew them sideways.

Larry turned to the motor and pulled out the choke. Chris stood up, reached over Larry's shoulder and yanked the starter rope. The engine fired. "Give it gas!" He sat back down, facing forward.

Larry pushed in the choke, accelerated and guided the boat close along the edge of the reeds where the water wasn't so rough. The rain let up, but though visibility improved, Chris felt bereft of his vision. The inner light that had guided him to this point in Canada, in life, had been blown out and replaced by a dazzle of panic. "Faster," he cried, gripping the sides, leaning forward, straining for speed.

Larry didn't speed up. Chris turned to tell him again, but Larry spoke first: "If we go any faster, we'll lift the prop out of the water." They were out in high waves now. Larry's left hand was behind him on the throttle; his right hand rested on his forward knee. He sat up straight, his eyes not on Chris but beyond him, on the other boat. Intense, squinting, far-seeing eyes, lit with purpose.

Chris faced forward just as Blackie fell—or rather was slung—out of the boat. He shot up and over the side and hung for an instant in the air, face-down, one leg bent up behind him—a puppet dangling from tangled strings—and then he splashed into the water ahead of the boat, where Chris couldn't see if he sank or swam.

"Faster!"

Larry accelerated slightly.

As they moved with the wind, with the waves, their progress seemed slower than it was. Languidly the boat climbed the back of each wave and rode the crest for three or four seconds before dipping and climbing the next wave. When the bow fell, the stern rose and lifted the propeller almost clear, the blades turning in froth and the boat stalling; when the bow rose, the propeller dug deep into the water and the boat surged ahead as the following wave boiled at the stern and fell away.

Blackie's boat was thirty yards off now and Chris saw, on its far side, Blackie throwing his arm over the gunwale and trying to climb in. The boy—wisely—made no move to help him, realizing that if he gave up his grip, he too would be flung out. The boy's mouth was open wide in a scream that mingled with the rush of the wind as Blackie lost his hold, his arm disappearing and the boat moving forward over him.

"Oh, God." Chris turned to Larry.

Larry, biting his lip, nodded. Then his eyes brightened. "Look!"

Blackie had reappeared on the waves, now on the near side. By what miracle had he remained afloat? His boots must be full of water, yet he was buoyant. Again he flung his arm up to grip the boat, but a wave pushed it out of reach. His forward lunge carried him face-down into the water. Chris and Larry moved steadily, undulantly, closer—twenty feet, ten, five. As they passed beside Blackie, Chris reached into a wave and clutched with both hands the shoulder of Blackie's jacket. Straining to tug him out of the water, he tumbled to his knees and hung over the side, pulling Blackie along with the boat—which Larry had slowed but dared not stop lest it swing broadside to the waves.

Blackie, turning face-up, resisted Chris's grip. Dragged on his back and engulfed by a wave, he choked and put all his strength and panic into a blow to Chris's face—a blinding smash in the teeth. The pain, too shocking, too intense, to strike all at once, came to Chris in stages; it spread into his nose and up into his left eye and back along his jaw to his left ear while he bled from the searing cut in his upper lip. But still, he held onto Blackie, who, head and shoulders out of the water now, was shaking the water from his face and throwing an arm feebly over the side and then (the last of his energy having gone into his uppercut) hanging limply from Chris's arms.

Chris's arms ached. "Stop," he said to Larry.

"I can't, we'll be swamped. Just hang on."

Now they were passing the bow of the other boat. The boy, having got up from his sitting position, had turned and was kneeling on the coils of rope. Thrusting his head out over the point of the bow, he held his mouth open in the wide oval of his last scream while preparing to scream again.

"Throw me some rope," Larry commanded the boy as he passed him, close enough—for a moment—to touch hands.

The boy ignored the order. He stood and put one foot up on the gunwale as though to spring from boat to boat.

"Don't jump," said Larry. "Throw me some rope, we'll pull you."

The boy scooped up an armful of rope at his feet. It was dripping wet, and though he flung it with force, it fell heavily short of the other boat, uncoiling itself on the waves, a snake of bristly hemp.

"It's all right," cried Larry, moving away. "Hang on tight, you'll float to shore."

The boy screamed.

"It's all right, you're halfway there already."

The boy's boat wasn't rocking so steeply now because it was half full of water; it wallowed in the waves, rising and falling like a heavy tub. If the boy didn't panic, if he wedged himself back into the point of the bow, he would be borne safely to land. But he couldn't force himself into the bow, couldn't force himself to turn his back on the men. Again he screamed and again he lifted one foot to the gunwale. The leap would have been impossible—the boats were ten yards apart—but he was on the verge of trying it.

"Get down!" cried Larry. "I'll come back."

By this time Chris had managed to drape both of Blackie's arms inside the boat. Still clutching the jacket with one hand, Chris reached down to grip Blackie's belt. His belt was gone. His pants and boots were gone. Upon plunging into the lake, Blackie had apparently unbuckled his belt, to which his hip boots were strapped, and had kicked off his pants with his boots. Chris leaned out farther and slipped his hand under Blackie's thigh, trying to haul him over, but he was too heavy. Chris hadn't leverage enough to keep himself from falling into the water. Instead, he slipped his arms under Blackie's arms and they hugged tightly, face to face, the ridge of the gunwale cutting across their chests.

"Hang on, I'm going to circle back," said Larry. "If I don't, the kid'll jump." He made a quick right turn and rode the back of a broad wave, turned right again and headed into the wall of the wave behind it, splitting the water with the bow. He cut into more waves—the boat shuddering each time—then he turned again and circled behind the boy's boat and came forward past its bow for the second time. With his left hand clamped to the throttle, where it had been since they left the island, Larry leaned over and snatched the rope out of the water. He looped it over the motor.

"Get off the rope!" he called to the boy.

The boy sprang onto the bow seat, kneeling there with his outstretched arms clutching the sides, watching in fear as Larry moved away and the rope payed out over the side. "Come back!" the boy pleaded.

When the rope became taut, the lead boat stalled. The trailing boat, containing so much of the lake, was a heavy drag. Larry turned the throttle to high speed. The boats moved ahead, the trailing boat swinging around and pointing itself toward land. The boy braced himself once again in the bow, facing back toward the island, which had vanished behind a moving curtain of rain. His boat, end to end with the waves, no longer rocked like a cradle; it tipped like a rocking horse. Each time the bow rose, the boy looked down at the water as it receded over the stern and carried off one or two dead ducks.

In maneuvering for the rope, the lead boat, too, had taken on water and now it rode low in the lake—so low that Blackie was able to throw a leg over the side and topple in on top of Chris. They untangled themselves and sat amidships, dazed. Blackie faced forward quaking with cold, his nose running, his cheek and mustache bloody from having rubbed against Chris's wound, the rest of his face a new color for him—cream—fear and the elements having washed the pigment out of his skin.

Chris faced aft, his left hand pressed over his nose and lip, his right hand cupped at his chin. Into his cupped hand he spit a tooth. He peered at it seriously, soberly, for several seconds; studied it with such intensity that he seemed unaware that he was sitting belly-deep in water, the hem of his poncho afloat front and back; examined it so closely, like a jewel, that Larry laughed.

Reaching inside his poncho and tucking the tooth carefully into his shirt pocket, Chris raised his eyes to Larry. Whether from exhaustion or the blow to his face, Chris's vision was fuzzy. At first he thought the amusement and strength in Larry's wet face were an illusion. Larry's eyes were sharp. He wasn't looking inward for a change; he was searching, instead of his soul, the shoreline ahead. Chris squinted through the rain. This was no illusion, this face from which years had dropped away. This was Larry restored by danger and adrenaline. The restoration made Chris's heart leap, and because he associated heart leaps with Rachel, he instantly thought of her, imagined what she would think—feel—if she could see Larry now, at the helm, his jaw set high in triumph as he moved the hunting party from peril to safety. Larry transformed. How long did such transformations last? Was there a chance this one might be preserved, or would it perish with the moment? Was it transportable from lake to land? From Delta Marsh to Rookery? To Rachel?

"Hang on for the big one," said Larry.

They were climbing a great wave. From its crest the others looked harmless. As they went over the top, the propeller spun in the air. The boat stalled. Then it swirled down ahead of the wave and water came rushing over the stern and lifted Larry off his seat like a cork. Skin and bones and buoyant, he might have been swept away with the ducks and oars and backpack had his left hand not been clamped around the throttle, had his right hand not been gripped fiercely by Chris, who—in the split second before Larry regained his seat and righted the boat in the blinding spray—was swept up in a wild new fear:

He feared for Larry's life.

Albert saw them coming. When the first boat ran aground, he waded into the surf and helped Blackie to his feet and led him—his bare legs quaking with cold— up the beach and lowered him to the stones above the surfline. Then he ran back to assist Chris in dragging Larry ashore. When the second boat washed in, Albert carried the boy in his arms as far as the grass and told him to run to the house. The boy did so, tripping on his rubber coat as he went.

Larry, leaning on Chris, chanted, "Wait till I tell Rachel about this, wait till I tell Rachel and Bruce." He pointed to Blackie, who was kneeling on the stones and trying to stand. "Cover him with your poncho, Chris, he'll die of exposure." Larry was jerky in Chris's arms, overcome by chills and ecstasy. "God, wait till Rachel hears about this."

"Come to the house, you guys," said Albert, returning down the beach to Blackie, helping him to his feet. "Come to the house and change clothes and get warm."

Larry clung to Chris, both arms around his shoulders. "Just get me to the car, Chris. I just want to sit down."

"Go ahead," Chris told Albert. "Take care of Blackie and the boy. We'll be waiting in the car."

Helping Larry over the stones, Chris found that his face hurt worse when he removed his hand and exposed his wound to the air, so he kept as much of his upper lip as possible in his mouth. His tongue told him that his lip was split halfway to the base of his left nostril. He spit blood, swallowed blood.

The boy scampered up to the front door of the house and opened it. Light from the hallway spilled out into the dark afternoon. Close behind the boy trailed Blackie, wearing one black sock and stumbling swiftly along in Albert's arms.

At the car Larry did not release his grip when Chris opened the door for him. He locked his arms around Chris's shoulders. Chris made a move to lower him into the seat, but Larry clung tighter, more desperately, not in a spasm of pain but in an attempt to convey a message he had no words for. It was clear to Chris that Larry was seized by an emotion so rare in his recent experience that if he had been asked to identify it, to call it by name, he couldn't have done so. He might have said it was excitement, or relief from despair, or pride, or distraction from pain and death; and he would have been correct, but only insofar as someone is correct who would explain the nature of the universe by naming four or five of its planets. Larry recognized only in part what possessed him. But Chris saw the whole of it, at close range, in his face.

What possessed him was happiness.

7

"GIFTS."

Chris woke to the pain in his face. Through the windshield he saw the moon. Through the back window fell the floodlight from customs station.

"Gifts," Larry said again from his nest in the back seat. "I don't have any gifts for Rachel and Bruce."

Chris sat up, feeling his face, the soft swelling of his cheek, that hard swelling across his lip, the blood caked. How could his wound be stitched shut with his lip so badly swollen? Because he had stopped in Winnipeg only for gasoline and a small bag of ice, not for medical attention, was he destined to go through life with a mutilated face?

He had held the ice to his face all the way to the border, driving with a sense of urgency, hurrying Larry home before he wilted. Somewhere between the island and the mainland, killing Larry had become inconceivable. The mere *thought* had become inconceivable. Waiting in the car at Lawler's (he and Larry soaked, the heater on high), Chris had tried to reassemble the arguments and emotions that had led to his murder plan, but all such arguments and emotions were scattered and out of reach. Renewed in spirit or not renewed in spirit, Larry would live till he died.

North of the border the pain in Chris's face had kept him alert at the wheel, but by the time he reached customs his cheek and lip were chilled to numbness, and the receding pain made way for fatigue—the aftermath of overexertion and undernourishment; three days of too much adventure and too little food and sleep. As soon as

292

the customs officer had finished inspecting the car ("No ducks? No geese? Not even any *chickens*?"), Chris had driven around behind the building and fallen across the front seat. That had been at 10:00 P.M.

"In the old days, when I went off hunting for the weekend, I always used to bring them something. When you and I met in Owl Brook to hunt, I used to buy some sort of trinket for Rachel and a T-shirt or something for Bruce, remember?"

"Yep." Chris turned on the dashlights. Two o'clock. The pain was back, but it wasn't in his lip so much as inside his mouth, where his tooth had been. Probing the void with his tongue, he settled himself behind the wheel and started the car.

"What time is it, Chris?"

"Two."

"I've been sleeping most of the way from Blackie's. What time did we get away from there?"

"About seven."

"How are you feeling?"

"Tolerable." Chris drove onto the highway. Heading south, he speeded up, full of purpose again, certain of Rachel's delight if he could deliver Larry home renewed. Chris, for love of her, was determined that she see her husband whole once more. Not that he would ever again be *truly* whole—he would doubtless be dead in a year— but never in the past *three* years had Larry expressed anything like the high spirits that had him talking excitedly as the car heated up in Lawler's driveway; there, while they waited for the LaVois and the plumber's son to come out of the house, Larry reviewed, rehearsed, relished the tale of saving the lives of a man and a boy. Never in the past three years had he expressed anything like the warmth with which he held the plumber's son in his arms as they said goodbye at the bunkhouse door. Someday Chris would describe the scene to Rachel. After changing clothes and packing the car, Chris left Larry in the bunkhouse and went into the kitchen. There he paid Mrs. LaVoi for their food and lodging and guide service (he could hear Blackie sneezing beyond the curtained doorway) while Gladdy and Poo Poo insisted on patching his wound with tape and gauze. Then, as he passed through the dining room where the hunters were eating duck, he noticed that the twelve-year-old was telling his spellbound elders of the day's adventure. When the boy saw that Chris was about to leave camp without supper, he interrupted his story to follow him into the bunkhouse and say goodbye. That was where Larry hugged him.

"I think the gift Rachel liked best from those years was a pair of gold earrings, Chris. She still wears them."

Chris drove on, silent. Soon Larry went back to sleep.

Gifts, thought Chris, staring ahead at the moonlit road. The sprig of apple blossom—too slight a gift for a woman who had lost her son. A certain silver necklace in a jeweler's window in Rookery—too great a gift for a woman married to one's best friend. Often Chris had paused at that window and admired the necklace that would have gone so well with Rachel's blue-gray eyes, would have looked so lovely at her throat. It was a necklace of silver triangles that glittered like icicles or flames, depending on whether the light they reflected was cloud-light or sunlight, cold or warm. He had decided to buy it for her as soon as she was free of Larry. As soon as he himself was free of Larry. But now he was giving her Larry instead.

At 3:00 A.M. Chris stopped and woke Larry and asked him for two of his headache pills. The pain was spreading through the bones of his face.

Half an hour later the pain grew sharper. He ate one of Larry's tranquilizers. Within minutes this capsule drained away not only his pain but his vitality as well. He was too sleepy to drive. He pulled off the highway and parked at the edge of a hayfield, where both men slept until daylight.

"Breakfast?" said Larry, sitting up in the back seat. They were passing Buster's Truck Corral. It was 8:00 A.M.

"You'd have to chew mine for me."

Larry chuckled.

Chris glanced at him in the mirror. Larry's eyes were still unclouded and lively.

Larry hunched forward. Crossing his arms on the back of the front seat, he began to say something about Blackie overboard but interrupted himself: "My God, Chris!" He was astonished at Chris's face in the mirror, the bandage off, the dried blood, the left eye swollen nearly shut. "You need a doctor. Drive to Mercy—Rachel can pick me up there."

Chris shook his head. "I'll drop you off at home; then I'll go to the hospital." He had to deliver this gift in person, though his determination to do so had become, by now, cold stubbornness, not love. At least not love that he could feel. For he had left all feeling behind him in the North, in the night. He was too tired now to feel anything but the great ache that was his face, and even that seemed too old and stiff and familiar to require much of his attention. "When I'm through at the hospital, I'll come back with your gear."

Larry, high on heroism as well as twelve hours of sleep and an underdose of medication, said, "All right, hurry up then. I want to assault my wife."

The Sunday streets were empty. The morning was bright and bracing. Turning into the Quinns' street, Chris saw Rachel standing in the yard in her white jogging shorts. She was facing away; her red hair and her tanned legs shone in the sun as she raked elm leaves into a pile at curbside. She turned to say something to Bruce, who was coming out the front door wearing a seersucker sportcoat—the Gospel Quartet was to perform this morning at Parkview Methodist—and Chris—the car drawing near—was enchanted by her profile.

"Better watch where you're going," said Larry.

Chris brought the car back in line, close along the curb. Rachel turned, saw the car, flung down her rake. For an instant, spotting Chris alone in the front seat (his hand over his mouth), she may have thought that Larry had not survived the hunt—an instant of perplexing emotions crossed her face: alarm? grief? relief?—and then she saw Larry in the back seat. He was opening the door while the car still moved and he was saying, "Wait till I get my hands on you, my autumn prairie flower." Chris stopped beside the leafpile and Larry, grasping at the doorframe, grasping at Rachel, brought himself to his feet. He teetered for a moment on the curb as he slammed the door, and then he threw his weight upon his wife, his arms around her neck, his lips on hers, bearing her down into the leaves as Chris drove off.

"Oh, Larry." She laughed, sunk in the leafpile, sunk under Larry, who pressed out of her a wild screech of delight.

EPILOGUE

1

LARRY STIFFENED AND DIED on schedule.

By midsummer 1980 he had lost his power of locomotion (he lived in bed in the living room) and he had partially lost his power of speech (he stammered trying to think of words) and his arms and legs and spine had grown stiff as rake handles. During the last week of his life he was bendable only at the waist and at the base of his fingers.

Beginning in early August Chris visited the Quinns every evening for what amounted to a month-long deathwatch. The hot days of late summer passed with a remarkable lack of emotion: Rachel was determined not to brood, Larry was drugged, Bruce was in and out of the house with friends (mostly out), and Chris was holding life at arm's length. Psychological distance, which had proved so useful during the dissolution of his marriage and the rebuilding of the Rookery counseling department, came in handy now as he watched the two people he loved best in the world bid each other a lingering farewell.

He kept his distance from Larry. Both men seemed to understand that talk was unnecessary, that merely occupying the same room for two or three hours in the evening was all this stage of their companionship required of them, that a periodic meeting of eyes was communication enough. Sitting beside Larry's bed in the heat—Larry asleep, Rachel at the theater—Chris sipped iced tea and read novels. Otherwise his days were occupied with his revision of *Handbook for Counselors*, a second edition of which was to be published in the fall. Out of respect for Larry's unfulfilled desire to write a book, he never worked on the manuscript at Larry's bedside.

As for Rachel, he suppressed the lust she aroused in him on certain days when the heat and humidity grew nearly unbearable (no air conditioning—Larry permanently chilly) and she wore very little around the house and moved in provocative ways. With Chris sitting nearby, she would sometimes stand at the bed for a minute or more with her eyes closed, her hand resting on Larry's brow, or holding his hand, and then suddenly break off her meditation with a switch of her tail—a brief, lewd wag. These displays of sexual animation were involuntary; perhaps she was vaguely aware of them, perhaps she even sensed how Chris was ravished by them, but she could no more hold them in check than she could refrain from running every day in the valley. For just as a few years ago she had taken up running in an instinctive response to Larry's lameness, now, while Larry stiffened and slept, she seemed enlivened by a new surge of energy. Chris observed how, as Larry's flesh turned gray, Rachel's became more sunbronzed and supple, how, as Larry's face hardened into a noncommittal mask, Rachel's smile (if less wide, if more abstracted) became readier; he observed how, as death haunted the house, a subtle aura of death-defying sexuality followed Rachel through the rooms. He understood that in this house—in this marriage—where she had worked so hard for harmony and achieved it, she was now engaged in the ultimate work of holding death at bay. She was foredefeated—she knew that—but her vitality was a bold perennial force rooted deep in her soul; it grew in the fatal shade; it blossomed in the heat.

The night before Larry died his condition seemed no graver than it had been for the past five or six days. He lay flat without a pillow and slept with his eyes half-open, his fingers twitching. Chris sat between the bed and the front window, reading. Bruce, home from tennis, was upstairs soaking in the tub.

At eleven Rachel returned from the Playhouse, where she and the crew had struck the last set of the summer season. She wore jeans and a sleeveless blouse and tiny earrings of gold wire. Her hair was cut short and swept left to right across her forehead. She dropped into the soft rocking chair on the opposite side of the bed from Chris and said:

"I shouldn't be telling you this, you two"—she was beaming with amusement—"because you're always picking on Bernard and you never give him credit for being the sensible boss he is." In contrast with her heat-flushed face her gray eyes sparkled like pools of cool water. "But if you don't hear it from me, you're bound to hear it from somebody else. Bernard's in trouble with the police, would you believe it? And not only that, he has thirty truck drivers mad at him. Oh, it's too awful." She giggled.

Chris closed his book. Larry, his nose pointed at the ceiling, rolled his eyes as far as they would go toward Rachel. She stood up so he could see her. She took his hand.

"You know how Bernard loves to play with his CB radio. Sometimes in the evening he'll sit in his office for two or three hours at a time, talking to truckers going through on the freeway."

"Saint..." said Larry, his voice husky from disuse. "Saint Bernard."

"Yes, Saint Bernard—that's his handle," she explained to Chris, who was oddly comforted to realize that as familiar as he had become with the Quinns they still shared certain scraps of information that he wasn't privy to. Bernard Beckwith's handle, for instance. It was no longer possible to envy Larry and Rachel their secrets and intimacies, they had become so pitifully few.

"Imagine calling yourself... a saint," said Larry. "The ego of it."

"Oh, he doesn't mean 'saint' in that sense. He calls himself Saint Bernard after the dogs in the Alps that rescue lost travelers. You see, it's Bernard's dream that someday a great disaster will strike Rookery and he'll be instrumental in saving a lot of lives with his CB radio. He subscribes to a magazine that tells how people have been spared from floods and tornadoes and other calamities because they were warned on their CB's."

"Beckwith the hero," said Chris, trying to imagine it.

"Beckwith..." Larry stammered. "The drip."

"So tonight he got his chance. Truckers coming through the city from the east told him there was a grass fire burning about six miles down the road. The smoke was so thick over the highway they could go only five miles an hour. So Bernard immediately began calling all trucks coming from the west. 'Breaker one nine,' he said, 'breaker one nine, this is Saint Bernard with a warning, do you read me? Ten four.' His office door was open and we could hear him as we worked onstage. My crew thinks he's kind of odd, you know.

"Well, one after another the truckers read him. We could hear their voices as well as Bernard's. There was Tailgate Charlie and the Lone Fender and four or five Rubber Duckies, and Bernard told each of them to take Exit Twenty-three off the freeway and drive through the city to the third stoplight and turn east on County Road Four and they'd have clear sailing around the north side of the fire. He must have given these directions two dozen times. My crew was in stitches. They mimicked him and made up ridiculous handles for themselves and they kept telling each other 'ten four.' I joined in, I have to admit it, and finally we all collapsed on the stage from laughing so hard. Oh, it was silly.

"But then we heard the voices over the CB start to sound angry, and Bernard's voice rose to a very high pitch. Well, it turned out that instead of saving all those truckers from a disaster on the freeway, he was creating a disaster on County Road Four. See, what Bernard didn't know was that the grass fire had started up north on the riverbank and had crossed that very road and burned away the wooden flooring of the bridge. So he had this procession of about thirty trucks moving out along Four, which is narrow and dark and very bumpy— and that's lucky because if it hadn't been narrow and dark and bumpy the trucker in the lead would have been going too fast to stop when he came to the burned-out bridge. As it was, he slammed on his brakes and came to a stop with the front tires of his cab hanging over the water, and the thirty trucks behind him slammed on *their* brakes and there they all sat, bumper to bumper in the wilderness with the nearest crossroad for turning around three miles behind them."

Larry's blanket began to quiver with his silent laughter. Chris laughed. Rachel laughed. Bruce came down from his room to see what was funny. So little *had* been funny lately.

"And they're still out there. The state patrol has been called in to help the thirty truckers back up to that crossroad so they can turn around." Rachel sat down and rocked. "The most horrid things were coming over the CB." She lowered her voice, pulled in her chin and frowned. "'Saint Bernard, now hear this, have you ever tried to back up a rig three miles in the dark, you stupid asshole?'"

Larry didn't die laughing—he lived for several more hours—but that's how Chris last saw him alive: laughing. Leaving for home, Chris glanced back: Bruce was standing beside the bed, looming over it, laughing; Rachel was leaning forward in her rocker, her face buried in the blanket, laughing; Larry, his eyes closed, his face a mask, expressed his laughter in the squeaks of his bouncing bed.

Larry died at dawn. Rachel, having spent the night in the rocker, awoke with a start, too late to hear (yet somehow knowing that only a few seconds had passed since he emitted it) the long bubbly exhalation announcing her widowhood.

For several minutes she held Larry's hand loosely, staring across the bed at the dim daylight filtering through the drawn drapes. Then she went upstairs and sat on Bruce's bed. She coaxed him awake and up to a sitting position before hugging him hard.

"Did he die?" asked Bruce, barely conscious.

She nodded. She kissed him. She went down to the phone in the kitchen and dialed Chris's number. Waiting for Chris to answer, she felt, in retrospect, how quickly Larry's hand had grown cold in her own. A terrible ache surged up in her breast, an ache that redoubled itself with each ring, so by the time Chris picked up the phone and said hello he heard at first an inhuman moan and then several sighs of breathy weeping and then, very loud:

"Chris! . . ." followed by a dead stillness like the pause between thunderclaps . . . "Chris, I've lost my leading man!"

2

$G_{IFTS.}$

Larry's files were full of his research and it would be tragic, said John Hildahl, if the world were denied the gift of his book. Hildahl, a young history professor at Rookery State College, had been at first a devoted student of Larry's and subsequently a devoted colleague. Since learning, three years ago, that Chris was Larry's friend, he had taken every opportunity to ask Chris about him—was he feeling better? Was he finally starting on his book? Would he been interested in a collaborator? For three years the answer was always no, but Hildahl, having seen nothing of Larry since his retirement, seemed unwilling to believe it.

Today John Hildahl was Chris's partner at the front coffin grip. The other four pallbearers, like Hildahl, were historians, and as they rode from the mortuary to Parkview Methodist Church in a long black car, they talked about Larry's research. Hildahl still wanted to be Larry's collaborator and see Larry's book—his gift to the profession—in print. Chris promised to speak to Rachel in his behalf.

From the pallbearers' pew at the front of the church Chris spent most of the funeral gazing out through the wall of glass that overlooked the pathways of the city park, for more compelling than the minister's tedious eulogy was the movement of people between the flower beds and goldfish pools on this bright, mild September day. Young mothers were pushing babies in strollers; candystripers were pushing rest-home residents in

305

wheelchairs; a long line of young art students meandered down the street, each boy and girl carrying a new sketch book and a new pencil and gawking at the familiar benches and bushes and sky as if they had never seen them before, and no doubt they hadn't.

"His gift was teaching," said the minister, a Reverend Richard Blee, who wore a white robe and a false liturgical smile. "This man whom today we commit to God's care was a most gifted teacher."

Chris had been surprised when Rachel chose Parkview Methodist for this service—neither she nor Larry had been a churchgoer—but she explained—last night —that she was honoring Bruce's request. Bruce, whose quartet often sang here, was very fond of Reverend Blee.

"And I must say, the man was very prompt in phoning me with words of consolation," she told Chris in her crowded living room on the eve of the funeral. "I was touched, really, by his concern. And did you know that I was a Methodist myself one time, that as a girl I sang in a Methodist choir? I had Methodism before I had Larry, so why not an hour or so of Methodism after he's gone? And you realize Larry left no instructions. He didn't have the slightest interest in what became of him once he was dead. He said for all he cared I could set him afloat down the Badbattle River."

"A most gifted teacher." Chris—his eyes outdoors— weighed the minister's words. While they had the hollow ring that one expected to hear at funerals, they were closer to the truth than Reverend Blee could possibly know. Larry's gift, Chris knew, was the gift of balance between scholarship and instruction. While he loved losing himself in the musty records of early Minnesota (the daybooks of logging camps, the logbooks of Lake Superior steamers), he never lost his touch with students. The more history he learned, the more skillful he became at imparting it, and simultaneous with his burrowing into antiquity was his stalking the minds of the young. The only way a student could avoid having his intellect stirred was to drop Larry's course, as dolts sometimes did. Coming on campus after Larry was gone, Chris learned that his friend had spent his career making his work look as easy as breathing. It was only after he had lost his job (and, with it, his will to learn and to write) that it became clear how essential teaching had been to his happiness.

Breathing, too, looked easy, thought Chris, but try living without it.

The funeral drew to a close and he followed the mourners down the aisle. Carrying the body out into the sunshine and down the steps of the church, Chris imagined setting Larry afloat down the Badbattle River, and he had to smile in spite of himself.

The procession of cars followed Badbattle Drive into the valley and came to a stop between the river and the main gate of the cemetery. After placing Larry over an open grave in the shade of an enormous white pine, Chris and the five historians stepped back and watched the mourners assemble opposite them. Chris counted thirty-three people. Bruce, in his seersucker jacket, was red-eyed. Rachel, in a green dress, was not. Coming up to stand beside Rachel were her mother and her mother's new husband, Sam. They had flown in from Arizona yesterday, and Chris had been introduced to them last night in Rachel's living room, where Sam concocted round after round of large, potent drinks consisting of tequila, soy sauce and lime juice.

Behind the family stood the college president and a dean and two librarians and Bernard Beckwith. And there were six of Bruce's classmates and eight of Rachel's friends from the Playhouse. There were three wives from Rachel's neighborhood and seven strangers who might have gone to school with Larry. At second glance Chris saw that one of the seven was Carmelita Nelson from Buster's Truck Corral. She was weeping copiously into her hands.

The graveside prayer was a long one. Chris's and Rachel's eyes met. Rachel smiled quickly and turned her head away, toward her mother.

In an era when most people wore the same clothes to

funerals that they wore to weddings, Rachel's mother and her husband struck Chris as conspicuously mournful. Rachel's mother wore a black dress and black gloves; a veil was fitted over her face and cinched under her chin with tiny black ribbons—a show of grief not entirely authentic, for this woman's resentment of Larry reached back nearly twenty years to the time when he plucked her daughter out of her girlhood and made a wife of her before she was graduated from high school. Further, she resented Larry for contracting a mortal disease at a time in life when he should have been coming into his full vigor (her first husband, Rachel's father, had had the decency not to develop heart trouble until he was fifty-one) and she resented Larry for taking so long to die of it (her first husband's heart had stopped beating promptly on the first anniversary of his first chest pain) and she resented Larry for leaving Rachel so little money. But this last injustice she could rectify; or rather Sam could rectify it, his petroleum stock making them rich beyond anything she had imagined when she was married the first time.

The prayer continued. Bruce shuddered. Sam stepped around and gave him a comforting pat on the shoulder. Sam was Mexican-American. Chris could see at a glance that Sam's line, though he claimed it was traceable back to Ferdinand and Isabella, included several Indians and perhaps a Chinese. He was handsome and short; his black eyes sparkled with warm humor; his black suit was perfectly tailored to the hump on his back. From the moment they met yesterday, Sam and Bruce had become the best of friends. Having married Bruce's only surviving grandparent, Sam had obviously been determined even before arriving in Rookery to like the boy, and he stepped off the plane with a two-hundred-dollar wristwatch for his birthday. With that for openers, he and the boy went on to discover how much they had in common: an interest in singing, an interest in Christ as their personal savior, an interest in football. Sam, in fact, was obsessed by football, and when he learned that Bruce, though enrolled, was less than eager to attend Rookery

State College (its shabby treatment of Larry, its shabby won-lost record), he urged him to come to Tempe and attend his own alma mater, Arizona State. Sam was empowered to make certain promises about athletic scholarships. "Play tackle for the Sun Devils and you'll get a free ride through college," he had told Bruce late last evening as he mixed yet another round of drinks for his new wife and Rachel and Chris and Bernard Beckwith and four or five of the Playhouse cast and crew. This post-mortuary gathering at the Quinn house, intended to mark Larry's passing and to console Rachel and Bruce, might have been an opening-night celebration, so deafening was the din.

"But what if I don't make the team?" Bruce asked above the stereo and the chatter.

"If you don't make the team, so what? *I'll* pay your bills. I'll make room for you in one of my duplexes and all you need to do in return is cut the grass and water it."

At this, Bruce crossed the living room to Rachel, who was standing where the head of Larry's bed had been. In one hand she held a drink and in the other she held the hand of a handsome actor who was instructing her in a spurious-sounding accent: "Veep, my darlink, you'll feel much better if you veep."

"Mother," said Bruce, "let's move to Arizona."

"Ahhhhhh-men," said Reverend Blee under the white pine.

There was a moment of stiff silence, then a few moments of hand-squeezing, and then Rachel startled everyone by springing back from the grave and pivoting and striding off, not toward the main gate but deeper into the cemetery, her red hair and green summer dress flashing brightly where she stepped through patches of sunlight.

"Mother," called Bruce, to remind her she had come in a car.

She stopped and turned. "Please ride with your grandmother, I'll see you at home." She noticed Chris break away from the five historians and approach her.

She waited for him. She put out her hand to him. She said, "I'm going to Arizona."

He wasn't surprised. Last midnight he had ben privy to the family discussion. "For how long?"

"Long enough to oversee Bruce's enrollment at Arizona State." She put a hand to her hair, fluffing the wave at her right temple. "Long enough to mark the division between being married and not being married."

He nodded. He understood. He thought of the silver necklace. He would give her time instead.

"And long enough for Sam to serve me a whole bunch of those lime drinks."

"You'll be back for the Playhouse season?"

"Possibly. That would give me nearly a month away."

"If not, I'll come looking for you."

"No, please, Chris, I want to be deliberate about my next move. I want to make sure I've come out of this whole and entire. Maybe I'll want more than a month. Maybe I'll want a year. Or maybe only a few days—who knows?"

They turned from each other and stood surveying the cemetery. Below them, along the road, car doors slammed, engines ignited. Several faces were turned up in their direction.

They faced each other again. A breeze moved the boughs above them, opening a stream of sunlight against which Rachel shielded her eyes as she looked at Chris. He wore a tan suit, a tan and blue tie. The scar on his upper lip, though almost a year old, was still raw-looking. His hair was longer than it had been a year ago; it curled over his ears. And it was grayer.

"Be strong," he said.

"I'll be fine, Chris. I feel good." Actually now that Larry was settled in his grave she felt better than she wanted to say. "All I need is time. I haven't had the luxury of time since I was seventeen."

"Write me as soon as you get to Tempe. Or call."

"I will."

Chris took her by the shoulders. This was the woman whose husband he had nearly murdered, the woman who had said she loved him. But all that was long ago. More than a year had gone by since they last embraced. After bringing Larry home from Delta Marsh not only alive but renewed, Chris had been discreet and kept his distance, watching from the wings as Larry and Rachel played out their final year as man and wife.

A long year. Although Larry's resurgence of self-esteem had burned high for several weeks after his lifesaving adventure, it had flickered out in the dark snowy days of December. At that point Chris had expected Larry to pass into the Doldrums again—the Doldrums Nonpareil—but instead Larry had dropped into an unruffled calm, a lazy comfort, an apathy of mind and body brought on by the dissolution of his nervous system and by the growing strength of his medication. Now he was dead. Rachel was free. Rachel was bound—away.

She said goodbye. Chris said goodbye. They exchanged a long look weighted with all they had shared. They parted with a smile—his grim, hers wavering. She turned and set off at a quick walk toward the high gate, her green dress flowing around her knees, her short hair bouncing. Fighting back the urge to run after her, he watched the levitational spring in her step as she followed—without looking back—the narrow and curving lane among the dead.

3

September 7, 1980. Article in this morning's *Call* about the recession and its effect on city finances. Cutbacks planned across the board. Uncertainty in high places on the question of the Playhouse, the mayor doubting its survival beyond next spring.

No call from Rachel. Her second day in Tempe.

September 9, 1980. Letter from president to all department chairmen: college staff to be reduced by 14½ professors, effective at end of academic year. Lopping off one counselor, in other words, despite my pleas.

September 10, 1980. Larry dead a week. Why did putting him to death seem right to me one day, wrong the next? One day I sat on the island and saw beyond the edge of the world. Next day clouds moved in and cut off my vision. Sometimes a man can see too far.

Note from Fresno. Karen asks if I can manage an extra hundred dollars this month for Kay—community college tuition.

September 11, 1980. Still no word from Rachel. I try to focus my mind's eye on her face, but at least one detail always eludes me—an ear, an eyebrow—and I have to open an old playbill and study her photo.

In Owl Brook I knew her as a girl and wife. In Rookery I've known her as a mother—to Larry as well as Bruce. Now she's in Arizona playing daughter. Next?...

4

O_N $_THE$ $_SECOND$ $_SATURDAY$ in September Chris woke up to a premonition: today he would hear from Rachel. She had been gone a week without writing or calling.

He had just finished shaving when the phone rang. "Hi," he said gleefully. During her absence he had been feeling absurdly cheerful, as though a lid had been lifted from his spirit, a feeling of release dating from the day and hour when Larry was encased in earth.

"Have you got any gifts for the missions, Mr. Mac-Kensie?" It was the building superintendent's wife with her annual appeal for old clothes. Some women from her church were downstairs, she said, gathering up castoff clothing. The poor of the world would be forever grateful. Anything would do except shoes and underwear.

"Yes, I have a few things. I'll bring them right down."

From his wardrobe he took his hunting jacket and canvas pants and wool shirt and rubber poncho. His gun and shells and backpack were sunk in Lake Manitoba, but these hunting clothes had been hanging there, troubling him, since last October. Much as he wished to be rid of them, he had delayed throwing them out, as though he had needed a reminder of the day when he nearly put two men and a boy to death. Nonsense—he had reminders enough without this clutter in his closet. Every morning he had to shave carefully around his badly healed scar. Every meal he had to be careful what he bit into with his false tooth.

Searching deeper, he found a sportcoat long out of style and a pair of yellow pajamas that didn't fit him. He found a sweatshirt and sweatpants from his tennis-playing days in Clement Hill. He put on the sweatsuit and went to the mirror. He was reminded of a time when he was trim. In Clement Hill he had weighed 175 and played tennis by the hour. Now he was a 188-pound weakling. He was short of breath. He needed to run. He *would* run, damn it. Beginning this morning he would jog in the valley every day, rain or shine, the way Rachel had done. He would take himself in hand and be fit again. He would cut his drinking by half.

Downstairs in the vestibule, Chris in his gray sweatsuit (elastic at the wrists and ankles) was introduced to three elderly women. As they took his clothes, item by item, and thanked him profusely, he pictured some Pakistani shepherd tending his flock in this poncho, some toothless old Laplander crossing the tundra with the collar of this tweed sportcoat turned up to warm his ears, some Kenyan dancing for rain in these yellow pajamas.

The mailman came in and joined the crowd in the vestibule, responding to greetings with a silent nod.

Chris said, "Anything for MacKensie?"

He handed him a letter from Rachel.

"Ah." Chris carried the letter down the hallway to the back door and out under the birch trees. It was the sort of day September does so well: the sun underplaying its power, withholding its harshness and heat and casting a cool golden light over the city; small clouds floating neatly along the rim of the deep blue sky; the air perfectly still unless you wanted to walk somewhere, in which case a breeze came to life and went with you, nudging you behind the ears.

Chris went down the hillside into the valley and sat on a bench beside the bike path. He opened the letter. She called him "My dearest Chris." She said Tempe was hot, hot. She said most days she lay in the sun reading plays, imagining herself the leading lady. She would like to do more acting this year. Bruce was a Sun Devil. He had been snatched from her by the football coach and was living in the players' dormitory. She hoped he wasn't neglecting his studies. She never saw him. Her mother's condo was a bit crowded. Sam was much the easier of the two to get along with. Last night she had sat up late with Sam and got plastered on lime drinks. She had brought her jogging outfit to Arizona, but she didn't feel like jogging. Would Chris do her a favor and check Larry's grave to see if his stone had been put in place yet? The monument people said they would do it Saturday morning. "Being loved"—this was a postscript—"is a pleasure, and loving is a pleasure, but neither is a *great* pleasure by itself. They are *great* pleasures only in combination with each other."

The postscript held Chris on the bench for a long time. He gave it six interpretations: she loved him, but not so much as she once had. She loved him more than ever. She didn't love him. She didn't love him *yet*. She didn't know if she loved him or not. She was uncertain of his love for her.

He stood up and put the letter in the pocket of his sweatpants. He did four jumping jacks. He touched his toes, as it were. He ran downstream along the bike path, conscious of carrying thirteen extra pounds over his best tennis weight, yet feeling wholesome as his lungs pumped and his heart pounded and his sneakers slapped the tar. He ran to the footbridge at the foot of the valley before he ran out of breath.

Leaning on the bridgerail, he read the letter again, pondered the postscript again. He rejected one of the six interpretations as improbable: that she loved him not at all. Another he rejected as impossible: that she was uncertain of his love for her. There, he was down to four.

He left the bridge and headed for the cemetery at a lazy lope.

Rachel saw him coming. She was standing next to the monument truck, which was parked near Larry's grave, and she was talking to the monument crew—a small old man smoking a crooked cigarette of his own making and a boy about Bruce's age who was learning the trade. The two of them had mixed a bucket of cement, poured it into the rectangular wooden form at the head of Larry's grave, troweled it flat and were waiting for it to set before they lowered onto it the granite stone lying on the bed of the truck:

LAWRENCE A QUINN
1932-1980

The old man blew smoke out his nose and said softly, "Was this your husband, ma'am?"

"Yes." Rachel nodded, smiling a faint smile.

The old man and the boy turned and read the stone, then turned back to Rachel, appraising her, calculating the years. In her sandals and blue wraparound skirt and jacket of white denim she looked very young.

The old man said, "Quite some bit older than you, wasn't he?"

"Some." Her eyes were on Chris, who was turning in at the main gate and walking across the grass toward the truck. He was within three graves of the truck when he saw her.

"My God, Rachel, you're back."

"I got in last night. I couldn't think in Tempe."

He stepped around the slab of drying concrete and cupped her smile in both his hands. He kissed her. He stepped back and looked her over. He regarded the stone on the truck (the buffed granite gray and marbly, the lettering unadorned) and instantly he felt a vast gulf open up between himself and his old friend Larry Quinn, a division even greater than that between life and death; it was like the distance between two men who had never met. "Lawrence A" was a stranger's name.

He tugged at Rachel's hand and drew her away from the monument men.

Watching them stroll off across the graves, the old man stepped on his cigarette and took the boy by the arm and said, "I've seen a lot of fast women in my day, sonny, but she takes the cake. This one dead a week and already she snares herself a new one."

The boy nodded seriously, learning the trade.

Rachel and Chris sat down in a circle of sunny grass.

"Arizona is a great place for lying inert while your skin tans and turns to leather, but it's no place for me to sort out my thinking, Chris. My brain works better when I'm doing something, and when I'm doing it on familiar ground. I can think in this valley. I can think at the Playhouse. I can think in my kitchen. Chris, have you had breakfast? Would you join me in my kitchen for muffins?"

"I love muffins."

"And would you help me decide on the opening play of the season? I've got three in mind—all with strong female leads. I'm going to act again. I'm going to open the season by plunging into a leading role. I've got to *emote*, Chris. There's a lot of pressing business to take care of now that I'm alone—insurance and doctor bills and Larry's research—but the first thing I have to do is *emote*. We'll decide over muffins how I can best do that. And after we've chosen the play, I'd love it if you could help me memorize—feed me lines. Larry was always good about that. He'd take the part of the leading man..." She snapped the elastic around his ankle. "So you've become a runner?"

"I feel like getting in shape."

"I've quit running. With Larry dead I don't have the urge—figure that one out." She leaned back on her elbows and looked up through the boughs of a birch. "With Larry dead I feel altogether different, Chris. I feel damn relieved if you don't mind my saying so. But on the other hand I feel half-bored all the time. Tempe was boring. I didn't know anybody but Sam and Mother. As I said in my letter, Bruce was abducted by the football coach. You got my letter?"

Chris opened the letter and read to her: "Being loved is a pleasure, and loving is a pleasure, but neither is a *great* pleasure by itself."

"Yes. What does that mean, Chris?"

"That's *my* question."

She kicked off her sandals and dropped her head farther back, her chin pointed at the sky, her hair hanging.

"Then neither of us knows. But someday I'm sure we'll figure it out—we just need time. At least *I* do. How much time can you give me, Chris?"

"How much do you need?"

"Lots."

"That's exactly how much I can give you. Though my days in Rookery might be numbered. It's clear that one counselor will lose his job next spring, and it's up to me to decide who. I've been offered a position with General Mills."

"Minneapolis?"

"Yes. I could relieve the anxieties of seven counselors by packing up my aptitude tests and going to General Mills."

"Starting when—in the spring?"

"Midsummer."

She sat up, nodding approvingly.

He didn't tell her that her interest in Twin Cities theater was a factor in his talks with General Mills. He was certain she would outgrow Rookery, even if the Playhouse continued to prosper. While serving these past few years as maid, mother, analyst and nurse, she had outshone all the stars in Rookery. Unencumbered now, she would rise swiftly.

She picked a blade of grass and bit it in two. "When I think about Larry, do you know how I see him? I see him coming home from Canada last fall so full of his old self that I couldn't believe it. Remember when he got out of the car and rolled me in the leaves? I thought I was dreaming. That set the tone for his whole last year. Instead of spending the year in the pits, he felt good about himself for weeks at a time. The doctor says it was the medicine, but I don't believe it. It was because he had helped save those lives in Canada. You knew the trip would be a big thing in his life, didn't you, Chris? You must have known, the way you insisted on taking him with you."

He looked deeply into her gray eyes. "Yes, I thought it would be a big thing in his life."

"And to think I believed it would be the end of him. I

never told you this, but when you two left for Canada that morning, I had the strongest feeling that I'd never see him again. When I watched you drive off, I felt as though you were taking him away forever."

Chris recalled the moment—Rachel in her blue robe, her pirouette in his rearview mirror. He hadn't recognized it as her *danse macabre*.

"Chris, did it ever enter your mind that that trip might be too much for him?"

He folded the letter and put it in his pocket. "It did, actually."

She picked grass off her tongue. "Come on, help me pick a play and then I'll feed you muffins while you feed me lines." She stood and slipped into her sandals.

Walking uphill, he took her hand and felt wonderfully in touch with life. For too long, as a safeguard against disappointment, he had been wary of life, had kept his distance from it, had been entering it and leaving it like a bit player with stagefright. But now, with Rachel, he saw the possibility of stepping out of the wings and embracing it again. So much depended on what role she would choose for herself.

What role for him.

What play.

Jon Hassler

"A WRITER GOOD ENOUGH TO RESTORE YOUR FAITH IN FICTION."

—*The New York Times*